Praise for The Deal

"Elle has masterfully captured the feelings, the romance and the unbridled sexiness of the New Adult genre with this book! You will swoon for Garrett!"
— Alice Clayton, New York Times bestselling author of WALLBANGER

"Hannah and Garrett are funny, relatable, and their chemistry on the page is palpable enough to linger off of it. The Deal reminds me of all the reasons I love romance. It'll make you laugh, maybe even tear up, but most of all leave you with that warm good book feeling at the end"
— Jane Litte, Dear Author

"Elle Kennedy engages your senses from the very first sentence! Deliciously steamy and heart-achingly tender, The Deal is an absolute winner"
— Katy Evans, New York Times bestselling author

"The Deal is everything you could ask for in a New Adult. Sexy, sweet, and emotionally satisfying. I loved this book and did not want it to end!"
— Kristen Callihan, USA Today bestselling author

"I loved this book! Garrett is dreamy. If you love NA, you must read The Deal!" - Monica Murphy, New York Times bestselling author

Also available from Elle Kennedy

Out of Uniform
Heat of the Moment
Heat of Passion
Heat of the Storm
Heat It Up
Heat of the Night
The Heat is On
Feeling Hot
Getting Hotter
Hotter than Ever
A Little Bit of Hot
As Hot As It Gets

After Hours
One Night of Sin
One Night of Scandal
One Night of Trouble

DreamMakers
All Fired Up
Love Is A Battlefield
Don't Walk Away

A full list of Elle's contemporary and suspense print titles is available on her website www.ellekennedy.com

The Deal

An Off-Campus Novel

Elle Kennedy

Edited by Gwen Hayes
Proofed by Sharon Muha
Cover Art © Sarah Hansen, Okay Creations

1

Hannah

He doesn't know I'm alive.

For the millionth time in forty-five minutes, I sneak a peek in Justin Kohl's direction, and he's so beautiful it makes my throat close up. Though I should probably come up with another adjective—my male friends insist that men don't like being called *beautiful.*

But holy hell, there's no other way to describe his rugged features and soulful brown eyes. He's wearing a baseball cap today, but I know what's beneath it: thick dark hair, the kind that looks silky to the touch and makes you want to run your fingers through it.

In the five years since the rape, my heart has pounded for only two guys.

The first one dumped me.

This one is just oblivious.

At the podium in the lecture hall, Professor Tolbert delivers what I've come to refer to as the Disappointment Speech. It's the third one in six weeks.

Surprise, surprise, seventy percent of the class got a C-plus or lower on the midterm.

Me? I aced it. And I'd be lying if I said the big red *A!* circled on top of my midterm hadn't come as a complete shock. All I did was scribble down a never-ending stream of bullshit to try to fill up the booklet.

Philosophical Ethics was supposed to be a breeze. The prof who used to teach it handed out brainless multiple choice tests and a final "exam" consisting of a personal essay that posed a moral dilemma and asked how you'd react to it.

But two weeks before the semester started, Professor Lane dropped dead from a heart attack. I heard his cleaning lady found him on the bathroom floor—naked. Poor guy.

Luckily (and yep, that's total sarcasm) Pamela Tolbert stepped in to take over Lane's class. She's new to Briar University, and she's the kind of prof who wants you to make connections and "engage" with the material. If this was a movie, she'd be the young, ambitious teacher who shows up at the inner city school and inspires the fuckups, and suddenly everyone's putting down their AKs and picking up their pencils, and the end credits scroll up to announce how all the kids got into Harvard or some shit. Instant Oscar for Hilary Swank.

Except this isn't a movie, which means that the only thing Tolbert has inspired in her students is hatred. And she honestly can't seem to grasp why nobody is excelling in her class.

Here's a hint—it's because she asks the types of questions you could write a frickin' grad school thesis on.

"I'm willing to offer a makeup exam to anyone who failed or received a C-minus or lower." Tolbert's nose wrinkles as if she can't fathom why it's even necessary.

The word she just used—*willing*? Yeah, right. I heard that a ton of students complained to their advisors about her, and I suspect the administration is forcing her to give everyone a redo. It doesn't reflect well on Briar when more than half the students in a course are flunking, especially when it's not just the slackers. Straight-A students like Nell, who's sulking beside me, also bombed the midterm.

"For those of you who choose to take it again, your two grades will be averaged. If you do worse the second time, the first grade will stand," Tolbert finishes.

"I can't believe you got an A," Nell whispers to me.

She looks so upset that I feel a pang of sympathy. Nell and I aren't best pals or anything, but we've been sitting next to each other since September so it's only reasonable that we've gotten to know each other. She's on the pre-med path, and I know she comes from an overachieving family who would tar and feather her if they found out about her midterm grade.

"I can't believe it either," I whisper back. "Seriously. Read my answers. They're ramblings of nonsense."

"Actually, can I?" She sounds eager now. "I'm curious to see what the Tyrant considers A material."

"I'll scan and email you a copy tonight," I promise.

The second Tolbert dismisses us, the lecture hall echoes with let's-get-the-hell-outta-here noises. Laptops snap shut, notebooks slide into backpacks, students shuffle out of their seats.

Justin Kohl lingers near the door to talk to someone, and my gaze locks in on him like a missile. He's beautiful.

Have I mentioned how beautiful he is?

My palms go clammy as I stare at his handsome profile. He's new to Briar this year, but I'm not sure which college he transferred from, and although he wasted no time becoming the star wide receiver on the football team, he's not like the other athletes at this school. He doesn't strut through the quad with one of those I'm-God's-gift-to-the-world smirks or show up with a new girl on his arm every day. I've seen him laugh and joke with his teammates, but he gives off an intelligent, intense vibe that makes me think there are hidden depths to him. Which just makes me all the more desperate to get to know him.

I'm not usually into jocks, but something about this one has turned me into a mindless pile of mush.

"You're staring again."

Nell's teasing voice brings a blush to my cheeks. She's caught me drooling over Justin on more than one occasion, and she's one of the few people I've admitted the crush to.

My roommate Allie also knows, but my other friends? Hell no. Most of them are music or drama majors, so I guess that makes us the artsy crowd. Or maybe emo. Aside from Allie, who's had an on-again/off-again relationship with a frat boy since freshman year, my friends get a kick out of trashing Briar's elite. I don't usually join in (I like to think gossiping is beneath me) but...let's face it. Most of the popular kids are total douchebags.

Case in point—Garrett Graham, the other star athlete in this class. Dude walks around like he owns the place. I guess he kind of does. All he has to do is snap his fingers and an eager girl appears at his side. Or jumps into his lap. Or sticks her tongue down his throat.

He doesn't look like the BMOC today, though. Almost everyone else has gone, including Tolbert, but Garrett remains in his seat, his fists curled tightly around the edges of his booklet.

He must have failed too, but I don't feel much sympathy for the guy. Briar is known for two things—hockey and football, which isn't much of a shocker considering Massachusetts is home to both the Patriots and the Bruins. The athletes who play for Briar almost always end up in the pros, and during their years here they get everything handed to them on a silver platter—including grades.

So yeah, maybe it makes me a teeny bit vindictive, but I get a sense of triumph from knowing that Tolbert is failing the captain of our championship-winning hockey team right along with everyone else.

"Wanna grab something from the Coffee Hut?" Nell asks as she gathers her books.

"Can't. I've got rehearsal in twenty minutes." I get up, but I don't follow her to the door. "Go on ahead. I need to check the schedule before I go. Can't remember when my next tutorial is."

Another "perk" of being in Tolbert's class—along with our weekly lecture, we're forced to attend two thirty-minute tutorials a week. On the bright side, Dana the TA runs those, and she has all the qualities Tolbert lacks. Like a sense of humor.

"'Kay," Nell says. "I'll see you later."

"Later," I call after her.

At the sound of my voice, Justin pauses in the doorway and turns his head.

Oh. My. God.

It's impossible to stop the flush that rises in my cheeks. This is the first time we've ever made eye contact, and I don't know how to respond. Say hi? Wave? Smile?

In the end, I settle for a small nod of greeting. *There*. Cool and casual, befitting of a sophisticated college junior.

My heart skips a beat when the corner of his mouth lifts in a faint grin. He nods back, and then he's gone.

I stare at the empty doorway. My pulse explodes in a gallop because *holy shit*. After six weeks of breathing the same air in this stuffy lecture hall, he's finally noticed me.

I wish I were brave enough to go after him. Maybe ask him to grab a coffee. Or dinner. Or brunch—wait, do people our age even *have* brunch?

But my feet stay rooted to the shiny laminate floor.

Because I'm a coward. Yep, a total chicken-shit coward. I'm

terrified that he'll say no, but I'm even more terrified he'll say *yes*.

I was in a good place when I started college. My issues solidly behind me, my guard lowered. I was ready to date again, and I did. I dated several guys, but other than my ex, Devon, none of them made my body tingle the way Justin Kohl does, and that freaks me out.

Baby steps.

Right. Baby steps. That was my therapist's favorite piece of advice, and I can't deny that the strategy helped me a lot. Focus on the small victories, Carole always advised.

So…today's victory…I nodded at Justin and he smiled at me. Next class, maybe I'll smile back. And the one after that, maybe I'll bring up the coffee, dinner or brunch idea.

I take a breath as I head down the aisle, clinging to that feeling of victory, however teeny it may be.

Baby steps.

Garrett

I failed.

I fucking failed.

For fifteen years, Timothy Lane handed out A's like mints. The year *I* take the class? Lane's ticker quits ticking, and I get stuck with Pamela Tolbert.

It's official. The woman is my archenemy. Just the sight of her flowery handwriting—which fills up every inch of available space in the margins of my midterm—makes me want to go Incredible Hulk on the booklet and rip it to shreds.

I'm rocking A's in most of my other courses, but as of right now, I'm getting an F in Philosophical Ethics. Combined with the C-plus in Spanish history, my average has dropped to a C-minus.

I need a C-plus average to play hockey.

Normally I have no problem keeping my GPA up. Despite what a lot of folks believe, I'm not a dumb jock. But hey, I don't mind letting people think I am. Women, in particular. I guess they're turned on by the idea of screwing the big brawny caveman who's only good for one thing, but since I'm not looking for anything serious, casual hookups with chicks that only want my dick suit me just fine. Gives me more time to focus on hockey.

But there won't *be* any more hockey if I don't bring up this grade. The worst thing about Briar? Our dean demands excellence—academically *and* athletically. While other schools might be more lenient toward athletes, Briar has a zero-tolerance policy.

Fuckin' Tolbert. When I spoke to her before class asking for extra credit, she told me in that nasally voice of hers to attend the tutorials and meet with the study group. I already do both. So yeah, unless I hire some whiz kid to wear a mask of my face and take the makeup midterm for me…I'm screwed.

My frustration manifests itself in the form of an audible groan, and from the corner of my eye I see someone jerk in surprise.

I jerk too, because here I thought I was wallowing in my misery alone. But the girl who sits in the back row has stuck around, and she's making her way down the aisle toward Tolbert's desk.

Mandy?

Marty?

I can't remember her name. Probably because I've never bothered to ask for it. She's cute, though. A helluva lot cuter than I realized. Pretty face, dark hair, smokin' body—shit, how have I never noticed that body before?

But I'm noticing now. Skinny jeans cling to a round, perky ass that just screams "squeeze me," and her V-neck sweater hugs a seriously impressive rack. I don't have time to admire either of those appealing visuals because she catches me staring and a frown touches her mouth.

"Everything okay?" she asks with a pointed look.

I grumble something under my breath. I'm not in the mood to talk to anyone at the moment.

One dark eyebrow rises in my direction. "Sorry, was that English?"

I ball up my midterm and scrape my chair back. "I said everything's fine."

"Okay, then." She shrugs and continues down the steps.

As she picks up the clipboard that contains our tutorial schedule, I fling my Briar Hockey jacket on, then shove my pathetic midterm into my backpack and zip it up.

The dark-haired girl heads back to the aisle. Mona? Molly? The M sounds right, but the rest is a mystery. She has her midterm in hand, but I don't sneak a peek because I assume she failed just like everyone else.

I let her pass before I step into the aisle. I suppose I can say it's the gentleman in me, but that would be a lie. I want to check out her ass again, because it's a damn sexy ass, and now that I've seen it I wouldn't mind another look. I follow her up to the exit, suddenly realizing how frickin' tiny she is—I'm one step below her yet I can see the top of her head.

Just as we reach the door, she stumbles on absolutely nothing and the books in her hand clatter to the floor.

"Shit. I'm such a klutz."

She drops to her knees and so do I, because contrary to my previous statement, I *can* be a gentleman when I want to be, and the gentlemanly thing to do is help her gather her books.

"Oh, you don't have to do that. I'm fine," she insists.

But my hand has already connected with her midterm, and my jaw drops when I see her grade.

"Fucking hell. You aced it?" I demand.

She gives a self-deprecating smile. "I know, right? I thought I failed for sure."

"Holy shit." I feel like I've just bumped into Stephen fuckin' Hawking and he's dangling the secrets to the universe under my nose. "Can I read your answers?"

Her brows quirk up again. "That's rather forward of you, don't you think? We don't even know each other."

I roll my eyes. "I'm not asking you to take your clothes off, baby. I just want to peek at your midterm."

"*Baby*? Goodbye forward, hello presumptuous."

"Would you prefer *miss*? *Ma'am* maybe? I'd use your name but I don't know it."

"Of course you don't." She sighs. "It's Hannah." Then she pauses meaningfully. "*Garrett*."

Okay, I was waaaay off on the M thing.

And I don't miss the way she emphasizes my name as if to say, *Ha! I know yours, asshole!*

She collects the rest of her books and stands up, but I don't hand over her midterm. Instead, I hop to my feet and start flipping through it. As I skim her answers, my spirits plummet even lower, because if this is the kind of analysis Tolbert is looking for, I'm screwed. There's a reason I'm a history major, for chrissake—I deal in facts. Black and white. This happened at this time to this person and here's the result.

Hannah's answers focus on theoretical shit and how the philosophers would respond to the various moral dilemmas.

"Thanks." I give her the booklet, then hook my thumbs in the belt loops of my jeans. "Hey, listen. Do you...would you consider..." I shrug. "You know..."

Her lips twitch as if she's trying not to laugh. "Actually, I *don't* know."

I let out a breath. "Will you tutor me?"

Her green eyes—the darkest shade of green I've ever seen and surrounded by thick black eyelashes—go from surprised to skeptical in a matter of seconds.

"I'll pay you," I add hastily.

"Oh. Um. Well, yeah, of course I'd expect you to pay me. But..." She shakes her head. "I'm sorry. I can't."

I bite back my disappointment. "C'mon, do me a solid. If I fail this makeup, my GPA will implode. Please?" I flash a smile, the one that makes my dimples pop out and never fails to make girls melt.

"Does that usually work?" she asks curiously.

"What?"

"The aw-shucks little boy grin... Does it help you get your way?"

"Always," I answer without hesitation.

"*Almost* always," she corrects. "Look, I'm sorry, but I really don't have time. I'm already juggling school and work, and with the winter showcase coming up, I'll have even less time."

"Winter showcase?" I say blankly.

"Right, I forgot. If it's not about hockey, then it's not on your radar."

"Now who's being presumptuous? You don't even know me."

There's a beat, and then she sighs. "I'm a music major, okay? And the arts faculty puts on two major performances every year, the winter showcase and the spring one. The winner gets a five thousand dollar scholarship. It's kind of a huge deal, actually. Important industry people fly in from all over the country to see it. Agents, record producers, talent scouts.... So, as much as I'd love to help you—"

"You would not," I grumble. "You look like you don't even want to *talk* to me right now."

Her little you-got-me shrug is grating as hell. "I have to get to rehearsal. I'm sorry you're failing this course, but if it makes you feel better, so is everyone else."

I narrow my eyes. "Not *you*."

"I can't help it. Tolbert seems to respond to my brand of bullshit. It's a gift."

"Well, I want your gift. Please, master, teach me how to bullshit."

I'm two seconds from dropping to my knees and begging her, but she edges to the door. "You know there's a study group, right? I can give you the number for—"

"I'm already in it," I mutter.

"Oh. Well, then there's not much else I can do for you. Good luck on the makeup test. *Baby*."

She darts out the door, leaving me staring after her in frustration. Unbelievable. Every girl at this college would cut her frickin' arm off to help me out. But this one? Runs away like I just asked her to murder a cat so we could sacrifice it to Satan.

And now I'm right back to where I was before Hannah-not-with-an-M gave me that faintest flicker of hope.

Royally screwed.

2

Garrett

My roommates are piss drunk when I walk into the living room after study group. The coffee table is overflowing with empty beer cans, along with a nearly depleted bottle of Jack that I know belongs to Logan because he subscribes to the *beer is for pussies* philosophy. His words, not mine.

At the moment, Logan and Tucker are battling each other in a heated game of *Ice Pro*, their gazes glued to the flat screen as they furiously click their controllers. Logan's gaze shifts slightly when he notices me in the doorway, and his split second of distraction costs him.

"Hell to the yeah!" Tuck crows as his defenseman flicks a wrist shot past Logan's goalie and the scoreboard lights up.

"Aw, for fuck's sake!" Logan pauses the game and levels a dark glare at me. "What the hell, G? I just got deked out because of you."

I don't answer, because now *I'm* distracted—by the half naked make out session happening in the corner of the room. Dean's at it again. Bare-chested and barefoot, he's sprawled in the armchair while a blonde in nothing but a lacy black bra and booty shorts sits astride him and grinds against his crotch.

Dark blue eyes peer over the chick's shoulder, and Dean smirks in my direction. "Graham! Where've you been, man?" he slurs.

He goes back to kissing the blonde before I can answer the drunken question.

For some reason, Dean likes to hook up everywhere *but* his bedroom. Seriously. Every time I turn around, he's in the midst of some form of debauchery. On the kitchen counter, the living room couch, the dining room table—dude's gotten it on in every inch of the off-campus house the four of us share. He's a total slut and completely unapologetic about it.

Granted, I'm not one to talk. I'm no monk, and neither are Logan and Tuck. What can I say? Hockey players are horny motherfuckers. When we're not on the ice, we can usually be found hooking up with a puck bunny or two. Or three, if your name is Tucker and it's New Year's Eve of last year.

"I've been texting you for the past hour, man," Logan informs me.

His massive shoulders hunch forward as he swipes the whiskey bottle from the coffee table. Logan's a bruiser of a defenseman, one of the best I've ever played with, and also the best friend I've ever had. His first name is John, but we call him Logan because it makes it easier to differentiate him from Tucker, whose first name is also John. Luckily, Dean is just Dean, so we don't have to call him by his mouthful of a last name: Heyward-Di Laurentis.

"Seriously, where the hell have you been?" Logan grumbles.

"Study group." I grab a Bud Light from the table and pop the tab. "What's this surprise you kept blabbing about?"

I can always tell how plastered Logan is based on the grammar of his texts. And tonight he must be shit-faced, because I had to go full-on Sherlock to decrypt his messages. *Suprz* meant surprise. *Gyabh* had taken longer to decode, but I *think* it meant *get your ass back here?* But who knows with Logan.

From his perch on the couch, he grins so broadly it's a wonder his jaw doesn't snap off. He jerks his thumb at the ceiling and says, "Go upstairs and see for yourself."

I narrow my eyes. "Why? Who's up there?"

Logan snickers. "If I told you, then it wouldn't be a surprise."

"Why do I get the feeling you're up to something?"

"Jeez," Tucker pipes up. "You've got some major trust issues, G."

"Says the asshole who left a live raccoon in my bedroom on the first day of the semester."

Tucker grins. "Aw, come on, Bandit was fucking adorable. He was your welcome back to school gift."

I flip up my middle finger. "Yeah, well, your *gift* was a bitch to get rid of." Now I scowl at him because I still remember how it took three pest control guys to de-raccoon my room.

"For fuck's sake," Logan groans. "Just go upstairs. Trust me, you'll thank us for it later."

The knowing look they exchange eases my suspicion. Kind of. I mean, I'm not about to let down my guard completely, not around *these* assholes.

I steal two more cans of beer on my way out. I don't drink much during the season, but Coach gave us the week off to study for midterms and we still have two days of freedom left. My teammates, lucky bastards, seem to have no problem downing twelve beers and playing like champs the next day. Me? Even a buzz gives me a rip-roaring headache the morning after and then I skate like a toddler with his first pair of Bauers.

Once we're back to a six-days-a-week practice schedule, my alcohol consumption will drop to the usual one/five limit. One drink on practice nights, five after a game. No exceptions.

I plan on taking full advantage of the time I have left.

Armed with my beers, I head upstairs to my room. The *master* bedroom. Yup, I was not above playing the I'm-your-captain card to snag it, and trust me, it was worth the argument my teammates put up. Private bath, baby.

My door is ajar, a sight that snaps me right back into suspicion mode. I warily peer up at the frame to make sure there isn't a bucket of blood up there, then give the door a tiny shove. It gives way and I inch through it, fully prepared for an ambush.

I get one.

Except it's more of a visual ambush, because *damn*, the girl on my bed looks like she stepped out of a Victoria's Secret catalog.

Now, I'm a guy. I don't know the names of half the shit she's wearing. I see white lace and pink bows and lots of skin. And I'm happy.

"Took you long enough." Kendall shoots me a sexy smile that says *you're about to get lucky, big boy*, and my cock reacts accordingly, thickening beneath my zipper. "I was giving you five more minutes before I took off."

"I made it just in time then." My gaze sweeps over her

drool-worthy outfit, and then I drawl, "Aw, babe, is that all for me?"

Her blue eyes darken seductively. "You know it, stud."

I'm well aware that we sound like characters from a cheesy porno. But come on, when a man walks into his bedroom and finds a woman who looks like *this*? He's willing to reenact any trashy scene she wants, even one that involves him pretending to be a pizza guy delivering pies to a MILF.

Kendall and I first hooked up over the summer, out of convenience more than anything else because we both happened to be in the area during the break. We hit the bar a couple times, one thing led to another, and the next thing I know I'm fooling around with a hot sorority girl. But it fizzled out before midterms started, and aside from a few dirty texts here and there, I haven't seen Kendall until now.

"I figured you might want to have some fun before practice starts up again," she says, her manicured fingers toying with the tiny pink bow in the center of her bra.

"You figured right."

A smile curves her lips as she rises to her knees. Damn, her tits are practically pouring out of that lacy thing she's wearing. She crooks a finger at me. "C'mere."

I waste no time striding toward her. Because...again...I'm a *guy*.

"I think you're a tad overdressed," she remarks, then grasps the waistband of my jeans and teases the button open. She tugs on the zipper and a second later my dick springs into her waiting hand. I haven't done laundry in weeks so I've been going commando until I get my shit together, and from the way her eyes flare with heat, I can tell she approves of the whole no-boxers thing.

When she wraps her fingers around me, a groan slips out of my throat. Oh yeah. There's nothing better than the feel of a woman's hand on your cock.

Nope, I'm wrong. Kendall's tongue comes into play, and holy shit, it's *so* much better than her hand.

An hour later, Kendall snuggles up beside me and rests her head on my chest. Her lingerie and my clothes are strewn on the bedroom floor, along with two empty condom packages and the bottle of lube we hadn't needed to crack open.

The cuddling makes me apprehensive, but I can't exactly shove her away and demand she hit the road, not when she clearly put a lot of effort into this seduction.

But that worries me too.

Women don't get all decked out in expensive lingerie for a hookup, do they? I'm thinking *no,* and Kendall's next words validate my uneasy thoughts.

"I missed you, baby."

My first though is *shit.*

My second thought is *why?*

Because in all the time we've been hooking up, Kendall hasn't made a single effort to get to know me. If we're not having sex, she just talks non-stop about herself. Seriously, I don't think she's asked me a personal question about myself since we met.

"Uh..." I struggle for words, any sequence of them that doesn't consist of *I, miss, you,* and *too.* "I've been busy. You know, midterms."

"Obviously. We go to the same college. I was studying, too." There's an edge to her tone now. "Did you miss me?"

Fuck me sideways. What am I supposed to say to that? I'm not going to lie, because that'll only lead her on. But I can't be a dick about it and admit she hasn't even crossed my mind since the last time we hooked up.

Kendall sits up and narrows her eyes. "It's a yes or no question, Garrett. Did. You. Miss. Me."

My gaze darts to the window. Yup, I'm on the second floor and actually contemplating jumping out the frickin' window. That's how badly I want to avoid this convo.

But my silence speaks volumes, and suddenly Kendall flies off the bed, her blond hair whipping in all directions as she scrambles for her clothes. "Oh my God. You are *such* an ass! You don't care about me at all, do you, Garrett?"

I get up and make a beeline for my discarded jeans. "I do care about you," I protest. "But..."

She angrily shoves her panties on. "But what?"

"But I thought we were clear about what this was. I don't want anything serious." I shoot her a pointed look. "I told you that from the start."

Her expression softens as she bites her lip. "I know, but...I just thought..."

I know exactly what she thought—that I'd fall madly in love with her, and our casual hookup would transform into the fucking *Notebook*.

Honestly, I don't know why I bother laying down ground rules anymore. In my experience, no woman enters into a fling believing it's going to *stay* a fling. She might say otherwise, maybe even convince herself she's cool with a no-strings sex-fest, but deep down, she hopes and prays it'll lead to something deeper.

And then I, the villain in her personal rom-com, swoops in and bursts that bubble of hope, despite the fact that I never lied about my intentions or misled her, not even for a second.

"Hockey is my entire life," I say gruffly. "I practice six days a week, play twenty games a year—more if we make it to the post-season. I don't have time for a girlfriend, Kendall. And you deserve a helluva lot more than I can give you."

Unhappiness clouds her eyes. "I don't want a casual fling anymore. I want to be your girlfriend."

Another *why* almost flies out of my mouth, but I bite my tongue. If she'd shown any interest in me outside the carnal sense, I might believe her, but the fact that she hasn't makes me wonder if the only reason she wants a relationship with me is because I'm some kind of status symbol to her.

I swallow my frustration and offer another awkward apology. "I'm sorry. But that's where I'm at right now."

As I zip up my jeans, she refocuses her attention on getting her clothes on. Though *clothes* is a bit of a stretch—all she's sporting is lingerie and a trench coat. Which explains why Logan and Tucker were grinning like idiots when I got home. Because when a girl shows up at your door in a trench coat, you know damn well there's not much else underneath it.

"I can't see you anymore," she finally says, her gaze finding mine. "If we keep doing...this...I'll only get more attached."

I can't argue with that, so I don't. "We had fun, though, right?"

After a beat, she smiles. "Yeah, we had fun."

She bridges the distance between us and leans up on her tiptoes to kiss me. I kiss her back, but not with the same degree of passion as before. I keep it light. Polite. The fling has run its course, and I'm not about to lead her on again.

"With that said..." Her eyes twinkle mischievously. "Let me know if you change your mind about the girlfriend thing."

"You'll be the first person I call," I promise.

"Good."

She smacks a kiss on my cheek and walks out the door, leaving me to marvel over how easy that went. I'd been steeling myself for a fight, but aside from that initial burst of anger, Kendall had accepted the situation like a pro.

If only all women were as agreeable as her.

Yup, totally a jab at Hannah there.

Sex always stirs up my appetite, so I head downstairs in search of nourishment, and I'm happy to find there's still leftover rice and fried chicken courtesy of Tuck, who is our resident chef because the rest of us can't boil water without burning it. Tuck, on the other hand, grew up in Texas with a single mom who taught him to cook when he was still in diapers.

I settle at the eat-in counter, shoving a piece of chicken in my mouth just as Logan strolls in wearing nothing but plaid boxers.

He raises a brow when he spots me. "Hey. I didn't think I'd see you again tonight. Figured you'd be VBF."

"VBF?" I ask between mouthfuls. Logan likes to make up acronyms in the hopes that we'll start to use them as slang, but half the time I have no idea what he's babbling about.

He grins. "Very busy fucking."

I roll my eyes and eat a forkful of wild rice.

"Seriously, Blondie's gone already?"

"Yup." I chew before continuing. "She knows the score." The score being, no girlfriends and definitely no sleepovers.

Logan rests his forearms on the counter, his blue eyes gleaming as he changes the subject. "I can't fucking wait for the St. Anthony's game this weekend. Did you hear? Braxton's suspension is over."

That gets my attention. "No shit. He's playing on Saturday?"

"Sure is." Logan's expression turns downright gleeful. "I'm gonna enjoy smashing that asshole's face into the boards."

Greg Braxton is St. Anthony's star left wing and a complete piece of shit human being. The guy's got a sadistic streak that he's not afraid to unleash on the ice, and when our teams faced off in the pre-season, he sent one of our sophomore D-men to the emergency room with a broken arm. Hence his three game suspension, though if it were up to me, the psycho would've been slapped with a lifetime ban from college hockey.

"You need to throw down, I'll be right there with you," I promise.

"I'm holding you to that. Oh, and next week we've got Eastwood heading our way."

I really should pay more attention to our schedule. Eastwood College is number two in our conference (second to us, of course) and our matchups are always nail-biters.

And shit, it suddenly dawns on me that if I don't ace the Ethics redo, I won't be on the ice for the Eastwood game.

"Fuck," I mumble.

Logan swipes a piece of chicken off my plate and pops it in his mouth. "What?"

I haven't told my teammates about my grade situation yet because I'd been hoping my midterm grade wouldn't hurt me too bad, but now it looks like fessing up is unavoidable.

So with a sigh, I tell Logan about my F in Ethics and what it could mean for the team.

"Drop the course," he says instantly.

"Can't. I missed the deadline."

"Crap."

"Yup."

We exchange a glum look, and then Logan flops down on the stool beside mine and rakes a hand through his hair. "Then you gotta shape up, man. Study your balls off and ace this motherfucker. We need you, G."

"I know." I grip my fork in frustration, then put it down, my appetite vanishing. This is my first year as captain, which is a major honor considering I'm only a junior. I'm supposed to follow in my predecessor's footsteps and lead my team to another national championship, but how the hell can I do that if I'm not on the ice with them?

"I've got a tutor lined up," I assure my teammate. "She's a frickin' genius."

"Good. Pay her whatever she wants. I'll chip in if you want."

I can't help but grin. "Wow. You're offering to part with all your sweet, sweet cash? You must *really* want me to play."

"Damn straight. It's all about the dream, man. You and me in Bruins jerseys, remember?"

I have to admit, it's a damn nice dream. It's what Logan and I have been talking about since we were assigned as roommates in freshman year. There's no doubt in my mind that I'll go pro after I graduate. No doubt about Logan getting drafted, either. The guy's faster than lightning and a goddamn beast on the ice.

"Get that fucking grade up, G," he orders. "Otherwise I'll kick your ass."

"Coach will kick it harder." I muster up a smile. "Don't worry, I'm on it."

"Good." Logan steals another piece of chicken before wandering out of the kitchen.

I scarf down the rest of my food, then head back upstairs to find my phone. It's time to ramp up the pressure on Hannah-not-with-an-M.

3

Hannah

"I really think you should sing that last note in E major," Cass insists. He's like a broken record, throwing out the same unreasonable suggestion each time we finish running through our duet.

Now, I'm a pacifist. I don't believe in using fists to solve your problems, I think organized fighting is barbaric, and the idea of war makes me queasy.

Yet I'm *thisclose* to punching Cassidy Donovan in the face.

"The key is too low for me." My tone is firm, but it's impossible to hide my annoyance.

Cass runs a frustrated hand through his wavy dark hair and turns to Mary Jane, who's fidgeting awkwardly on the piano bench. "You know I'm right, MJ," he pleads at her. "It'll pack more of a punch if Hannah and I end in the same key instead of doing the harmony."

"No, it'll have a bigger impact if we do the harmony," I argue.

I'm ready to rip my own hair out. I know exactly what Cass is up to. He wants to end the song on *his* note. He's been pulling shit like this ever since we decided to team up for the winter performance, doing everything he can to single out his own voice while shoving me into the background.

If I'd known what a fucking prima donna Cass was, I would've said *hell no* to a duet, but the jackass decided to show his true colors *after* we started rehearsals, and now it's too late to back out. I've invested too much time in this duet, and honestly, I truly do love the song. Mary Jane wrote an incredible piece, and a part of me really doesn't want to let her down. Besides, I know for a fact that the faculty prefers duets to solos, because the last four scholarship-winning performances have been duets. The judges go cuckoo-bananas for complex harmonies, and this composition has them in spades.

"MJ?" Cass prompts.

"Um..."

I can see the petite blonde melting under his magnetic stare. Cass has that effect on women. He's infuriatingly handsome, and his voice happens to be phenomenal. Unfortunately, he's fully aware of both these assets and has no qualms using them to his advantage.

"Maybe Cass is right," MJ murmurs, avoiding my eyes as she betrays me. "Why don't we try the E Major, Hannah? Let's just do it once and see which one works better."

Benedict Arnold! I want to shout, but I bite my tongue. Like me, MJ has been forced to deal with Cass's outrageous demands and "brilliant" ideas for weeks now, and I can't blame her for trying to strike a compromise.

"Fine," I grumble. "Let's try it."

Triumph lights Cass's eyes, but it doesn't stay there long, because after we sing the song again, it's clear that his suggestion stinks. The note is far too low for me, and instead of causing Cass's gorgeous baritone to stand out, my part sounds so clumsily off that it draws attention away from his.

"I think Hannah should stick to the original key." Mary Jane looks at Cass and bites her lip, as if she's afraid of his reaction.

But although the guy is arrogant, he's not stupid. "Fine," he snaps. "We'll do it your way, Hannah."

I grit my teeth. "Thank you."

Fortunately, our hour is up, which means the rehearsal space is about to belong to one of the first-year classes. Eager to get out of there, I quickly gather my sheet music and slip into my pea coat. The less time I have to spend with Cass, the better.

God, I can't stand him.

Ironically, we're singing a deeply emotional love song.

"Same time tomorrow?" He eyes me expectantly.

"No, tomorrow is our four o'clock day, remember? I work

Tuesday nights."

Displeasure hardens his face. "You know, we could've mastered this song a long time ago if your schedule wasn't so...inconvenient."

I arch a brow. "Says the guy who refuses to rehearse on weekends. Because *I* happen to be free both Saturday *and* Sunday nights."

His lips tighten, and then he saunters off without another word.

Dick.

A heavy sigh echoes behind me. I turn around and realize MJ is still at the piano, still biting her lip.

"I'm sorry, Hannah," she says softly. "When I asked you guys to sing my song, I didn't realize Cass would be so difficult."

My annoyance thaws when I notice how upset she is. "Hey, it's not your fault," I assure her. "I wasn't expecting him to be this much of a jerk either, but he's an amazing singer, so let's just try to focus on that, okay?"

"You're an amazing singer, too. That's why I chose the two of you. I couldn't imagine anyone else bringing the song to life, you know?"

I smile at her. She really is a sweet girl, not to mention one of the most talented songwriters I've ever met. Every piece that's performed in the showcase has to be composed by a songwriting major, and even before MJ approached me, I had already planned on asking to use one of her songs.

"I promise you, we're going to sing the shit out of your song, MJ. Ignore Cass's bullshit tantrums. I think he just likes arguing for the sake of arguing."

She laughs. "Yeah, probably. See you tomorrow?"

"Yep. Four o'clock sharp."

I give her a little wave, then leave the choir room and head outside.

One of my favorite things about Briar is the campus. The buildings, ancient and covered with strands of ivy, are connected to each other by cobblestone paths lined with sweeping elms and wrought-iron benches. The university is one of the oldest in the country, and its alumni roster contains dozens of influential people, including more than one president.

But the best thing about Briar is how safe it is. Seriously, our crime rate is next to zero, which probably has a lot to do with Dean Farrow's dedication to the safety of his students. The school invests a ton of money in security in the form of strategically placed cameras and guards that patrol the grounds twenty-four hours a day. Not that it's a prison or anything. The security guys are friendly and unobtrusive. In all honesty, I barely notice them when I'm wandering around campus.

My dorm is a five-minute walk from the music building, and I breathe a sigh of relief when I walk through Bristol House's massive oak doors. It's been a long day, and all I want to do is take a hot shower and crawl into bed.

The space I share with Allie is more of a suite than a regular dorm room, which is one of the perks of being upperclassmen. We have two bedrooms, a small common area, and an even smaller kitchen. The only downside is the communal bathroom we share with the four other girls on our floor, but luckily none of us are slobs, so the toilets and showers usually stay squeaky clean.

"Hey. You're back late." My roommate pokes her head into my bedroom, sucking on the straw poking out of her glass. She's drinking something green and chunky and absolutely gross looking, but it's a sight I've grown accustomed to. Allie has been "juicing" for the past two weeks, which means that every morning I wake up to the deafening whir of her blender as she prepares her icky liquid meals for the day.

"I had rehearsal." I kick off my shoes and toss my coat on the bed, then proceed to strip down to my underwear despite the fact that Allie is still in the doorway.

Once upon a time, I had been too shy to get naked in front of her. When we shared a double in freshman year, I spent the first few weeks changing under my blanket or waiting until Allie left the room. But the thing about college is, there's no such thing as privacy, and sooner or later you just have to accept that. I still remember how embarrassed I was the first time I saw Allie's bare breasts, but the girl has zero modesty, and when she'd caught me staring, she just winked and said, "I've got it going on, huh?"

After that, I didn't bother with the under-the-blanket routine anymore.

"So listen..."

Her casual opening raises my guard. I've lived with Allie for two years. Long enough to know that when she starts a sentence with "So listen," it's usually followed by something I don't want to hear.

"Hmmm?" I say as I grab my bathrobe from the hook on the door.

"There's a party at Sigma house on Wednesday night." Her blue eyes take on a stern glint. "You're coming with me."

I groan. "A frat party? No way."

"Yes way." She folds her arms over her chest. "Midterms are over, so you don't get to use that as an excuse. And you promised you'd make an effort to be more social this year."

I *had* promised that, but...here's the thing. I don't like parties.

I was raped at a party.

God, I hate that word. Rape. It's one of the few words in the English language that has a visceral effect when you hear it. Like a bone-jarring slap to the face or the chill of ice water being dumped over your head. It's ugly and demoralizing, and I try so hard not to let it control my life. I've worked through what happened to me. Believe me, I have.

I know it wasn't my fault. I know I didn't ask for it or do something to invite it. It didn't steal my ability to trust people or cause me to fear every man that crosses my path. Years of therapy helped me see that the burden of blame lies solely on *him*. There was something wrong with *him*. Not me. Never me. And the most important lesson I learned is that I'm not a victim—I'm a survivor.

But that's not to say the assault didn't change me. It absolutely did. There's a reason I carry pepper spray in my purse and have 911 ready to dial on my phone if I'm walking alone at night. There's a reason I don't drink in public or accept beverages from anyone, not even Allie, because there's always a chance she might unwittingly be handing me a cup that's been tampered with.

And there's a reason I don't go to many parties. I guess it's my version of PTSD. A sound or a smell or a glimpse of something harmless makes the memories spiral to the surface. I hear music blaring and loud chatter and raucous laughter. I smell stale beer and sweat. I'm in a crowd of people. And suddenly I'm fifteen years old again and right back at Melissa Mayer's party, trapped in my own personal nightmare.

Allie softens her tone when she sees my distressed face.

"We've done this before, Han-Han. It'll be like all those other times. You'll never be out of my sight, and neither of us will drink a single drop. I promise."

Shame tugs at my gut. Shame and regret and a touch of awe, because man, she truly is an incredible friend. She doesn't have to stay sober and remain vigilant just to make me feel comfortable, but she does it every time we go out, and I love her deeply for it.

But I hate that she has to do it.

"Okay," I relent, not just for her sake, but my own. I *had* promised her I'd be more social, but I also promised myself that I would make an effort to try new things this year. To lower my guard and stop being so damn afraid of the unfamiliar. A frat party might not be my idea of a great time, but who knows, maybe I'll end up enjoying it.

Allie's face brightens. "Boo-yah! And look, I didn't even have to play my trump card."

"What trump card?" I ask suspiciously.

A grin lifts the corners of her mouth. "Justin is going to be there."

My pulse speeds up. "How do you know?"

"Because Sean and I ran into him in the dining hall and he said he'll be there. I guess a bunch of the meatheads were already planning on coming."

I scowl at her. "He's not a meathead."

"Aw, look how cute you are, defending a football player. Hold on—let me go outside to see if pigs are flying in the sky."

"Ha ha."

"Seriously, Han, it's *weird.* I mean, don't get me wrong, I'm totally on board with you crushing on someone. It's been, what, a year since you and Devon broke up? But I just don't understand how you, of all people, are into a jock."

Discomfort climbs up my spine. "Justin is…he's not like the rest of them. He's different."

"Says the girl who's never spoken a single word to him."

"He's different," I insist. "He's quiet and serious and from what I've seen, he doesn't bang anything in a skirt the way his teammates do. Oh, and he's smart—I saw him reading Hemingway in the quad last week."

"It was probably a required reading."

"It wasn't."

She narrows her eyes. "How do you know that?"

I feel the blush rising in my cheeks. "Some girl asked him about it in class the other day, and he told her Hemingway is his favorite author."

"Oh my God. You're eavesdropping on his conversations now? You're such a creeper." Allie heaves out a sigh. "Okay, that's it. Wednesday night you're exchanging actual dialogue with the guy."

"Maybe," I say noncommittally. "If the opportunity arises..."

"I'll *make* it arise. Seriously. We're not leaving that frat house until you talk to Justin. I don't care if it's just you saying hey, how are ya. You're *talking* to him." She jabs her finger in the air. "Capiche?"

I snicker.

"Capiche?" she repeats in a strict tone.

After a beat, I release a defeated breath. "Capiche."

"Good. Now hurry up and take a shower so we can watch a couple episodes of *Mad Men* before bed."

"*One* episode. I'm too exhausted for any more than that." I grin at her. "Capiche?"

"Capiche," she grumbles before waltzing out of my room.

I chuckle to myself as I gather the rest of my shower supplies, but I'm sidetracked yet again—I've barely taken two steps to the door when a cat meows in my purse. The high-pitched wail is the ringtone I chose for text messages because it's the only one annoying enough to get my attention.

I set my toiletry case on the dresser, rifle through my bag until I locate my cell phone, then scan the message on the screen.

Hey, it's Garrett. Wanted to hammer out the deets re: tutoring sched.

Oh, for fuck's sake.

I don't know whether to laugh or groan. The guy's tenacious, I'll give him that. Sighing, I quickly shoot back a text, short and not at all sweet.

Me: *How'd u get this number?*

Him: *Study grp signup sheet.*

Crap. I'd signed up for the group at the start of the semester, but that was before Cass decided we *had* to rehearse on Mondays and Wednesdays at the exact time the study group meets up.

Another message pops up before I can respond, and whoever said it isn't possible to detect a person's tone via text was totally wrong. Because Garrett's tone is full on irritable.

Him: *If u just showed up to study grp, I wouldn't have to text u.*

Me: *U don't have to text me at all. Actually, I'd prefer if u didn't.*

Him: *What'll it take to get u to say yes?*

Me: *Absolutely nothing.*

Him: *Great. So you'll do it for free.*

The groan I've been holding slips out.

Me: *Not happening.*

Him: *How bout tmrw night? I'm free at eight.*

Me: *Can't. I have the Spanish Flu. Highly contagious. I just saved your life, dude.*

Him: *Aw, I appreciate the concern. But I'm immune to pandemics that wiped out 40-mil ppl from 1918 to 1919.*

Me: *How is it u know so much about pandemics?*

Him: *I'm a history major, baby. I know tons of useless facts.*

Ugh, again with the baby thing? All righty. Clearly it's time to put an end to this before he gets his flirt on.

Me: *Well, nice chatting with u. Good luck on the makeup exam.*

When several seconds tick by and Garrett doesn't respond, I give myself a mental pat on the back for successfully getting rid of him.

I'm about to walk out the door when a picture message meows out of my phone. Against my better judgment, I click to download it, and a moment later, a bare chest fills my screen. Yep. I'm talking smooth tanned skin, sculpted pecs, and the tightest six-pack I've ever seen.

I can't help but snort out loud.

Me: *FFS. Did u just send me a pic of your chest?!*

Him: *Yup. Did it work?*

Me: *In icking me out? Yes. Success!*

Him: *In changing your mind. I'm trying to butter u up here.*

Me: *Ew. Go butter up someone else. PS--I'm posting that pic on my-bri.*

I'm referring, of course, to MyBriar, our school's equivalent of Facebook, which ninety-five percent of the student body is on.

Him: *Go for it. Lots of chicks will be happy to have it in their spank banks.*

Me: *Lose this number, dude. I mean it.*

I don't wait for a response. I just toss my phone on the bed and go take a shower.

4

Hannah

Briar University is five miles from the town of Hastings, Massachusetts, which has one main street and only about two-dozen shops and restaurants. The town is so miniscule it's a miracle I managed to land a part-time job there, and I thank my lucky stars for it every day because most students are forced to make the hour-long drive to Boston if they want to work during the school year. For me, it's either a ten-minute bus ride or a five-minute drive, and then I'm at Della's, the diner I've been waitressing at since freshman year.

Tonight I'm lucky and get to drive over. I have an arrangement with Tracy, one of the girls who lives on my floor. She lets me use her car whenever she doesn't need it as long as I return it with a full tank of gas. It's a sweet deal, especially in the winter when the whole area turns into a snow-covered skating rink.

I don't particularly like my job, but I don't hate it either. It pays well and it's close to campus, so really, I can't complain.

Scratch that—tonight I'm definitely allowed to complain. Because thirty minutes before my shift ends, I find Garrett Graham in one of my booths.

Seriously.

Does this guy *ever* give up?

I have no desire to go over there and serve him, but I don't have much of a choice. Lisa, the other waitress on duty, is busy tending to a group of faculty members at a table across the room, and my boss Della is behind the baby-blue Formica counter dishing out slices of pecan pie to three freshman girls sitting on the tall swivel stools.

I set my jaw and march up to Garrett, making my displeasure obvious as I meet his twinkling gray eyes. He runs a hand through his cropped dark hair and flashes a lopsided grin.

"Hey there, Hannah. Fancy meeting you here."

"Yeah, fancy," I mutter, yanking my order pad out of my apron pocket. "What can I get you?"

"A tutor."

"Sorry, that's not on the menu." I smile sweetly. "We serve really good pecan pie, though."

"You know what I did last night?" he says, without acknowledging the sarcasm.

"Yep. You were text stalking me."

He rolls his eyes. "Before that, I mean."

I pretend to think it over. "Um...you hooked up with a cheerleader? No, you hooked up with the girls' hockey team. No, wait, they're probably not ditzy enough for you. I stick with my original guess—cheerleader."

"Sorority sister, actually," he says smugly. "But I'm talking about what I did before that." He raises one dark eyebrow. "But I'm very intrigued by your interest in my sex life. I can give you details about that another time if you want."

"I don't."

"Another time," he echoes in a dismissive tone, folding his hands on the blue-and-white-checkered tablecloth.

He's got big hands with long fingers, short nails, and knuckles that are slightly red and cracked. I wonder if he's been in a fight recently, but then I realize the busted-up knuckles are probably a hockey player thing.

"I was at study group yesterday," he informs me. "There were eight other people there, and you know what the highest mark in the group was?" He blurts out the answer before I can hazard a guess. "C-plus. And our combined average was a *D*. How am I supposed to pass this makeup if I'm studying with people who are as dumb as I am? I *need* you, Wellsy."

Wellsy? Is that a nickname? And how on earth does he know that my last name is Wells? I never told—argh. Damn sign-up sheet.

Garrett notices my surprised look and cocks his brows again. "I learned a lot about you in study group. Got your number, your full name, even found out where you work."

"Congratulations, you really are a stalker."

"Nope, just thorough. I like to know what I'm up against."

"Jesus Harold Christ! I'm not tutoring you, okay? Go bug somebody else." I point at the menu in front of him. "Are you ordering? Because if not, then please go away and let me do my job in peace."

"Jesus Harold Christ?" Garrett snickers before picking up the laminated menu and giving it a cursory glance. "I'll have a turkey club." He sets the menu down, then reaches for it again. "And a bacon double cheeseburger. Just the burger, no fries. Actually, I changed my mind—yes to the fries. Oh, and a side order of onion rings."

My jaw almost hits the floor. "You're seriously going to eat all that?"

He grins. "Of course. I'm a growing boy."

Boy? Nuh-uh. I'm only noticing it now—probably because I've been too distracted by how insufferable he is—but Garrett Graham is all *man.* There's nothing boyish about him, not his chiseled good looks or his tall frame or that ripped chest of his, which suddenly flashes to mind as I remember the picture he sent me.

"I'll also take a slice of that pecan pie and a Dr. Pepper to drink. Oh, and some tutoring."

"Not on the menu," I say cheerfully. "But the rest is coming right up."

Before he can argue, I abandon his booth and head to the back counter to place his order with Julio, our night cook. A nanosecond later, Lisa rushes over and addresses me in a hushed voice.

"Oh my God. You know who that is, right?"

"Yep."

"It's Garrett Graham."

"I know," I answer dryly. "That's why I said *yep.*"

Lisa looks outraged. "What is wrong with you? Why aren't you freaking out right now? *Garrett Graham* is *sitting* in your *booth.* He *talked* to you."

"Holy shit, he did? I mean, his lips were moving, but I didn't realize he was talking."

I roll my eyes and walk over to the drink station to pour

Garrett's drink. I don't look his way, but I can feel those smoky gray eyes following my every movement. He's probably sending telepathic orders for me to tutor him. Well, too bad for him. There's no way I'm wasting the little spare time I have on a college hockey player who thinks he's a rock star.

Lisa trails after me, oblivious to my sarcasm and still gushing about Graham. "He's so gorgeous. Like unbelievably gorgeous." Her voice lowers to a whisper. "And I hear he's amazing in bed."

I snort. "He probably started that rumor himself."

"No, Samantha Richardson told me. She hooked up with him last year at the Theta kegger. Said it was the best sex of her life."

I have no response, because I couldn't care less about the sex life of some girl I don't even know. Instead, I shrug and hold out the Dr. Pepper. "You know what? Why don't you take his booth?"

The way Lisa gasps, you'd think I just handed her a check for five million dollars. "Are you sure?"

"Yep. He's all yours."

"Oh my God." She takes a step forward as if she's going to hug me, but then her gaze darts to Garrett and she appears to have second thoughts about broadcasting her terribly unwarranted joy. "I owe you *so* big for this, Han."

I want to tell her that she's actually doing me the favor, but she's already dashing toward the booth to wait on her prince. I watch in amusement as Garrett's expression clouds over at Lisa's approach. He picks up the glass she sets in front of him, then meets my gaze and slants his head.

As if to say, you're not getting rid of me *that* easily.

Garrett

She's not getting rid of me *that* easily.

Clearly Hannah Wells hasn't been around many athletes.

We're a stubborn lot, and the main thing we all have in common? We never, ever give up.

God help me, but I'm going to convince this girl to tutor me, even if I die trying.

But now that Hannah has dumped me off on the other waitress, it's a long while before I get another opportunity to plead my case. For the next twenty minutes, I endure the blatant flirting and undisguised interest of the curly-haired brunette who's serving me, but although I'm polite to her, I don't flirt back.

The only person I'm interested in tonight is Hannah, and my gaze sticks to her like glue as she works the room. I wouldn't put it past her to make a run for it when I'm not looking.

Her uniform is kinda hot, if I'm being honest. Powder-blue dress with a white collar, big buttons down the front, and a short white apron around her waist. Looks like an outfit right out of *Grease*, which I guess makes sense considering Della's is a 50s-themed diner. I can easily picture Hannah Wells fitting in during that era. Her dark, shoulder-length hair has a slight wave to it, and her bangs are pinned to the side with a blue barrette, giving the hairstyle an old-fashioned vibe.

As I watch her work, I wonder what her story is. I asked around at study group, but nobody knew much about her. One guy told me she's from a small town in the Midwest. Someone else said she dated some guy in a band all through sophomore year. Other than those two meager details, she's a total mystery.

"Can I get you anything else?" my waitress asks eagerly.

She's looking at me like I'm a celebrity or some shit, but I'm used to the attention. Fact: when you're the captain of a Division I hockey team that's won two consecutive national titles, people know who you are. And women want to fuck you.

"No, thanks. Just the bill, please."

"Oh." Her disappointment is unmistakable. "Sure. Coming right up."

Before she can go, I voice a gruff question. "Do you know when Hannah's shift is over?"

Her disappointed expression transforms into one of disbelief. "Why?"

"She's in one of my classes. I wanted to talk to her about an assignment."

The brunette's face relaxes, but a flicker of suspicion lingers in her eyes. "She's off now, but she can't leave until her table does."

I glance over at the only other occupied table in the diner, where a middle-aged couple is sitting. The man has just pulled out his wallet, while his wife peers at the bill through her horn-rimmed glasses.

I pay for my food, bid my waitress goodbye, then head outside to wait for Hannah. Five minutes later, the older couple waltzes out of the diner. A minute after that, Hannah appears, but if she sees me lurking near the door, she doesn't let on. She simply buttons up her coat and takes off toward the side of the building.

I waste no time hurrying after her. "Wellsy, wait up."

She looks over her shoulder, frowning deeply. "For the love of God, I'm *not* tutoring you."

"Sure you are." I shrug. "I just need to figure out what you want in return."

Hannah whirls around like a dark-haired tornado. "I want to not tutor you. *That's* what I want."

"All right, so it's obvious you're not interested in money," I muse as if she hasn't spoken. "Has to be something else then." I mull it over for a beat. "Booze? Weed?"

"No, and no, and get lost."

She starts walking again, her white sneakers slapping the sidewalk as she marches toward the gravel lot at the side of the diner. She makes a beeline for the silver Toyota hatchback parked right next to my Jeep.

"Okay then. I guess you're not into party favors."

I follow her to the driver's side, but she completely ignores me as she unlocks the door and tosses her purse into the passenger seat.

"How about a date?" I offer.

That gets her attention. She straightens up like someone shoved a metal rod up her spine, then swivels her head in astonishment. "What?"

"Ah. I've got your attention."

"No, you've got my disgust. You actually think I want to go out with you?"

"Everyone wants to go out with me."

She bursts out laughing.

Maybe I should feel insulted by the response, but I like the sound of her laughter. It's got a musical quality to it, a husky pitch that tickles my ears.

"Just out of curiosity," she says, "after you wake up in the morning, do you admire yourself in the mirror for one hour or two?"

"Two," I reply cheerfully.

"Do you high five yourself?"

"Of course not." I smirk. "I kiss each of my biceps and then point to the ceiling and thank the big man upstairs for creating such a perfect male specimen."

She snorts. "Uh-huh. Well, sorry to burst your bubble, Mr. Perfect, but I'm not interested in dating you."

"I think you're misunderstanding, Wellsy. I'm not looking to make a love connection with you. I know you're not into me. If it makes you feel better, I'm not into you either."

"That does make me feel better. I was starting to worry I might actually be your type, and that's too terrifying to even contemplate."

When she tries to duck into the car, I curl my fingers over the doorframe to keep it open. "I'm talking about image," I clarify.

"Image," she echoes.

"Yeah. Do you think you'd be the first girl who went out with me to boost her popularity? Happens all the time."

Hannah laughs again. "I'm perfectly content with my current rung on the social ladder, but thanks so much for offering to 'boost my popularity.' You're a prince, Garrett. Really."

Frustration scrambles up my throat. "What'll it take to change your mind?"

"Nothing. You're wasting your time." She shakes her head, looking as frustrated as I feel. "You know, if you take all the effort you're using to harass me and channel it to your studies, you'd get an A-plus-plus-plus on that midterm."

She shoves my hand out of the way, slides into the driver's seat, and shuts the door. A second later, the engine roars to life, and I'm pretty sure that if I hadn't stepped back in time, she would've run right over my foot.

I wonder if Hannah Wells was an athlete in another life, because she is one stubborn woman.

Sighing, I stare at her blinking red taillights and try to figure out my next move.

Absolutely nothing comes to mind.

5

Hannah

Allie stays true to her word. It's twenty minutes into the party, and she's yet to leave my side, despite the fact that her boyfriend has been begging her to dance with him since the second we arrived.

I feel like a jackass.

"Okay, this is ridiculous. Go dance with Sean already." I have to shout in order to be heard over the music, which, shockingly enough, is pretty decent. I expected shitty dance beats or vulgar hip-hop, but whoever's manning the stereo system seems to have an affinity for indie rock and Brit punk.

"Naah, it's fine," Allie shouts back. "I'll just chill here with you."

Right, because lurking against the wall like a creeper and watching me cling to the bottle of Evian I brought from the dorm is *way* more fun than spending time with her boyfriend.

The living room is teeming with people. Frat brothers and sorority sisters galore, but tonight there's a lot more variety than you usually find at a Greek event. I spot several drama majors near the pool table. A few girls from the field hockey team chatting by the fireplace. A group of guys that I'm pretty sure are freshman standing at the built-in bar. All the furniture has been pushed against the wood-paneled walls to create a makeshift dance floor in the center of the room. Everywhere I look, I see people dancing and laughing and shooting the shit.

And poor Allie is stuck to me like Velcro, unable to enjoy a second of the party *she* wanted to go to.

"Go," I urge her. "Really. You haven't seen Sean since midterms started. You deserve to spend some quality time with your man."

She hesitates.

"I'll be fine. Katie and Shawna are right over there—I'll hang out with them for a bit."

"Are you sure?"

"Positive. I came here to socialize, remember?" Grinning, I give her a tiny smack on the butt. "Get outta here, babe."

She grins back and starts to walk away, then holds up her iPhone and waves it in the air. "SOS if you need me," she calls out. "And don't leave without telling me!"

The music drowns out my response, but she catches my nod before she hurries off. I see her blond head weaving through the crowd, and then she's at Sean's side and he's happily dragging her into the throng of dancers.

See? I can be a good friend too.

Except now I'm all alone, and the two girls I was planning on latching onto are chatting with two very cute guys. I don't want to interrupt the flirt fest, so I search the crowd for anyone else I might know—even Cass would be a sight for sore eyes at this point—but I don't spot any familiar faces. Stifling a sigh, I hunker down in my little corner and spend the next few minutes people-watching.

When several guys glance my way with unabashed interest, I have to curse myself for allowing Allie to choose my outfit tonight. My dress isn't indecent by any means, just a knee-length green shift with a modest neckline, but it hugs my curves more tightly than I'm comfortable with, and the black heels I paired it with make my legs look a lot longer than they actually are. I didn't put up an argument about the outfit because I'd wanted to catch Justin's eye, but in my eagerness to make it on his radar, I didn't think about all the other radars I might appear on, and the attention I'm getting makes me nervous.

"Hey."

I turn my head as a cute guy with wavy brown hair and light-blue eyes sidles up to me. He's wearing a polo shirt and holding a red plastic cup in his hand, and he's smiling at me as if we know each other.

"Uh. Hey," I answer.

When he notices my quizzical expression, his smile widens. "I'm Jimmy. We have British Lit together?"

"Oh. Right." I honestly don't remember seeing him before, but there are about two hundred students in that class, so all the faces blur into each other after a while.

"You're Hannah, right?"

I nod, shifting in discomfort, because his gaze has already lowered to my chest a dozen times in the five seconds we've been talking.

Jimmy pauses as if he's trying to think of something else to say. I can't think of anything either because I suck at small talk. If he was someone I was interested in, I'd ask him about his classes, or if he has a job, or what kind of music he's into, but the only guy I care about at the moment is Justin—and he still hasn't shown up.

The fact that I'm searching the crowd for him makes me feel like a total loser. Truth be told, Allie's not the only one wondering what my deal is. I'm wondering too, because seriously, why am I so obsessed with this guy? He doesn't know I exist. And he's a jock, to boot. I may as well be interested in Garratt Graham, for fuck's sake. At least *he* offered to go out with me.

And what do you know—the second I think about Garrett, the devil himself enters the room.

I didn't expect to see him tonight, and I immediately duck my head so he doesn't spot me. Maybe if I concentrate hard enough, I'll chameleon into the wall behind me and he won't know I'm here.

Luckily, Garrett is oblivious to my presence. He stops to talk to a couple of guys, then saunters toward the bar on the other side of the room, where he's immediately swarmed by half a dozen girls who bat their eyelashes and thrust their boobs out to get his attention.

Beside me, Jimmy rolls his eyes. "Jeez. The big man on campus routine gets old, huh?"

I realize he's looking at Garrett too, and the disgust on his face is unmistakable. "You're not a fan of Graham's?" I say dryly.

"You want the truth or the house line?"

"House line?"

"He's a member of this frat," Jimmy explains. "So

technically that makes us *brothers*." He air-quotes the word. "And a Sigma man loves *all* his brothers."

I have to grin. "Okay, so that's the house line. What's the truth?"

The music swells, so he leans in closer. His lips are centimeters from my ear as he confides, "Can't stand the guy. His ego's bigger than this house."

Look at that—I've met a kindred spirit. Another person who's not a card-carrying member of Team Garrett.

Except the conspiratorial smile I give him is clearly taken the wrong way, because Jimmy's eyes go heavy-lidded. "So...wanna dance?" he drawls.

I don't. At all. But just as I open my mouth to say no, I glimpse a flash of black from the corner of my eye. Garrett's black T-shirt. Crap. He's spotted me and now he's heading our way. Judging by his determined stride, he's ready to do battle with me again.

"Sure," I blurt out, eagerly grabbing Jimmy's hand. "Let's dance."

A slow smile spreads across his mouth.

Uh-oh. Maybe I sounded a bit too eager there.

But it's too late to change my mind, because he's leading me toward the dance floor. And just my luck—the song changes the second we get there. The Ramones have been replaced by a Lady Gaga track. Not a fast one, either, but the slow version of "Poker Face." Great.

Jimmy plants both his hands on my hips.

After a beat, I reluctantly hold onto his shoulders, and we begin to sway to the music. It's awkward as hell, but at least I managed to evade Garrett, who is now regarding us with a frown, his hands hooked in the belt loops of his faded blue jeans.

When our gazes meet, I shoot him a half-smile and a what-can-you-do look, and he immediately narrows his eyes as if he knows I'm dancing with Jimmy just so I don't have to talk to him. Then a pretty blonde touches his arm, and he breaks the eye contact.

Jimmy twists his head to see who I'm looking at. "You know Garrett?" He sounds more than a little wary.

I shrug. "He's in one of my classes."

"Are you friends?"

"Nope."

"Good to hear."

Garrett and the blonde duck out of the room just then, and I mentally pat myself on the back for my successful evasion tactics.

"Does he live here with you guys?" God, this song is taking forever, but I'm trying to make conversation because I feel like I have to finish out the dance after being so "enthusiastic" about it.

"No, thank fuck," Jimmy answers. "He's got a house off-campus. He's always bragging about it, but I bet you his father pays his rent."

I wrinkle my forehead. "Why do you say that? Is his family rich or something?"

Jimmy looks surprised. "You don't know who his dad is?"

"No. Should I?"

"It's Phil Graham." When the groove in my forehead deepens, Jimmy elaborates. "Forward for the New York Rangers? Two-time Stanley Cup champ? Hockey legend?"

The one hockey team I know anything about is the Chicago Blackhawks, and that's only because my dad is a rabid fan and makes me watch the games with him. Ergo, I have zero knowledge of a man who played for the Rangers, what, twenty years ago? But I'm not surprised to hear that Garrett hails from hockey royalty. He's got that superior sense of entitlement down pat.

"I wonder why Garrett didn't go to college in New York then," I say politely.

"Graham Sr. finished out his career in Boston," Jimmy explains. "I guess the family decided to stay in Massachusetts after he retired."

The song blessedly comes to an end, and I hastily excuse myself by pretending I need to use the washroom. Jimmy makes me promise to dance with him again, then winks and wanders off toward the beer pong table.

Since I don't want him to know I lied about the bathroom, I follow through on the pee charade by leaving the living room to loiter in the front parlor for a bit, which is where Allie finds me a few minutes later.

"Hey! Are you having a good time?" Her eyes are bright and her cheeks are flushed, but I know she hasn't been drinking. She promised to stay sober, and Allie never breaks her promises.

"Yeah, I guess. I think I'm taking off soon, though."

"Aw no, you can't go yet! I just saw you dancing with Jim Paulson—you looked like you were having fun."

Really? I guess I'm a much better actress than I thought.

"He's cute," she adds with a meaningful look.

"Naah, he's not my type. Too preppy."

"Well, I know someone who *is* your type." Allie wiggles her eyebrows before lowering her voice to a teasing whisper. "And don't turn around, but he just walked through the door."

My heart takes off like a kite in a windstorm. *Don't turn around*? Don't people realize that saying that is guaranteed to make someone do the exact opposite?

I swivel my head toward the front door, then swivel it right back because *oh my God*. She's right. Justin has finally shown up.

And since the glimpse I stole was far too fleeting, I rely on Allie to fill in the blanks. "Is he alone?" I murmur.

"He's with a few of his teammates," she murmurs back. "None of them brought dates, though."

I do my best impression of a person who's just talking to a friend and is in no way crushing on the guy standing ten feet away. And it works, because Justin and his buddies walk right past Allie and me, their loud laughter quickly swallowed up by a swell of music.

"You're blushing," she teases.

"I know." I groan softly. "Fuck. This crush is so stupid, A. Why are you letting me embarrass myself like this?"

"Because I don't think it's stupid at all. And it's not embarrassing—it's healthy." She grabs my arm and proceeds to drag me back to the living room. The stereo volume is lower now, but animated chatter continues to buzz through the room.

"Seriously, Han, you're young and beautiful, and I want you to fall in love. I don't care who it's with as long as—why is Garrett Graham staring at you?"

I follow her startled gaze and smother another groan when Garrett's gray eyes lock onto mine.

"Because he's stalking me," I grumble.

Her eyebrows soar. "For real?"

"Pretty much, yeah. He's failing Ethics, and he knows I did well on the midterm so now he's demanding I tutor him. The guy can't take no for an answer."

She snickers. "I think you might be the only girl who's ever turned him down."

"If only the rest of the female population was as smart as I am."

I gaze past Allie's shoulder and scan the room for Justin, and my pulse speeds up when I spot him by the pool table. He's wearing black pants and a gray cable-knit sweater, and his hair is messy, falling onto his strong forehead. God, I love that just-rolled-out-of-bed look he has going on. He's not all gelled up like his buddies, nor is he wearing his football jacket like the rest of them.

"Allie, get your cute ass over here!" Sean shouts from the Ping-Pong table. "I need my pong partner!"

A pretty blush blooms on her cheeks. "Wanna watch us kick some beer pong butt? Minus the beer," she adds quickly. "Sean knows I'm not drinking tonight."

I'm hit with another jolt of guilt. "That's no fun," I say lightly. "You've gotta have the beer to play the pong."

She firmly shakes her head. "I promised you I wouldn't drink."

"And I'm not planning on sticking around for much longer," I counter. "So there's no reason for you not to get your buzz on."

"But I want you to stay," she protests.

"How about this? I'll stay for another half hour, but only if you allow yourself to have some actual fun. I know we made a deal in freshman year, but I'm not holding you to it anymore, A."

I mean every word, because I really do hate that she has to babysit me every time we go out. It's not fair to her. And after two years at Briar, I know it's time for me to lower my guard, at least a little bit.

"Come on, I want to see you show off those mad beer pong skills." I link my arm through hers, and she laughs as I drag her over to Sean and his friends.

"Hannah!" Sean says in delight. "You playing?"

"Nope," I reply. "Just cheering on my bestie."

Allie joins Sean at one end of the table, and for the next ten minutes, I watch the most intense beer pong match on the planet unfold. But the entire time, I'm wholly aware of Justin, who's chatting with his teammates across the room.

Eventually, I wander off because I finally do need to use the restroom. There's one on the main floor near the kitchen, but the line is crazy long and it's ages before I get a turn. I quickly do my business, then walk out of the bathroom—and slam into a hard male chest.

"You should really watch where you're going," a husky voice remarks.

My heart stops.

Justin's dark eyes twinkle with humor as he places his hand on my arm to steady me. The moment he touches me, heat sears my flesh and unleashes a flurry of goose bumps.

"Sorry," I stammer.

"No worries." Smiling, he pats his chest down. "I'm still in one piece."

I suddenly notice that there's no one waiting to use the washroom anymore. It's just Justin and me in the hallway, and God, he's even better looking close up. He's also much taller than I realized—I have to tilt my head to meet his eyes.

"You're in Ethics with me, aren't you?" he asks in that deep, sexy voice of his.

I nod.

"I'm Justin."

He introduces himself as if there might actually be someone at Briar who *doesn't* know his name. But I find his modesty is adorable.

"I'm Hannah."

"How'd you do on the midterm?"

"I got an A," I admit. "You?"

"B minus."

I can't hide my surprise. "Really? I guess we're the lucky ones, then. Everyone else bombed it."

"I think it makes us smart, not lucky."

His grin makes me melt. Seriously. I'm a puddle of goo on the floor, unable to look away from those magnetic dark eyes. And he smells fantastic, like soap and lemony aftershave. Would it be inappropriate if I pressed my face in his neck and inhaled him?

Uh...yeah. It would.

"So..." I try to think of something clever or interesting to say, but I'm too nervous to be witty at the moment. "You play football, huh?"

He nods. "Wide receiver. Are you a fan?" A dimple appears in his chin. "Of the game, I mean."

I'm not, but I suppose I could lie and pretend to like his

sport. Except that's a risky move, because then he might try to talk "shop" with me, and I don't know enough about football to carry a whole conversation about it.

"Not really," I confess with a sigh. "I've seen a game or two, but honestly, it's too slow for my liking. Seems like you guys play for five seconds, and then someone blows a whistle and you stand around for hours before the next play starts."

Justin laughs. He's got a great laugh. Low and husky and I feel it right down to my toes. "Yeah, I've heard that complaint before. It's different when you're playing it, though. A lot more intense than you'd think. And if you're invested in a team or certain players, you pick up the rules a lot faster." He slants his head. "You should come to one of our games. I bet you'd have fun."

Holy shit. He's inviting me to one of his games?

"Uh, yeah, maybe I will—"

"Kohl!" a loud voice interrupts. "We're up!"

We both turn as a blond behemoth pokes his head out of the living room doorway. It's one of Justin's teammates, and he's wearing a look of extreme impatience.

"Coming," Justin calls back, then gives me a rueful smile as he takes a step toward the bathroom. "Big Joe and I are about to kick some ass in pool, but I've gotta hit the can first. Talk later?"

"Sure." I keep my tone casual, but there's nothing casual about the way my heart is racing.

As Justin shuts the door behind him, I hurry back to the living room on shaky legs. I'm dying to tell Allie about what just happened, but I don't get the chance. The second I walk into the room, six-foot-two and two hundred pounds of Garrett Graham block my path.

"Wellsy," he says cheerfully. "You're the last person I expected to see here tonight."

As usual, his presence causes my guard to snap into place. "Yeah? Why's that?"

He shrugs. "I didn't think frat parties were your scene."

"Well, you don't know me, remember? Maybe I'm partying it up on Greek Row every night."

"Liar. I would've seen you here before."

He crosses his arms over his chest, a pose that causes his biceps to flex. I glimpse the bottom of a tattoo peeking out from his sleeve, but I can't tell what it is, only that it's black and looks intricate. Flames maybe?

"So, about this tutoring thing... I thought we should take a moment to set up a schedule."

Aggravation shoots up my spine. "You don't give up, do you?"

"Never."

"Then you need to start, because I'm not tutoring you." I'm distracted now. Justin has reentered the room, his long, lithe body moving through the crowd as he makes his way to the pool table. He's halfway there when a pretty brunette intercepts him. To my dismay, he stops to talk to her.

"Come on, Wellsy, help a guy out," Garrett begs.

Justin laughs at something the girl says. Same way he was laughing with me a minute ago. And when she touches his arm and leans in close, he doesn't back away.

"Look, if you don't want to commit to the whole semester, at least help me pass this midterm. I'll owe you one."

I'm no longer paying Garrett even a lick of attention. Justin leans in to whisper in the girl's ear. She giggles, her cheeks turn a rosy shade of pink, and my heart plummets to the pit of my stomach.

I was so sure we'd been, I don't know, *connecting*, but now he's flirting with someone else?

"You're not even listening to me," Garrett accuses. "Who are you looking at, anyway?"

I tear my eyes off Justin and the brunette, but not fast enough.

Garrett grins when he notices where my gaze was. "Which one?" he demands.

"Which one what?"

He cocks his head at Justin, then shifts it five feet to the right, where I notice Jimmy talking to one of his frat brothers. "Paulson or Kohl—which one do you want to bone?"

"Bone?" He has my attention again. "Ugh. Who says stuff like that?"

"Fine, should I rephrase? Which one do you want to fuck or screw or drill or *make love to,* if that's your thing."

I set my jaw. This guy is such an asshole.

When I don't answer, he answers for me. "Kohl," he decides. "I saw you dancing with Paulson earlier and you definitely weren't making googly eyes at him."

I don't confirm or deny it. Instead I take a step away. "Have a good night, Garrett."

"I hate to break it to you, but it ain't gonna happen, Wellsy. You're not his type."

Anger and embarrassment flood my belly. Wow. Had he really just said that?

"Thanks for the tip," I say coolly. "Now if you'll excuse me..."

He tries reaching for my arm but I bulldoze past him and leave him in my proverbial dust. I do a quick search of the room for Allie, halting in my tracks when I spot her making out with Sean on the couch. I don't want to interrupt them, so I spin on my heel and head toward the front door instead.

My fingers are shaky as I text Allie to let her know I'm taking off. Garrett's blunt assertion—*you're not his type*—echoes in my mind like a depressing mantra.

Truth is, it's exactly what I needed to hear. So what if Justin spoke to me in the hallway? Obviously it meant nothing, because in the next breath he turned around and flirted with someone else. It's time for me to face reality. It's not going to happen with me and Justin, no matter how badly I want it to.

It was stupid of me to come here tonight.

Waves of embarrassment course through me as I leave the Sigma house and step into the cool night breeze. I regret not bringing a coat, but I hadn't wanted to carry it around all night, and I figured I could deal with the October chill for the five-second walk from the cab to the front door.

Allie messages back as I step onto the porch, offering to come outside and keep me company until the taxi arrives, but I order her to stay with her boyfriend. Then I pull up the number for the campus taxi service, and I'm just about to dial when I hear my name. A maddening variation of it, that is.

"Wellsy. Wait up."

I take the porch steps two at a time, but Garrett is a lot taller than me, which means his stride is longer, and he catches up to me in no time.

"Come on, wait." His hand latches onto my shoulder.

I shrug it off and turn to glare at him. "What? You're in the mood to insult me some more?"

"I wasn't trying to insult you," he protests. "I was just

stating a fact."

That stings. "Gee. Thanks."

"Fuck." He looks frustrated. "I insulted you again. I didn't mean to do that. I'm not trying to be a dick, okay?"

"Of course you're not *trying*. You just are."

He has the nerve to grin, but his humor fades fast. "Look, I know the guy, all right? Kohl's friends with one of my roommates, so he's been over at my place a few times."

"Goodie for you. You can date him then because I'm not interested."

"Yes, you are." He sounds very sure of himself, and I hate him for that. "All I'm saying is, Kohl has a type."

"All right, I'll humor you. What's his type then? And not because I'm interested in him or anything," I add hastily.

He smiles knowingly. "Uh-huh. Of course you're not." Then he shrugs. "He's been at this college for, what, almost two months? So far I've seen him hook up with one cheerleader and two members of Kappa Beta. Know what that tells me?"

"No, but it tells *me* that you spend way too much time keeping track of who other dudes are dating."

He ignores the barb. "It tells me Kohl is interested in chicks with a certain social status."

I roll my eyes. "If this is another offer to make me popular, I'm gonna have to pass."

"Hey, if you want to get Kohl's attention, you've gotta do something drastic." He pauses. "So yes, I'm reoffering to go out with you."

"I re-pass. Now if you'll excuse me, I need to call a cab."

"No, you don't."

My phone had gone idle, so I quickly type in my password to unlock it.

"Seriously, don't bother," Garrett says. "I can drive you home."

"I don't need a ride."

"That's what cabs *do*. They give you *rides*."

"I don't need a ride from *you*," I amend.

"You'd rather pay ten bucks to get home instead of accepting a free ride from me?"

His sarcastic remark is right on target. Because yes, I most certainly trust a campus-employed cabbie to drive me home more than I trust Garrett Graham to do it. I don't get into cars with strangers. Period.

Garrett's eyes narrow as if he's read my mind. "I'm not going to try anything, Wellsy. It's just a ride home."

"Go back to the party, Garrett. Your frat brothers are probably wondering where you are."

"Trust me, they don't give a shit where I am. They're only interested in finding a tipsy chick to stick their dicks in."

I gag. "God. You are disgusting, you know that?"

"Nope, just honest. Besides, it's not like I said *I'm* looking to do that. I don't need to get a woman drunk for her to sleep with me. They come to me sober and willing."

"Congratulations." I yelp when he snatches the phone out of my hand. "Hey!"

To my amazement, he turns the camera toward his face and snaps a picture.

"What are you doing?"

"There," he says, handing the phone back. "Feel free to text that sexy face to your entire contact list and inform them I'm driving you home. That way if you show up dead tomorrow everyone will know who did it. And if you want, you can keep your finger on the emergency call button the whole time in case you need to call the cops." He heaves out an exasperated breath. "Can I please take you home now?"

Although I'm not excited about standing outside alone and coatless to wait for the taxi, I still put up one last protest. "How much have you had to drink?"

"Half a beer."

I raise my eyebrows.

"My limit is one," he insists. "I've got practice tomorrow morning."

My resistance crumbles at his earnest expression. I've heard a lot of rumors about Garrett, but none involving alcohol or drugs, and the campus cab service is notorious for taking its sweet ass time, so really, it won't kill me to spend five minutes in a car with the guy. I can easily give him the silent treatment if he annoys me.

Or rather, *when* he annoys me.

"All right," I concede. "You can take me home. But this doesn't mean I'm tutoring you."

His smile is the epitome of smug. “We’ll discuss it in the car.”

6

Garrett

Hannah Wells is into a football player. I can't wrap my head around it, but I've already offended her once tonight, so I know I have to tread carefully if I'm going to win her over.

I wait until we're in my Jeep and buckled up before I voice the cautious question. "So, how long have you wanted to fu—make love to Kohl?"

She doesn't answer, but I can feel her death glare boring into the side of my face.

"Has to be a fairly recent thing since he just transferred two months ago." I purse my lips. "Okay, let's assume it's been a month."

No answer.

I glance over and see that she's glowering even harder now, but even with that forbidding expression, she still looks hot. She's got one of the most interesting faces I've ever seen—her cheeks are a little too round, her mouth a little too pouty, but combined with her smooth olive skin, vivid green eyes, and the tiny beauty mark over her top lip, she looks almost exotic. And that body...man, now that I've noticed it, I can't *un*-notice it.

But I remind myself that I'm not driving her home in the hopes of scoring. I need Hannah too much to screw it up by sleeping with her.

After practice today, Coach pulled me aside and gave me a ten-minute lecture about the importance of keeping my grades up. Well, *lecture* is too generous a description—his exact words had been "maintain your average or I'll shove my foot so far up your ass you'll be able to taste my shoe polish in your mouth for years to come."

Like the smartass I am, I asked if people actually still use shoe polish, and he responded with a string of colorful expletives before storming off.

I'm not exaggerating when I say that hockey is my entire life, but I guess that's bound to happen when your father is a fucking superstar. The old man had my future planned out when I was still in the womb—learn to skate, learn to shoot, make it to the pros, the end. Phil Graham has a reputation to uphold, after all. I mean, just think about how badly it'd reflect on him if his only son didn't grow up to be a professional hockey player.

Yes, that's sarcasm you're detecting. And here's a confession: I hate my father. No, I *despise* him. The irony is, the bastard thinks everything I've done has been for him. The intense training, the full-body bruises, killing myself twenty hours a week in order to better my game. He's arrogant enough to believe that I put myself through all that for *him*.

But he's wrong. I do it for me. And to a lesser extent, I do it to *beat* him. To be *better* than him.

Don't get me wrong—I love the game. I live for the roar of the crowd, the crisp air chilling my face as I hurtle down the ice, the hiss of the puck as I release a slap shot that lights the lamp. Hockey is adrenaline. It's excitement. It's...soothing, even.

I look at Hannah again, wondering what it'll take to persuade her, and it suddenly occurs to me I've been thinking about this Kohl thing the wrong way. Because yeah, I don't think she's his type, but how is he *hers*?

Kohl plays it off like he's the strong, silent type, but I've hung out with him enough times to see through the act. He uses that man of mystery bullshit to draw girls in, and once they bite, he turns on the charm and lures them right into his pants.

So why the hell is a levelheaded girl like Hannah Wells salivating over a bigshot like Kohl?

"Is this just a physical thing or do you actually want to date him?" I ask curiously.

Her exasperated sigh echoes in the car. "Can we please not talk about this?"

I flick the right turn signal and drive away from Greek Row, heading for the road that leads back to campus.

"I was wrong about you," I tell her in a frank tone.

"What's that supposed to mean?"

"It means I thought you were upfront. Ballsy. Not someone who's too much of a pussy to admit she's into a guy."

I hide a grin when I see her jaw harden. I'm not surprised that I hit a nerve. I'm pretty good at reading people, and I know without a shred of doubt that Hannah Wells isn't the kind of woman who backs down from a challenge, not even a veiled one.

"Fine. You win." She sounds like she's speaking through clenched teeth. "Maybe I'm into him. A teeny, tiny bit."

My grin breaks free. "Gee, was that so hard?" I ease my foot off the gas as we approach a stop sign. "Why haven't you asked him out then?"

Alarm ripples through her voice. "Why would I do that?"

"Uh, because you just said you're into him?"

"I don't even know him."

"How else are you going to get to know him if you don't ask him out?"

She shifts in her seat, looking so uncomfortable I can't help but laugh.

"You're scared," I tease her, unable to keep the delight out of my voice.

"I am not," she says instantly. Then she pauses. "Well, maybe a little. He...he makes me nervous, okay?"

It takes some effort to mask my surprise. I hadn't expected her to be so...honest, I guess. And the vulnerability she's radiating is slightly unsettling. I haven't known her long, but I've gotten used to her sarcasm and confidence. The uncertainty on her face seems out of place.

"So you're going to wait around for him to ask you?"

She scowls at me. "Let me guess—you think he won't."

"I *know* he won't." I give a little shrug. "Men are all about the chase, Wellsy. You're making it too easy for him."

"Hardly," she says dryly. "Considering I haven't even told him I'm interested."

"Oh, he knows."

That startles her. "No, he doesn't."

"A man always knows when a woman wants him. Believe me, you don't have to say it out loud for him to pick up on the vibes you're sending out." I grin. "Hell, it only took five seconds for me to figure it out."

"And you think if I go out with you, he'll magically be interested in me?" She sounds skeptical, but no longer hostile, which is a promising sign.

"It'll definitely help your cause. You know what intrigues guys even more than the chase?"

"I can't wait to hear it."

"A woman who's out of reach. People want what they can't have." I can't help but smirk. "Case in point—you wanting Kohl."

"Uh-huh. Well, if I can't have him, then why bother going on a date with you?"

"You can't have him *now*. Doesn't mean you'll *never* have him."

I reach another stop sign, and I'm annoyed to see that we're almost back at campus. Shit. I need more time to persuade her, so I drive a bit slower and hope she doesn't notice I'm going ten under the limit.

"Trust me, Wellsy, if you show up on my arm, he'll notice." I pause, pretending to think it over. "Tell you what—there's this party next Saturday and Loverboy will be there."

"One, don't call him that. And two, how do you know where he'll be?" she says suspiciously.

"Because it's Beau Maxwell's birthday bash. You know, the quarterback? The whole team will be there." I shrug. "And so will we."

"Mmm-hmmm. And what happens when we get there?"

She's playing it off as casual, but I know I've got her exactly where I want her.

"We mingle, have a few beers. I'll introduce you around as my date. Chicks will want to murder you. Guys will wonder who you are and why you haven't been on their radars before. Kohl will wonder too, but we're going to ignore him."

"And why would we do that?"

"Because it'll drive him crazy. Make you seem even more unattainable."

She bites her lip. I wonder if she knows how easy it is to read her emotions. Annoyance, anger, embarrassment. Her eyes reveal everything and it fascinates me. I work so hard to mask what I'm feeling—a lesson I learned from childhood—but Hannah's face is an open book. It's kinda refreshing.

"You have a lot of confidence in yourself," she finally remarks. "Do you honestly think you're such hot shit that the mere act of going to a party with you will turn me into a celebrity?"

"Yes." I'm not being arrogant, just truthful. After two years at this school, I know the kind of cred I have.

Though honestly? Sometimes I don't feel half as cool as people think I am, and I'm pretty sure that if any of them took the time to actually get to know me, they'd probably change their opinion. It's like that pond I skated on when I was a kid—from a distance, the ice looked so shiny and smooth, until you got close enough to it, and suddenly all the uneven edges and crisscrossed skate marks became visible. That's me, I guess. Covered with skate marks that nobody ever seems to notice.

And jeez, clearly I'm feeling way too philosophical tonight.

Next to me, Hannah has gone quiet, chewing on her lip as she considers my proposal.

For a split second, I almost tell her to forget it. It seems... *wrong* that this girl cares what a douche like Kohl thinks about her. Hannah's intelligence and razor-sharp tongue is wasted on a guy like that.

But then I think of my team, and all the guys that are counting on me, and I force myself to ignore my misgivings.

"Think about it," I coax. "The makeup is next Friday, which gives us a week and a half to study. I'll write the exam, and then on Saturday night we'll go to Maxwell's party and show Loverboy how sexy and desirable you are. He won't be able to resist, trust me."

"One, don't call him that. Two, stop telling me to trust you. I don't even know you." But despite the grumbling, I can see her capitulating. "Look. I can't commit to tutoring you for the whole semester. I honestly don't have time."

"It'll just be this week," I promise.

She hesitates.

I don't blame her for doubting me. Truth is, I'm already thinking of how I can convince her to hold my hand for the duration of Tolbert's course, but...one battle at a time.

"So do we have a deal?" I prompt.

Hannah stays quiet, but just when I've given up hope, she sighs and says, "All right. We've got a deal."

Hot damn.

A part of me is genuinely shocked that I managed to wear her down. I've been badgering her for what feels like an eternity, and now that I've won, it's almost like experiencing a sense of loss. Figure that out.

Nevertheless, I give myself a mental high five as I drive into the lot behind the dormitories. "What dorm are you in?" I ask as I put the Jeep in park.

"Bristol House."

"I'll walk you in." I start to unbuckle my seatbelt, but she shakes her head.

"It's fine. I don't need a bodyguard." She holds up her phone. "All prepped to dial 911, remember?"

A short silence falls over us.

"Well." I stick out my hand. "It was a pleasure doing business with you."

She stares at my hand like I'm a carrier for Ebola. I roll my eyes and withdraw the gesture.

"I work until eight tomorrow," she says. "We can meet up when I'm done. You don't live in the dorms, right?"

"No, but I can come to you."

She blanches as if I've offered to shave her head. "And have people think we're friends? No way. Text me your address. I'll come to your place."

I've never met anyone who's so repulsed by my popularity, and I have no idea what to make of it.

I think I might like it.

"You'll be the most popular girl on your floor if I came over, you know."

"Text me your address," she says firmly.

"Yes, ma'am." I beam at her. "I'll see you tomorrow night."

All I get in return is a sour look and a flash of her profile as she turns to open her door. She hops out of the car without a word, then reluctantly taps on the passenger window.

Stifling a grin, I press the button to roll down the window. "Forget something?" I mock.

"Thank you for the ride," she says primly.

And then she's gone, her green dress fluttering in the night breeze as she hurries toward the darkened buildings.

7

Hannah

Normally I pride myself on having a good head on my shoulders and making sound decisions, but agreeing to tutor Garrett? Stupider than stupid.

I'm still cursing myself for it as I make the drive over to his house the following evening. When he cornered me at the Sigma party, I had every intention of telling him to fuck off and leave me alone, and then he'd dangled Justin under my nose like a carrot, and I caved like a cheap tent.

Great. And now I'm mixing metaphors.

I think it might be time for me to face a grim truth: I have zero common sense when it comes to Justin Kohl. Last night I left the party with the sole purpose of forgetting about him, and instead of doing that, I allowed Garrett Graham to fill me with the most destructive emotion known to mankind—hope.

Hope that Justin might notice me. Hope that he might want me. Hope that I might've finally met someone who can make me *feel* something.

It's embarrassing how besotted I am with the guy.

I park my borrowed car in the driveway behind Garrett's Jeep and next to a shiny black pick-up, but I leave the engine running. I keep wondering what my old therapist would think if she knew about the deal I'd struck with Garrett. I want to say she'd be against it, but Carole was all about empowerment. She always encouraged me to take control of my life and grab hold of any opportunity that allows me to put the attack behind me.

So here's what I know: I've dated two guys since the rape. I slept with both of them. And neither of them made me feel as hot and achy as Justin Kohl does with one heavy-lidded look.

Carole would tell me that's an opportunity worth exploring.

Garrett's townhouse is two stories tall, with a white stucco exterior, a stoop instead of a porch, and a front lawn that's surprisingly tidy. Despite my reluctance, I force myself to get out of the car and walk to the door. Rock music blares inside the house. A part of me hopes that nobody hears me ring the bell, but muffled footsteps echo behind the door and then it swings open and I find myself looking at a tall guy with spiky blond hair and a chiseled face right off the cover of *GQ*.

"Why, hello there," he drawls as he looks me up and down. "My birthday's not until next week, but if this is an early b-day gift, I sure ain't complaining, baby doll."

Of course. I should have known Garrett would be rooming with someone as obnoxious as he is.

I curl my fingers over the strap of my oversized messenger bag, wondering if I can make it back to my car before Garrett knows I'm here, but my dastardly plan is foiled when he appears in the doorway. He's barefoot, clad in faded jeans and a threadbare gray T-shirt, and his hair is damp as if he's just come out of the shower.

"Hey, Wellsy," he says breezily. "You're late."

"I said eight-fifteen. It's eight-fifteen." I stare coldly at Mr. GQ. "And if you were implying that I was a hooker, then call me insulted."

"You thought she was a hooker?" Garrett turns to glare at his friend. "That's my *tutor*, bro. Show some respect."

"I didn't think she was a hooker—I thought she was a *stripper*," the blond retorts, as if that makes it better. "She's wearing a costume, for fuck's sake."

He does have a point. My waitress uniform isn't exactly subtle.

"PS, I want a stripper for my birthday," GQ announces. "Just decided now. Get on it."

"I'll make a couple calls," Garrett promises, but the second his friend wanders off, he confides, "He's not getting a stripper. We all chipped in to get him a new iPod. He dropped his in the koi pond behind Hartford House."

When I snicker, Garrett pounces like a mountain lion. "Holy

shit. Was that a laugh? I didn't think you were capable of showing amusement. Can you do it again and let me film it?"

"I laugh all the time." I pause. "Mostly *at* you, though."

He grabs his chest in mock pain as if I've shot him. "You're terrible for a guy's ego, y'know that?"

I roll my eyes and shut the door behind me.

"Let's go up to my room," he says.

Shit. He wants to study in his bedroom? While I'm sure that's probably a wet dream for every girl at this school, I'm apprehensive about being alone with him.

"G, is that the tutor?" a male voice shouts as we pass what I deduce is the living room. "Hey, tutor, get in here! We need to have a little chat."

My alarmed gaze flies to Garrett, but he just grins and guides me to the doorway. The living room just screams *bachelor pad* with its two leather couches set up in an L-shape, a complicated-looking entertainment system, and a coffee table littered with beer bottles. A dark-haired guy with vivid blue eyes rises from the couch. He's as handsome as Garrett and GQ, and from the way his long body saunters my way, he's fully aware of his appeal.

"So listen," Blue Eyes announces in a stern voice. "My boy needs to ace this test. You better make that happen."

My lips twitch. "Or what?"

"Or I'll be very, very upset." His sultry gaze does a slow and deliberate sweep of my body, lingering on my chest before traveling back up. "You don't want to upset me, do you, gorgeous?"

Garrett snorts. "Don't waste your time, man. She's immune to flirting. Trust me, I've tried." He turns to me. "This is Logan. Logan, Wellsy."

"Hannah," I correct.

Logan thinks it over before shaking his head. "Naah. I like Wellsy."

"You met Dean in the hall, and that's Tucker," Garrett adds, pointing to the auburn-haired guy on the couch, who—surprise, surprise—is as good-looking as the rest of them.

I wonder if "sexy as fuck" is a requirement for living in this house.

Not that I'd ever ask Garrett. His ego is big enough as it is.

"'Sup, Wellsy," Tucker calls out.

I smother a sigh. Wonderful. I guess I'm Wellsy now.

"Wellsy is the star of the Christmas recital," Garrett tells his friends.

"Winter showcase," I grumble.

"Isn't that what I said?" He waves a dismissive hand. "Okay, let's do this shit. Later, boys."

I follow Garrett up the narrow staircase to the second floor. His room is at the end of the hall, and from the sheer size of it and the private bath, it must be the master bedroom.

"You mind if I change out of this uniform?" I ask awkwardly. "I've got my street clothes in my bag."

He flops on the edge of the monstrous bed and leans back on his elbows. "Go right ahead. I'll sit here and enjoy the show."

I clench my teeth. "I meant in the washroom."

"That's no fun."

"Nothing about this is *fun*," I mutter.

The bathroom is a lot cleaner than I expect, and the faint traces of woodsy aftershave hang in the air. I quickly change into yoga pants and a black sweater, tie my hair into a ponytail, and shove my uniform in my bag.

Garrett is still on the bed when I return. He's engrossed with his phone, doesn't even glance up when I dump an armful of books on his bed.

"To quote your annoying self, are you ready to do this shit?" I say sarcastically.

He speaks in an absent-minded tone. "Yeah. One sec." His long fingers tap out a message, and then he drops the phone on the mattress. "Sorry. I'm paying attention now."

My seating options are limited. There's a desk under the window but only one chair, which is buried under a mountain of clothes. Same goes for the armchair in the corner of the room. The floor is hardwood and looks uncomfortable.

The bed, it is.

I reluctantly sit cross-legged on the mattress. "Okay, so I think we should run through all the theories first. Make sure you know the important points of each one, and then we can start applying them to the list of conflicts and moral dilemmas."

"Sounds good."

"Let's start with Kant. His ethics are pretty straightforward."

I open the binder of readings Tolbert handed out at the start of the year and flip through the pages until I find all the material on Immanuel Kant. Garrett slides his big body to top of the bed and rests his head on the wooden frame, letting out a heavy sigh as I plop the readings in his lap.

"Read," I order.

"Out loud?"

"Yep. And once you're done, I want you to summarize what you just read. Think you can handle that?"

There's a beat, and then his bottom lip quivers. "This might be the wrong time to tell you, but...I can't read."

My jaw falls open. Holy shit. He can't be seri—

Garrett barks out a laugh. "Relax, I'm fucking around with you." Then he scowls at me. "You actually thought I couldn't *read*? Jesus Christ, Wellsy."

I offer a sweet smile. "Wouldn't have surprised me in the slightest."

Except Garrett *does* end up surprising me. Not only does he read the material in a smooth, articulate voice, he proceeds to summarize Kant's Categorical Imperative almost word-for-word.

"Do you have a photographic memory or something?" I demand.

"Nope. I'm good with facts." He shrugs. "I just have a tough time applying the theories to the moral situations."

I cut him some slack. "It's total bullshit, if you ask me. How can we be sure what these philosophers—who are all long dead—would think about Tolbert's hypotheticals? For all we know, they'd evaluate it on a case-by-case basis. Right and wrong isn't black and white. It's more complex than—"

Garrett's phone buzzes.

"Shit, one sec." He glances at the screen, frowns, and sends another text. "Sorry, you were saying?"

We spend the next twenty minutes going over the finer points of Kant's ethical views.

Garrett sends about five more texts during that time.

"Oh my God," I burst out. "Am I going to have to confiscate that thing?"

"Sorry," he says for the zillionth time. "I'll put it on silent."

Which achieves nothing because he leaves the phone on his binder and the damn thing lights up every time a new message comes in.

"So basically, logic is the backbone of Kantian ethics—" I halt when the phone screen flashes again. "This is ridiculous. Who keeps texting you?"

"Nobody."

Nobody, my ass. I grab the phone and click on the message icon. There's no name, just a number, but it doesn't take a rocket scientist to figure out the messages are from a female. Unless there's some guy out there who wants to "lick Garrett all over."

"You're *sexting* during a tutoring session? What is wrong with you?"

He sighs. "I'm not sexting. *She's* sexting."

"Uh-huh. Let's blame *her*, shall we?"

"Read my responses," he insists. "I keep telling her I'm busy. It's not my fault she can't take the hint."

I scroll through the conversation and discover he's telling the truth. All the messages he's sent in the past thirty minutes have involved the words *busy* and *studying* and *talk later*.

Sighing, I bring up the touch keyboard and start typing. Garrett protests and tries to seize the phone from my hand, but he's too late. I've already pressed *send*.

"There," I announce. "All taken care of."

"I swear to God, Wellsy, if you..." He trails off as he reads the message.

This is Garrett's tutor. You're annoying me. We're done in thirty minutes. I'm confident you can keep your pants zipped until then.

Garrett meets my eyes and laughs so loudly I can't help but smile.

"That ought to be more effective than your half-assed leave me alones, don't you think?"

He chuckles again. "Can't argue with that."

"Hopefully that shuts your girlfriend up for a while."

"She's not my girlfriend. She's this puck bunny I hooked up with last year and—"

"Puck bunny?" I echo in horror. "You're *such* a pig. Is that actually what you call women?"

"When the woman is only interested in sleeping with a hockey player so she can brag to all her friends that she bagged a hockey player? Yeah, that's what we call 'em," he says with a bite to his voice. "If anything, *I'm* the one being objectified in this scenario."

"Whatever helps you sleep better at night..." I reach for the binder. "Let's move on to utilitarianism. We'll focus on Bentham for now."

Afterward, I quiz him on the two philosophers we've discussed tonight, and I'm pleased when he answers everything correctly, even the curveballs I throw at him.

Fine. So maybe Garrett Graham isn't as dumb as I thought he was.

By the time our hour is up, I'm confident that he didn't just memorize the information and spit it back at me. There's genuine comprehension there, as if the ethical ideas have truly sunk in for him. It's a shame the makeup exam isn't multiple choice, because there's no doubt in my mind he could pass it with flying colors.

"Tomorrow we'll tackle postmodernism." I sigh. "Which, in my humble opinion, is probably the most convoluted school of thought in human history. I've got rehearsal until six but I'm free afterward."

Garrett nods. "I'm done with practice around seven. So how about eight?"

"I'm good with that." I shove my books back in my bag, then duck into the bathroom to pee before I hit the road. When I come out, I find Garrett scrolling through my iPod.

"You went through my bag?" I exclaim. "Seriously?"

"Your iPod was hanging out of the front pocket," he protests. "I was curious to see what was on it." His gray eyes remain glued to the screen as he starts reading names out loud. "Etta James, Adele, Queen, Ella Fitzgerald, Aretha, Beatles—man, this is wicked eclectic." He suddenly shakes his head in dismay. "Hey, did you know there's One Direction on here?"

"No, really?" I ooze sarcasm. "It must have downloaded itself."

"I think I've lost all respect for you. You're supposed to be a *music* major."

I snatch the iPod from his hands and stuff it in the bag. "One Direction does some great harmonies."

"Strongly disagree." His chin lifts decisively. "I'll make you a playlist. Obviously you need to learn the distinction between good music and shitty music."

I speak through clenched teeth. "I'll see you tomorrow."

Garrett's tone is preoccupied as he heads to the iMac on his desk. "How do you feel about Lynyrd Skynyrd? Or do you only like bands where the guys coordinate their outfits?"

"Good night, Garrett."

I'm ready to tear my hair out as I march out of the room. I can't believe I agreed to a week and a half of this.

God help me.

8

Hannah

Allie calls the next evening as I storm out of the music building fuming over another disastrous rehearsal with Cass.

"Whoa," she says when she hears my curt tone. "What's up your ass?"

"Cassidy Donovan," I answer angrily. "Rehearsal was a fucking nightmare."

"Is he trying to steal all the good notes again?"

"Worse." I'm too pissed to rehash what happened, so I don't bother. "I want to murder him in his sleep, A. No, I want to murder him when he's awake so he can see the joy on my face when I do it."

Her laughter tickles my ear. "Shit. He pissed you off good, huh? Want to vent about it over dinner?"

"Can't. I'm seeing Graham tonight." Another appointment I'm not keen on keeping. All I want to do right now is take a shower and watch TV, but knowing Garrett, he'll hunt me down and yell at me if I dare to cancel on him.

"I still can't believe you caved about the tutoring thing," Allie marvels. "He must be very persuasive."

"Something like that," I say vaguely.

I haven't told Allie about my arrangement with Garrett, mostly because I want to delay her inevitable teasing when she finds out how desperate I am to get Justin to notice me. I know I won't be able to hide the truth from her forever—she's definitely going to have questions when she finds out I'm going to a *party* with the guy. But I'm confident I can come up with a good excuse by then.

Some things are too embarrassing to admit, even to your best friend.

"How much is he paying you?" she asks curiously.

Like an idiot, I throw out the first number that comes to mind. "Uh, sixty."

"*Sixty dollars* an hour? Holy crap. That's insane. You better take me out for a steak dinner when you're done!"

A steak dinner? Shit. That's like three shifts' worth of diner money for me.

See, this is why people shouldn't lie. It always comes back to bite you in the ass.

"Sure," I say lightly. "Anyway, I gotta go. I don't have Tracy's car tonight so I need to call a cab. I'll see you in a couple hours."

The campus taxi takes me to Garrett's, and I make arrangements to get picked up in an hour and a half. Garrett told me to just let myself in when I come over because nobody ever hears the bell over the blaring TV or stereo, but the house is quiet when I walk inside.

"Graham?" I call out from the entryway.

"Upstairs," comes his muffled reply.

I find him in his bedroom, clad in sweatpants and a white wifebeater that shows off his perfectly formed biceps and strong forearms. I can't deny that his body is...appealing. He's big, not in a bulky linebacker way, but long and sleek and leanly muscular. His sleeveless shirt provides an eyeful of the tattoo on his right upper arm—black flames that curl up to his shoulder and coil around his bicep.

"Hey. Where are your roommates?"

"It's Friday night—where do you think they are? Partying." He sounds glum as he pulls the class readings from the backpack on the floor.

"And you're choosing to study," I remark. "I'm not sure if I should be impressed or feel sorry for you."

"I don't party during the season, Wellsy. Already told you that."

He had, but I hadn't really believed him. How is he *not* partying every night? I mean, look at the guy. He's drop dead gorgeous and more popular than the Bieber. Well, at least before Beebs went off the rails and abandoned his poor monkey in a foreign country.

We settle on the bed and get right down to work, but each time Garrett takes a few minutes to read over a theory, my mind drifts back to tonight's rehearsal. Anger continues to simmer in my belly, and although I'm ashamed to admit it, my bad mood leaks into the study session. I'm crabbier than I mean to be, and much harsher than necessary when Garrett misinterprets the material.

"It's not that complicated," I mutter when he completely misses the point for the third time. "He's saying—"

"All right, I get it now," he cuts in, aggravation creasing his forehead. "No need to snap at me, Wellsy."

"Sorry." I briefly close my eyes to calm myself. "Let's just move on to the next philosopher. We'll come back to Foucault at the end."

Garrett frowns. "We're not moving on to anything. Not until you tell me why you've been biting my head off since you got here. What, did Loverboy ignore you in the quad or something?"

His sarcasm only intensifies my annoyance. "No."

"Are you on your period?"

"Oh my God. You are *the worst*. Just read, will you?"

"I'm not reading a damn thing." He crosses his arms. "Look, there's an easy fix for this bitch fest of yours. All you have to do is tell me why you're mad, I'll assure you you're being ridiculous, and then we can study in peace."

I've underestimated Garrett's stubbornness. But I really ought to know better, seeing as how I've been bested by his tenacity on more than one occasion. I don't particularly want to confide in him, but my argument with Cass is like a dark cloud over my head, and I need to dispel the stormy energy before it consumes me.

"He wants a *choir*!"

Garrett blinks. "Who wants a choir?"

"My duet partner," I say darkly. "AKA the bane of my existence. I swear, if I wasn't afraid I might break my hand, I'd punch him right in his smug, stupid face."

"You want me to teach you how to throw down?" Garrett presses his lips together as if he's trying hard not to laugh.

"I'm tempted to say yes. Seriously, this guy is impossible to work with. The song is fantastic, but all he does is nitpick every microscopic detail. The key, the tempo, the arrangement, the frickin' *clothes* we're going to wear."

"Okay…so what's this about a choir?"

"Get this—Cass wants a choir to accompany us for the last chorus. A fucking choir. We've been rehearsing this piece for *weeks*, Garrett. It was supposed to be simple and understated, just the two of us showcasing our voices, and suddenly he wants to make a huge production out of it?"

"He sounds like a diva."

"He totally is. I'm ready to rip his head off." My anger is so visceral it coats my throat and makes my hands tremble. "And then, if that's not infuriating enough, two minutes before rehearsal ends he decides we should change the arrangement."

"What's wrong with the arrangement?"

"Nothing. *Nothing* is wrong with the arrangement. And Mary Jane—the girl who *wrote* the fucking song—is just sitting there saying nothing! I don't know if she's scared of Cass or in love with him or who the hell knows what, but she's no help at all. She clams up whenever we start fighting, when what she should be doing is voicing an opinion and trying to resolve the issue."

Garrett purses his lips. Sort of like the way my grandma does when she's deep in thought. It's kind of adorable.

But he'd probably kill me if I told him he just reminded me of my grandmother.

"What?" I prompt when he doesn't speak.

"I want to hear this song."

Surprise filters through me. "What? Why?"

"Because you've been babbling about it since the moment I met you."

"This is the first time I've ever brought it up!"

He responds with that flippant hand-waving thing again, which I'm starting to suspect he does often. "Well, I want to hear it. If this Mary Jane chick doesn't have the balls to offer legitimate criticism, then I'll do it." He shrugs. "Maybe your duet partner—what's his name again?"

"Cass."

"Maybe Cass is right and you're just too stubborn to see it."

"Trust me, he's wrong."

"Fine, then let me be the judge. Sing both versions of the

song for me—the way it is now, and the way Cass wants it—and I'll tell you what I think. You play, right?"

I furrow my brow. "Play what?"

Garrett rolls his eyes. "Instruments."

"Oh. Yeah, I do. Piano and guitar...why?"

"I'll be right back."

He ducks out of the room and I hear his footsteps thud in the hall, followed by the sound of a door creaking open. He returns with an acoustic guitar in hand.

"Tuck's," he explains. "He won't mind if you play it."

I grit my teeth. "I'm not serenading you."

"Why not? You feeling self-conscious or something?"

"No. I just have better things to do." I give him a pointed look. "Like help you pass your midterm."

"We're almost done with postmodernism. All the hard stuff starts next session." His voice takes on a teasing note. "C'mon, we've got time. Let me hear it."

Then he flashes that boyish grin, and damned if I don't cave. He really has mastered that little boy look. Except he's not a little boy. He's a man with a big, strong body and a chin that lifts in determination. Teasing grins aside, I know Garrett will harass me all night if I don't agree to sing.

I accept the guitar and plop it in my lap, giving it a few test strums. It's in tune, a bit tinnier than the acoustic I have at home, but the sound is great.

Garrett climbs on the bed and lies down, resting his head on a mountain of pillows. I've never met anyone who sleeps with so many pillows. Maybe he needs them to cradle his massive ego.

"Okay," I tell him. "This is how we're doing it now. Pretend there's a guy joining me in the first chorus, and then singing the second verse."

I know a lot of singers who are too shy to perform in front of strangers, but I've never had that problem. Ever since I was a kid, music has always been an escape for me. When I sing, the world disappears. It's just me and the music and a deep sense of tranquility that I've never been able to find anywhere else, no matter how hard I try.

I take a breath, play the opening chords, and start to sing. I don't look at Garrett because I'm already somewhere else, lost in the melody and the words, wholly focused on the sound of my voice and the resonance of the guitar.

I love this song. I truly do. It's hauntingly beautiful, and even without Cass's rich baritone to complement my voice, it still packs the same punch, the same heart-wrenching emotion that MJ poured into the lyrics.

Almost immediately, my head clears and my heart feels lighter. I am whole again, because the music has made me that way, just like it did after the rape. Whenever things got too overwhelming or painful, I'd go to the piano or pick up my guitar, and I'd know joy wasn't out of reach. It was always within my grasp, always available to me as long as I was able to sing.

Several minutes later, the final note lingers in the air like a trace of sweet perfume, and I float back to the present. I turn to Garrett, but his face is expressionless. I don't know what I was expecting him to do. Praise me? Mock me?

But I hadn't expected silence.

"Do you want to hear Cass's version?" I hedge.

He nods. That's it. A quick jerk of the head and nothing more.

His shuttered face unsettles me, so this time I close my eyes when I sing. I move the bridge to where Cass argued it should be, add a second chorus like he insisted, and I honestly don't think I'm biased when I say I prefer the original. This second version drags, and the extra chorus is overkill.

To my surprise, Garrett agrees with me once I've finished. "It's too long when you do it like that," he says gruffly.

"I know, right?" I'm thrilled to hear him validate my own concerns. God knows MJ can't speak her mind around Cass.

"And forget the choir. You don't need it. Hell, I don't think you need *Cass*." He shakes his head in amazement. "Your voice is…fuck, Wellsy, it's beautiful."

My cheeks heat up. "You think so?"

His impassioned expression tells me he's dead serious. "Play something else," he orders.

"Um. What do you want to hear?"

"Anything. I don't care." I'm startled by the intensity in his voice, the emotion now glittering in his gray eyes. "I just need to hear you sing again."

Wow. Okay. My entire life people have been telling me I'm talented, but other than my parents, nobody has ever *pleaded* with me to sing to them.

"Please," he says softly.

So I sing. An original piece this time, but it's still rough so I end up switching to another song. I play "Stand By Me." It's my mom's favorite song, the one I sing to her every year for her birthday, and the memory carries me away to that peaceful place again.

Halfway through the song, Garrett's eyes flutter shut. I watch the steady rise and fall of his chest, my voice cracking from the emotion behind the lyrics. Then my gaze travels to his face, and I notice a small white scar on his chin, bisecting the stubble shadowing his jaw. I wonder how he got it. Hockey? An accident when he was a kid?

His eyes stay closed for the duration of the song, and as I strum the last chord, I've decided he must be asleep. I let the last note trail off, then set down the guitar.

Garrett's eyes pop open before I can rise from the bed.

"Oh. You're awake." I swallow. "I thought you were sleeping."

He slides up into a sitting position, his tone laced with sheer awe. "Where did you learn to sing like that?"

I shrug awkwardly. Unlike Cass, I'm far too modest to sing my own praises. "I don't know. It's just something I've always been able to do."

"Did you take lessons?"

I shake my head.

"So you just opened your mouth one day and *that* came out?"

A laugh slips out. "You sound like my parents. They used to say there must have been a mix-up at the hospital nursery and they got the wrong kid. Everyone in my family is tone deaf. They still can't figure out who I got the music gene from."

"I need to get you to sign an autograph for me. That way when you're cleaning up at the Grammys, I can sell it on eBay and make a killing."

I let out a sigh. "The music business is tough, dude. For all I know, I'll crash and burn if I try to make a go at it."

"You won't." Conviction rings in his voice. "And by the way? I think you're making a mistake singing a duet for the showcase. You should be on that stage alone. Seriously, if you sit there with a single spotlight on you and sing like you just did now? You'll give everyone in the audience chills."

I think Garrett might be right. Not about the chills thing, but that I made a mistake teaming up with Cass. "Well, it's too late. I'm already committed."

"You could always back out," he suggests.

"No way. That's a dick move."

"I'm just saying, if you back out now, you still have time to come up with a solo. If you wait too long, you'll be screwed."

"I can't do that." I eye him in challenge. "Would you let your teammates down if they were counting on you?"

He answers without hesitation. "Never."

"Then what makes you think *I'd* do that?"

"Because Cass isn't your teammate," Garrett says quietly. "From the sound of it, he's been working exclusively against you from the start."

Again, I'm afraid he's right, but it really is too late to make a change. I committed to the duet, and now I have to follow through on it.

"I agreed to sing with him," I say firmly. "And my word means something." I glance at Garrett's alarm clock and curse when I notice the time. "I have to go. My cab's probably waiting outside." I quickly slide off the bed. "Just have to pee first."

He snickers. "TMI."

"People pee, Garrett. Deal with it."

When I come out of the bathroom a few minutes later, Garrett wears the most innocent expression on the planet. So of course, I'm instantly mistrustful. I stare at the books strewn on the mattress, then at the messenger bag I left on the floor, but nothing seems out of place.

"What did you do?" I demand.

"Nothing," he says nonchalantly. "Anyway, I have a game tomorrow night, so our next session will have to be Sunday. Is that cool? Late afternoon-ish?"

"Sure," I answer, but I still can't fight the sneaking suspicion he's up to something.

It isn't until I walk into my dorm room fifteen minutes later that I discover my suspicions were warranted. My jaw drops in outrage when a text from Garrett comes in.

Him: *Confession: I deleted all the 1 Direction from your iPod when u were in the can. You're welcome.*

Me: *WHAT?? I'm going to kiss u!*

Him: *With tongue?*

It takes me a second to realize what happened, at which point I'm completely mortified.

Me: *Kill u! I meant KILL u. Damn autocorrect.*

Him: *Surrrrrre. Let's blame it on autocorrect.*

Me: *Shut it.*

Him: *I think someone wants to kiss me...*

Me: *Goodnight, Graham.*

Him: *U sure you don't want to come back here? Give our tongues some exercise?*

Me: *Ew. Never.*

Him: *Uh-huh. PS—check your email. I sent u a zip file of music. Actual music.*

Me: *Which will be going straight to my trash folder.*

I'm grinning to myself as I send the message, and Allie chooses that exact moment to wander into my room.

"Who are you texting?" She's drinking one of her nasty juices, and the straw pops out of her mouth as she gasps. "Holy shit! Is it Justin?"

"Naah, just Graham. He's being an annoying jackass as per usual."

"What, you two are friends now?" she teases.

I falter. It's on the tip of my tongue to voice a denial, but it feels wrong when I remember I spent the past two hours confiding in Garrett about my issues with Cass and then serenading him like a frickin' troubadour. And honestly, as insufferable as he is at times, Garrett Graham isn't as bad as I thought he was.

So I offer a rueful grin and say, "Yeah. I guess we are."

9

Garrett

Greg Braxton is a beast. I'm talking six-five, two hundred and twenty pounds of pure power, and the kind of speed and precision that's going to land him a plum contract with an NHL team one day. Well, only if the league is willing to overlook all the time he spends in the sin bin. It's the second period and Braxton has already taken three penalties, one of which resulted in a goal courtesy of Logan, who skates past the penalty box to give Braxton a smug little wave. Big mistake, because now Braxton's back on the ice, and he's got an axe to grind.

He slams me into the plexi so hard it jars every bone in my body, but I luckily get the pass off and shake the disoriented cobwebs from my brain in time to see Tuck flick a wrist shot past St. Anthony's goalie. The scoreboard lights up, and even the groans and boos from the crowd don't diminish the sense of victory coursing through my veins. Away games are never as exhilarating as home games, but I feed off the energy of the crowd, even when it's negative.

When the buzzer signals the end of the period, we head into the locker room leading St. Anthony's 2-0. Everyone is riding the high of the two-period shutout, but Coach Jensen won't let us celebrate. Doesn't matter that we're ahead—he never lets us forget what we're doing wrong.

"Di Laurentis!" he shouts at Dean. "You're letting number thirty-four toss you around like a rag doll! And you—" Coach glares at one of our sophomore D-men. "You've given them *two* breakaways! Your job is to shadow those assholes. Did you see that hit Logan delivered at the start of the period? I expect that kind of physical play from you, Renaud. No more pansy-ass hip checks. Hit 'em like you mean it, kid."

As Coach marches to the other end of the locker room to dish out more criticism, Logan and I exchange grins. Jensen is a total hard-ass, but he's damn good at his job. He gives praise when praise is deserved, but for the most part, he pushes us hard and makes us better.

"That was a brutal hit." Tuck shoots me a sympathetic look as I lift my jersey to gingerly examine my left side.

Braxton absolutely pummeled me, and I can already see a bluish discoloration forming on my skin. Gonna leave a helluva bruise.

"I'll live," I answer with a shrug.

Coach claps his hand to signal it's time to get back on the ice, and the skate guards come off as we file down the tunnel.

As I make my way to the box, I can feel his eyes on me. I don't seek him out, but I know what I'll find if I do. My father, hunkered down in his usual seat at the top of the bleachers, his Rangers cap pulled low over his eyes, his lips set in a tight line.

St. Anthony's campus isn't too far from Briar, which means my father only had to drive an hour from Boston to get here, but even if we'd been playing hours away at a weekend invitational during the snowstorm of the century, he'd still be there. My old man never misses a game.

Phil Graham, hockey legend and proud father.

Yeah fucking right.

I know damn well he doesn't come to the games to watch his son play. He comes to watch an extension of *himself* play.

Sometimes I wonder what would have happened if I sucked ass. What if I couldn't skate? Couldn't shoot? What if I'd grown up to be a scrawny twig with the coordination of a Kleenex box? Or if I'd been into art or music or chemical engineering?

He probably would've had a coronary. Or maybe convinced my mother to give me up for adoption.

I swallow the acrid taste of bitterness as I join my teammates.

Block him out. He's not important. He's not here.

It's what I remind myself every time I swing my body over that wall and plant my skates on the ice. Phil Graham is nothing to me. He stopped being my father a long time ago.

The problem is, my mantra isn't foolproof. I can block him out, yes, and he's not important to me, hell yes. But he *is* here. He's always here, damn it.

The third period is intense. St. Anthony's is playing for their lives, desperate to keep from being shut out. Simms is under attack from the word *go*, while Logan and Hollis scramble to hold off St. A's starting line from rushing our net.

Sweat drips down my face and neck as my line—me, Tuck and a senior nicknamed Birdie—go on the offensive. St. Anthony's defense is a joke. The D-men bank on their forwards to score and their goalie to stop the shots they ineptly let into their zone. Logan tangles with Braxton behind our net and comes out victorious. His pass connects with Birdie, who's lightning fast as he hurtles toward the blue line. Birdie flips the puck to Tucker and the three of us fly into enemy territory on an odd man rush, bearing down on the hopeless defensemen who don't know what hit 'em.

The puck flies in my direction and the roar of the crowd pulses in my blood. Braxton comes tearing down the ice with me in his sights, but I'm not stupid. I unload the puck to Tuck, hip-checking Braxton as my teammate dekes out the goalie, fakes a shot, then slaps it back to me for the one-timer.

My shot whizzes into the net and the clock runs down. We beat St. Anthony's 3-0.

Even Coach is in good spirits as we file into the locker room after the third. We've shut out the other team, stopped the beast that is Braxton, and added a second win to our record. It's still early in the season, but we're all seeing championship stars in our eyes.

Logan flops down on the bench beside me and bends over to unlace his skates. "So what's the deal with the tutor?" His tone is casual as fuck, but I know him well, and there's nothing casual about the question.

"Wellsy? What about her?"

"Is she single?"

The question catches me off-guard. Logan gravitates toward girls who are rail-thin and sweeter than sugar. With her endless curves and total smartass-ness, Hannah doesn't fit either of those bills.

"Yeah," I say warily. "Why?"

He shrugs. All casual again. And again, I see right through it. "She's hot." He pauses. "You tapping that?"

"Nope. And you won't be either. She's got her sights on some douchebag."

"They together?"

"Naah."

"Doesn't that make her fair game then?"

I stiffen, just slightly, and I don't think Logan notices. Luckily, Kenny Simms, our wizard of a goalie, wanders over and puts an end to the convo.

I'm not sure why I'm suddenly on edge. I'm not into Hannah in that way, but the idea of her and Logan hooking up makes me uneasy. Maybe because I know what a slut Logan can be. I can't even count the number of times I've seen a chick do a walk of shame out of his bedroom.

It pisses me off to picture Hannah sneaking out of his room with sex-tousled hair and swollen lips. I didn't expect it to happen, but I kinda like her. She keeps me on my toes, and last night when I heard her sing... Shi-it. I've heard the words *pitch* and *tone* thrown around on *American Idol*, but I don't know squat about the technical aspects of singing. What I do know is that Hannah's throaty voice had given me fucking chills.

I push all thoughts of Hannah from my head as I hit the showers. Everyone else is riding the victory high, but this is the part of the night I dread. Win or lose, I know my father will be waiting in the parking lot when the team heads for our bus.

I leave the arena with my hair damp from the shower and my hockey bag slung over my shoulder. Sure enough, the old man is there. Standing near a row of cars, his down jacket zipped up to his collar and his cap shielding his eyes.

Logan and Birdie flank me, crowing about our win, but the latter stops in his tracks when he spots my dad. "You gonna say hello?" he murmurs.

I don't miss the eager note in his voice. My teammates can't understand why I don't shout to the whole fucking world that my father is *the* Phil Graham. They think he's a god, which I guess makes me a demi-god for having the good fortune to be sired by him. When I first came to Briar, they used to harass me for his autograph, but I fed them some line about how my father is wicked private, and fortunately they've quit badgering me to introduce them.

"Nope." I keep walking toward the bus, turning my head just as I pass the old man.

Our eyes lock for a moment, and he nods at me.

One little nod, and then he turns away and lumbers toward his shiny silver SUV.

It's the same old routine. If we win, I get a nod. If we lose, I get nothing.

When I was younger, he would at least put on a fatherly show of support after a loss, a bullshit smile of encouragement or a consolatory pat on the back if anyone happened to be looking at us. But the moment we were alone, the proverbial gloves would come off.

I climb onto the bus with my teammates and breathe a sigh of relief when the driver pulls out of the lot, leaving my father in our rearview mirror.

I suddenly realize that depending on how the Ethics exam goes, I might not even be playing next weekend. The old man definitely won't be happy about that.

Good thing I don't give a shit what he thinks.

10

Hannah

My mom calls on Sunday morning for our weekly phone chat, which I've been looking forward to for days. We rarely have time to talk during the week because I'm in class all day, rehearsing in the evenings, and fast asleep by the time Mom finishes her night shift at the grocery store.

The worst thing about living in Massachusetts is not being able to see my parents. I miss them so frickin' much, but at the same time, I needed to get far, far away from Ransom, Indiana. I've only been back once since my high school graduation, and after that visit, we all agreed it would be better if I didn't come home anymore. My aunt and uncle live in Philadelphia, so my parents and I fly there for Thanksgiving and Christmas. The rest of the time, I speak to them on the phone, or if I'm lucky, they're able to scrape together enough money to come see me.

It's not the most ideal arrangement, but they understand why I can't come home, and I not only understand why they can't leave, I know I'm to blame for it. I also know I'm going to spend the rest of my life trying to make it up to them.

"Hey, sweetie." My mother's voice slides into my ear like a warm embrace.

"Hey, Mom." I'm still in bed, snuggled up in a blanket cocoon and staring up at the ceiling.

"How did you do on the Ethics midterm?"

"I got an A."

"That's wonderful! See, I told you there was nothing to worry about."

"Trust me, there was. Half the class failed." I roll onto my side and rest the phone on my shoulder. "How's Dad?"

"He's good." She pauses. "He picked up extra shifts at the mill, but..."

My body tenses. "But what?"

"But it doesn't look like we'll be able to get to Aunt Nicole's for Thanksgiving, sweetie."

The pain and regret in her voice cuts me like a knife. Tears prick my eyes, but I blink them away.

"You know we just had to fix the leak in the roof, and our savings took a hit from that," Mom says. "We don't have money for airfare."

"Why don't you drive?" I ask weakly. "It's not that long..." Uh-huh, just a fifteen-hour drive. Not long at *all*.

"If we do that, your father will need to book more time off, and he can't afford to give up the hours."

I bite my lip to keep the tears at bay. "Maybe I can..." I quickly calculate how much savings I've got. Definitely not enough for three plane tickets to Philly.

But it *is* enough for one ticket to Ransom.

"I can fly home," I whisper.

"No." Her response is swift and unequivocal. "You don't have to do that, Hannah."

"It's just for one weekend." I'm trying to convince myself, not her. Trying to ignore the panic that claws its way up my throat at the thought of going back there. "We don't have to drive into town or see anyone. I can just hang out at the house with you and Dad."

There's another long pause. "Is that what you really want? Because if it is, then we'll welcome you home with open arms, you know that, sweetie. But if you're not one hundred percent comfortable with it, then I want you to stay at Briar."

Comfortable? I'm not sure it's possible for me to ever feel comfortable in Ransom again. I was a pariah before I left, and the one time I came back to visit, my father landed in jail for assault. So no, going back is about as appealing as cutting off my arm and feeding it to wolves.

My silence, however brief, is all the answer my mother needs. "You're not coming back," she says sternly. "Your dad and I would love to see you on Thanksgiving, but I'm not putting my own happiness ahead of yours, Hannah." Her voice cracks. "It's bad enough that we're still living in this godforsaken town. There's no reason for you to ever step foot here again."

Yeah, no reason for me to do that at all. Except for my *parents*. You know, the people who raised me, who love me unconditionally, who stood by me through the most horrific experience of my life.

And who are now stuck in a place where everyone despises them…because of *me*.

God, I want them to be free of that town. I feel so guilty that I was able to leave, and worse, that I left them *behind*. They're planning on moving the first chance they get, but the real estate market has been on a downswing, and with the second mortgage they took in order to pay our legal fees, they'll go bankrupt if they try to sell the house now. And although the renovations my dad is doing will boost the house's value, they're also taking money out of his pocket in the meantime.

I swallow the lump in my throat, wishing like hell that circumstances were different. "I'll send you the money I've got saved up," I whisper. "You can put it toward the mortgage."

The fact that she doesn't object tells me they're in an even worse position than they've been letting on.

"And if I win the showcase scholarship," I add, "I'll be able to pay my residence and meal fees for next year, so you and Dad won't have to worry about it." I know that will help them out even more, because the full scholarship I got from Briar only covers my tuition. My folks have been taking care of the other expenses.

"Hannah, I don't want you worrying about money. Your dad and I will be okay, I promise. Once we finish the updates on the house, we'll be in a much better position to list it. In the meantime, I want you to enjoy college, sweetie. Stop worrying about us, and start focusing on *you*." Her tone becomes playful. "Are there any new boyfriends I should know about?"

I smile to myself. "Nope."

"Oh come on, there has to be *someone* you're interested in."

My cheeks heat up as I think about Justin. "Well. There is. I mean, we're not dating or anything, but I wouldn't be against it. If he was interested."

Mom laughs. "Then ask him out."

Why does everyone think that's so easy for me to do?

"Yeah, maybe. You know me, I like to take things slow." Or rather, not at all. I haven't gone on a single date since Devon and I broke up last year.

I quickly change the subject. "Tell me about that new manager you were bitching about in your last email. It sounds like he's driving you nuts."

We chat about Mom's cashier job for a while, though it hurts like hell to hear about it. She used to be an elementary school teacher, but she'd been let go after my scandal, and the bastards in the school system had even found a loophole that made it possible for them to pay her the shittiest severance possible. Which had gone straight to my family's mountain of debt—and had barely made a dent in it.

Mom tells me about my dad's new obsession with building model planes, regales me with the antics of our dog, and bores me with details of the vegetable garden she's planting in the spring. Noticeably absent from the conversation is any mention of friends or dinners in town or the community events all small towns are known for. Because like me, my parents are also the town pariahs.

Unlike me, they didn't race out of Indiana like their asses were on fire.

In my defense, I had desperately needed a fresh start.

I just wish they were able to get one, too.

By the time we hang up, I'm caught between overwhelming joy and profound sorrow. I love talking to my mother, but knowing I won't see her and Dad on Thanksgiving makes me want to cry.

Fortunately, Allie pops into my bedroom before I surrender to the sadness and end up spending the rest of the day bawling in bed. "Hey," she says cheerfully. "Wanna grab breakfast in town? Tracy says we can take her car."

"Only if we go anywhere but Della's." There's nothing worse than eating where you work, especially since more often than not, Della ropes me into staying for a shift.

Allie rolls her eyes. "There's nowhere else that serves breakfast. But fine. Let's just eat in the dining hall."

I hop out of bed, and Allie hops right into it, sprawling on the blanket as I walk to the dresser to grab some clothes.

"Who were you on the phone with? Your mom?"

"Yeah." I slip a soft blue sweater over my head and smooth out the hem. "I'm not seeing them for Thanksgiving."

"Aw, I'm sorry, babe." Allie sits up. "Why don't you come to New York with me?"

It's a tempting offer, but I promised my mom I'd send her money, and I don't want to completely deplete my savings account by blowing it on a train ticket and a weekend in New York. "I can't afford it," I answer ruefully.

"Crap. I'd pay your way if I could, but I'm broke because of that Mexico trip me and Sean took in the spring."

"I wouldn't let you pay for me, anyway." I grin. "We're going to be starving artists when we graduate, remember? We need to save all the pennies we can."

She sticks out her tongue. "No way. We're going to be famous right out of the gate. You'll sign a multi-record deal, and I'll be starring in a rom-com alongside Ryan Gosling. Who, by the way, will fall madly in love with me. And then we'll live in a Malibu beach house together."

"You and me?"

"No, me and *Ryan*. You can come visit, though. You know, when you're not hanging out with Beyoncé and Lady Gaga."

I laugh. "You do dream big."

"It'll happen, babe. Just you watch."

I sincerely hope so, especially for Allie's sake. She's planning on moving out to L.A. the second she graduates, and honestly, I can totally picture her starring in a romantic comedy. She's not Angelina Jolie-beautiful, but she's got a cute, fresh-faced look and comedic timing that would play well in those quirky romantic roles. The only thing that worries me is...well, she's too soft. Allie Hayes is hands-down the most compassionate person I've ever met. She turned down a free ride to UCLA's drama program in order to stay on the east coast because her father has multiple sclerosis and she wanted to be able to get to New York at a moment's notice if he ever needed her.

Sometimes I'm afraid Hollywood will eat her alive, but she's as strong as she is sweet, and she's also the most ambitious person I've ever met, so if anyone can make their dreams come true, it's Allie.

"Let me brush my teeth and wash up, and then we can go." I glance over my shoulder on my way to the door. "Are you around tonight? I'm tutoring until six, but I thought we could watch some *Mad Men* afterward."

She shakes her head. "I'm having dinner with Sean. I'll probably crash at his place tonight."

A grin tugs on my lips. "So you guys are getting serious again, huh?" Allie and Sean have broken up three times since freshman year, but the two of them always seem to wind up in each other's arms again.

"I think so," she admits as she follows me into the common room. "We've both grown up a lot since the last break-up. But I'm not really thinking about the future. We're good together right now, and that's good enough for me." She winks. "And it doesn't hurt that the sex is fan-fucking-tastic."

I muster up another smile, but deep down, I can't help but wonder what that feels like. The fantastic sex part.

My sex life hasn't exactly been sunshine and rainbows and sparkly tiaras. It's been fear and anger and years of therapy, and when I was finally ready to try my hand at the whole sex thing, it certainly didn't work out the way I wanted. Two years after the rape, I slept with a college freshman I met at a coffee shop in Philly when I was visiting my aunt. We spent the whole summer together, but the sex was awkward and lacking passion. At first I thought maybe we just didn't have chemistry...until the same thing happened with Devon.

Devon and I had the kind of chemistry that could set a room on fire. I was with him for eight months, insanely attracted to the guy, but no matter how hard I tried, I wasn't able to get past my...fine, I'll call a spade a spade. My sexual dysfunction.

I couldn't have an orgasm with him.

It's so fucking mortifying even thinking about it. And even more humiliating when I remember how frustrating it was for Devon. He tried to please me. God, he tried. And it's not like I can't have orgasms on my own—because I can. Easily. But I just couldn't make it happen with Devon, and eventually he grew tired of working so hard and not seeing any results.

So he dumped me.

I don't blame him. Must be a major hit on your manhood when your girlfriend doesn't enjoy your sex life.

"Hey, you're white as a sheet." Allie's concerned voice jerks me back to the present. "Are you all right?"

"I'm fine," I assure her. "Sorry, I spaced out."

Her blue eyes soften. "You're really upset about not seeing

your parents for Thanksgiving, huh?"

I eagerly take the exit she gives me, nodding in agreement. "Like you said, it sucks." I manage a shrug. "But I'll see them at Christmas. That's something, at least."

"It's everything," she says firmly. "Now brush your teeth and make yourself beautiful, babe. I'll have coffee waiting for you when you come back."

"Aw gee, you're the best wifey ever."

She grins. "Just for that, I'm spitting in your coffee."

11

Garrett

Hannah shows up around five in a thick parka with a fur hood and bright red mittens. The last I checked, there wasn't a speck of snow on the ground, but now I'm wondering if I somehow slept through a blizzard when I was taking my catnap.

"Did you just fly in from Alaska?" I ask as she unzips the puffy parka.

"No." She sighs. "I'm wearing my winter coat because I couldn't find my other one. I thought I might have left it here." She glances around my bedroom. "I guess not, though. Ugh. I hope I didn't leave it in the music room. I just know one of those freshman girls is going to steal it. And I *love* that coat."

I snicker. "What's your excuse for the mittens?"

"My hands were cold." She cocks her head. "What's your excuse for the ice pack?"

I realize I'm still holding an ice pack to my side, right where Greg Braxton's behemoth body had slammed into me. I'm bruised to shit, and Hannah gasps when I lift the bottom of my shirt to show her the fist-sized purple bruise on my skin.

"Oh my God! Did that happen at your game?"

"Yup." I slide off the bed and head for my desk to grab my Ethics books. "St. Anthony's has the Incredible Hulk on their team. He loves to wail on us."

"I can't believe you willingly put your body through this," she marvels. "It can't be worth it, can it?"

"It is. Trust me, a few scrapes and bruises are nothing compared to the thrill of being on the ice." I glance over at her. "Do you skate?"

"Not really. I mean, I *have* skated. But I usually just go around in circles on the rink. I've never had to hold a stick or chase a puck around."

"Is that what you think hockey is?" I ask with a grin. "Holding a stick and chasing a puck?"

"Of course not. I know there's a lot of skill involved, and it's definitely intense to watch," she admits.

"It's intense to play."

She perches on the edge of my bed, tilting her head curiously. "Have you always wanted to play? Or is it something your dad forced you into?"

I tense. "What makes you think that?"

Hannah shrugs. "Someone told me your dad is like a hockey superstar. I know there are a lot of parents out there who force their kids to follow in their footsteps."

My shoulders are even stiffer now. I'm surprised she hasn't brought up my father before now—I doubt there's anyone at Briar who *doesn't* know I'm Phil Graham's son—but I'm also startled by how perceptive she is. Nobody has ever asked me if I actually enjoy playing hockey. They just assume I *must* love it because my father played.

"He pushed me into it," I confess in a gruff voice. "I was skating before I even hit the first grade. But I kept playing because I love the sport."

"That's good," she says softly. "I think it's important to be doing what you love."

I'm afraid she might ask more questions about my father, so I clear my throat and change the subject. "So which philosopher should we start with—Hobbes or Locke?"

"You pick. They're both incredibly boring."

I chuckle. "Way to make me enthusiastic about it, Wellsy."

But she's right. The next hour is brutal, and not just because of the mind-numbingly dull theories. I'm absolutely starving because I slept through lunch, but I refuse to end the session until I've mastered the material. When I studied for the midterm before, I focused only on the major points, but Hannah makes me examine every last detail. She also forces me to rephrase each theory, which I have to admit, gives me a better handle on the convoluted crap we're studying.

After we'd muddled through it all, Hannah quizzes me on everything we've read these past few days, and when she's satisfied I know my stuff, she closes the binder and nods.

"Tomorrow we'll start applying the theories to actual ethical dilemmas."

"Sounds good." My stomach grumbles so loudly it practically shakes the walls, and I wince.

She snorts. "Hungry?"

"Famished. Tuck does all the cooking in the house, but he's not home tonight so I was going to order a pizza." I hesitate. "Do you want to stick around? Have a couple slices and maybe watch something?"

She looks surprised by the invitation. It surprises me too, but honestly, I wouldn't mind the company. Logan and the others went out to hit up a party, but I wasn't in the mood to tag along. And I've managed to get ahead on all my course readings, so I've got shit all to do tonight.

"What do you want to watch?" she asks warily.

I gesture to the stack of Blu-Rays next to my TV. "Dean just got every season of *Breaking Bad*. I keep meaning to watch it but I never have time."

"Is that the show about the heroine dealer?"

"Meth cooker. I hear it's fucking awesome."

Hannah runs her fingers through her hair. She seems reluctant to stay, but equally reluctant to go.

"What else do you have to do tonight?" I prompt.

"Nothing," she says glumly. "My roommate is spending the night at her boyfriend's, so I was just going to watch TV anyway."

"So do it here." I grab my cell phone. "What do you like on your pizza?"

"Um…mushrooms. And onions. And green peppers."

"So pretty much all the boring toppings?" I shake my head. "We're getting bacon and sausage and extra cheese."

"Why bother asking me what I like if you're not going to order any of it?"

"Because I was hoping you'd have better taste than that."

"I'm sorry you find vegetables boring, Garrett. Why don't you give me a call when you get scurvy?"

"Scurvy is a deficiency of Vitamin C. You don't put sunshine or oranges on pizza, sweetheart."

In the end, I compromise by ordering two pizzas, one with Hannah's boring-ass toppings, the other loaded with meat and cheese. I cover the mouthpiece and glance at her. "Diet Coke?"

"What do I look like, a pansy? Regular Coke, thank you very much."

Chuckling, I place our order, then put in the first disc of *Breaking Bad*. We're twenty minutes in when the doorbell rings.

"Wow. Fastest pizza delivery guy ever," Hannah remarks.

My stomach is not complaining in the slightest. I head downstairs and grab our food, then pop into the kitchen to grab paper towels and a bottle of Bud Light from the fridge. At the last second, I grab an extra bottle in case Hannah wants one.

But when I offer it to her upstairs, she vehemently shakes her head. "No, thank you."

"What, you're too much of a prude to have one beer?"

Discomfort flickers in her eyes. "I'm not a big drinker, okay?"

I shrug and crack open my beer, taking a deep swig as Hannah rips a piece of paper towel off the roll and pries a gooey vegetable-covered slice out of the box.

We settle on the bed to eat, neither of us speaking as I turn the show back on. The pilot episode is amazing, and Hannah doesn't object when I click on the next one.

There's a female in my bedroom and neither of us is naked. It's strange. But kinda nice. We don't talk much during the show—we're too engrossed by what's happening on the screen—but once the second episode ends, Hannah turns to me and gapes.

"Oh my God, imagine not knowing that your husband is cooking meth? Poor Skylar."

"She's definitely going to find out."

Hannah gasps. "Hey. No spoilers!"

"That's not a spoiler," I protest. "It's a prediction."

She relaxes. "Okay, good."

She picks up her Coke can and takes a deep swig. I've already demolished my pizza, but Hannah's is only half done, so I steal a piece and take a big bite.

"Ohhhh, look who's eating my *boring* pizza. Can anyone say hypocrite?"

"It's not my fault you eat like a bird, Wellsy. I can't let food go to waste."

"I had four slices!"

I have to concede, "Yeah, that actually makes you a total pig compared to the girls I know. The most they ever eat is half a starter salad."

"That's because they need to stay rail-thin so guys like you will find them attractive."

"There's nothing attractive about a woman who's all skin and bones."

"Uh-huh, I'm sure you're *so* turned off by skinny women."

I roll my eyes. "No. I'm just saying I prefer 'em curvy." I swallow my last bite before reaching for another slice. "A man likes having something to grab onto when he's...you know." I arch my eyebrows at her. "It goes both ways, though. I mean, wouldn't you rather sleep with a guy who's built over one who's a twig?"

She snorts. "Is this the part where I compliment you on your super hot bod?"

"You think I'm super hot? Thanks, baby."

"No, *you* think you're super hot." She purses her lips. "But I suppose you have a point. I'm not attracted to scrawny guys."

"Then I guess it's a good thing Loverboy is shredded like lettuce, huh?"

She sighs. "Would you stop calling him that?"

"Nope." I chew thoughtfully. "I'll be honest. I don't know what you see in him."

"Why, because he's not Mr. Big Man on Campus? Because he's serious and smart and not a raging manwhore?"

Shit, I guess she's bought into Kohl's act. If I had a hat, I'd probably tip it off to the guy for successfully creating a persona that drives women wild—the nerd athlete.

"Kohl isn't what he seems," I say roughly. "I know he comes off as the smart, mysterious jock, but there's something...slimy about him."

"I don't think he's slimy at all," she objects.

"Right, because you've had a plethora of deep, meaningful conversations with him," I crack. "Trust me, he's putting on a show."

"Agree to disagree." She smirks. "Besides, you're in no position to judge who I'm interested in. From what I hear, you only date airheads."

I smirk right back. "You're wrong."

"Am I?"

"Yup. I only *sleep* with airheads. I don't date."

"Slut." She pauses, curiosity etching into her face. "How come you don't date? I'm sure every girl at this college would kill to be your girlfriend."

"I'm not looking for a relationship."

That perplexes her. "Why not? Relationships can be really fulfilling."

"Says the woman who's single."

"I'm single because I haven't found anyone I connect with, not because I'm anti-relationship. It's nice having someone to spend time with. You know, talking, cuddling, all that mushy stuff. Don't you want that?"

"Eventually. But not right now." I flash a cocky grin. "If I ever feel the need to talk to someone, I've got you."

"So your airheads get the sex, and I'm the one who has to listen to you babble?" She shakes her head. "I feel like I'm getting the short end of that deal."

I wiggle my eyebrows. "Aw, you want the sex too, Wellsy? I'm happy to give it to you."

Her cheeks turn the brightest shade of red I've ever seen, and I burst out laughing.

"Relax. I'm just kidding. I'm not stupid enough to bone my tutor. I'll end up breaking your heart, and then you'll feed me false information, and I'll fail the midterm."

"Again," she says sweetly. "You'll fail the midterm *again*."

I flip up my middle finger, but I'm grinning as I do it. "You taking off now or should I put on Episode 3?"

"Episode 3. Definitely."

We get comfortable on the bed again, me on my back with my head on three pillows, Hannah on her stomach at the foot of the bed. The next episode is intense, and once it's done, we're both eager to watch the next one. Before I know it, we're done with the first disc and moving on to the second. In between cliffhangers, we discuss what we've just seen and make predictions, and honestly? I haven't had this much platonic fun with a girl in...well, *ever*.

"I think his brother-in-law is on to him," Hannah muses.

"Are you kidding me? I bet they save that reveal for the end. I think Skylar's gonna find out soon, though."

"I hope she divorces him. Walter White is the devil.

Seriously. I hate him."

I chuckle. "He's an anti-hero. You're supposed to hate him."

The next episode comes on, and we shut up immediately, because this is the kind of show that requires your full attention. The next thing I know, we've reached the season finale, which ends with a scene that leaves us wide-eyed.

"Holy shit," I exclaim. "We're done with the first season."

Hannah bites her lip and steals a glance at the alarm clock. It's nearly ten o'clock. We've just watched seven episodes without so much as a bathroom break.

I expect her to announce it's time for her to go, but she sighs instead. "Do you have season two?"

I can't control my laughter. "You want to keep watching?"

"After that finale? How can we not?"

She makes a good point.

"At least the premiere," she says. "Don't you want to see what happens?"

I totally do, and so I don't object when she gets up to load the next disc. "You want a snack or something?" I offer.

"Sure."

"I'll go see what we have."

I find two microwave popcorn pouches in the kitchen cupboard, nuke them both, and head back upstairs with two bowls of popcorn in my hands.

Hannah has stolen my spot, her dark hair fanned on my stack of pillows, legs stretched out in front of her. Her red and black polka dot socks make me grin. I've noticed she doesn't wear designer clothing or preppy getups like most of the females at this school, or the trashy party clothes you see on Greek Row and at the campus bars on weekends. Hannah is all about skinny jeans and leggings and tight-fitting sweaters, which might look elegant if she didn't always throw in a flash of bright color. Like the socks, or the mittens, or those quirky hair clips she wears.

"Is one of those for me?" She gestures to the bowls I'm holding.

"Yup."

I hand one over, and she sits up and shoves her hand inside, then giggles. "I can't eat popcorn without thinking about Napoleon."

I blink. "The emperor?"

She laughs harder. "No, my dog. Well, my family's dog. He's in Indiana with my parents."

"What kind of dog?"

"A huge mutt crossed with a gazillion breeds, but he mostly looks like a German shepherd."

"Does Napoleon like popcorn?" I ask politely.

She grins. "He loves it. We got him when he was a puppy, and this one time—I was about ten—my parents took me to the movies, and he broke into the cupboards when we were out and managed to get into a box of microwave popcorn packets. There were like fifty of them in there. My mom is all about sales, so if there's ever a great deal at the grocery store, she'll buy up the entire shelf of whatever product is on sale. I guess that month it was Orville Redenbacher's. I swear, that dog ate every single one of them, packaging included. He was pooping out whole kernels and bits of paper for days."

I snicker.

"My dad was freaking out," she says. "He thought Napoleon would get food poisoning or something, but the vet said it was no biggie and that it would all come out eventually." She pauses. "Do you have any pets?"

"No, but my grandparents had a cat when I was growing up. Her name was Peaches and she was batshit crazy." I shovel a handful of popcorn into my mouth, chuckling as I chew. "She was sweet to me and my mom, but she fucking hated my dad. Which isn't surprising, I guess. My grandparents hated him too, so she must have been following their lead. But man, she terrorized the old bastard."

Hannah grins. "What'd she do?"

"Scratch him any chance she got, piss on his shoes, that kind of stuff." I suddenly burst out laughing. "Oh shit, the best thing she ever did? It was Thanksgiving and we were at my grandparents' place in Buffalo, and we're all gathered at the table about to eat when Peaches comes in through the cat door. Right behind the house was this ravine, so she used to prowl around there. Anyway, she waltzes inside and she's got something in her mouth, but none of us can tell what it is."

"Oh God. I don't like where this is going."

I'm grinning so hard it hurts. "Peaches jumps up on the table like she's the queen of the castle or some shit, strolls along the edge of the tablecloth, and dumps a dead rabbit on my father's plate."

Hannah gasps. "Seriously? Gross!"

"Gramps is pissing himself laughing, and Gran is freaking out because she thinks all the food on the table is contaminated now, and my dad..." My humor fades as I remember the look on the old man's face. "Let's just say he wasn't pleased."

Understatement of the year. A chill runs up my spine as I recall what happened when we got back to Boston a few days later. What he did to my mother as punishment for "shaming" him, as he'd accused her of doing during his rage.

The only saving grace is that Mom died a year later. She wasn't there to witness it when he turned his rage on me, and I'm grateful for that every day of my life.

Beside me, Hannah goes somber as well. "I'm not seeing my parents for Thanksgiving."

I glance over, studying her face. It's obvious she's upset, and her soft confession distracts me from the crushing memories pressing down on my chest. "Do you usually go home?"

"No, we go to my aunt's for the holidays, but my folks can't afford it this year, and I...can't afford to go to them."

There's a false note there at the end, but I can't imagine what she might be lying about.

"It's okay," she murmurs when she sees the sympathy on my face. "There's always Christmas, right?"

I nod, though for me, there are no holidays. I'd rather slit my wrists than go home and spend the holidays with my father.

I set my popcorn bowl on the nightstand and pick up the remote. "Ready for season two?" I ask in a casual voice. The conversation has gotten too heavy, and I'm eager to derail it.

"Bring it on."

This time I sit beside her, but there's still two feet of space between us. It's messed up how much I'm enjoying this. Just hanging out with a girl without worrying about how I'm going to get rid of her or that she's going to start making demands on me.

We watch the premiere episode of season two, followed by the next one, and then the next one...and the next thing I know, it's three in the morning.

"Oh crap, is that the time?" Hannah blurts out. As she voices the question, a huge yawn overtakes her face.

I rub my weary eyes, unable to fathom how it got this late without either one of us noticing. We've literally watched a season and a half of television in one sitting.

"Shit," I mumble.

"I can't believe how late it is." She yawns again, which triggers a yawn of my own, and then we're both sitting in my dark bedroom—I don't even remember turning off the light—yawning like two people who haven't slept in months.

"I should go." She stumbles off the bed and rakes her hands through her hair. "Where's my phone? I need to call a cab."

My next yawn nearly breaks my jaw. "I can drive you," I say groggily, sliding off the mattress.

"No way. You had two beers tonight."

"Hours ago," I object. "I'm good to drive."

"No."

Exasperation courses through me. "I'm not letting you take a cab and walk through campus at three in the fucking morning. Either I drive you, or you stay here."

She looks startled. "I'm not staying here."

"Then I'm driving you. No argument."

Her gaze travels to the two Bud bottles on the nightstand. I sense her reluctance, but I also see the exhaustion lining her features. After a moment, her shoulders droop and she lets out a breath. "Fine. I'll crash on your couch."

I'm quick to shake my head. "No. It's better if you sleep in here."

Wrong thing to say, because her body goes stiffer than a board. "I'm not sleeping in your bedroom."

"I live with three hockey players, Wellsy. Who, by the way, still aren't home from a night of partying. I'm not saying it'll happen, but there's a chance one of them might stumble into the living room drunk off their asses and grope you or something if they find you on the couch. I, on the other hand, have no interest in groping you." I gesture to my massive bed. "This thing can sleep seven. You won't even know I'm here."

"You know, a gentleman would offer to sleep on the floor."

"Do I look like a gentleman to you?"

She laughs at that. "Nope." There's a beat of silence. "Okay, I'll crash here. But only because I can barely keep my eyes open, and I really don't want to wait for a taxi."

I walk over to my dresser. "You want something to sleep in? T-shirt? Sweatpants?"

"A T-shirt would be great." Even in the darkness, I can make out the flush on her cheeks. "Do you have an extra toothbrush?"

"Yup. Cabinet under the sink." I give her one of my old T-shirts, and she disappears into the bathroom.

I strip off my shirt and jeans and climb into bed in my boxers. As I get comfortable, I hear the toilet flush and the faucet turn on and off, and then Hannah returns, her bare feet softly slapping the hardwood. She stands at the side of the bed for so long that I finally groan in irritation.

"Would you get in bed already?" I grumble. "I don't bite. And even if I did, I'm half asleep. So quit looming over me like a weirdo and get in here."

The mattress dips slightly as she climbs on the bed. There's a tug on the blanket, a rustling and a sigh, and then she's lying beside me. Well, not quite. She's all the way on the other side of the bed, no doubt clinging to the edge of the mattress so she doesn't fall off.

I'm too tired to make a sarcastic remark so I just mumble, "Night" and close my eyes again.

"Night," she murmurs back.

A few seconds later, I'm dead to the world.

12

Garrett

I'm addicted to that moment right before I wake up, when the wispy cobwebs in my brain thread together to form a coherent ball of consciousness. It's the ultimate WTF moment. Disorienting and foggy, with half my brain still lost in whatever dream I'm having.

But something is different about this morning. My body feels warmer than usual, and I become aware of the sweetest smell. Strawberries maybe? No, cherries. Definitely cherries. And something tickles the bottom of my chin, something soft and hard at the same time. A head? Yup, there's a head nestled in the crook of my neck. And a slender arm draped across my stomach. A warm leg hooked on my thigh and a soft breast resting on my left pec.

My eyes open gradually and I find Hannah snuggled up against me. I'm on my back with both my arms wrapped around her, holding her tight to my body. No wonder my muscles are so stiff. Did we sleep like this all night? I remember being on opposite sides of the bed when I fell asleep, so far apart that I half expected to wake up and find Hannah on the floor.

But now we're tangled in each other's arms. It's nice.

I'm growing more alert. Alert enough to register that last thought. It's *nice*? What the fuck am I thinking? Cuddling is an act reserved solely for girlfriends.

And I don't do girlfriends.

But I don't release her either. I'm fully awake now, breathing in her scent and basking in the heat of her body.

I glance at the alarm clock, which is due to go off in five

minutes. I always wake up ahead of the alarm, as if my body knows it's time to get up, but I still set it as a precaution. It's seven. I've only gotten four hours of sleep, but I feel oddly rested. At peace. I'm not ready to let go of that feeling yet, so I just lie there with Hannah in my arms and listen to her steady breathing.

"Is that a *boner*?"

Hannah's horrified voice slices through the serene silence. She shoots into a sitting position, then stumbles back down. Yup, Ms. Graceful trips while lying down, because her leg is still slung over my thighs. And yup, there's definite morning wood happening in my southern region.

"Relax," I say in a sleep-gravelly voice. "It's just a morning chub."

"A morning chub?" she echoes. "Oh my God. You're so..."

"Male?" I supply dryly. "Yes, I am, and that's what happens to men in the morning. It's biology, Wellsy. We wake up with wood. If it makes you feel better, I am in no way turned on right now."

"Fine, I'll accept your biology excuse. Now can you please explain why you decided to cuddle with me in the middle of the night?"

"I didn't *decide* a damn thing. I was asleep. For all I know, you're the one who crawled on top of *me*."

"I would never. Not even in my sleep. My subconscious knows better than that." She jabs her finger in the center of my chest, then dives off the bed in a blur of motion.

The moment she's gone, I experience a sense of loss. I'm no longer warm and cozy, but cold and alone. As I sit up and stretch my arms over my head, her green eyes fix on my bare chest and her nose wrinkles in distaste.

"I cannot believe my head was on that thing all night."

"My chest is not a *thing*." I give her a pointed look. "Other women seem to like it just fine."

"I'm not other women."

No, she isn't. Because other women don't entertain me as much as she does. I suddenly wonder how I ever made it through life without Hannah Wells' sarcastic barbs and annoyed grumbles.

"Stop grinning," she snaps.

I'm grinning? Didn't even realize it.

She narrows her eyes as she fumbles for her clothes. My T-shirt hangs to her knees, emphasizing just how small she is.

"Don't you dare tell anyone about this," she orders.

"Why not? It'll only boost your street cred."

"I don't want to be another one of your puck bunnies, and I don't want people thinking I am, understood?"

Her use of the term makes me grin harder. I like that she's picking up the hockey lingo. Maybe one of these days, I'll even convince her to come to a game. I have a feeling Hannah would be a great heckler, which is always an advantage at home games.

Though knowing her, she'd probably heckle *us* and give the other team the advantage.

"Well, if you really don't want anyone to think that, then I suggest you get dressed fast." I cock a brow. "Unless you want my teammates to witness your walk of shame. Which they will, because we have practice in thirty minutes."

Panic lights her eyes. "Crap."

I have to say, this is the first time a girl's been worried about getting caught in my bedroom. Normally they strut out like they've just bagged Brad Pitt.

Hannah takes a breath. "We studied. We watched TV. I went home late. That's what happened. Got it?"

I fight back laughter. "As you wish."

"Did you really just *Princess Bride* me?"

"Did you really just use *Princess Bride* as a verb?"

She glowers at me, then points a finger in my direction. "I expect you to be dressed and ready to go when I get out of that bathroom. You're driving me home before your roommates wake up."

A chuckle of amusement slips out as she marches into the washroom and slams the door.

Hannah

I'm functioning on four hours of sleep. Kill me now. On the bright side, nobody saw Garrett drop me off at the dorms earlier, so at least my honor is still intact.

My morning classes drag on forever. I have a theory class followed by a music history seminar—both require me to actually pay attention, which is hard to do when I can barely keep my eyes open. I've already chugged three coffees today, but instead of giving me an energy boost, the caffeine just drained the meager energy I had to begin with.

I grab a late lunch in one of the campus dining halls, choosing a corner table in the back and sending out *leave me alone* vibes because I'm too damn tired to make conversation with anyone. The food succeeds in waking me up a little, and I'm early when I walk through the huge oak doors of the philosophy building.

I near the Ethics lecture hall and stop in my tracks. None other than Justin is loitering in the wide corridor, his dark eyebrows knitted as he texts on his phone.

Even though I showered and changed at the dorm, I still feel like a total slob. My outfit consists of yoga pants, a green hoodie, and red rain boots. The weather forecast called for rain that didn't come, so now I feel like an idiot for my choice of footwear.

Justin, on the other hand, is sheer perfection. Dark jeans hug his long, muscular legs and his black sweater stretches across his broad shoulders in a delicious way that makes me shiver.

My heart beats faster the closer I get. I'm trying to decide if I should say hello or just nod in greeting, but he solves that dilemma by speaking first.

"Hey." His mouth curves in a half smile. "Nice boots."

I sigh. "It was supposed to rain."

"That wasn't sarcasm. I'm totally digging the boots. They remind me of home." He notices my quizzical look and quickly elaborates. "I'm from Seattle."

"Oh. Is that where you transferred from?"

"Yep. And trust me, if it's *not* raining there, then something's wrong. Rain boots are a necessity for survival when you live in Seattle." He tucks his phone in his pocket, his voice taking on a casual note. "So what happened to you on Wednesday?"

I furrow my brow. "What do you mean?"

"The Sigma party. I looked for you when I was done playing pool, but you were already gone."

Oh my God. He was *looking* for me?

"Yeah, I left early," I answer, hoping I sound equally casual. "I had a nine o'clock class the next morning."

Justin slants his head. "I heard you left with Garrett Graham."

That catches me off guard. I hadn't thought anyone saw Garrett and me leave together, but clearly I was wrong. And apparently word travels faster than the speed of light at Briar.

"He gave me a ride home," I reply with a shrug.

"Oh. I didn't know you guys were friends."

I smile impishly. "There's a lot you don't know about me."

Holy shit. I'm flirting with him.

He smiles too, and the sexiest dimple I've ever seen appears in his chin. "I guess you're right." He pauses meaningfully. "Maybe we ought to change that."

Holy shit. He's flirting *back*.

And as much as I hate to admit it, I'm starting to think Garrett's hard-to-get theory actually holds water. Justin seems curiously fixated on the fact that I left the party with Garrett.

"So..." His eyes twinkle playfully. "What are you doing after cla—"

"Wellsy!"

I swallow a groan at the cheerful interruption from—who else—Garrett. A slight frown touches Justin's lips as Garrett strides up to us, but then he smiles and nods at the unwelcome intruder.

Garrett holds two foam cups in his hands, and he thrusts one at me with a grin. "Got you a coffee. I figured you might need it."

I don't miss the strange look Justin shoots in our direction, or the flicker of displeasure in his eyes, but I gratefully accept the cup and pop the lid, blowing on the hot liquid before taking a tiny sip. "You're a lifesaver," I breathe.

Garrett nods at Justin. "Kohl," he says in greeting.

The two of them exchange a manly hand slap type of thing, not a shake, but not quite a fist bump either.

"Graham," Justin says. "I heard you handed St. Anthony's asses to them this weekend. Nice win."

"Thanks." Garrett chuckles. "I heard you got *your* ass handed to you against Brown. Bummer."

"There goes our perfect season, huh?" Justin says ruefully.

Garrett shrugs. "You guys'll bounce back. Maxwell's arm is ridiculous."

"Tell me about it."

Since I rate sports talk on the same level of boring as politics and gardening, I take a step toward the door. "I'm heading in. Thanks for the coffee, Garrett."

My pulse continues to race as I enter the lecture hall. It's funny, but my life suddenly seems to be moving at lightning speed. Before the Sigma party, the most contact I had with Justin was one measly nod from ten feet away—and that was over a two-month span. Now, in less than a week, we've had two conversations, and either I was imagining it, or he was about to ask me out before Garrett interrupted.

I slide into my usual seat next to Nell, who greets me with a smile. "Hey," she says.

"Hey." I unzip my bag and grab a notebook and pen. "How was your weekend?"

"Brutal. I had a huge chem test this morning, and I pulled an all-nighter to study for it."

"How'd you do?"

"Oh, I definitely aced it." She smiles happily, but the joy fades fast. "Now I just need to do better on this makeup on Friday, and all will be right in the world again."

"You got my email, right?" I had sent Nell a copy of my midterm earlier in the week, but she hadn't emailed back.

"I did. Sorry I didn't respond, but I was focused on chem. I'm planning on reading through your answers tonight."

A shadow falls over us, and the next thing I know, Garrett slides into the seat beside me. "Wellsy, you got an extra pen?"

Nell's eyebrows nearly hit the ceiling, and then she stares at me like I've sprouted a goatee in the past three seconds. I don't blame her. We've been seat buddies since school started, and not once have I even looked in Garrett Graham's direction, let alone talked to him.

Nell isn't the only one who's fascinated by this new seating arrangement. When I look across the aisle, I find Justin watching us with an indecipherable expression on his face.

"Wellsy? Pen?"

I shift my gaze back to Garrett. "You came to class unprepared? Shocker." I reach into my bag again and rummage around for a pen, then slap it into his hand.

"Thanks." He offers that cocky grin of his before opening his notebook to a fresh page. Then he leans forward and peeks over at Nell. "I'm Garrett."

She gapes at the hand he's sticking out at her before reaching over to shake it. "Nell," she says. "Nice to meet you."

Tolbert arrives just then, and as Garrett turns his attention to the podium, Nell shoots me another WTF look. I bring my lips close to her ear and murmur, "We're kinda friends now."

"I heard that," Garrett pipes up. "And there's no 'kinda' about it. We're best friends, Nelly. Don't let Wellsy tell you otherwise."

Nell giggles softly.

I just sigh.

Our lecture today focuses on some seriously heavy issues. Mainly, the conflict between an individual's conscience versus responsibility to society. Tolbert uses the Nazis as our example.

Needless to say, it's a depressing hour and a half.

After class, I'm dying to finish my conversation with Justin, but Garrett has other ideas. Rather than let me linger—or rather, let me make a beeline for Justin—he firmly takes my arm and helps me to my feet. I steal a look at Justin, who walks briskly down the aisle as if he's trying to catch up to us.

"Ignore him." Garrett's voice is barely audible as he guides me out the door.

"But I want to talk to him," I protest. "I'm pretty sure he was going to ask me out before."

Garrett just plows forward, his hand like an iron vise around my forearm. I have to sprint to keep up with his long strides, and I'm annoyed as hell when we emerge into the cool October air.

I'm tempted to look over my shoulder to see if Justin is behind us, but I know Garrett will chastise me if I do, so I resist the urge.

"What the hell?" I demand, shaking his hand off me.

"You're supposed to be unattainable, remember? You're making it too easy for him."

Aggravation rumbles inside me. "The whole point is to get

him to notice me. Well, he's noticed me. Why can't I stop playing games now?"

"You've piqued his interest," Garrett says as we walk down the cobblestone path toward the courtyard. "But if you want to *keep* his interest, you need to make him work for it. Men like a challenge."

I want to argue with him, except I think he might be right.

"Just play it cool until Maxwell's party," he advises.

"Yes, sir," I grumble. "Oh, and by the way, I'm canceling on you tonight. I'm exhausted from our marathon last night, and if I don't get some sleep I'll be a zombie for the rest of the week."

Garrett doesn't look happy. "But we were going to start the hard stuff today."

"Tell you what, I'll email you a sample essay question, something Tolbert would come up with. Give yourself two hours to write it, and tomorrow we'll go over it together. That way I can get a sense of what we need to work on."

"Fine," he concedes. "I've got practice in the morning and then class. Come over at noon?"

"Sure, but I've gotta be out of there by three for rehearsal."

"Cool. See you tomorrow then." He ruffles my hair as if I'm a five year old, then saunters off.

A wry smile tugs on my lips as I watch him go, his silver and black hockey jacket plastering to his chest as he walks into the wind. I'm not the only one looking—several females also swing their heads in his direction, and I can practically see their panties melt away as he flashes that rogue grin around.

Rolling my eyes, I head off in the opposite direction. I don't want to be late for rehearsal, especially since Cass and I still haven't reached an agreement about his ludicrous choir idea.

But when I walk into the music room, Cass is nowhere to be seen.

"Hey," I greet MJ, who's at the piano studying sheets of music.

Her blond head pops up, a strained smile on her face. "Oh, hey." She pauses. "Cass isn't coming today."

Annoyance erupts in my belly. "What do you mean he's not coming?"

"He texted me a few minutes ago. He has a migraine."

Yeah right. I know for a fact that a bunch of our classmates,

Cass included, went out for drinks last night, because one of them texted me an invite when Garrett and I were watching *Breaking Bad*. It's easy to put two and two together—Cass is hung-over and that's why he bailed.

"We can still rehearse, though," MJ says. This time her smile reaches her eyes. "It might be nice to run through the song without stopping to argue every five seconds."

"Yeah, except whatever we do today, he'll just veto tomorrow." I plop into a chair near the piano and pin her down with a hard look. "The choir idea is bullshit, MJ. You *know* it is."

She nods in defeat. "I know."

"Then why didn't you back me up?" I demand, unable to mask my resentment.

A blush appears on her pale cheeks. "I…" She gulps visibly. "Can you keep a secret?"

Shit. I don't like where this is going. "Sure…"

"Cass asked me out."

"Oh." I try not to sound surprised, but it's hard to hide it. MJ is a sweet girl, and she's certainly not unattractive, but she's also the last person I'd consider Cass Donovan's type.

As much as I loathe him, Cass is drop dead gorgeous. He's got the kind of album-cover-friendly face that will sell a lot of records one day, no doubt about that. And look, I'm not saying the plain girl can't get the hot guy. I'm sure it happens all the time. But Cass is a pompous, image-obsessed jerk. Someone that superficial would never be caught dead with a mousy thing like Mary Jane, no matter how sweet she is.

"It's okay," she says with a laugh. "I know you're surprised. I was too. He asked me before rehearsal that day." She sighs. "You know, the choir day."

Annnnd all the puzzle pieces swiftly slide together. I know exactly what Cass is up to, and it takes some serious effort to swallow my anger. It's one thing to coax MJ into backing him up during our fights, it's another to lead the poor girl on.

But what am I supposed to say to her? *He only asked you out so you'd support all his crazy ideas for the showcase*?

I refuse to be an asshole, so I paste on the most polite smile I can muster and ask, "Do you *want* to go out with him?"

Her cheeks go even redder, and then she nods.

"Really?" I say skeptically. "But he's such a diva. Like,

giving Mariah Carey a run for her money diva. You know that, right?"

"I know." She looks embarrassed now. "But that's only because he's so passionate about singing. He's actually a nice guy when he wants to be."

When he *wants* to be? She says it like it's the endorsement of the year, but the way I see it, people should be nice because they *are*, not because it's a calculated move on their part.

But I keep that opinion to myself, too.

I adopt a tactful tone. "Are you afraid that if you disagree with his ideas, he'll renege on the date?"

She winces. "It sounds pathetic when you phrase it like that."

Um, how else does she want me to phrase it?

"I just don't want to make any waves, you know?" she mumbles, looking uncomfortable.

No, I don't know. At all.

"This is your song, MJ. And you shouldn't have to censor your opinions just to make Cass happy. If you hate the choir idea as much as I do, then tell him. Trust me, men appreciate a woman who speaks her mind."

Yet even as I say the words, I know Mary Jane Harper is not that woman. She's shy and awkward and spends most of her time hiding behind a piano or curled up in her dorm room writing love songs about boys who don't return the sentiment.

Oh shit. Something suddenly occurs to me. Is our song about *Cass*?

I'm icked out at the thought that the emotional lyrics I've been singing for months might actually be about a guy I loathe.

"I don't *hate* the choir idea," she hedges. "I don't love it, either, but I don't think it's terrible."

And in that moment, I know without a doubt there's going to be a three-tiered fucking choir standing behind Cass and me at the winter showcase.

13

Garrett

I'm working at the kitchen counter tonight, frustrated as fuck as I read over the practice essay Hannah "graded" for me earlier. She left my house with orders for me to redo the paper, but I'm having a tough time with it. The answer is simple, damn it—if someone commands you to murder millions of people, you say *no thanks, I'll pass*. Except going by the criteria laid out in this bullshit theory, there are pros and cons for both sides, and I can't wrap my head around it. I guess I suck at putting myself in someone else's shoes, and that's kind of disheartening.

"Question," I announce as Tuck wanders into the kitchen.

"Answer," he replies instantly.

"I haven't asked the question yet, asshole."

Grinning, he washes his hands at the sink and then ties a neon pink apron around his waist. Logan, Dean and I gave him the frilly monstrosity as a joke for his birthday, on the argument that if he was going to be our mother hen, he might as well look the part. Tucker countered by insisting he's masculine enough to pull off any item of clothing we throw his way, and now he wears the damn thing like a badge of macho honor.

"Okay, I'll bite," he says as he heads to the fridge. "What's the question?"

"All right, so you're a Nazi—"

"Fuck that," he interjects.

"Let me finish, will ya? You're a Nazi, and Hitler has just ordered you to commit an act that goes against everything you believe in. Do you say, *cool beans, boss, I'll kill all these people for you*, or do you say *fuck off*, and risk getting killed yourself?"

"I tell him to fuck off." Tuck pauses. "Actually, no. I put a bullet in his head. Problem solved."

I groan. "I know, right? But *this* asshole—" I point to the book on the counter "—believes that government exists for a reason, and citizens need to trust their leader and obey his orders for the good of the society. So in theory, there's an argument to be made for genocide."

Tuck pulls a tray of chicken drumsticks from the freezer. "Bullshit."

"I'm not saying I agree with that line of thinking, but I'm supposed to argue this guy's point of view." I drag a frustrated hand over my scalp. "I fucking hate this class, man."

Tuck unwraps the meat tray and places it in the microwave. "The redo is on Friday, huh?"

"Yup," I say glumly.

He hesitates. "Are you going to play in the Eastwood game?"

I brighten up, because this morning I received official word from Coach that I'll definitely be on the ice on Friday. Apparently the midterm grades aren't entered into the system until the following Monday, so at the moment, my average is still what it needs to be.

Come Monday, if my Ethics grade is a D or lower, I'll be benched until I turn things around.

Benched. Jesus. Just thinking about it makes me queasy. All I want to do is lead my team to another Frozen Four victory and make it to the pros. No, I want to *excel* in the pros. I want to prove to everyone that I got there on my own merit and not because I happen to be a famous hockey player's son. It's all I've *ever* wanted, and I feel sick knowing that my goals, that everything I've worked so hard for, is in jeopardy because of one stupid class.

"Coach said I'm playing," I tell Tuck, who high fives me so hard my palm stings.

"Hell yeah," he exclaims.

Logan enters the kitchen, an unlit cigarette dangling from the corner of his mouth.

"You better not smoke that in here," Tucker warns. "Linda

will ream your ass."

"I'm going out back," Logan promises, because he knows better than to piss off our landlady. "Just wanted to let you guys know that Birdie and the guys are coming over tonight to watch the Bruins game."

I narrow my eyes. "What guys?"

Logan blinks innocently. "You know, Birdie, Pierre, Hollis, Niko—if he can stop being pussy whipped for long enough to leave his dorm—um, Rogers and Danny. Connor. Oh, Kenny, too, and—"

I stop him before he can name every guy on our roster. "So the whole team, you mean," I say dryly.

"And their girlfriends, those who have 'em." He glances at Tuck and me. "It's cool, right? Won't be an all-nighter or anything."

"As long as it's BYOB, I'm cool," Tuck answers. "And if Danny is coming then you better lock up the liquor cabinet."

"We can move the hooch to G's room," Logan says with a snort. "God knows he won't drink a drop of it."

Tuck glances over at me with a grin. "Poor baby. When are you gonna learn to handle your liquor like a man?"

"Hey, I handle the drinking part just fine. It's the morning after that does me in." I smirk at my teammates. "Besides, I'm your captain. Somebody has to stay sober to keep your crazy asses in line."

"Thanks, Mom." Logan pauses, then shakes his head. "Actually, no, *you're* the mom," he tells Tucker, grinning at Tuck's apron before turning back at me. "Guess that makes you the dad. You two are positively domestic."

We both flip him the finger.

"Aw, are Mommy and Daddy mad at me?" He gives a mock gasp. "Are you guys gonna get a divorce?"

"Fuck off," Tuck says, but he's laughing.

The microwave beeps, and Tucker pulls out the defrosted chicken, then proceeds to cook our dinner while I do my homework at the counter. And damned if the whole thing isn't domestic as hell.

14

Hannah

"Hey, Han-Han." Allie surprises me at work tonight, sliding into my booth with a beaming smile. When Sean slides in next to her, I have a tough time fighting a grin. They're sitting on the same side of the booth? Whoa, they *must* be getting serious again, because only couples who are madly in love do that.

"'Sup, Hannah," Sean says as he slings his arm around Allie's slender shoulders.

"Hey." I've been dealing with pain-in-the-ass customers all evening, so I'm genuinely happy to see some friendly faces. "You guys want something to drink while you look at the menu?"

"Chocolate milkshake, please," Allie announces.

Sean holds up his index and middle fingers. "Two straws," he adds with a wink.

I laugh. "God, you two are so sweet you're giving me a toothache."

But I'm happy to see them happy. For a frat boy, Sean is actually pretty decent, and he's never fucked around on Allie, as far as I know. Their past breakups were always her decision—she'd thought they were too young to be so serious—and Sean had been infinitely patient with her every time.

I prepare their lovers milkshake, then deliver it to the booth with an extravagant bow. "Madam, monsieur."

"Thanks, babe. Hey, so listen," Allie says as Sean studies the menu. "Some of the girls on our floor are having a Ryan Gosling movie marathon tomorrow night."

Sean groans. "*Another* Gosling fest? I don't know what

chicks see in that guy. He's scrawny as shit."

"He's beautiful," Allie corrects before glancing at me again. "You in?"

"Depends what time."

"Tracy's got a late class, but she'll be back by nine. So around then?"

"Shit. I'm tutoring at nine."

Allie's face clouds with disappointment. "Can't you try to tutor earlier?" She wiggles her eyebrows as if trying to entice me. "Val's making sangrias..."

I have to admit, I *am* enticed. It's been a while since I've hung out with the girls *or* consumed anything alcoholic. I might not drink at parties (and for a damn good reason) but I don't mind getting my buzz on every now and then.

"Let me call Garrett on my break. I'll see if he's free earlier."

Sean looks up from the menu, interested in the conversation again. "So you and Graham are best buds now?"

"Naah. It's just a tutor/tutoree relationship."

"Nuh-uh," Allie teases. She turns to her boyfriend. "They're totally friends. They *text* and everything."

"Fine. We're friends," I say grudgingly. When Sean gives me a knowing grin, I promptly scowl at him. "*Just* friends. So banish all those dirty thoughts from your mind."

"Oh come on, can you really blame me? He's the captain of the hockey team and he goes through girls faster than he goes through a roll of toilet paper. You *know* everyone's gonna think you're his next conquest."

"They can think whatever they want." I offer a little shrug. "But it's not like that with us."

Sean seems unconvinced, which I chalk up to being a guy thing. I doubt there's a guy out there who believes that men and women are capable of being purely platonic.

I leave Allie and Sean and tend to my other customers. When my break rolls around, I pop into the staff room in the back to call Garrett. The dial tone goes on forever before he finally answers, his gruff "hello" overpowered by the loud music in the background.

"Hey, it's Hannah," I tell him.

"I know. I have Caller ID, dumbass."

"I was calling to see if we can change our tutoring time for tomorrow."

A swell of hip-hop blasts into my ear. "Sorry, what?"

I raise my voice so he can hear me better. "Can we meet up earlier tomorrow? I've got plans at nine, so I was hoping I could come by around seven. Is that cool?"

His response is drowned out by the deafening pounding of Jay-Z.

"Where are you?" I'm practically shouting now.

"Home," comes his muffled response. "We invited a few people over to watch the game."

A few people? It sounds like he's in the middle of Times Square.

"So you're coming at nine?"

I swallow my aggravation. "No, at *seven*. Is that okay?"

"Garrett, beer me!" a voice ripples over the line. Judging by the faint Texas drawl, it must be Tucker.

"Hold on, Wellsy. One sec." A rustling meets my ear, followed by a howl of laughter, and then Garrett comes back. "Okay, tomorrow at nine then."

"Seven!"

"Right, seven. Sorry, I can't hear you at all. I'll see you tomorrow."

He hangs up on me, but I don't care. I've discovered this past week that Garrett never takes the time to say goodbye on the phone. It annoyed me at first, but now I sort of appreciate his time-saving approach.

I shove my phone in my apron and reenter the main room to tell Allie I'm good to go for tomorrow night, and she squeals in response. "Yay! I can't *wait* to get my Gosling on. Hottest. Guy. Ever."

"I'm sitting right here, you know," Sean grumbles.

"Babe, have you *seen* that man's abs?" she demands.

He sighs.

The following night, I show up at Garrett's house at seven o'clock sharp and let myself in as usual. Before I head upstairs, I poke my head into the living room to say hi to Logan and the guys. Logan's not there, but Tuck and Dean are, and they glance up in confusion when they spot me.

"Hey, Wellsy." Tucker wrinkles his forehead. "Whatcha doing here?"

"Tutoring your captain, what else?" Rolling my eyes, I start to edge away from the doorway.

"You don't want to go up there, baby doll," Dean calls out.

I stop in my tracks. "Why not?"

His light-green eyes gleam in amusement. "Uh…he might have forgotten."

"Well, then I'll go up and remind him."

A minute later, I completely regret that course of action.

"Yo, Graham, let's get this over with so I can—" I halt midsentence, freezing like a deer in headlights after I open the door.

Embarrassment slams into me when I register what I'm seeing.

Garrett is lying on the bed in all his bare-chested glory…while a naked girl straddles his thighs.

Yep, Miss Thang is buck-naked, and she whirls around in a cloud of blond hair at the sound of my voice. Perky breasts assault my vision, but I don't have time to judge them one way or the other because her ear-piercing screech cuts through the air.

"*What the hell!*"

"Shit. I'm *so* sorry," I blurt out.

Then I slam the door and race downstairs like I'm being chased by a serial killer.

When I stumble into the living room a moment later, I'm greeted by two grinning faces. "We told you not to go up there," Tucker says with a sigh.

Dean's grin widens. "How was the show? We can't hear much from down here, but I have a feeling she's a screamer."

I'm so mortified that my cheeks feel like they're burning from the inside out. "Can you tell your slutty friend to call me when he's done? Actually, no. Tell him he's out of luck. My time is precious, damn it. I'm not tutoring him anymore when he obviously doesn't take my schedule seriously."

With that, I march out of the house, my emotions alternating between embarrassment and anger. Unbelievable. How is fooling around with some girl more important to him than passing his midterm? And what kind of jerk would do that when he *knows* I'm coming over?

I'm halfway to Tracy's car when the front door bursts open, and Garrett rushes out. He at least had the decency to put on a pair of jeans, but he's still not wearing a shirt. Or shoes, for that matter. He hurries over to me, his expression a mixture of sheepish and annoyed. "What the hell was that?" he demands.

"Are you kidding me?" I retort. "I should be asking *you* that question. You knew I was coming over!"

"You said nine!"

"I changed it to seven, and you know it." My lips twist in a scowl. "Maybe next time you should pay more attention to me when I call you."

He rakes a hand through his short hair, and his biceps bulge as he does it. The cold air causes goose bumps to rise on his smooth, golden skin, and my gaze is unwittingly drawn to the thin line of hair that arrows toward his unbuttoned waistband.

At the sight, an odd flicker of heat travels from my breasts to my core. My body suddenly feels tight and achy, my fingers tingling with the urge to...oh, for fuck's sake. *No.* So what if the guy is totally cut? That doesn't mean I want to ride him like a cowgirl.

He already has someone else doing that to him.

"I'm sorry, okay?" he grumbles. "I screwed up."

"No, *not* okay. One, you clearly don't respect my time, and two, you *clearly* don't want to pass this class, otherwise your pants would be zipped and your textbook would be open."

"Oh really?" he challenges. "So you expect me to believe that *you* study twenty-four-seven and never hook up with *anyone*?"

Discomfort churns in my stomach, and when I don't answer, suspicion floods his eyes. "You do hook up, don't you?"

An irritable breath escapes my lips. "Of course I do. Just...not in a while."

"What's a while?"

"A year. Not that it's any of your business." I set my jaw and unlock the driver's door. "Go back to your floozy, Garrett. I'm going home."

"Floozy?" he echoes. "That's a rude assumption, don't you think? She could be a Rhodes scholar, for all you know."

I raise one eyebrow. "Is she?"

"Well, no," he relents. "But Tiffany—"

I snort. Tiffany. *Of course* her name is Tiffany.

"—is a very smart girl," he finishes darkly.

"Uh-huh, I'm sure she is. Go back to Ms. Smart then. I'm outta here."

"Can we reschedule for tomorrow?"

I open the car door. "No."

"Is that so?" He clamps his hand over the doorframe. "Then I guess our date on Saturday is off too?"

He stares at me.

I stare right back.

But we both know he won't be the one backing down.

I suddenly flash back to the conversation I had with Justin in the hallway the other day. My cheeks heat up again, but this time it has nothing to do with the fact that I just caught Garrett with his pants down. Literally. Justin has finally acknowledged my existence, and if I bail on this party, I'll be passing up the opportunity to talk to him outside of school. It's not like we travel in the same circles, so unless I want to limit myself to a once-a-week interaction in Ethics, I need to be proactive and seek him out away from the lecture hall.

"Fine," I mumble to Garrett. "I'll see you tomorrow. At *seven*."

His mouth curves in a self-satisfied smile. "That's what I thought."

15

Garrett

I make sure to be home—and alone—when Hannah shows up on Thursday night. I'm more amused than embarrassed that she walked in on Tiff and me yesterday, and hey, at least it hadn't been for the money shot. Hannah's face would've been a hundred times redder if she'd heard Tiffany's screams of orgasm.

Honestly, a part of me wonders if Tiff had been faking those porn star moans. I don't claim to be a stud in bed, but I'm attentive as hell and I've never had any complaints in the past. But last night was the first time I felt like the chick in my bed was putting on a show. There'd been something incredibly… *unsatisfying* about the whole thing. I don't know if she was faking it or simply exaggerating her pleasure, but either way, I'm not too eager for a repeat performance.

Hannah knocks on my door, but she doesn't stop at one knock. She does it at least ten more times, and then two more even after I've shouted for her to come in.

The door swings open and Hannah stumbles inside, tightly covering her eyes with both palms. "Is it safe?" she asks loudly. Eyes still shut, she stretches her arms out in front of her like a blind person feeling their way through the darkness.

"You're such a fucking brat," I say with a sigh.

Her eyelids pop open, and she fixes me with a dark look. "I'm just being careful," she answers in a haughty tone. "God forbid I walk in on another one of your sex fests."

"Don't worry, we hadn't even gotten to the sex part. If you must know, we were still in the foreplay stage. Second and third base, to be exact."

"Gross. TMI."

"You asked."

"I did not." She settles cross-legged on the bed and pulls the class binder out of her bag. "Okay, enough chit chat. Let's read over your revised essay and then we'll outline a few practice ones."

I hand over the paper I'd fixed up, then lean back on the pillows as Hannah reads it. Once she's done, she looks over at me, and I can tell she's impressed. "This is pretty good," she admits.

Damned if I don't experience a burst of pride. I slaved over this Nazi paper, and Hannah's praise not only pleases me, but it also confirms that I'm getting better at putting myself in someone else's headspace.

"Actually, it's *really* good," she amends as she skims the conclusion again.

I mock gasp. "Holy shit. Was that a compliment?"

"Nope. I take it back. It sucks ass."

"Too late." I wag my finger at her. "You think I'm smart."

She lets out a heavy sigh. "You're smart when you apply yourself." She pauses. "Okay, so this might be a total dick thing to say, but I always assumed the school was easier on athletes. Academically, I mean. You know, handing out free A's because you guys are *so* important."

"I wish. I know a few guys on the Eastwood team whose professors don't even read their papers—they just slap an A on them and hand them back. But the Briar profs make us work for it. Assholes."

"How are you doing in your other courses?"

"A's across the board, and a pesky C in Spanish history, but that'll change once I turn in my final paper." I smirk. "Guess I'm not the dumb jock you thought I was, huh?"

"I never thought you were dumb." She sticks out her tongue. "I thought you were a jackass."

"*Thought*?" I pounce on her use of the past tense. "Does that mean you've seen the error of your ways?"

"Naah, you're still a jackass." She grins. "But at least you're a smart one."

"Smart enough to ace this midterm?" My spirits sink as I voice the question. The makeup is tomorrow, and I'm starting to stress about it again. I'm not sure I'm ready, but Hannah's confidence eases some of my uncertainty.

"Definitely," she assures me. "As long as you keep your own bias out of it and stick to what the philosophers would do, I think you'll be fine."

"I better be. I really need this grade, Wellsy."

Her voice softens. "The team's that important to you?"

"It's my whole life," I say simply.

"Your life? Whoa. You're putting a lot of pressure on yourself, Garrett."

"You want to talk about pressure?" Bitterness colors my tone. "Pressure is being seven years old and forced to go on a high-protein diet to promote growth. Pressure is being woken up at the crack of dawn six days a week to skate and run drills while your father blows a whistle in your face for two hours. Pressure is being told that if you fail, you'll never be a real man."

Her face goes stricken. "Shit."

"Yeah, that about sums it up." I try to push the memories away, but they keep flashing through my mind, tightening my throat. "Trust me, the pressure I put on myself is nothing compared to what I had to deal with growing up."

She narrows her eyes. "You told me you love hockey."

"I do love it." My voice goes hoarse. "When I'm on the ice, it's the only time I feel...*alive*, I guess. And believe me, I'm going to work my ass off to get to where I want to be. I...fuck, I can't fail."

"What happens if you do?" she counters. "What's your backup plan?"

I frown. "I don't have one."

"Everyone needs a Plan B," Hannah insists. "What if you get injured and can't play anymore?"

"I don't know. I guess I'd be a coach. Or maybe a sportscaster."

"See, you *do* have a plan, then."

"I guess so." I eye her curiously. "What's your Plan B? If you don't make it as a singer?"

"Honestly, sometimes I don't know if I even *want* to be a singer. I mean, I love it, I really do, but doing it professionally is a whole other story. I'm not crazy about the idea of living out of a suitcase or spending all my time on a tour bus. And yeah, I like singing in front of an audience, but I'm not sure I want to be on stage in front of thousands of people on a nightly basis." She shrugs, looking thoughtful. "Sometimes I think I'd rather be a songwriter. I enjoy composing music, so I wouldn't mind working behind the scenes and letting someone else do the whole *star* thing. If that doesn't work out, I could go into teaching." She gives a self-deprecating smile. "And if that fails, I could always try my hand at stripping."

I sweep my gaze up and down her body, making a big show out of licking my lips. "Well, you've definitely got the tits for it."

She rolls her eyes. "Pervert."

"Hey, I'm just stating a fact. Your tits are great. I don't know why you don't flaunt 'em more. You know, throw a few low-cut tops into your wardrobe rotation."

A pink blush blooms in her cheeks. I love how quickly she goes from serious and sassy to shy and innocent.

"By the way, you can't do that on Saturday," I inform her.

"What, strip?" she says mockingly.

"No, blush like a tomato every time I make a lewd comment."

Hannah arches one brow. "How many lewd comments do you plan on making?"

I grin. "Depends on how much I have to drink."

She lets out an exasperated breath, and a strand of dark hair comes loose from her ponytail and falls onto her forehead. Without thinking, I reach out and tuck the errant strand behind her ear.

The instantaneous tensing of her shoulders brings a frown to my lips. "You can't do that either. Freeze up when I touch you."

Alarm flits through her eyes. "Why would you touch me?"

"Because I'm supposed to be your *date*. Have you met me? I'm a handsy guy."

"Well, you can keep your hands to yourself on Saturday," she says primly.

"Good plan. And then Loverboy will think we're just friends. Or enemies, depending on how jumpy you get."

She bites her lip, and her visible agitation only makes me tease her harder. "Oh, and I might kiss you, too."

Now she glares at me. "No way."

"Do you or do you not want Kohl to think you're into me? Because if you do, you'll need to at least try to act like it."

"That's going to be tough," she says with a smirk.

"Bullshit. You like me lots."

She snorts.

"I'm totally digging that snorting thing you do," I tell her frankly. "It's kind of a turn on."

"Would you quit it?" she grumbles. "He's not in the room right now. You can save the flirting for Saturday."

"I'm trying to get you used to it." I pause as if I'm mulling something over, but really, I'm getting a huge kick out of making Hannah squirm. "Actually, the more I think about it, the more I'm wondering if we should warm up."

"Warm up? What the hell does that mean?"

I slant my head. "What do you think I do before a game, Wellsy? Just show up at the rink and throw my skates on? Of course not. I practice six days a week to get ready. Ice time, weight room, watching game tapes, strategy meetings. Think of all the advance prep that goes into it."

"This isn't a game," she says irritably. "It's a fake date."

"But it needs to look real for Loverboy."

"Would you stop calling him that?"

Nope, I have no plans to stop. I like how angry it makes her. In fact, I like pissing her off, period. Every time Hannah gets mad, her green eyes blaze and her cheeks turn the cutest shade of pink.

"So yeah," I say with a nod. "If I'm going to be touching and kissing you on Saturday, I think it's imperative that we rehearse." I lick my lips again. "Thoroughly."

"I honestly can't decide if you're messing with me right now." She blows out an annoyed breath. "Either way, I'm not letting you touch *or* kiss me, so wipe all those dirty ideas out of your head. If you want some action, call Tiffany."

"Yeah, that's not gonna happen."

There's a bite to Hannah's tone. "Why not? You seemed pretty into her last night."

"It was a one-time hook up. And stop trying to change the subject." I grin at her. "Why don't you want to kiss me?" I narrow my eyes. "Oh shit. There's only one explanation I can think of." I pause. "You're a bad kisser."

Her jaw drops in outrage. "I most certainly am *not*."

"Yeah?" I lower my voice to a seductive pitch. "Prove it."

16

Hannah

Somehow I've traveled back in time to my third-grade playground days. Unless there's another explanation for why Garrett is goading me into kissing him.

"I don't have to prove a damn thing," I inform him. "I happen to be a *fantastic* kisser. Sadly, you will never get to find out."

"Never say never," he answers in a singsong voice.

"Thanks for that, Justin Bieber. But yeah, not going to happen, dude."

He sighs. "I get it. You're intimidated by my potent masculinity. Chin up, it happens all the time."

Oh brother. I can still remember the days—all of a week ago—when Garrett Graham wasn't a fixture in my life. When I didn't have to listen to his cocky remarks or see his rogue grins or get drawn into a flirt battle I have no interest in.

Except Garrett happens to be very, very good at one particular thing: throwing down the gauntlet.

"Fear is a fact of life," he says solemnly. "Don't let it get you down, Wellsy. Everyone experiences it." He leans back on his elbows like a bigshot. "Tell you what, I'll give you a free pass. If you're too scared to kiss me, I won't make you."

"Scared?" I rumble. "I'm not scared, dumbass. I just don't *want* to."

Another sigh rolls out of his chest. "Then I guess we're back to self-confidence issues. Don't worry, there are a lot of bad kissers in this world, sweetheart. I'm sure with practice and perseverance, you'll one day be able to—"

"Fine," I interrupt. "Let's do it."

His mouth slams shut, eyes widening in surprise. *Ha.* So he didn't expect me to call his bluff.

Our gazes lock in a stare-down for the ages. He's waiting for me to back down, but I'm confident I can wait him out. Maybe it's childish of me, but Garrett has already gotten his way about this tutoring thing. This time *I* want to win.

But I've underestimated him yet again. His gray eyes darken to smoky metallic silver, and suddenly there's heat in his gaze. Heat, and a gleam of self-assurance, as if he's certain I won't go through with it.

I hear that certainty in the dismissive tone he uses when he finally speaks. "All right, show me what you've got then."

I falter.

Fucking hell. He can't be serious.

And I can't actually be *considering* meeting this inane challenge. I'm not attracted to Garrett, and I don't want to kiss him. End of story.

Except...well, it doesn't feel like the end of *anything*. My body is engulfed with flames, and my hands are trembling not from nerves, but anticipation. When I picture his mouth pressed against mine, my heart races faster than a drum-and-bass track.

What the hell is the matter with me?

Garrett inches closer. Our thighs are touching now, and either I'm hallucinating it, or I can actually see his pulse throbbing in the center of his throat.

He can't possibly *want* this...can he?

My palms grow damp, but I resist wiping them on the front of my leggings because I don't want him to know how unnerved I am. I'm wholly aware of the heat radiating from his jean-clad thigh, the faint scent of his woodsy aftershave, the slight curve of his mouth as he awaits my next move...

"Come on," he mocks. "We don't have all night, baby."

Now I'm bristling. Screw it. It's just a kiss, right? I don't even have to like it. Shutting that smart mouth of his will be reward enough.

Arching a brow, I reach up and touch his cheek.

His breath hitches.

I sweep my thumb over his jaw, stalling, waiting to see if

he'll stop me, and when he doesn't, I slowly bring my mouth to his.

The second our lips meet, the strangest thing happens. Pulsing waves of heat unfurl inside me, starting at my mouth and then rippling down my body, tingling in the tips of my breasts before traveling even lower. He tastes like the peppermint gum he's been chewing all night and the minty flavor suffuses my taste buds. My lips part of their own volition, and Garrett takes full advantage by sliding his tongue inside. When my tongue tangles with his, he makes a low, growling noise in the back of his throat, and the erotic sound vibrates through my body.

Immediately, I'm hit with a jolt of panic that spurs me to break the kiss.

I suck in a shaky breath. "There. How was that?" I'm trying to sound unaffected by what just happened, but the slight wobble in my voice betrays me.

Garrett's eyes are molten. "Not sure. It wasn't long enough for me to properly judge. I'm gonna need more to go on."

His big hand cups my cheek.

This should be my cue to leave.

Instead, I lean in for another kiss.

And it's just as eerily incredible as the first. As his tongue slicks over mine, I stroke his cheek, and God, that's a big mistake because the scratchy feel of his stubble on my palm intensifies the pleasure already wreaking havoc on my body. His face is strong and masculine and *sexy*, and the sheer maleness of him triggers another burst of need. I need more. I didn't expect to, but damn it, I *need* more.

With an anguished moan, I angle my head to deepen the kiss, and my tongue eagerly explores his mouth. No, not eagerly—*hungrily*. I'm hungry for him.

Garrett threads his fingers through my hair and tugs me closer, one powerful arm curling around my hip to keep me in place. My breasts are now crushed against his rock-hard chest, and I can feel the wild hammering of his heart. His excitement matches my own. The raw, husky groan he releases tickles my lips and sends my pulse careening.

Something's happening to me. I can't stop kissing him. He's too addictive. And even though this might have started with me somewhat in charge, I'm no longer in control.

Garrett's mouth moves over mine with skill and confidence

that steals the breath from my lungs. When he nibbles on my bottom lip, I feel an answering tug in my nipples, and press one palm to his chest to ground myself, to try to keep from floating away in a mindless cloud of pleasure. His hot lips leave mine and travel along my jaw line, dipping down to my neck, where he plants open-mouthed kisses that leave shivers in their wake.

I hear a tortured whimper, and I'm startled to realize it came from me. I'm desperate to feel his mouth on mine again. I thrust one hand in his hair to bring him back to where I want him, but the dark strands are too short to grab onto. All I can do is pull his head forward, which summons a low chuckle from him.

"Is this what you want?" he rasps, and then his lips find mine, and he thrusts that talented tongue into my mouth again.

A moan leaves my throat at the exact moment the bedroom door swings open.

"Hey, G, I need to borrow a—"

Dean grinds to a halt.

With a squeak of horror, I tear my mouth away from Garrett's and shoot to my feet.

"Oops. Didn't mean to interrupt." Dean's grin takes up his entire face, and his twinkling green eyes make my cheeks scorch.

I snap back to reality faster than you can say *biggest mistake ever*. Holy shit. I've just been caught making out with Garrett Graham.

And I was *enjoying* it.

"You're not interrupting," I blurt out.

Dean looks like he's fighting back laughter. "No? Because it sure seems like it."

Despite the tight knot of embarrassment lodged in my throat, I force myself to glance at Garrett, silently pleading for backup, but his expression catches me off guard. Deep intensity and a flash of annoyance, but the latter is directed at Dean. And thrown into the mix is something akin to fascination, as if he can't believe what he and I just did.

I can't believe it either.

"So this is what you two do when you're up here," Dean drawls. "All that deep, intensive *tutoring*." He air-quotes the last word, chuckling in delight.

His teasing irks me. I don't want him thinking that Garrett and I are...involved. That we've been fooling around for the past week behind everyone's backs.

Which means I have to nip his suspicions in the bud. ASAP.

"Actually, Garrett's just helping me brush up on my make-out skills," I tell Dean in the most casual voice I can muster. At this point, telling the truth is far less humiliating than letting his imagination run wild, but the confession sounds insane when I utter it out loud. Yep, just honing my kissing skills with the captain of the hockey team. No biggie.

Dean snickers. "That so?"

"Yes," I say firmly. "I have a date coming up and your friend here thinks I don't have any moves. Trust me, we're not into each other. At all." I realize that Garrett still hasn't said a single word, and I turn to him for confirmation. "Right, Garrett?" I ask pointedly.

He clears his throat, but his voice is still gravelly as hell when he speaks. "Right."

"Okay..." Dean's eyes gleam. "Then I'm calling your bluff, baby doll. Show me your moves."

I blink in surprise. "What?"

"If a doctor told you you've got ten days to live, you'd go for a second opinion, wouldn't you? Well, if you're worried about being a crappy kisser, you can't just take G's word for it. You need a second opinion." His brows lift in challenge. "Let me see what you've got."

"Stop being a jackass," Garrett mutters.

"No, he has a point," I answer awkwardly, and my brain screams, *What*?

He has a *point*? Apparently Garrett's body-melting kisses have turned me into a crazy person. I'm shaken up and confused, and most of all, I'm worried. Worried that Garrett will know I...what? That I'd never been so turned on from a kiss before? That I loved every second of it?

Yes, and yes. That's *precisely* what I don't want him to know.

So I saunter over to Dean and say, "Give me a second opinion."

He seems startled for a second, before breaking out in another grin. He rubs his hands together, then cracks his knuckles as if he's preparing for a fight, and the ridiculous gesture makes me laugh.

When I reach him, his bravado falters. “I was just kidding, Wellsy. You don’t have to—”

I cut him off by leaning on my tiptoes and pressing my mouth to his.

Yep, that’s me, just another college coed kissing one guy after the other.

This time, there’s no heat. No tingles. No sense of overpowering desperation. Kissing Dean is nothing compared to the way it felt kissing Garrett, but Dean seems to enjoy it, because he lets out a groan when I part my lips. His tongue enters my mouth, and I let it. Only for a few seconds, and then I step back and put on my most nonchalant face.

“Well?” I prompt.

His eyes are completely glazed over. “Uh.” He clears his throat. “Uh...yeah...I don’t think you have anything to worry about.”

He looks so stunned that I can’t help but smile, but my humor dissolves when I turn to see Garrett rising from the bed, his chiseled face darker than a thundercloud.

“Hannah,” he starts roughly.

But I can’t listen to the rest. I don’t want to think about that kiss anymore. Or ever. The mere memory of it makes my head spin and my heart pound.

“Good luck on the makeup tomorrow.” The words rush out in a fast stream of nervousness. “I’ve gotta take off now, but let me know how it goes, ’kay?”

Then I quickly gather up my things and hurry out of the room.

17

Hannah

"You lost a bet," Allie says dubiously.

"Yep." I sit at the edge of the bed and lean over to zip up my left boot, deliberately avoiding my roommate's gaze.

"And now you're going out with him."

"Uh-huh." I rub my thumb over the side of the boot and pretend I'm wiping away a smudge on the leather.

"You're going out with Garrett Graham."

"Mmm-hmmm."

"I call shenanigans."

Of course she does. A date with Garrett Graham? I might as well have announced I'm marrying Chris Hemsworth.

So no, I don't blame Allie for looking so flabbergasted. The *I lost a bet* excuse was the best one I'd been able to come up with, and it's feeble at best. Now I'm wondering if I should just fess up and tell her about Justin.

Or better yet, if I should cancel the date altogether.

I haven't seen Garrett since... *the big mistake*...as I'm now referring to the kiss. He texted me yesterday after he wrote the makeup exam. Four measly words, two of which aren't even real: "*easy peasy lemon squeezy.*"

I won't lie, I was thrilled to hear it had gone well. But not thrilled enough to initiate an actual conversation, so I simply sent back one word—"*nice*"—and that was the only contact we had up until twenty minutes ago, when he messaged to say he was on his way to pick me up for the party.

As far as I'm concerned, the kiss didn't happen. Our lips

didn't touch, and my body didn't ache. He didn't groan when my tongue filled his mouth, and I didn't whimper when his lips latched onto that sensitive spot on my neck.

It didn't happen.

But...well, if it didn't happen, then there's no reason for me to bail on the party, now is there? Because no matter how confused and stricken the ki—*the big mistake* had left me, I'm still eager for a chance to see Justin outside of class.

I can't bring myself to tell Allie the truth, though. I'm usually so confident in other areas of my life. Singing, schoolwork, friends. When it comes to relationships, I revert back to that traumatized fifteen-year-old who required three years of therapy before she was able to feel normal again. I know Allie would disapprove if she knew I was using Garrett to get to Justin, and right now, I'm not in the mood to be lectured.

"Trust me, shenanigans are Garrett's middle name," I say dryly. "The guy treats life like a game."

"And you, Hannah Wells, are playing along?" She shakes her head, incredulous. "Are you sure you don't have a thing for this guy?"

"Garrett? No way," I say immediately.

Uh-huh. Because you alwaaaaaays make out with guys you don't like.

I banish the internal taunt. Nope, I didn't make out with Garrett. I was simply meeting a challenge.

The mocking voice rears its head again. *And you felt absolutely nothing, right?*

Argh, why isn't there an off switch for that sarcastic part of your brain? Except I know that doing that won't erase the truth. I *did* feel something when we kissed. Those tingles that Justin evokes in me? I felt them the other night with Garrett. They were different, though. The butterflies didn't just float around in my belly—they took flight and raced through my entire body, making every inch of me pulse with pleasure.

But it meant nothing. In the span of ten days, Garrett went from being a stranger to a nuisance to a friend, but that's as far as I'm willing to take it. I don't want to date him, no matter how good a kisser he is.

Before Allie can grill me further, Garrett texts to inform me he's here. I'm about to tell him to wait in the car, but I guess we have different definitions of *here*, because a loud knock sounds on the door a second later.

I sigh. "That's Garrett. Can you let him in? I just want to put my hair up."

Allie grins and disappears. As I run a brush through my hair, I hear voices in the living area, followed by a squeaky protest and then heavy footsteps heading to my bedroom.

Garrett appears in the doorway wearing dark blue jeans and a black sweater, and something terrible happens. My heart turns into a dolphin and does a stupid little flip of excitement.

Excitement, for fuck's sake.

God, that ki—*mistake* really messed with my head.

He scrutinizes my clothes before raising one eyebrow. "Is that what you're wearing?"

"Yes." I bristle. "Got a problem with that?"

He tilts his head to the side like he's Tim fucking Gunn judging an outfit on *Project Runway*. "I'm totally digging the jeans and boots, but the shirt has gotta go."

I examine my loose blue-and-white striped sweater but I honestly don't see the issue. "What's wrong with it?"

"It's too baggy. I thought we talked about how you need to show off your stripper tits."

A strangled cough comes from behind him. "Stripper tits?" Allie echoes as she steps into the room.

"Ignore him," I tell her. "He's a chauvinist."

"No, I'm a guy," he corrects, then proceeds to flash his trademark grin. "I want to see some cleavage."

"I like this sweater," I protest.

Garrett glances at Allie. "Hi, I'm Garrett. What's your name again?"

"Allie. Hannah's roommate and BFF."

"Great. Well, can you tell your roomie and BFF that she looks like a reject from a sailing show?"

She laughs, and then, to my horror—*Benedict Arnold*!—she agrees with him. "It wouldn't hurt to wear something more form-fitting," she says tactfully.

I scowl at her.

Garrett beams. "See? We're all in agreement. Go big or go home, Wellsy."

Allie looks from me to Garrett, and I know exactly what

she's thinking. But she's wrong. We're not into each other, and we're certainly not dating. But I suppose it's better she think *that* than know I'm going out with him to impress someone else.

Garrett strides to my closet like he owns it. When he pokes his dark head inside, Allie shoots me a grin. She seems highly entertained by all this.

He flips through the hangers to examine my wardrobe, then pulls out a sheer black top. "How about this?"

"No way. It's see-through."

"Then why do you own it?"

Good question.

He holds up another hanger, this time a red sweater with a gaping V-neck. "This one," he says with a nod. "You look great in red."

Allie's eyebrows hit the ceiling, and I curse Garrett for putting all these unnecessary ideas in her head. But at the same time, my chest goes warm and gooey, because...*he thinks I look great in red*? As in, he's actually noticed what I've worn in the past?

Garrett tosses me the shirt. "Okay, get changed. We want to be fashionably late, not asshole late."

Allie snickers.

I glare at them both. "Can I please have some privacy?"

They're either oblivious to my annoyance or they're choosing to ignore it, because I hear them chatting easily in the living room. I suspect Allie is grilling him about our "date," and I hope to God that Garrett sticks to the bet story. When his husky laughter floats into my bedroom, an involuntary shiver skitters up my spine.

What is *happening* to me? I'm losing sight of what I want. No, of *who* I want. Justin. Justin frickin' Kohl. I shouldn't be kissing Garrett—or *Dean*, for that matter—and getting distracted by the strange rush of heat he unleashes inside me.

It's time to get my head on straight and remember why I agreed to this charade in the first place.

Starting right now.

Garrett

Beau Maxwell lives off campus with four of his teammates. Their house is only a few blocks from mine, but a helluva lot bigger, and it's packed like a hockey arena on game night when Hannah and I walk inside. Deafening hip-hop blasts from the speaker system, and several warm, sweaty bodies jostle us as we venture deeper into the house. All I can smell is alcohol, sweat, and cologne.

I pat myself on the back for convincing Hannah to wear that red top, because holy fucking hell, it looks amazing on her. The material is so thin it outlines every sweet curve of her chest, and that neckline...Sweet Jesus. Her tits are practically pouring out of it, like they're trying to pop out and say hello. I don't know if she's wearing a pushup bra or if her breasts are really that big, but either way, they're bouncing like crazy with every step she takes.

Several people wander over to say hello to me and there's a shit ton of curious stares in Hannah's direction. She fidgets at my side, clearly feeling out of place. My chest goes softer than butter when I glimpse the deer-in-the-headlights look in her eyes.

I reach for her hand, which prompts her gaze to fly up to mine in surprise.

Bringing my lips close to her ear, I murmur, "Relax."

Leaning in is a big mistake, because she smells fantastic. That sweet, familiar cherry fragrance mingles with the faint hint of lavender and something uniquely feminine. It takes a serious amount of willpower not to press my nose into her neck and inhale her. Or taste her with my tongue. Lick and kiss the hot flesh of her throat until she moans.

Oh man. I'm in big trouble. I haven't been able to stop thinking about that kiss. Every time the memory floats into my head, my pulse races and my balls tighten, and all I want to do is kiss the crap out of her again.

The overpowering lust, however, is accompanied by a sense of crushing rejection. Because, clearly, I was the only one affected by that damn kiss. If Hannah had felt something, even in the slightest, she wouldn't have stuck her tongue down Dean's throat two seconds later. *Dean.* One of my best friends.

But she's not here with Dean tonight, now is she? Nope,

she's my date, and we're here to make another guy jealous—why *can't* I give in to temptation? This might be the only chance I get.

So I plant a soft kiss on the side of her throat before whispering, "You're gonna be the center of attention tonight, babe. Smile and pretend you're enjoying it."

I steal another kiss, this time on the corner of her jaw, and she sucks in a breath. Her eyes widen, and either I'm imagining it, or there's a glimmer of heat there.

Before I can interpret what I'm seeing, one of the linebackers interrupts us. "Graham! Yo, good to see you, man!" Ollie Jankowitz lumbers over and slaps my back, and the contact jars my entire body because the dude is monster-sized.

"Hey, Ollie," I say before nodding at Hannah. "Do you know Hannah?"

He wears a blank look for a second. Then his eyes dip to her chest, and a slow smile stretches across his bearded face. "I do now." He sticks out one meaty paw. "Hey, I'm Oliver."

She awkwardly shakes his hand. "Hi. It's nice to meet you."

"Got anything to drink in this place?" I ask Ollie.

"Kegs are in the kitchen. Lots of other party favors floating around, too."

"Nice. Thanks, man. I'll catch up with you in a bit."

I lace my fingers through Hannah's and lead her to the kitchen, which is packed with drunken frat brothers. I haven't spotted Beau yet, but I know we'll run into him eventually.

I'm not too thrilled at the prospect of seeing Kohl, though.

I grab two plastic cups from the stack on the granite counter and make my way to one of the kegs. The frat boys protest, but when they notice who's pushing them aside, they part for me like the Red fucking Sea. Just another perk of being the captain of Briar's revered hockey team. I pour two beers, then duck away from the crowd and hold a cup out to Hannah, who adamantly shakes her head.

"It's a party, Wellsy. Won't kill you to have one measly beer."

"No," she says firmly.

I shrug and take a sip of the watery alcohol. The beer is cheap as fuck, but that's probably a good thing. Means there's no chance of me getting wasted off this shit, not unless I drink a whole keg to myself.

As the kitchen empties out, Hannah leans against the counter and sighs. "I hate parties," she says glumly.

"Maybe that's because you refuse to drink," I tease.

"Go ahead and bring on the prude jokes. I don't mind."

"I know you're not a prude." I wag my eyebrows. "A prude doesn't kiss the way you do."

Her cheeks redden. "What the hell does that mean?"

"It means you've got a sexy tongue and you know how to use it." Ah shit, wrong thing to say. Because now I'm hard. Luckily, my jeans are tight enough to keep my erection from tenting like an asshole.

"Sometimes I think you say things just to make me blush," Hannah accuses.

"Nope. I'm just being honest." A swell of voices wafts past the kitchen, and I find myself praying that nobody walks in. I like being alone with Hannah.

And even though there's no reason to put on a show when we're alone, I still move closer and sling one arm around her shoulder as I take another sip of water-beer.

"In all seriousness, why are you so anti-drinking?" I ask gruffly.

"I'm not anti-drinking." She pauses. "I actually kind of like it. In moderation, of course."

"Of course," I echo, rolling my eyes before reaching for the second cup I left on the counter. "Would you have a beer already?"

"No."

I have to laugh. "You just said you liked it."

"I don't mind drinking in my room with Allie, but I never do it at parties."

"Oh jeez. So you sit at home like a wino when you drink?"

"No." She looks exasperated. "Just…drop it, will you?"

"Do I ever drop anything?"

Her exasperation turns to defeat. "Look, I get paranoid about what might be in my cup, all right?"

Insult prickles my skin. "For fuck's sake, you think I'd *roofie* you?"

"No, of course not."

Her swift response eases my concerns, but when she adds, "Not you, anyway," it triggers my suspicion.

"Did…" I frown deeply. "Did that happen to you?"

Hannah's face goes stricken for a beat, and then she slowly shakes her head. "It happened to a friend of mine in high school. She was drugged."

My jaw falls open. "Seriously?"

She nods. "Someone slipped her GHB at a party…and, um…let's just say it wasn't a good night for her, okay?"

"Oh shit. That's all kinds of fucked up. Was she okay?"

Hannah looks sad. "Yeah. She was fine." She gives an awkward shrug. "But it made me distrustful about drinking in public. Even if I pour the drink myself…who knows what will happen if I turn away, even for a second. I refuse to take that chance."

My voice thickens. "You know I'd never let that happen to you, right?"

"Um, yeah. Sure, I do." But she doesn't sound fully convinced, and I can't bring myself to be offended about it because I suspect her friend's experience really screwed with Hannah's head. And with good reason.

I've heard horror stories like that before. As far as I know, it hasn't happened at Briar, but I know it goes on at other colleges. Girls unwittingly ingesting E or Rohypnol, or getting shit-faced out of their minds while immoral creeps take advantage of them in that state. I honestly don't understand guys who would do that to a woman. As far as I'm concerned, they should all be behind bars.

But now that I know the reason behind her no-drinking rule, I quit bugging Hannah about having a beer, and we head back to the main room. Hannah's eyes scan the crowd, and I instantly stiffen because I know she's looking for Kohl.

Fortunately, he's nowhere to be seen.

We mingle for a while. Every time I introduce her to someone, they look surprised, as if they can't understand why I'm with her and not some ditzy sorority girl. And more than one guy ogles Hannah's breasts before winking at me as if to say *good job*.

I officially take back my earlier claim—I wish I *hadn't* convinced her to wear that top. For some reason, the appreciative stares she's receiving really piss me off. But I swallow the possessive caveman urges and try to enjoy the party. The crowd is more football than hockey, but I still know almost everyone there, which causes Hannah to mutter, "Jeez. How do you *know* all these people?"

I smirk at her. "I told you I'm popular. Hey, there's Beau. Come on, let's go over and say hi."

Beau Maxwell is the typical college quarterback. He's got it all—the looks, the swagger, and most important, the talent. But although anyone else in his position might think it's their right to be a total douchebag, Beau's actually kinda decent. He's a history major like me, and he looks genuinely happy to see me tonight.

"G, you made it! Here, try this." He holds out a bottle of...*something*. The bottle is black and has no label, so I have no clue what he's offering.

"What is it?" I ask with a grin.

Beau grins back. "Moonshine courtesy of Big Joe's sister. This shit is *potent*."

"Yeah? Then get it the hell away from me. I've got a game tomorrow afternoon. Can't show up with a moonshine hangover."

"Fair enough." He bats his baby blues at Hannah. "You want some, honey?"

"No, thanks."

"Beau, Hannah. Hannah, Beau," I introduce.

"Why do you look so familiar?" Beau demands, looking her up and down. "Where do I know you fr—oh shit, I know. I saw you sing in the spring showcase last year."

"Really? You were there?"

Hannah sounds simultaneously surprised and pleased, and I wonder if maybe I've been living on a different planet or some shit, because how am I the only one who doesn't know about these showcases?

"Damn straight I was there," Beau declares. "And you were awesome. You sang...what was it again? "Stand By Me," I think?"

She nods.

I wrinkle my forehead as I glance at her. "I thought you were only allowed to sing originals."

"That's a senior level requirement," she explains. "Freshmen and sophomores can sing whatever they want because they're not in the running for the scholarships."

"Yeah, my sister had to sing an original," Beau tells us. "She was in the senior group. Joanna Maxwell? Do you know her?"

Hannah gasps. "Joanna's your sister? I heard she landed a part on Broadway this summer."

"She did!" Beau beams with pride. "My big sis is a

Broadway star. How 'bout that?"

We're drawing even more stares now that we're chatting with the birthday boy, but Hannah seems oblivious to it. I, on the other hand, am annoyingly aware of the attention—from one person in particular. Kohl has just entered the living room, and his lips pinch when our gazes meet. I nod in hello, then turn my head and very deliberately plant a kiss on Hannah's cheek.

Her head jerks up in surprise, so I justify the random gesture by saying, "I'll be right back. Going to grab another beer."

"Okay." She instantly turns back to Beau and they continue chatting about his sister.

I'm not sensing any romantic interest on her part, though, which brings an odd pang of relief. The real threat is across the room, and he marches purposefully in our direction the second I step away from Hannah and Beau.

I intercept Justin before he can reach the chatting duo, giving him a casual slap on the arm. "Kohl. Great party, huh?"

His nod is absent-minded, his gaze still focused beyond my shoulder at Hannah. Fuck. Can he actually be interested in her? I figured this big charade of ours wouldn't result in anything I needed to worry about, but evidently my plan is working too well. Kohl only has eyes for Hannah, and I don't like it. Not one bit.

I glance at his empty hands and grin. "Come on, let's get you a drink."

"Naah, I'm good." He's already brushing past me, heading right where I don't want him to go.

The moment Hannah notices Justin, her cheeks turn pink and a startled look crosses her eyes, but she recovers quickly and greets him with a hesitant smile.

Oh *hell* no. My back snaps straighter than a hockey stick. I want to stalk over there and yank her away from Kohl. Or better yet, yank her right into my arms and kiss the living daylights out of her.

I do neither—because this time I'm the one being intercepted.

Kendall appears in my path, her long blond hair braided over one shoulder, the tail end of it dangling in her cleavage. She's dressed to the nines in a teeny red dress and impossibly high heels, but her expression is stormy as fuck.

"Hi," she says tightly.

"Hey." I clear my throat. "How's it going?"

Her lips flatten in displeasure. "Seriously? You're on a *date* and *that's* what you say to me?"

Shit. Half my attention remains on Hannah, who is now laughing at something Kohl said. Thankfully Beau is still there to serve as a buffer, but I'm not happy to see her and Justin looking so chummy.

The rest of my attention is on Kendall, who I'm suddenly afraid might make a scene.

"You said you didn't want a girlfriend," she hisses out.

"I don't," I'm quick to reply.

She's so pissed she's actually trembling. "Then how do you explain *her*?" One manicured finger lifts in Hannah's direction.

Great. Well, now I'm screwed. I can't insist that it's *not* a date, because Kohl is supposed to think it is. But if I say it *is* a date, Kendall might very well slap me.

I lower my voice. "She's not my girlfriend. It's a date, yeah, but it's not a serious thing, okay?"

"No, *not* okay. I'm really into you! And if you're not into me, then fine. But at least have the decency to—"

"Why?" I'm unable to stop the question that had bitten at my tongue last week when she and I called it quits.

Kendall blinks in confusion. "Why what?"

"Why are you into me?"

She scowls at me, as if she's genuinely insulted that I would ask that.

"You don't even know me," I say softly. "You haven't *tried* to get to know me."

"That's not true," she objects, her scowl dissolving into a worried frown.

I let out a troubled breath. "We've never even had a real conversation, Kendall, and we've seen each other dozens of times since the summer. You haven't asked me a single question about my childhood, or my family, or my classes. My teammates, my interests—hell, you don't even know my favorite color, and that's the kind of thing you find out in Getting to Know You 101."

"Yes, I do," she insists.

I sigh again. "Yeah? What is it then?"

She hesitates for a beat, then says, "Blue."

"Actually, it's black," another voice pipes up, and then

Hannah appears at my side, and I'm so fucking relieved that I almost give her a bear hug.

"Sorry to interrupt," she chirps, "but…dude, where's our beer? Did you get lost on your way to the kitchen or something?"

"I got sidetracked."

Hannah glances at Kendall. "Hi. I'm Hannah. Sorry, but I need to steal him away for a second. Thirst calls."

The fact that Kendall doesn't object tells me that my point has hit home, and Kendall's expression is a mixture of shame and guilt as Hannah takes my arm and drags me into the hallway.

Once we're out of sight, I lower my voice and say, "Thanks for the save. She was either about to burst into tears, or kick me in the balls."

"I'm sure the latter would've been well-deserved," Hannah replies with a sigh. "Let me guess—you broke her heart."

"No." Annoyance rises in my throat. "But it turns out our amicable parting wasn't as amicable as I thought it was."

"Ah. I see."

I narrow my eyes. "So my favorite color is black, huh? What makes you think that?"

"Because every frickin' shirt you own is black." She shoots a pointed look at my sweater.

"Maybe that's because black goes with everything—did you ever think about *that*?" I smirk. "Doesn't mean it's my favorite color."

"Fine, I'll bite. What's your favorite color then?"

I let out a sigh. "It's black."

"*Ha!* I knew it." Hannah sighs, too. "So, what, do we have to hide in the hall for the rest of the night now to avoid that girl?"

"Yup. Unless you want to take off?" I say hopefully. I've lost all enthusiasm for this party, especially now that Kohl has arrived. Before she can answer, I strengthen my case by adding, "Kohl took the bait, by the way. So if we take off now, you'll leave him wanting more, which was the plan, right?"

Hesitation digs a line into her forehead. "Yeah, I guess. But…"

"But what?"

"I was enjoying talking to him."

Damned if that doesn't feel like a knife to the heart. But why? I'm not interested in Hannah. Or at least I hadn't been before. All I'd wanted was her tutoring services, but now…now I don't know *what* I want.

"What did you guys talk about?" I ask, and hope she doesn't hear the edge in my voice.

Hannah shrugs. "Class. Football. The showcase. He asked me if I want to have coffee sometime and study for Ethics together."

Uh, *what*?

"Are you shitting me?" I burst out. "He's macking on my date right in front of me?"

Amusement dances in her eyes. "We're not actually together, Garrett."

"*He* doesn't know that." I can't control the anger simmering in my gut. "You don't hit on another man's date. Period. That's a dick move."

A frown touches her lips.

I eye her. "Would you want to go out with a guy who does something that shady?"

"No," she admits after a long beat. "But…" She appears to be thinking it over. "There wasn't anything overtly sexual about the invitation. If he was hitting on me, he would've asked me to dinner. Coffee and studying can be construed as a friend thing."

She could be right, but I know how guys think. That son of a bitch was hitting on her in plain sight of the guy she came to the party with.

Dick. Move.

"Garrett…" Her voice becomes wary. "You know that kiss didn't mean anything, right?"

The question catches me off guard. "Uh. Yeah. Of course I know that."

"Because we're just friends…right?"

The pointed note in her tone irks, but I know now is not the time to argue about this. Whatever *this* is.

So I nod and say, "Right."

Relief floats through her eyes. "Good. Okay, well, maybe we *should* go. I think we've done enough mingling."

"Sure. Whatever you want."

"Let's just say bye to Beau first. You know, I really like that guy. He's not at all what I expected…"

She continues to chatter my ear off as we go back to the

living room, but I don't hear a single word. I'm too busy dealing with the truth bomb that's just been dropped on my head.

Yes, Hannah and I are friends. In fact, she's the only female friend I've ever had. And yes, I want to *keep* being Hannah's friend.

But...

I also want to sleep with her.

18

Hannah

I've been neglecting my friends since I started tutoring Garrett, but now that he's written the midterm, my free time belongs to me again. So the night after Beau Maxwell's party, I meet up with the usual suspects at the campus coffeehouse, excited to reconnect with everyone. And it's obvious they missed me just as hard.

"Han-Han!" Dexter jumps out of his chair and pulls me into a bear hug. And when I say bear hug, I mean it, because Dex is a giant of a guy. I always tease him that he looks exactly like the kid from *The Blind Side* and should therefore be playing linebacker for the football team, but Dex doesn't have an athletic bone in his body. He's a music major like me, and trust me, the dude can *sing*.

Megan is the next one to greet me, and as usual, a smartass remark pops out of her smartass mouth. "Were you abducted by aliens?" she demands even as she hugs me so tightly I can hardly breathe. "I hope the answer to that is yes and that they anal-probed you for ten hours straight, because you deserve it for ignoring me for more than a *week*."

I laugh at the vivid picture she's painted. "I know. I'm a total shit. But I had a tutoring gig this week and it's kept me busy."

"Oh, we all know who's been keeping you busy," Stella pipes up from her seat next to Dex. "Garrett Graham, Han? Really?"

I stifle a sigh. "Who told you? Allie?"

Stella rolls her eyes in the most theatrical fashion. I think it's a drama student thing—it's like they can't say a solitary word or make a single gesture without hamming it up. "Of course she did. Unlike you, Allie doesn't keep any secrets from us."

"Oh, shut it. I've just been busy with tutoring and rehearsal. And whatever Allie said about Garrett, it's not true." I unzip my winter coat and drape it over the empty chair beside Meg's. "I'm helping him pass Ethics. That's all."

Meg's boyfriend Jeremy wiggles his eyebrows at me over the rim of his coffee mug. "You know this makes you the enemy now, right?"

"Aw, come on," I protest. "That's just mean."

"Says the traitor," teases Meg. "How dare you fraternize with a meathead? How. Dare. You."

I can see from their playful expressions that it's all in good fun. Or at least it is before Garrett texts me.

My phone meows, and I grin the second I pull it out of my purse.

Garrett: *U totally should've come to the post-game party tonite. Some chick just dumped a pitcher of beer over Dean's head.*

I snort out loud and shoot back a quick text, because I *have* to know more.

Me: *OMG. Why? (tho I'm sure he deserved it).*

Him: *Guess he forgot to tell her they weren't exclusive.*

Me: *Of course. Men.*

Him: *Men…finish that sentence…Men are awesome? Thanks, baby. I accept this award on behalf of all of us.*

Me: *The award for biggest douchebag? Yeah, you're the perfect spokesman.*

Him: *Awwww. I'm hurt. I'm not a DB* ☹

The notion that I might have hurt his feelings causes guilt to trickle through me.

Me: *You're right. You're not. I'm sorry.* ☹

Him: *Ha. You're the biggest softie on the planet. I wasn't hurt at all.*

Me: *Good, because the apology was for show.*

"Hannah Wells, please report to the principal's office!"

My head jerks up, and I discover all four of my friends grinning at me again.

Dex, who'd voiced the booming command, addresses the group. "Oh, look, she's paying attention to us."

"Sorry," I say guiltily. "I will officially put my phone away for the duration of this get-together."

"Hey, you'll never guess who we saw at Ferro's last night," Meg says, referring to the Italian restaurant in town.

"Here we go," her boyfriend sighs. "Can't you go five seconds without gossiping, babe?"

"Nope." She flashes him a jovial smile before turning to me. "Cass and Mary Jane," she announces. "They were on a *date*."

"Did you know they were together?" Stella demands.

"I know he asked her out," I admit. "But I was hoping she'd be smart enough to say no."

But I'm not surprised to hear that MJ had done the opposite. And now I'm certainly not looking forward to Monday's rehearsal, because if Cass and MJ are a "couple" now? I'll never win an argument about the duet ever again.

"Is that ass-hat still causing trouble at rehearsals?" Dex asks with a frown.

"Yup. It's like he's made it his mission in life to piss me off. But we don't rehearse on the weekends, so I have a reprieve from his bullshit until Monday. How's your piece going?"

Dex's expression turns serious. "It's great, actually. Jon's been really good about listening to my suggestions. He's not crazy possessive over the song, you know? But he also has no problem saying no to my ideas, which I also appreciate."

Well, at least one of us lucked out in the songwriter department. MJ seems perfectly content to let Cass light a match to her song and set it on fire.

"Okay, I totally want to hear more, but I need to grab a

coffee first." I hop out of my seat and pick up my purse. "Does anyone want anything while I'm up there?"

After everyone shakes their heads, I head to the counter and stand at the end of the long line. The coffee house is surprisingly packed for a Sunday night, and I'm startled when several people in line nod or say hello to me. I don't know a single one, but I smile awkwardly and nod back, then pretend to text on my phone because I don't want to get drawn into a conversation with a stranger. Maybe I met them at Beau's party? All the introductions Garrett made are a total blur to me, though. The only people whose names and faces I remember are Beau and Justin and a few of the other football players.

There's a soft tap on my shoulder, and I turn around to find myself peering up at Justin's vivid blue eyes.

Speak of the devil.

"Oh, hi," I squeak out.

"Hey." He slides his hands into the pockets of his football jacket. "How's it going?"

I try to sound casual despite my racing heart. "Good. You?"

"I'm great. But...I *am* curious about something." He slants his head in the most adorable way, and when a lock of dark hair falls onto his forehead, I fight the urge to brush it away. "What exactly do you have against parties?" he asks with a grin.

I blink. "What?"

"I've run into you at two parties now, and both times you left early." He pauses. "Actually, both times you left with *Graham*."

Discomfort coils around my spine. "Uh, yeah. Well, he's got a car. I can't pass up a free ride."

The second I say it, I realize how dirty that sounded, but unlike Garrett, who would have pounced on the *ride* remark in a heartbeat, Justin doesn't even crack a smile. If anything, he looks disturbed.

He's quiet for a moment before lowering his voice. "You know what? I'm just gonna come out and ask—are you and Graham friends, or is it something more?"

My phone rings the second he voices the question, proving that iPhones have the absolute worst timing. As Justin Timberlake's "Sexy Back" blares from the speaker, everyone in line looks over with a grin. *Why* is "Sexy Back" blaring out of my phone? Well, because a very obnoxious hockey player programmed it in as his ringtone, and I've been too lazy to change it.

Justin's gaze drops to my phone, and since the screen is facing upward, he doesn't miss the name flashing across it in huge block letters.

GARRETT GRAHAM.

"I guess that answers my question," he says wryly.

I quickly press the *ignore* button. "No. Garrett and I aren't together. And just so you don't think I'm a total weirdo, I didn't assign him that ringtone. He did."

Justin still looks dubious. "So you're not dating him?"

Since the whole point of going to Beau's party with Garrett was to make me seem desirable, I stick to the lie. "We're casually seeing each other, but we're not exclusive or anything. We see other people, too."

"Oh. Okay."

The line shifts closer to the counter, and we shuffle right along with it.

"Does that mean you're allowed to have dinner with me sometime?" Justin asks with a faint smile.

A pang of alarm lights my belly. I can't quite make sense of it, so I decide to ignore it. "I'm allowed to do whatever I want. Like I said, Garrett and I aren't together. We just hang out sometimes."

God, that sounds sleazy. I know what guys think when they hear that. I might as well have said, *I'm just sleeping with him, no strings attached.*

However, Justin doesn't seem put off by that. His hands move from his pockets to the belt loops of his cargo pants in a slightly awkward pose. "Look. Hannah. I think you're pretty cool." He shrugs. "I'd like to get to know you better."

My heart skips a beat. "Really?"

"Totally. And I'm fine if you're dating other people at the same time, but..." His expression becomes intense. "If you and I go out a couple times and we have the kind of connection I think we're going to have, then I'm gonna want to invoke an exclusive clause pretty damn soon."

I can't help but smile. "I didn't realize football players were interested in monogamy," I tease.

He chuckles. "My teammates sure as hell aren't, but I'm not like them. If I'm into a girl, I want her to be with me and *only* me." I don't know what to say to that, but fortunately he goes on before

I can respond. "But it's way too early to talk about stuff like that, huh? How about we start with dinner?"

Oh my God. He's asking me out. Not for coffee, not to study, but an actual *date*.

I should be doing internal cartwheels or something, and yet I can't shake the apprehension churning in my stomach, the muffled little alarm bells that are telling me to say…no. But that's crazy. I've been obsessing over this guy since school started. I *want* to go out with him.

I exhale a slow breath. "Sure, that sounds great. When?"

"Well, I'm kinda swamped this week. I have two papers to write, and then I'll be in Buffalo with the team this weekend. How about a week from now? Next Sunday, maybe?"

My phone busts out its rendition of "Sexy Back."

A frown touches Justin's lips, but it fades when I hastily press *ignore* again.

"Next Sunday is great," I say firmly.

"Awesome."

We reach the counter, and I order a large mocha latte, but before I can reach for my wallet, Justin comes up beside me, places his own order, and proceeds to pay for both of us. "My treat."

His husky voice sends a shiver racing through me.

"Thank you."

As we move to the other end of the counter to wait for our drinks, he does that cute head-tilting thing again. "Are you sticking around here, or do you want me to walk you back to your dorm? Wait—you're in the dorms, right? Or do you live off-campus?"

"I'm in Bristol House."

"Hey, we're next door neighbors. I'm in Hartford."

The barista slides our orders on the counter. Justin reaches for his cup, then grins at me. "Shall we walk back together, milady?"

Okay. Well, that was…cheesy. And he didn't thank the girl at the counter when she handed him his coffee. I don't know why that bothers me, but it does.

Still, I force a smile, even as I give the rueful shake of my head. "I would, but I'm here with friends."

His eyes twinkle. "You're just a social butterfly, aren't you?"

I laugh awkwardly. "Not really. I haven't seen my friends in a while. I've been too busy to go out."

"Not too busy to see Graham," he points out. There's a teasing note in his voice, but I also hear something sharper. Jealousy? Or maybe it's resentment. But then he smiles again and playfully takes my phone from my hand. "I'm putting my number in here. Text me yours when you get a chance, and we'll figure out the details for next week."

My heart speeds up, but this time it's from nervous excitement. I can't believe we're actually going on a date.

Justin finishes entering his number into my contact list just as the phone rings in his hand.

Surprise! It's Garrett again.

"Maybe you should just answer it," Justin mutters.

He might be right. Three calls in two minutes? That could definitely mean an emergency.

Or it could mean that Garrett is just trying to annoy me as usual.

"I'll see you Sunday." Justin hands the phone back, smiles again (but it looks mega awkward this time), and then walks off.

I move away from the counter and answer the call before it jumps over to voice mail. "Hey, what's up?" I say irritably.

"Finally!" Garrett's aggravated voice slides into my ear. "Why do you even *own* a phone if you don't bother picking it up when someone calls? You better have a good reason for ignoring me, Wellsy."

"Maybe I was in the shower," I grumble. "Or peeing. Or doing yoga. Or streaking naked through the quad."

"Were you doing any of those things?" he challenges.

"No, but I *could* have been. It's not like I spend my days sitting around and waiting for you to call, jackass."

He ignores the barb. "What's with all the voices? Where are you?"

"Coffee Hut. I'm catching up with some friends." I leave out the part where Justin asked me out on a date. For some reason, I don't think Garrett will approve, and I'm not in the mood to argue with him. "So what's so important you had to call me five trillion times?"

"Dean's birthday is tomorrow and the team is going to Malone's. We'll probably end up going back to our place afterward. You in?"

I laugh. "You're asking me if I want to go to a bar and watch a bunch of hockey players get loaded? Why would you ever think that's something I'd enjoy?"

"You have to come," he says firmly. "My midterm grade comes back tomorrow, remember? Which means I'll either be celebrating or commiserating. Either way, I want you there."

"I don't know..."

"Please?"

Wow. Garrett knows the word *please*? Shocking.

"All right," I relent, because for some stupid reason, I can't say no to this guy. "I'll come."

"Hells yeah. Pick you up at eight?"

"Sure."

I hang up, wondering how in the span of five minutes, I've made not one, but *two* dates. One with the guy I like, and the other with the guy I kissed.

I wisely keep both those details to myself as I rejoin my friends.

19

Hannah

It's becoming glaringly obvious that Garrett was right. He *is* an image booster. As I walk down the cobblestone path toward the Philosophy building, at least fifteen people call out to me. *Hi, how are ya, looking good.* I'm greeted by so many smiles, waves and hellos that I feel like I've just stepped foot on a whole other planet. A planet called *Hannah*, because everyone seems to know me. But I have no clue who *they* are, though I must have met them at Beau's party.

Discomfort twists my stomach, along with a wave of self-consciousness that has me picking up my pace. Unsettled by all the attention, I practically sprint to class and slide into my seat next to Nell. Garrett and Justin haven't arrived yet, which is a bit of a relief. I'm not sure I feel like talking to either of them right now.

"I heard you went out with Garrett Graham this weekend," is the first thing Nell says to me.

Sweet baby Jesus. Can I not go a single second without being reminded of the guy?

"Uh, yeah," I say vaguely.

"That's it? *Yeah*? Come on, I want all the dirty details."

"There aren't any." I shrug. "We just hang out sometimes." Apparently, this is now my go-to response.

"What about your *other* crush?" Nell nods meaningfully toward the opposite aisle.

I follow her gaze and realize that Justin has just shown up. He settles in his seat and pulls a Macbook out of its case, and as if he senses my gaze on him, he lifts his head and smiles.

I smile back, and then Tolbert saunters in, and I break eye contact as I focus on the podium.

Garrett's late, which is unlike him. I know he was out with his teammates last night and didn't have practice this morning, but there's no way he would've slept in until four o'clock. I discreetly pull out my phone to text him, but his message reaches me first.

Him: *Dealing with an emergency. I'll show up for the second half. Take notes for me until I get there?*

Me: *Everything OK??*

Him: *Yeah. Cleaning up Logan's mess. Long story. Tell u later.*

I take copious notes during the lecture, more for Garrett's sake than my own, since I've already read ahead and have the latest theory memorized. As Tolbert drones on, my mind drifts. I think about my impending dinner date with Justin, and that uneasy sensation returns, bringing a queasy feeling to my stomach.

Why am I so nervous about it? It's just dinner. And that's *all* it's going to be. Other girls might put out on the first date, but I'm certainly not one of them.

But Justin is a football player. The girls he dates probably get naked before the menus even arrive. What if he expects that from me?

What if he…

No, I firmly tell myself. I refuse to believe he's the kind of guy who would pressure someone to sleep with him.

At the forty-five minute mark, Tolbert calls for a break, and all the smokers in the class bolt out as if they've been trapped in a mine for two weeks. I head outside too, not to smoke, but to look for Garrett, who still hasn't made an appearance.

Justin trails after me into the corridor. "I'm grabbing a coffee. Want one?"

"No, thanks."

His lips curve as he meets my eyes. "Are we still on for

Sunday?"

"Yep."

He gives a pleased nod. "Good."

I can't help but admire his butt as he walks off. His cargo pants aren't super tight, but they hug his ass nicely. His body really is amazing. I just wish I had a better sense of his personality. I still find it difficult to read him, and that bugs me.

That's why you're having dinner with the guy—to get to know him.

Right. I force myself to remember that as I shift my attention back to the front doors, right as Garrett strides through them. His cheeks are flushed from the cold and his hockey jacket is zipped all the way up to the collar.

His black Timberlands thud on the shiny floor as he heads toward me. "Hey, what'd I miss?" he asks.

"Not much. Tolbert's talking about Rousseau."

Garrett glances at the lecture hall entrance. "Is she in there?"

I nod.

"Okay, good. I'm gonna see if she can give me my midterm back now instead of at the end of class. I'm still dealing with that emergency, so I can't stay."

"Are you going to tell me what happened or should I start guessing?"

He grins. "Logan lost his fake ID. He needs it in case we get carded tonight, so I'm driving him to Boston to meet this guy who does 'em on the spot." He pauses. "You've got ID, right? The bouncer at Malone's knows me and the guys, so we shouldn't have a problem getting in, but you might."

"Yeah, I have ID. And by the way, why is Dean having his birthday party on a *Monday*? How late do you guys plan on staying out?"

"Probably not too late. I'll make sure you get home whenever you're ready to go. And it's on a Monday because Maxwell stole Dean's thunder by having *his* party on Saturday. That, and we don't have ice time on Tuesdays. The team's in the weight room, and when you're hung over, it's a lot easier to lift weights than skate."

I roll my eyes. "Wouldn't it be easier to just not be hung over?"

He snickers. "Tell that to the birthday boy. But don't worry, I'm the DD tonight. I'll be stone cold sober. Oh, and I wanted to talk to you about something, but one sec, let me just speak to Tolbert first. Be right back."

A moment after Garrett disappears into the lecture hall, Justin reappears holding a foam coffee cup. "Heading back in?" he asks me as he walks to the doorway.

"I'll be there soon. I'm just waiting for someone."

Two minutes later, Garrett pops into the corridor, and I take one look at his expression and know he's about to deliver good news.

"You passed?" I squeal.

He raises his exam booklet over his head like he's acting out a scene from the *Lion King*. "A-fucking-minus!"

I gasp. "Holy shit! Really?"

"Yup."

Before I can blink, Garrett tugs me into his arms and hugs the breath out of my lungs. I throw my arms around his neck, then burst out laughing when he lifts me right off my feet and spins me around so many times I get dizzy.

Our exuberant display draws several curious stares, but I don't care. Garrett's joy is contagious. When he finally sets me down, I snatch the paper from his hand. After all those hours I invested in his tutoring, it kind of feels like this is my grade too, and my chest overflows with pride as I skim through his A-minus-worthy words.

"This is amazing," I tell him. "Does that mean your GPA is back where it should be?"

"Damn right it is."

"Good." I narrow my eyes. "Now make sure it stays that way."

"It will—*if* you promise to help me study for every quiz and outline every paper."

"Hey, our arrangement is over, dude. I promise nothing. But..." As always, I capitulate in the presence of Garrett Graham. "I'll help you maintain the grade as a token of my friendship, but only when I have the time."

With a smile, he draws me in for another hug. "I couldn't have done it without you, you know." His voice has gone husky, and I feel his warm breath tickling my temple. He eases back, those magnetic gray eyes focusing on my face, and then his head dips slightly, and for one nerve-wracking second I think he might kiss me.

I abruptly step out of the embrace. "So I guess we *are* celebrating tonight," I say lightly.

"You're still coming, right?" There's a chord of intensity in his voice now.

"Did I literally not just say that?" I grumble.

Relief flits through his expression. "Listen...I wanted to run something by you."

I check my phone and realize there's only three minutes before class starts again. "Can you do it later? I should go back in."

"It'll just take a minute." His gaze locks with mine. "Do you trust me?"

Wariness ripples through me, but when I answer, it's with unwavering certainty that startles me. "Of course I do."

Gosh, I really do. Even though I've only known him for a short time, I *trust* this guy.

"I'm glad." His voice thickens, and he clears his throat before continuing. "I want you to have a drink tonight."

I stiffen. "What? Why?"

"Because I think it will be good for you."

"So wait, *that's* why you invited me to Dean's thing tonight?" I say sarcastically. "To get me drunk?"

"No." Garrett shakes his head, visibly frazzled. "To help you see that it's okay to let down your guard sometimes. Look, I'm the DD tonight, but I'm offering to be more than just your driver. I'll be your bodyguard, and your bartender, and most importantly, your friend. I promise to look out for you tonight, Wellsy."

I am oddly touched by his speech. But it's completely unwarranted.

"I'm not some alcoholic who *has* to drink, Garrett."

"I don't think that at all, dumbass. I just wanted to make sure you knew that if you decide to have a beer or two, you don't have to worry. I'm on it." He hesitates. "I know your friend had a bad experience with drinking in public, but I promise, I'd never let that happen to you."

I wince when he says "your friend," but luckily, I don't think he notices. A part of me wishes I never fed him that old *this happened to my friend* excuse, but I can't bring myself to regret it.

Only my closest friends know about what happened to me, and yeah, I might trust Garrett, but I don't feel comfortable telling him about the rape.

"So if you want to drink tonight, I promise nothing bad will happen to you." He sounds so genuine that my heart squeezes with emotion. "Anyway, that's all I wanted to say. Just...think about it, okay?"

My throat is so tight I can barely get a word out. "Okay." I exhale a wobbly breath. "I'll think about it."

Garrett

Hockey players take up every inch of available space at Malone's, a bar that doesn't have much space to begin with. The place is so tiny that most of the time it's standing room only.

Tonight there's barely enough room to breathe, let alone stand.

The whole team has shown up for Dean's birthday bash, and Mondays happen to be karaoke night at the bar, so the cramped room is loud as fuck and jammed with bodies. On the plus side, none of us had to flash our fake IDs at the door.

I suddenly realize that in a few months, my fake ID will be useless. And once I turn twenty-one in January, I'll be rewarded with more than just legal adult status—I'll finally have access to the trust my grandparents left me, which means I'll be one step closer to ridding myself of my old man.

Hannah walks in about twenty minutes after the guys and me. I didn't pick her up because her rehearsal ran late and she insisted she was fine taking a cab. She'd also insisted on going back to her dorm first to shower and change, and when I lay eyes on her, I whole-heartedly support that decision. She looks fucking gorgeous in her leggings, high-heeled boots and ribbed T-shirt. All black, of course, but as she gets closer, I'm on the lookout for her trademark flash of color—and I find it when she turns her head to greet Dean. A huge yellow hairclip with little blue stars holds her dark hair back. Half of it is still loose and frames her flushed face.

"Hey," she says. "It's sweltering in here. I'm glad I didn't bother with a coat."

"Hey." I lean in and smack a kiss on her cheek. I would have loved to target those luscious lips, but even though I consider this a date, I'm pretty sure Hannah doesn't. "How was rehearsal?"

"The usual." She offers a glum look. "The usual being shitty."

"What did Cass the Ass do this time?"

"Nothing major. Just acting like his jackass self." Hannah sighs. "I won the argument about where to put the bridge in the arrangement, but he won about the second chorus. You know, for when the choir comes in."

I groan loudly. "Oh, for fuck's sake, Wellsy. You *caved* on that?"

"It was two against one," she says darkly. "MJ decided her song *absolutely* required a choir for maximum effect. We start rehearsing with them on Wednesday."

She's very obviously pissed, so I squeeze her arm and say, "Do you want a drink?"

I see her slender throat bob as she gulps. She doesn't answer for a moment. She just looks into my eyes, as if she's trying to mentally bore her way into my brain. I end up holding my breath, because I know something important is about to happen. Hannah is either going to place her trust in my hands, or she's going to lock it up tight, which would be the equivalent of a bone-jarring hip-check, because damn it, I *want* her to trust me.

When she finally answers, her voice is so soft I can't hear her over the music.

"What?"

A breath escapes her lips, and then she raises her voice. "I said, *sure*."

With that one teeny word, my heart inflates like a goddamn helium balloon. *Hannah's trust, meet Garrett's hands.*

I fight to keep my happiness in check, settling for a nonchalant nod as I lead her toward the bar counter. "What'll it be? Beer? Whiskey?"

"No, I want something tasty."

"I swear to God, Wellsy, if you order peach schnapps or something girly like that, I will officially unfriend you."

"But I *am* a girl," she protests. "Why can't I have a girly drink? Ooh, maybe a piña colada?"

I heave out a sigh. "Fine. That's better than schnapps, at least."

At the counter, I order Hannah's drink and then proceed to scrutinize every move the bartender makes. Hannah also watches him with eagle eyes.

With two of the most vigilant patrons on the planet monitoring the piña-colada-making process from start to finish, there's absolutely no doubt about the drug-free status of the glass I place in Hannah's hand a few minutes later.

She takes a tiny sip, then smiles up at me. "Mmmm. Yummy."

The joy in my heart damn near overflows. "C'mon, let me introduce you to some of the guys."

I take her arm again and we wander toward the rowdy group at the pool table, where I introduce her to Birdie and Simms. Logan and Tucker spot us and walk over, and both of them greet Hannah with a hug. Logan's hug lasts a little too long, but when I meet his eyes, his expression is one of innocence. Maybe I'm just being paranoid.

But hell, I'm already competing with Kohl for Hannah's affections, and the last thing I want is my best friend throwing his hat in the ring.

Except...*am* I competing? I'm still not sure what I even want from her. I mean, fine, I want sex. I want it very, very badly. But if by some miracle she decides to give it to me, what then? What happens *after*? Do I stick a flag in the ground and claim her as my girlfriend?

Girlfriends are a distraction, and I can't afford any distractions right now, especially when two weeks ago I was in danger of losing my place on the team.

There aren't many things my father and I agree on, but when it comes to focus and ambition, we happen to be on the same page. I *will* go pro after I graduate. Until then, I need to concentrate on keeping my grades up and leading my team to another Frozen Four victory. Failure is not an option.

But watching Hannah hook up with some other guy?

Not an option, either.

Rock, meet hard place.

"Oh my God, this is *so* good," she announces as she takes another deep swig. "I totally want another one."

I chuckle. "How about you finish this one first, and then we can talk about a refill?"

"Fine," she huffs. Then she drains the rest of her drink in one of the most impressive feats of speed I've ever witnessed, licks her lips, and beams at me. "Okay. How about that refill?"

I can't fight the grin that stretches across my face. Man oh man. I have a feeling Hannah is going to be a very... *interesting* drunk.

I am absolutely right.

Three piña coladas later, Hannah is up on stage doing karaoke.

Yup. Drunk girl karaoke.

The only saving grace is that she's a phenomenal singer. I can't imagine how cringe-worthy it would be if she was drunk *and* tone-deaf.

The entire bar is going batshit crazy for Hannah's performance. She's belting out "Bad Romance" and almost everyone is singing along, including more than a few of my wasted teammates. I find myself grinning like an idiot as I gaze at the stage. There's nothing lewd about what she's doing. No coy almost-stripping, no suggestive dance moves. Hannah throws her head back happily, her cheeks flushed and eyes shining as she sings, and she's so beautiful it makes my chest hurt.

Fuck, I want to kiss her again. I want to feel her lips on mine. I want to hear that throaty noise she made the first time I sucked on her tongue.

Wonderful. And now I'm hard as a rock, splat in the middle of a bar teeming with my friends.

"She's amazing!" Logan shouts, sidling up to me. He's grinning too as he watches Hannah, but there's an odd gleam in his eyes. Looks a bit like...longing.

"She's a music major," is the dumbass response I come up with, because I'm too distracted by his expression.

Thunderous applause bursts out when Hannah's song ends. A second later, Dean climbs on the stage and whispers something in her ear. From what I can glean, he's trying to persuade her to sing a duet, but he keeps touching her bare upper arm as he works the charm, and there's no mistaking the flicker of unease in Hannah's eyes.

"That's my cue to rescue her," I say before threading my way through the crowd. When I reach the bottom of the low-rise stage, I cup my hands around my mouth and call out to Hannah. "Wellsy, get your sexy butt over here!"

Her expression lights up when she spots me. Without skipping a beat, she dives off the stage and into my waiting arms, laughing in delight as I spin her around. "Oh my God, this is so much fun!" she exclaims. "We need to come here *all the time*!"

As laughter tickles my throat, I study her face to gauge where she lands on my incredibly accurate drunk scale. One being sober and ten being *I'm going to wake up naked in Portland with no memory of how I got here*. Since her eyes are sharp and she's not slurring or stumbling, I decide she's probably at about a five—tipsy but aware.

And maybe it makes me an arrogant bastard, but I love being the one who got her to this point. Who she trusted enough to take care of her so that she could allow herself to let go and have a good time.

With another brilliant smile, she takes my hand and starts dragging me away from the tiny dance floor.

"Where are we going?" I ask with a laugh.

"I have to pee! And you promised to be my bodyguard, so that means you have to wait outside the door and stand guard." Those mesmerizing green eyes peer up at me, flickering with uncertainty. "You won't let anything bad happen to me, will you, Garrett?"

A lump the size of Massachusetts lodges in my throat. I swallow hard and try to speak past it. "Never."

20

Hannah

I can't believe I was ever nervous about coming to the bar tonight, because holy moly, I'm having a *blast*. At the moment, I'm crammed in a booth next to Garrett, and we're involved in a heated debate with Tucker and Simms, arguing about technology, of all things. Tucker won't budge on his position that young kids shouldn't be allowed to watch more than an hour of TV a day. I'm totally with him on that, but Garrett and Simms disagree, and the four of us have been bickering about it for more than twenty minutes now. I'm ashamed to admit it, but I honestly didn't expect all these hockey players to have articulate opinions about non-hockey-related matters, but they're a lot more insightful than I gave them credit for.

"Children need to be outside riding their bikes and catching frogs and climbing trees," Tucker insists, waving his pint glass in the air as if to punctuate his point. "It's not healthy for them to be cooped up indoors staring at a screen all day."

"I agree about everything except for the frogs part," I pipe up. "Because frogs are slimy and gross."

The guys burst out laughing.

"Sissy," Simms teases.

"Aw, come on, Wellsy, give the frogs a chance," Tucker protests. "Did you know that if you lick the right one you might get high?"

I stare at him in horror. "I have *zero* interest in licking a frog."

Simms hoots. "Not even to get the prince?"

Good-natured groaning rings out.

"Nope, not even then," I say firmly.

Tucker takes a deep swig of beer before winking at me. "How about licking something other than a frog? Or are you anti-licking altogether?"

My cheeks scorch at the innuendo, but the impish glimmer in his eyes tells me he's not trying to be crude, so I respond with my own dose of innuendo. "Naah, I'm pro-licking. As long as I'm licking something tasty."

Another round of hoots breaks out, but Garrett doesn't join in. When I glance over at him, I notice that his eyes have flared with heat.

I wonder if he's imagining my mouth on his...*nope, not going there.*

"Shit, someone needs to hog-tie that old dude so he stops monopolizing the jukebox," Tucker declares when yet another Black Sabbath song blasts through the bar.

We all turn toward the culprit—a local with a bushy red beard and the meanest scowl I've ever seen. The moment the karaoke machine shut down for the night, Red Beard had raced to the jukebox and shoved ten bucks worth of quarters inside it, keying in a rock playlist that has so far consisted of Black Sabbath, Black Sabbath, and more Black Sabbath. Oh, and one CCR song that Simms claimed he'd lost his virginity to.

Eventually our debate turns to hockey talk, as Simms tries to convince me that the goalie is the most important player on a hockey team, while Tucker boos him the entire time. The Black Sabbath song blessedly comes to an end, replaced by Lynyrd Skynyrd's "Tuesday's Gone," and as the opening strains echo through the bar, I feel Garrett stiffen beside me.

"What's wrong?" I ask.

"Nothing." He clears his throat, then slides out of the booth and tugs me up with him. "Dance with me."

"To this?" I'm baffled for a moment, until I remember what a huge hard-on he has for Lynyrd Skynyrd. Come to think of it, I'm pretty sure this song was on that playlist he emailed me last week.

Tucker snickers from his side of the booth. "Since when do you dance, G?"

"Since right now," Garrett mutters.

He leads me to the small area in front of the stage, which is completely empty because nobody else is dancing. Discomfort shifts inside me, but when Garrett holds out his hand, I hesitate for only a second before taking it. Hey, if he wants to dance, then we'll dance. It's the least I can do considering how amazing he's been tonight.

You can say a lot of things about Garrett Graham, but he's definitely a man of his word. He's been glued to my side all night, guarding my drinks, waiting outside the bathroom for me, making sure I don't get harassed by his friends or the locals we've met. He's totally had my back, and because of him, I was able to lower my guard for the first time in a very long time.

God. I can't believe I ever thought he *wasn't* a good guy.

"You know this song is like seven minutes long, right?" I point out as we step onto the dance floor.

"I know." His tone is casual. Unaffected. But I have the strangest feeling he's upset about something.

Garrett doesn't plaster his body to mine or try to grind up against me. Instead, we dance the way I've seen my parents do, with Garrett's hand on my hip and his other one curled around my right hand. I rest my free hand on his shoulder, and he leans in closer and presses his cheek to mine. His stubble is a teasing scratch against my face, bringing goose bumps to my bare arms. When I take a breath, his woody aftershave fills my lungs, and a rush of giddy dizziness washes over me.

I don't know what's happening to me. I feel hot and achy and—it's the alcohol, I assure myself. It has to be. Because Garrett and I agreed that we're just friends.

"Dean's enjoying himself," I comment, mostly because I'm desperate for a distraction from my out-of-control hormones.

Garrett follows my gaze toward the back booth, where Dean is sandwiched between two blondes who are very eagerly nibbling on his neck. "Yeah. Guess so."

There's a faraway look in his gray eyes. His absent tone makes it clear he's not interested in making conversation, so I fall silent and try hard not to let his overpowering masculinity affect me.

But every time his cheek grazes my face, the goose bumps get worse. And every time his breath puffs on my jaw, a flurry of shivers skitters through me. The heat of his body sears into me, his scent surrounds me, and I'm excruciatingly aware of his warm hand clutching mine. Before I can stop myself, I rub my thumb over the center of his palm.

Garrett's breath hitches.

Yep, it *has* to be the alcohol. There's no other explanation for the sensations coursing through my body. The ache in my breasts, the tight clenching of my thighs and the strange emptiness in my core.

When the song ends, I exhale a relieved breath and take a much-needed step back.

"Thanks for the dance," Garrett mumbles.

I might be tipsy, but I'm not drunk, and I instantly pick up on the sadness radiating from his broad chest.

"Hey," I say in concern. "What's wrong?"

"Nothing." His throat dips as he swallows. "It's just...that song..."

"What about it?"

"Brings back memories, that's all." He pauses for so long I don't think he's going to continue, but then he does. "It was my mom's favorite song. They played it at her funeral."

My breath catches in surprise. "Oh. Oh, Garrett, I'm sorry."

He shrugs as if he has no care in the world.

"Garrett..."

"Look, it was either dance to it, or bawl my eyes out, okay? So yeah, thanks for the dance." He sidesteps me as I reach for his arm. "I've gotta take a leak. Will you be okay here for a few minutes?"

"Yeah, but—"

He stalks off before I can finish.

I watch him go, battling a wave of sorrow that constricts my throat. I'm torn as I stand there staring at his retreating back. I want to go after him and force him to talk about it.

No, I *should* go after him.

I square my shoulders and hurry forward—only to freeze as I come face to face with my ex-boyfriend.

"Devon!" I squeak.

"Hannah...hey." Devon is visibly uncomfortable as our gazes lock.

It takes me a second to register that he's not alone. A tall, pretty redhead stands beside him...and they're holding hands.

My pulse speeds up because I haven't seen Devon since we

broke up last winter. He's a political science major, so we're not in any of the same classes, and our social circles don't usually intersect. We probably wouldn't have even met if Allie hadn't dragged me to that concert in Boston last year. It was a small venue, just a few local bands playing, and Devon happened to be the drummer in one of the bands. We spent the whole night talking, discovered that we both went to Briar, and he ended up driving Allie and me back to campus that night.

After that, he and I were inseparable. We were together for eight months, and I was wildly and unequivocally in love with him. He told me he loved me, too, but after he dumped me, a part of me wondered if maybe he'd only been with me out of pity.

Don't think that way.

The stern voice in my head belongs to Carole, and suddenly I long to hear it in person. Our therapy sessions ended once I left for college, and although we've had a few phone chats here and there, it's not the same as sitting in that cozy leather armchair in Carole's office, breathing in her soothing lavender scent and hearing her warm, reassuring voice. I no longer need Carole the way I used to, but right now, as I face off with Devon and his gorgeous new girlfriend, all the old insecurities come rushing back.

"How've you been?" he asks.

"Good. No, I'm great," I amend hastily. "How are you?"

"Can't complain." The smile he gives me looks forced. "Uh…the band broke up."

"Oh, shit. I'm sorry to hear that. What happened?"

He absently rubs the silver hoop in his left eyebrow, and I'm reminded of all the times I used to kiss that piercing when we were lying in bed together.

"Brad happened," Devon admits. "You know how he was always threatening to go solo? Well, he finally decided he didn't need us. He landed a record deal with this hot new indie label, and when they said they wanted their house band to back him, Brad didn't fight for us."

I'm not surprised to hear it. I always thought Brad was the most pompous asshole on the planet. Actually, he'd probably get along splendidly with Cass.

"I know it sucks, but I think you're better off," I tell Devon. "Brad would've screwed you over eventually. At least it happened now, before you signed anything, you know?"

"That's what I keep telling him," the redhead pipes up, then turns to Devon. "See, someone else agrees with me."

Someone else. Is that what I am? Not Devon's ex-girlfriend, not his friend, not even an acquaintance. I'm simply...someone else.

The way she diminishes my position in Devon's life makes my heart squeeze painfully.

"I'm Emily, by the way," the redhead says.

"It's nice to meet you," I reply awkwardly.

Devon looks as awkward as I feel. "So, uh, you've got the winter showcase coming up, huh?"

"Yep. I'm performing a duet with Cass Donovan." I sigh. "Which is beginning to look like a huge mistake."

Devon nods. "Well, you always did work better alone."

My stomach goes rigid. For some reason, it feels like he's making a jab at me. Like he's insinuating something. Like what he's really saying is *you have no problem getting YOURSELF off, right, Hannah? But you can't do it with a partner, can you?*

I know that's just my insecurities talking. Devon's not that cruel. And he *tried.* He tried so hard.

But insinuation or not, it still hurts.

"Anyway, it was nice to see you, but I'm here with friends, so..."

I nod toward the booth where Tucker, Simms and Logan are holed up, which brings a crease of confusion to Devon's forehead. "Since when do you hang out with the hockey crowd?"

"I'm tutoring one of the players, and...uh, yeah, we hang out sometimes."

"Oh. Cool. Okay, well...see you around."

"It was nice to meet you!" Emily chirps.

My throat closes up as they saunter off hand-in-hand. I swallow hard, then twirl in the opposite direction. I duck into the corridor that leads to the restroom, blinking away the hot tears that have welled up in my eyes.

God, why am I crying?

I quickly run through all the reasons why I shouldn't be crying.

Devon and I are over.

I don't want him anymore.

I've been fantasizing about someone else for months.

I'm going on a date with Justin Kohl this weekend.

But the reminders achieve nothing, and my eyes sting harder. Because who the fuck am I kidding? What chance do Justin and I possibly have? Even if we go out, even if we get close enough to be intimate, what happens when we have sex? What if all the issues I had with Devon sprout up again, like some annoying rash you can't get rid of?

What if there really *is* something wrong with me and I can never, ever have a normal sex life like a normal frickin' woman?

I blink rapidly to try to stop the flow of tears. I refuse to cry in public. I *refuse* to.

"Wellsy?"

Garrett emerges from the men's bathroom and frowns the moment he sees me. "Hey," he says urgently, cupping my chin. "What's the matter?"

"Nothing," I mumble.

"You're lying." His grip stays firm on my chin as he sweeps his thumbs underneath my eyes. "Why are you crying?"

"I'm not crying."

"I'm wiping away your *tears* right now, Wellsy. Ergo, you're crying. Now tell me what's wrong." His face suddenly pales. "Oh shit, did someone harass you or something? I was only gone a few minutes. I'm so sorry—"

"No, it's not that," I cut in. "I promise."

Garrett's features relax. But only slightly. "Then why are you upset?"

I choke back the lump in my throat. "I bumped into my ex out there."

"Oh." He looks startled. "The guy you were dating last year?"

I nod weakly. "He was with his new girlfriend."

"Shit. That must have been awkward."

"I guess." Hostility crawls through me like an army of tiny ants. "She's gorgeous, by the way. Like, really gorgeous." The bitter feeling intensifies, twisting my insides and hardening my jaw. "I bet she has orgasms that last for hours and probably screams out *I'm coming!* when she's in the throes of passion."

Alarm flickers through Garrett's eyes. "Uh. Yeah. Okay. I don't really understand that, but okay."

But it's not okay. It's *not*.

Why did I ever think I could be a normal college student? I'm *not* normal. I'm broken. I keep telling myself that the rape didn't destroy me, but it *did*. A piece of shit didn't just steal my virginity—he stole my ability to have sex and feel pleasure like a healthy, red-blooded woman.

So how the hell can I ever have a real relationship? With Devon, with Justin, with *anyone*, when I can't...

I abruptly shrug Garrett's hands off my face. "Forget it. I'm being stupid." Lifting my chin, I take a step toward the doorway. "Come on, I want another drink."

"Hannah—"

"I want another drink," I snap, and then I bulldoze past him and march all the way to the bar.

21

Garrett

Hannah is wasted.

Not only that, but she refuses to go home. It's one in the morning and the party has moved from the bar to my house, and no matter how hard I try, I can't convince Hannah to call it a night.

It's becoming crucial that I get her back to her dorm. My living room is full of hockey players and puck bunnies, all of whom score at least an eight on my drunk scale: rapidly on their way to throwing inhibition to the wind and making some huge-ass mistakes.

Dean has just dragged a laughing Hannah to the center of the living room and the two of them start dancing to ODB's "Baby, I like it Raw," which blasts out of the speakers at top-volume.

Hannah hadn't been moving suggestively when she'd belted out Lady Gaga earlier, but she sure as shit is moving suggestively now. She's gone from Disney Channel Miley Cyrus to Full-on Twerk Mode Miley, and it's officially time for me to put a stop to it before she moves straight to Let's Make a Sex Tape Miley. Wait—has Miley ever made a sex tape? Fuck, who am I kidding? Of course she has.

I march up to Hannah and Dean and forcibly break them apart, laying a firm hand on Hannah's shoulder. "I need to talk to you," I shout over the music.

She pouts. "I'm dancing!"

"We're dancing," Dean slurs.

I level a hard glare at my teammate. "Dance with someone

else," I snap.

As if on cue, a willing female partner appears like an apparition and yanks Dean into her arms. Dean all but forgets about Hannah, which allows me to drag her out of the living room without any further objections.

I curl my hand around her arm and lead her upstairs, and I don't release her until we're in the quiet safety of my bedroom. "Party's over," I announce.

"But I'm having fun," she whines.

"I know you are." I cross my arms. "You're having *too much* fun."

"You're mean." With an exaggerated sigh, Hannah flops down on the bed and falls onto her back. "I'm sleepy."

I grin. "Come on, I'll drive you back to the dorm."

"I don't wanna go." She sticks out her arms and legs and proceeds to do snow angels on my bed. "Your bed is so big and comfy."

Then her eyelids flutter closed and she goes still, another deep sigh escaping her lips.

I smother a groan as I realize she's seconds away from falling asleep, but then I decide it might be better if I let her crash here and drive her home in the morning. Because if I take her home now and she gets a second wind, I won't be there to keep her out of trouble.

"Fine," I say with a nod. "Stay here and sleep it off, Cinderella."

She snorts. "Does that make you my prince?"

"Damn straight." I duck into the bathroom and rummage around in the medicine cabinet until I find some ibuprofen. Then I pour a glass of water and head back to the bed, sitting at the edge as I force Hannah to sit up. "Take two of these and chug the water," I order, slapping the two pills into her palm. "Trust me, you'll thank me in the morning."

Shoving pills and water down someone's throat is nothing new to me. I do it often with my teammates. Dean, in particular, who takes drinking to a whole new level, and not just on his birthday.

Hannah obediently follows my instructions before collapsing on the mattress again.

"Good girl."

"I'm hot," she mumbles. "Why is it so hot in here?"

My heart literally stops beating when she starts wiggling out of her leggings.

The material snags on her knees, eliciting a loud groan from her. "*Garrett*!"

I have to chuckle. Taking pity on her, I lean in to help her out, peeling the pants off her legs and doing my best to ignore the smooth, silky skin beneath my fingertips.

"There you go," I say thickly. "Better?"

"Mmm-hmmm." She reaches for the hem of her shirt.

Sweet Jesus.

I tear my gaze off her and stumble toward my dresser to find her something to sleep in. I grab an old T-shirt, take a deep breath, and turn around to face her.

Her shirt is off.

Fortunately, she's wearing a bra.

Unfortunately, the bra is black and lacy and see-through, and I have a perfect view of her nipples behind that transparent fabric.

Don't look. She's drunk.

I heed the stern internal voice and forbid my gaze from lingering. And since there's no way in hell I can take off her bra without coming in my pants, I shove the T-shirt over her head and hope she's not one of those girls who hates sleeping in her bra.

"I had so much fun tonight," Hannah babbles happily. "See? I might be broken but I can still have fun."

I freeze. "What?"

But she doesn't answer. Her bare legs kick at the blanket and then she slides beneath it, rolling over on her side with a tiny sigh.

She passes out within seconds.

I battle a rush of unease as I turn off the light. She's broken? What the *hell* does that mean?

Frowning, I slip out of the bedroom and quietly close the door behind me. Hannah's cryptic words continue to echo in my head, but I don't have the opportunity to dwell on them because when I go downstairs, Logan and Dean waste no time dragging me into the kitchen for a round of shots.

"It's his birthday, dude." Logan says when I object. "You've gotta take a shot."

I cave in and accept the shot glass. The three of us clink our glasses together, slugging back the whiskey. The alcohol burns my throat and heats my stomach, and I welcome the hot buzz that floats through my body. This whole night, I've been...*off.* That stupid song. Hannah's tears at the bar. The confusing way she makes me feel.

I'm raw and on edge, and when Logan pours me another drink, this time I don't object.

After the third shot, I'm no longer thinking about how confused I am.

After the fourth one, I'm not thinking at all.

It's two-thirty in the morning when I finally drag my drunken ass upstairs. The party has all but fizzled. Only Dean's puck bunnies remain, lying on the couch with him in a tangle of bare arms and legs. I pass the kitchen and spot Tucker asleep at the counter, his hand still curled around an empty beer bottle. Logan had disappeared into his bedroom a while ago with a cute brunette, and as I walk past his room, I hear the kind of groans and moans that tell me he's VBF.

My bedroom is bathed in shadows when I walk inside. I blink a few times, and my eyes adjust to the darkness to find a Hannah-shaped lump on the bed. I'm too tired to brush my teeth or follow my own hangover-prevention regimen—I just strip to my boxers and climb in next to Hannah.

I try to be as quiet as possible as I get comfortable, but the rustling of the sheets causes Hannah to stir. A soft moan ripples through the darkness, and then she rolls over and a warm hand presses against my bare chest.

I stiffen. Or rather, my chest does. Down below, I'm softer than pudding. That's whiskey dick for you, which is damn sad considering I only had five shots. Man. Me and alcohol *really* don't mix.

Even if I wanted to take advantage of Hannah right now, I'd be totally useless. And shit, that's a totally repulsive thing to think, because I'd *never* take advantage of her. I'd rip my own dick off before forcing myself on someone.

But apparently there's only one person with honorable intentions in this bed tonight.

My pulse speeds up when soft lips latch onto my shoulder.

"Hannah..." I say warily.

There's a beat of silence. A part of me prays that she's asleep, but Hannah shoots down that hope by murmuring, "Uh-huh?" Her voice is throaty, and sexy as fuck.

"What are you doing?" I whisper.

Her lips meander from my shoulder to my neck, and then she sucks on my suddenly feverish flesh, finding a sweet spot that sends a zing of heat straight to my balls. Jesus. My cock might not be working properly right now, but that doesn't mean I'm incapable of feeling arousal. And holy hell, there's no word to describe how aroused I am as Hannah's greedy mouth explores my neck like she's sampling a damn buffet.

I smother a groan, touching her shoulder to still her. "You don't want to do this."

"Nuh-uh. You're wrong. I totally do."

The groan I've been holding rumbles out as she climbs on top of me. Her firm thighs straddle mine. Her hair tickles my collarbone as she leans forward.

My heart takes off in a fast, pounding gallop.

"Stop being difficult," she tells me.

Then she kisses me.

Oh *hell*.

I should stop her. I really, really should. But she's warm and soft and she smells so good I can't fucking think straight. Her mouth moves eagerly over mine, and I kiss her back hungrily, wrapping my arms around her and stroking her lower back as our lips mold together. She tastes like piña coladas, and she makes the sexiest sounds I've ever heard as she takes deep pulls on my tongue like she can't get enough.

"Hannah," I mumble against her eager lips. "We can't."

She licks my bottom lip, then bites it hard enough to summon a growl from my throat. Fuck. Fuck, fuck, *fuck*. I need to derail this lust train before it hurtles to the point of no return.

"I love your chest," she breathes, and holy hell, now she's rubbing her breasts against my pecs and I can feel her nipples poking right through her shirt.

I want to rip that fucking shirt off. I want to draw those puckered nipples deep into my mouth and suck. But I can't. I won't.

"No." I thrust my hand in her hair and bunch it between my fingers. "We can't do this. Not tonight."

"But I want to," she whispers. "I want you so bad."

She's just uttered the words every guy wants to hear—*I want you so bad*—but damn it, she's drunk and I can't let her do this.

Her tongue circles my earlobe and my hips shoot off the bed. Oh Jesus. I want to be inside her.

It takes superhuman strength on my part to push her off my body. She whimpers in protest, but when I gently touch her cheek, the whimper turns into a happy sigh.

"We can't do this," I say gruffly. "You trusted me to look out for you, remember? Well, this is me looking out for you."

I can't see her expression in the dark, but she sounds surprised as she says, "Oh." Then she nestles closer and I instantly tense. I'm prepared to lay down the law again, but she simply snuggles against my body and rests her head on my chest. "Okay. Goodnight."

Okay? Goodnight?

Does she actually think I'll be able to sleep after what just happened?

But she's not thinking at all. Nope, she's out like a light again, and as her steady breathing tickles my nipple, I swallow another groan and close my eyes, doing my best to ignore the hot lust pulsating in my groin.

It's a long, long time before I fall asleep.

22

Hannah

I wake up in Garrett Graham's arms for the second time in two weeks. Except this time...I want to be there.

Last night turned out to be a series of eye-opening experiences. I drank in public without having a panic attack. I was forced to accept that the rape screwed me up a lot more than I let myself admit.

And I decided that Garrett is the answer to all my problems.

My seduction attempt might have failed, but it wasn't because of a lack of desire on Garrett's part. I know exactly what was going through his mind—*Hannah's drunk and not thinking clearly.*

But he's wrong.

My brain was sharp as a tack last night. I kissed Garrett because I wanted to. I would've slept with him because I *wanted* to.

Now, in the light of day, I *still* want it. Seeing Devon left me feeling scared and uncertain. It made me question what would happen if I got involved with Justin. Made me wonder if I'm simply inviting more frustration and disappointment into my life.

As insane as it sounds, a test run with Garrett might be just what I need to work through my issues. He said so himself—he doesn't date girls, he sleeps with them. There's no risk of him falling in love with me or demanding a relationship. And it's not like we don't have any chemistry. We have so much of it we could inspire an entire R&B song.

It would be the perfect arrangement. I could have sex with a guy without getting bogged down by all the relationship pressure. With Devon, my sex issues were made a hundred times worse because of that pressure, because the sex part was tangled up with the love part.

With Garrett, it can be just about the sex. Trying to put the pieces of my sexuality back together without worrying about disappointing someone I love.

But first, I need him to agree to it.

"Garrett," I murmur.

He doesn't stir.

I scooch closer and stroke his cheek. His eyelids flutter, but he doesn't wake up.

"Garrett," I say again.

"Mmmmfhrhghd?"

His gibberish makes me smile. I lean in and press my lips to his.

His eyes fly open.

"Morning," I say innocently.

He blinks in rapid succession. "Did I dream that or did you really just kiss me?" he asks groggily.

"You didn't dream it."

Confusion fogs his eyes, but he's growing more alert. "Why?"

"Because I felt like it." I sit up and take a breath. "Are you one-hundred percent awake? Because there's something really important I need to ask you."

A huge yawn overtakes his face as he slides into an upright position. The blanket falls to his waist and his bare chest is revealed, and my mouth promptly goes dry. He's cut like a diamond. Hard edges and gleaming skin and pure masculinity.

"What's up?" he says in a sleep-gravelly voice.

There's absolutely no way to phrase this without sounding desperate and pathetic, so I simply blurt out the words and let them hang in the air.

"Will you have sex with me?"

After the longest pause imaginable, Garrett wrinkles his forehead. "Now?"

Despite the embarrassment tightening my stomach, I can't stop the laugh that pops out. "Um, no. Not now." Call me vain, but

I refuse to have sex with anyone when I have morning breath and bed head, and haven't shaved any pertinent areas. "Maybe tonight, though?"

Garrett's expression is like a *Wheel of Fortune* spin, going from shocked to incredulous to mystified, inching toward intrigued before finally landing on suspicious. "I think this might be a prank, but I can't figure out where you're going with it."

"It's not a prank." I meet his gaze head-on. "I want you to have sex with me." Okay, wait, that sounds wrong. "I mean, I want to have sex with you. I want us to have sex with each other."

His lips twitch.

Wonderful. He's trying not to laugh at me.

"Are you still drunk?" he asks. "Because if you are, I promise to play the rare gentleman card and never bring up this conversation again."

"I'm not drunk. I'm serious." I shrug. "Do you want to or what?"

Garrett stares at me.

"Well?" I prompt.

His dark eyebrows knit together in a frown. It's pretty obvious he has no idea what to make of my request.

"It's a simple yes or no answer, Garrett."

"Simple?" he bursts out. "Are you kidding me? There's nothing *simple* about this." He runs a hand through his hair. "Are you forgetting what you told me at Maxwell's party? The kiss meant nothing, we're just friends, blah, blah."

"I did not say *blah blah*," I grumble.

"But you said everything else." His jaw hardens. "What the hell changed from then to now?"

I swallow. "I don't know. I just changed my mind."

"Why?"

"Because I did." Aggravation pricks my chest. "What does it matter? Since when do guys cross-examine a girl about her motives for wanting to get naked?"

"Since you're not the kind of girl who gets naked!" he sputters.

I clench my teeth. "I'm not a virgin, Garrett."

"You're not a puck bunny either."

"So that means I'm not allowed to sleep with a guy I'm attracted to?"

He rakes both hands over his scalp now, looking equally aggravated. Then he takes a breath, exhales slowly, and meets my eyes. "Okay, here's the deal. I believe you're attracted to me. I mean—one, who isn't? And two, you moan like crazy whenever my tongue's in your mouth."

I bristle. "I do not."

"Agree to disagree." He folds his sleek, muscular arms over his sleek, muscular chest. "But I don't believe that you underwent some magical transformation where suddenly you want to jump my bones just for the hell of it. You know, for funsies." His head tilts thoughtfully. "What is it, then? Do you want to get back at your ex or something? Make Loverboy jealous again?"

"No," I say stiffly. "I just..." Frustration slams inside me. "I just want to do it, okay? I want to do *you*."

His expression is a peculiar combination of amused and annoyed. "Why?" he asks again.

"Because I *want* to, damn it. Why does there need to be some deep, philosophical meaning behind it?" But I can see from his face that I haven't convinced him, and I'm smart enough to know when to admit defeat. "You know what? Forget it. Forget I asked—"

He grabs hold of my arm before I can hop off the bed. "What the hell is going on, Wellsy?"

The concern in his eyes hurts more than his rejection. I practically begged him for sex and he looks *worried* for me.

God, I can't even proposition a guy right.

"Forget it," I mutter again.

"No."

I yelp when he suddenly pulls me onto his lap.

"We're not having this conversation anymore," I protest as I try to scramble off him.

He plants his hands on my waist to trap me in place. "Yes, we are."

His gray eyes bore into my face, searching, probing, and I'm mortified to feel tears pricking my eyelids.

"What's this about?" he says gruffly. "Tell me what's wrong, and I'll try to help."

A hysterical giggle flies out of my mouth. "No, you won't! I just *asked* for your help and you shot me down!"

He looks even more bewildered than before. "You didn't ask

me for help, Hannah. You asked me to fuck you."

"Same damn thing," I mumble.

"For fuck's sake, I have no frickin' idea what you're talking about!" He inhales slowly as if trying to calm himself down. "I swear to God, if you don't tell me what you're babbling about in the next two seconds, I'm going to lose my shit."

Misery lodges in my throat. I wish I never opened my mouth and asked him. I should have just snuck out of his room while he slept and pretended that I never threw myself at him last night.

But then Garrett reaches up and strokes my cheek with infinite tenderness, and something inside me cracks open.

I let out a shaky breath. "I'm broken, and I wanted you to fix me."

Alarm widens his eyes. "I…still don't understand."

Not many people know about what happened to me. I mean, it's not like I go around advertising that I was raped to everyone I meet. I have to trust someone implicitly in order to confess something so monumental.

If you told me a few weeks ago that I would be confiding in Garrett Graham about the most traumatic experience of my life, I would've peed my pants laughing.

And now here I am, doing just that.

"I lied to you at Beau's party," I admit.

His hand drops from my face, but his gaze stays locked on mine. "Okay…"

"I don't know anyone who was drugged in high school." My throat closes up. "*I* was the one who got drugged in high school."

Garrett's body goes rigid. "What?"

"When I was fifteen years old, a guy I went to school with drugged me." I gulp down the acid coating my windpipe. "And then he raped me."

A shocked breath hisses out of his mouth. Although he doesn't say a word, I can clearly see the tense set of his jaw, the hot fury in his eyes.

"It was…it…well, shit, I'm sure you can imagine how awful it was." I swallow again. "But… Please don't feel sorry for me, okay? It was awful and terrifying and it destroyed me at the time, but I worked through it. I'm not scared of all men, or angry at the world, or any of that stuff."

Garrett says nothing, but his expression is fiercer than I've ever seen it.

"I've put it behind me. I really have. But it broke something inside me, okay? I can't...I can't...you know." My cheeks are so hot it feels like I've come down with sunstroke.

He finally speaks, his voice coming out low and tortured. "No, I *don't* know."

I'm already in this deep, so I force myself to clarify. "I can't have an orgasm with a guy."

Garrett gulps. "Oh."

I press my lips together, trying hard to tamp down the embarrassment climbing up my throat. "I thought that maybe if you and me...if we...you know, fooled around a bit, I might be able to...I don't know...reprogram my body to...um, respond."

Oh God. The words are stuttering out before my brain can edit them, and my face goes up in flames as I realize how pitiful I sound. The realization that I've officially reached the rock bottom equivalent of sheer humiliation unleashes my tears.

As a strangled sob tears out of my mouth, I attempt a frantic scramble off Garrett's lap, but his arms tighten around me, one hand tangling in my hair to bring my head closer. I bury my face in his neck, trembling wildly as tears slide down my cheeks in salty waves.

"Hey, come on, don't cry," he begs. "It breaks my fucking heart to hear you cry."

But I can't stop. I gulp for air and shudder in his arms, and he strokes my hair and makes rough, soothing noises that only make me cry harder.

"I'm *broken*."

My voice is muffled against his neck, but I hear his voice loud and clear as he says, "You're not broken, baby. I promise."

"Then help me prove it," I whisper. "*Please*."

He gently pulls my head up. I meet his gaze and find nothing but raw emotion and shining sincerity.

"Okay," he whispers back. Then he lets out a long, unsteady breath. "Okay. I will."

23

Garrett

Half the guys in the weight room are hung-over as hell. I, surprisingly, am not one of them. Nope, this morning's revelations pretty much zapped away any headache or queasiness I might have felt.

Hannah was raped.

Those three words have been running through my head since I dropped her off at her dorm, and every time they pop up, red-hot fury blasts through me like a freight train. I wish she'd told me his name, his phone number, his fucking *address.*

But it's better that she hadn't, otherwise I'd probably be in my car right now on my way to commit murder.

Whoever he was, I hope to God he paid for what he did to Hannah. I hope to God he's rotting in jail at the moment. Or better yet, I hope he's fucking dead.

"Two more." Logan looms over me as I lie on the bench press. "Come on, man, you're slacking."

I blow out a breath and curl my fingers around the barbell. I channel all my rage into heaving the weights over my head, as Logan spots me from above. Once I finish the last set of reps, he drops the bar in the rack and sticks out his hand. I allow him to haul me to my feet and we switch places.

Christ, I need to get my head on right. Thank fuck we're not on the ice today because I'm not sure I even remember how to skate at the moment.

Hannah was raped.

And now she wants to have sex with me.

No, she wants me to *fix* her.

Holy mother of God. What was I thinking, agreeing to do this? I've wanted her naked ever since that first kiss, but not like this. Not as some kind of sexuality experiment. Not when I'm feeling this much pressure to...to what? Make it good for her? Not let her down?

"Any time now," comes Logan's mocking voice.

I snap out of my distressed thoughts and realize that he's waiting for me to drop the barbell into his outstretched hands.

Taking a breath, I force myself to focus on making sure Logan doesn't die on my watch rather than obsessing over Hannah.

"So I'm pissed at you," he tells me as he bends his arms and brings the bar low to his chest. Then he grunts out a breath and lifts.

"What did I do now?" I ask with a sigh.

"You told me you weren't interested in Wellsy."

My chest tenses, but I pretend to be unfazed as I count out his set. "I wasn't, at least not when you and I talked about it before."

Logan grunts with each upward extension of his arms. We're both lifting twenty pounds less than usual because last night's drink fest means neither one of us is operating at a hundred percent today.

"So, what, now you *are* interested?"

I swallow. "Yeah. I guess I am."

Logan doesn't say anything else. My fingers hover beneath the barbell as he finishes his reps.

I keep a close eye on the clock above the weight room door. It's almost five. Hannah finishes work at ten, and then she's coming straight over to my place.

So we can have sex.

The pressure in my gut gathers in strength, tightening into a massive knot. I have no idea if I can do this. I'm terrified of doing something wrong. Hurting her.

"I'm not surprised you saw the error of your ways," Logan finally says as we trade places again. "She's pretty damn cool. I knew that from the moment I met her."

Yeah, Hannah *is* cool. She's also beautiful and smart and funny.

And she's *not* broken.

The tightness in my stomach eases as I cling to that last thought. *That's* why I agreed to sleep with her, because no matter what happened to her in the past, no matter how many scars she still bears from that ordeal, I know without a shred of doubt that Hannah Wells is not broken. She's too strong to allow anyone—especially a piece of shit high school rapist—to break her.

No, what she's lacking is the ability to trust, and to some extent, confidence. She just needs someone to...guide her, for lack of a better word.

But shit, can that someone really be *me*? I don't know the first thing about the etiquette required for sleeping with a rape victim.

"So anyway, maybe I'm *not* pissed that you beat me to it," Logan tells me.

I shoot him a faint smile. "Gee, thanks."

He grins back. "With that said, I request an exemption from the part of the bro code that states I can't date someone after you've broken up with her."

My fingers stiffen on the bar. Fuck *that*. The thought of Logan hooking up with Hannah makes me want to go He-Man on the barbell and hurl it across the gym. But at the same time, I'm pretty sure there isn't a chance in hell of Hannah dating Logan, especially now that I know about her hang-ups.

So I shrug casually and say, "Exemption granted."

"Good. Now I'm adding ten pounds to this motherfucker, because, really, G, we're better than this."

The next thirty minutes fly by. The room empties out as the other guys head for the showers, but when I see that Birdie is still rocking chin-ups across the room, I make my way over to him.

"Hey, man, got a sec?" I call out, wiping my sweaty forehead with a towel.

He lets go of the bar, and his sneakers land on the blue gym mat. Then he grabs his own towel. "Sure. What's up?"

I hesitate. Hockey players aren't known for having girly heart-to-hearts. Most of the time, we indulge in locker room talk or shoot insults back and forth, with the rare serious convo thrown into the mix.

Jake "Birdie" Berderon is the exception to that rule. The tall, intense senior is the one you seek out for advice, the one you call when you're in a jam, the one who'd drop whatever he was doing just to help you out. Last season, after half our seniors graduated and nominations for team captain were being tossed around, I told Birdie that if he wanted the job, I'd back him one hundred percent. He shot me down, insisting that he sucks at pep talks and would rather skate than lead, but honestly, deep down I know that Birdie is our *real* leader. You won't ever find a better man than him. No joke.

I glance at the open doorway, then lower my voice. "This has to stay between us, okay?"

A wry grin lifts his lips. "Dude, if you knew how many secrets are floating around in this thick skull of mine, you'd freak. Trust me, I know how to keep my mouth shut."

I sink onto the long wooden bench against the wall and rest my hands on my knees. I don't know where to start, but I do know I can't tell him the truth. That's something only Hannah has the right to share.

"Have you ever slept with a virgin?" I hedge.

He blinks. "Uh. Okay. Well, yeah. I have." Birdie sits beside me. "Between you and me?" he says.

"Of course."

"Nat was a virgin when we first hooked up." Nat is actually Natalie, Birdie's girlfriend since freshman year. The two of them are one of those "it" couples that everyone makes fun of for being so nauseatingly perfect together while secretly envying their relationship.

I have to ask, "Were *you*?"

He grins. "Naah. I punched in my V-card at fifteen."

Fifteen. That's how old Hannah was when she… I suddenly wonder if that had been her first time, and horror claws up my throat. Jesus. Losing your virginity is a huge deal for some chicks—I can't even imagine what'd it feel like having it *taken* from you.

"Why? You've got a date with a hot virgin?" Birdie teases.

"Something like that." Considering he met Hannah last night at Malone's, I'm sure Birdie is putting two and two together in his head, but I know he won't blab about this to anyone.

And I figure this virgin story is safer than uttering the words *rape victim*. Because really, the approach to sleeping with the former can't be all that different from doing it with the latter.

In both instances, you need to be patient and respectful and thorough, right?

"So what did you do for Nat's first time?" I ask awkwardly.

"Honestly? I just tried to make her comfortable." Birdie shrugs. "She's not into all that mushy shit, like flowers and candles and rose petals all over the bed. She didn't want it to be a big deal." Another shrug. "Some girls *do* want to make a big production outta it, though. So in your case, I think the first thing you need to do is figure out what kind of girl she is. Low-key or mega romantic."

I think about Hannah and all the pressure she's under to be "normal"—which is probably a million times worse than the pressure *I'm* feeling at the moment—and I immediately know the answer.

"Low-key, definitely. I think candles and rose petals would make her nervous."

Birdie tips his head. "Then just go slow and make sure she's comfortable. That's the only advice I can give you." He pauses. "And include lots of foreplay, dude. Chicks need that shit. Got it?"

I chuckle. "Yes, sir."

"Any more questions? Because I stink to high heaven, and I desperately need a shower."

"Naah, that's it. Thanks, man."

Birdie slaps me on the shoulder and rises to his feet. "Don't stress too much about it, G. Sex is supposed to be fun, remember?" Then he winks and lumbers out of the weight room.

Don't stress? Jeez, how can I *not*?

I groan out loud, grateful that nobody is around to hear the panicky sound.

Make her comfortable. Go slow. Lots of foreplay. Don't stress.

Okay. I can do that.

Or at least I damn well *hope* I can.

24

Hannah

I almost throw up three times on the way over to Garrett's, but I choke back the nerves because I'm driving Tracy's car, and the last thing I want to do is pay to have my vomit scrubbed off her upholstery.

I honestly don't remember a second of my five-hour shift at Della's. Or my one-hour rehearsal with Cass earlier. Or how I got from one place to the other today. I've been on autopilot since I left Garrett's bedroom earlier, every conscious thought focused on what I'm about to do tonight.

Did I mention I'm nervous?

I shouldn't be, though. It's just sex. It's sex with a guy I'm attracted to, a guy I genuinely like and trust.

My hands shouldn't be trembling this badly, and my heart shouldn't be beating this fast. And yet intertwined with the nervousness is a sense of excitement. Anticipation. I'm even wearing matching bra and panties beneath my waitressing uniform. Yep, you know you're about to have sex when you're rocking black lace top and bottom, and your skin is silky smooth and ready to be touched.

Garrett's roommates aren't home when I walk into the house. Unless they're holed up in their bedrooms, but I don't think they are because there's nothing but silence in the upstairs hallway as I head toward Garrett's room.

I wonder if Garrett ordered them to disappear. Then I hope he didn't, because...well, that's like holding up a neon sign announcing that he and I are getting it on tonight.

"Hey," he says when I walk in.

My heart simultaneously does a nervous somersault and an appreciative flip. I can tell he took the time to get ready because his hair is still slightly damp from the shower, and his face is completely clean-shaven. I glance at his black track pants and tight gray undershirt, then at my garish uniform. Thanks to the jittery state I've been in all day, I forgot to bring a change of clothes.

Then again, we probably won't be wearing clothes for much longer.

"Hey." I gulp. "So...how do you want to do this? Should I take my clothes off?" I pause as something occurs to me. "Don't you dare ask me to do a striptease, because I'm nervous enough as it is and there's no way I can dance even *remotely* sexy right now."

Garrett bursts out laughing. "You have no idea how to set a mood, do you, Wellsy?"

I moan miserably. "I know. I'm just...nervous," I reiterate. Taking a breath, I wipe my clammy palms on the front of my skirt. "Can we just get started? You're standing there and looking at me, and it's freaking me out."

He approaches with a quiet chuckle, cupping my chin in his hands. "First, relax—there's nothing to be nervous about. Second, I don't expect, or particularly want, a striptease." He winks. "At least not tonight. And third, we're not starting anything right now."

I battle a pang of disappointment. "We're not?"

Garrett tosses me the same T-shirt I slept in last night. "Go change out of that *Grease* costume and put this on. I'll get the next disc ready." He wanders over to the TV and picks up the DVD case for *Breaking Bad*.

"You want to watch TV?" I say incredulously.

"Yup."

My mouth opens. Then closes. But it stays closed, because I suddenly realize what he's doing, and I whole-heartedly appreciate it.

He's trying to put me at ease.

It's working.

I duck into the bathroom to change, returning a moment later to join Garrett on the bed. He instantly puts his arm around me and pulls me closer, and his familiar masculine scent relaxes me.

"Ready?" he says lightly, holding up the remote.

I find myself smiling. "Yep."

The episode fills the screen, and I lean my head against his shoulder as I focus on the TV. Like the other times we've watched this show together, neither of us say much aside from the occasional gasp from me or a prediction from him, but unlike those other times, I'm only half paying attention. Garrett rubs his palm over my shoulder in a light, teasing caress that makes it incredibly hard to concentrate on the TV.

Halfway through the episode, he leans in and kisses my neck.

I don't say a word, but an involuntary sigh slips out. Goose bumps rise in the spot his lips have touched, and when he rests one big hand on my bare thigh, a jolt of heat singes my skin.

"What are you doing?" I murmur.

His lips travel along the length of my neck. "Setting the mood." He nips at my earlobe. "Unlike some people, *I* happen to know how to do that."

I stick my tongue out at him even though he can't see it. He's too busy tormenting me with his mouth, planting wet, open-mouthed kisses on the side of my throat.

Arousal starts deep in my core and spreads outward, dancing through my body and tingling in all my erogenous zones. Every time his lips kiss a new patch of skin, I shiver with pleasure. When his tongue tickles my jaw, I turn my head toward him and our mouths meet in the hottest kiss on the planet.

I love the way Garrett kisses. It's not sloppy or hurried, but skillful and slow and absolutely incredible. His lips brush mine, lazy and teasing, while his tongue sneaks inside every so often for a fleeting taste before seductively retreating. I slant my head and drive the kiss deeper, and I moan when the minty flavor of him infuses my tongue. A masculine rumble comes from the back of his throat, and my belly clenches in response.

His mouth stays locked to mine as he gently pushes me onto my back, settling on his side beside me. One warm hand cups my breast over the thin material of my T-shirt, and the zing of pleasure makes me squeak in joy.

"Tell me if I'm going too fast." His deep voice tickles my lips, and then his tongue spears through them to find mine again.

I'm on sensory overload. He's kissing me, squeezing my breasts, lightly rubbing my nipple with his thumb, and everything he's doing feels so good I don't know which sensation to focus on.

My pulse goes haywire when he glides his palm down my body. He hesitates when he reaches the hem of the T-shirt, then makes a husky sound and slips his fingers beneath it.

When his hand moves between my legs, I stop breathing.

When his fingers touch my clitoris over my panties, I whimper.

Garrett's hand stills. "Should I stop?"

"God. No. Keep going."

A raspy chuckle leaves his mouth, and then his hand begins to move again. Just when I think it can't feel any better, he proves me wrong by moving aside the scrap of fabric covering my sex and pressing his index finger directly on my clit.

My hips shoot up as if I've been struck by lightning. "Oooh. Keep doing that."

He rubs tiny circles around my sensitive flesh, gentle but firm, before sliding his finger lower to tease the moisture pooling in my core.

The groan he lets out races up my spine. "Oh fuck. You're so wet."

I am. I really am. And the ache between my legs is getting worse, throbbing harder as ripples of pleasure dance inside me. I'm stunned to feel the telltale signs of impending orgasm. This is the closest I've ever come to feeling like this, but I get distracted when I register the hard ridge pressing into my hip. The feel of Garrett's hard-on rubbing up against me is so erotic I can't think straight.

I'm desperate to touch him, and my hands move as if possessed, slipping under his waistband and into his boxers.

The second I encounter his erection, my jaw drops.

"Oh my God, are you *kidding* me?"

He looks startled. "What's wrong?"

"Are you taking human growth hormones or something?" I snatch my hand back, fighting another rush of nervousness. "There's no way that huge man monster is fitting inside me!"

Garrett's head abruptly drops in the crook of his arm as a shudder racks his body. At first I think he's pissed off. Or maybe even crying. It takes several seconds before I realize what's happening. He's *laughing*.

Scratch that—he's in *hysterics*.

His broad back quakes with laughter, causing the mattress to vibrate beneath us. When he finally speaks, his voice is wheezy and broken by loud guffaws. "*Man monster*?"

"Stop laughing at me. I'm serious," I insist. "I might have big boobs and a grabbable ass, but have you seen my hips? Tiny and narrow! Which stands to reason that my lady canal—"

A howl rips out of his mouth. "*Lady canal?*"

"—is narrow too. You're going to rip me in *half*."

He raises his head and there are honest-to-God tears in his eyes. "I think that's the nicest thing a girl has ever said to me," he chokes out.

"It's not funny, okay?"

He's still wheezing like crazy. "It totally is."

"You know what? We're not doing this. You've officially killed the mood."

"Me?" he demands between laughs. "You did that all by yourself, baby."

I sit up with an annoyed grumble. "Seriously, this was a stupid idea." Sighing, I search the mattress for the remote control. "Let's just watch the show."

"No way. We're already in this deep." His voice becomes gruff. "Give me your hand."

I eye him suspiciously. "Why?"

"Because I think if you get better acquainted with my man monster, you'll see that you don't have to be afraid of him."

I snort, but the humor dies when Garrett takes my hand and puts it directly inside his boxers.

The mood I killed? Roars right back to life as I gingerly wrap my fingers around his shaft. He's long and thick and pulsing beneath my fingertips, and that's all it takes for my body to tingle again.

I give him a tentative stroke, and he groans softly. "See? It's just a regular old penis, Wellsy."

My throat closes up with laughter. "There are so many things wrong with that sentence I don't even know where to start." I pause. "Exactly how old is your penis?"

"He's twenty, like me," Garrett answers seriously. "But he's way more mature than I am. What about your lady canal? Is she wiser than her years, or is she—"

I shut him up with a kiss.

It isn't long before I'm shivering with pleasure again. Garrett's hand returns to where I want it to be. Somehow my panties disappear, and one long finger slides inside me, making me gasp. My inner muscles clamp around him, and a bolt of heat sizzles up my spine.

Garrett's tongue fills my mouth, his erection rocking into my hand. I've never felt more in control, more desirable, because I know I'm the one responsible for those rough sounds he's making. He breaks the kiss to nibble on my shoulder, and the spark in my body burns hotter, so close to detonating that I'm moaning louder now.

But the arousal extinguishes when I open my eyes to find him watching me.

The tingles disappear, and I stiffen beneath his touch.

"What's wrong?" he murmurs.

"Nothing." I swallow. "Just...kiss me again." I yank his head down and part my lips to welcome his tongue.

Garrett strokes my clit with dexterity that awes me. It's like he knows exactly how much pressure to exert, when to rub faster, when to slow down. I grind into his talented hand, but when he groans again, the arousal fades once more.

I groan too, frustrated.

"What's going on, Wellsy?" His fingertips skim over my sex. "I know you're into this. I can feel it."

"I am. I..." My throat constricts as helplessness rises inside it. "I get close, and then it...it goes away." I'm mortified to feel the sting of tears. "That's what always happens."

"How can I get you there?" he says intently.

"I don't know. Just keep touching me. Please."

He does, and oh my God, he's so good at it. As two fingers move inside me in a slow glide, I shut my eyes again, but it doesn't matter. I can still feel him watching me.

Just like Aaron did when he took what I didn't want to give.

I was fully conscious during the rape. Sometimes, when I'm depressed or wallowing in self-pity, I actually curse the drugs for not knocking me out. Date rape drugs are supposed to *knock you out*, damn it. I'm not supposed to remember what happened to me. I wish I *didn't* remember.

But I do. The memories are hazier than normal memories,

but the sight of Aaron's wild eyes has been branded into my brain. I remember lying there on Melissa's parents' bed, feeling his heavy weight on top of me, feeling him thrusting inside me, hard and deep and painful. But it was like I was paralyzed. My arms and legs didn't seem to work, no matter how badly I wanted to hit or kick him. My vocal cords froze so I couldn't get a single scream out. All I could do was stare up at those smug brown eyes that were laced with pleasure and flashing with lust.

The vicious memories swarm my mind like a bee attack, stealing away the last traces of desire inside me. I know Garrett feels the change in my body, that I'm no longer warm and wet and pliant. That I'm stiffer than a board and colder than ice.

"This isn't working," he says hoarsely.

I sit up, fighting hard not to cry. "I know. I'm sorry. It's just...you're...you're looking at me... and..."

He offers a crooked grin. "Would it help if I close my eyes?"

"No," I say miserably. "Because I'll know you're still picturing me in your head."

With a sigh, he slides up and rests his head on the bed frame. He's still hard—I can see his erection straining beneath his track pants—but he seems oblivious to his own state of arousal as he slowly meets my eyes. "You don't trust me."

I'm quick to deny it. "I *do* trust you. I wouldn't be here if I didn't."

"Fine, I'll amend that. You don't trust me enough to fully let go."

My teeth sink into my bottom lip. I want to tell him he's wrong, but a part of me doesn't think he is.

"Sex is all about trust," he says. "Even if you don't love the other person, even if it's just a hookup, it still takes a serious amount of trust to open yourself up and let yourself go to that vulnerable place, you know? And there's nothing more vulnerable than coming." His mouth lifts in a dry smile. "At least that's what my Google search taught me."

"You *researched* this?" I yell.

Embarrassment reddens his cheeks. "I had to. I've never slept with anyone who's been...you know..."

"I know." I bite my lip even harder to stop myself from bursting into tears.

"After what happened to you, it's not surprising that you're scared to let yourself be vulnerable." He hesitates. "Were you a virgin?"

I press my lips together and nod.

"Yeah, I thought so." Garrett goes quiet for another beat. "I have an idea, if you're willing to hear it."

I can't talk because I'm too close to the I'm-gonna-bawl-my-eyes-out brink, so I settle for another nod.

"Instead of me giving you an orgasm, why don't you try to give one to yourself?"

I thought I'd maxed out my embarrassment credit card tonight, but clearly there's humiliation left to spare. "I do it all the time." My cheeks are flaming as I avoid his eyes.

"In front of me," he corrects. "Make yourself come in front of *me*." He pauses. "And I'll make myself come in front of you."

Oh my God.

I can't believe we're even having this discussion. That he's suggesting we *pleasure ourselves* in front of each other.

"Please excuse me while I go hang myself," I mutter. "Because I am so mortified right now."

"You shouldn't be." His gray eyes harden with intensity. "It'll be an exercise in trust. Seriously, I think it will be good. We'll both be making ourselves vulnerable, and you'll see that there's nothing to be afraid of."

Before I can respond, he hops off the bed and peels his shirt over his head. Then, without missing a beat, he yanks his pants off his hips.

My breath lodges in my lungs. I had been touching his erection before, but I hadn't actually seen it. And now I *am* seeing it, and he's long and hard and perfect. My body tingles at the sight of his naked body, and when my gaze slides up to meet his eyes, I glimpse nothing but healthy desire and sweet encouragement in those silvery gray depths. No dirty lust, no gleam of power, no savagery or malevolence.

He's not Aaron. He's Garrett, and he's putting himself on display for me, showing me that it's okay to let down your guard.

"Take off your shirt, Hannah. Let me see you." He grins. "I promise not to leer too hard at your stripper tits."

An unwitting smile springs to my lips. But I still don't move.

"Show me what you do to yourself when you're alone," he

coaxes.

"I…" The lump in my throat is too big to speak past.

His voice grows hoarse and seductive. "Show me, and I'll show you."

He wraps his fist around his cock, and a moan shudders out of my mouth.

I meet his gaze, and something about the certainty of his expression spurs me to action. My fingers shake uncontrollably as I reach for the bottom of my T-shirt and drag it over my head, leaving me in nothing but my bra.

Then I draw a deep breath and take the bra off, too.

25

Garrett

I've never jerked off in front of a girl before. I mean, I've given it a stroke or two before putting my cock in a more desirable place than my fist, but whacking it from start to finish? It's a first for me. And I'm nervous.

But I'd be lying if I said I also wasn't turned on something fierce.

I can't believe that Hannah is lying naked on my bed. She's fucking beautiful. Her body is soft and curvy in all the right places. Her breasts are absolute perfection, round and perky and tipped with reddish-brown nipples. My gaze lowers to the narrow strip of hair between her legs and I'm dying for her to part them. I want to see every inch of her.

But I don't want to come off like a perv, and I don't want to scare her off, so I keep my mouth shut. I'm hard as a rock, my cock throbbing in my fist as I try not to ogle the sexy naked girl on my bed.

"You're not talking," she accuses, her tone both teasing and nervous.

"I don't want to scare you off," I say hoarsely.

"Dude, you're standing there naked in front of me with your dick in your hand. If that doesn't scare me, I doubt anything you say will."

Good point. And damned if my dick doesn't tingle when she calls me *dude*. In fact, every word that comes out of her mouth gets me hot.

"Spread your legs," I tell her. "I want to see you."

She hesitates.

And then she does it, and my breath spirals out of my lungs. Fucking perfection. She's pink and pretty and glistening and perfect.

I'm going to come way too fast. It's a fact. But I do my damnedest to prolong the inevitable. I stroke myself in a painfully slow tempo, avoiding putting pressure on the tip of my cock, ignoring the sweet spot underneath it.

"Show me what you would do if I wasn't here," I murmur. "Show me how you'd touch yourself."

Her cheeks turn the sweetest shade of pink. Her lips are parted, just slightly, but wide enough that if I pressed my mouth to hers, I could slide my tongue between the pouty seam and taste her. I want to kiss her so badly, but I resist the urge. This moment is too delicate to risk panicking her again.

Very slowly, Hannah brings her hand between her legs.

A shockwave of pleasure shudders through me. "That's it, Wellsy. Touch yourself."

One fingertip brushes her clit. She rubs it. Her touch is measured, exploratory, like she's taking the time to find out what feels good.

I match her unhurried pace. My body craves release, but this is too important to blow. Literally *blow*, because I'm so fucking close I have to breathe through my nose and clench my ass cheeks to stop from exploding.

"Does that feel good?" My voice sounds low and strangled to my ears.

Hannah nods, her green eyes wide as saucers. A breathy noise slips out of her mouth, and I suddenly imagine that mouth wrapped around my dick, and I'm dangerously close to losing it. I snap into emergency jack-off mode, squeezing my shaft tight enough to bring a jolt of pain.

Hannah rubs herself even faster, her other hand skimming up her body to cup one firm breast. She toys with her nipple between her fingers and I bite back a growl. I want to suck on that puckered bud more than I want my next breath.

"What are you thinking about, Wellsy?" I voice the question not just for her sake, but mine. I need a distraction. ASAP.

Her gaze stays glued to the lazy movement of my hand. "I'm thinking about you."

Oh hell. Not *that* kind of distraction.

My strokes get faster as my hand takes on a life of its own. There's a naked woman on my bed and I can't fuck her. I *can't*, because tonight isn't about me. It's about Hannah.

"I'm thinking about how sexy you are," she whispers. "I'm thinking about how much I want to kiss you again."

I almost go to her and give her what she wants, but I'm terrified the spell will be broken if I do.

"What else?" I say thickly.

Her hand leaves her breast and travels over her flat belly, down the edge of her hips. God, she's tiny. I could probably span the entire width of her waist with both my hands.

"I'm thinking about your fingers inside me."

I'm thinking about the same damn thing, but I satisfy myself by watching *her* fingers. She pushes two of them into her pussy, while her other hand continues to tend to her clit. Her cheeks are even more flushed now. So are her breasts.

I realize she's getting close, and the satisfaction that courses through me is like nothing I've ever experienced. *I'm* doing this to her. I'm not touching her, but my presence is turning her on.

I pump my cock, squeezing the head on every upstroke. "I'm close," I warn her.

"Yeah?"

"So fucking close. I don't think I can hold off for much longer." Then I curse under my breath, because I can see the wetness coating her fingers every time she withdraws them. I'm dying here.

"Me too." Her eyes have gone hazy with pleasure, and she's rocking restlessly on my bed.

We're both making noise. I'm groaning, she's whimpering, sighing. The air is electric and my body is on fire.

"Oh...God..." She's panting for air now.

"Watch me," I mumble. "Watch what you're doing to me."

I stroke myself faster, and she cries out, "*Garrett*."

She comes with my name on her lips, and I come to the sound of it. Pleasure hurtles through me, coating my hand and my abs. The force of my release nearly knocks me off my feet, and I wildly grab the side of my desk, holding on tight as pulsing waves roar through my body.

When I crash back to Earth, I find Hannah watching me. She looks dazed and fascinated, and her breasts heave as she sucks in oxygen.

"Oh my God." Astonishment flashes across her face. "I can't believe..."

I blink, and suddenly there's a naked girl in my arms. She launches herself at me, unfazed by the wetness on my stomach, which now sticks to her skin.

She wraps her arms around my neck and buries her face in the center of my chest. "I came."

I choke out a laugh. "I saw."

"I came, and you were here, and..."

She peers up at me in awe. I always forget how short she is until we're standing face to face and she has to crane her neck to meet my eyes.

"Let's have sex," she announces.

Damned if my cock doesn't harden again. She feels it, her eyes widening as my heavy erection presses into her belly.

But clearly I'm a masochist, because I say, "No."

No?

It's official. I've gone insane.

"What do you mean, no?" she demands.

I hold my ground even in the face of her visible disappointment. "Tonight was a big step for you, but I think that's how we need to handle it from now on. In steps." I swallow, and force myself to add, "Baby steps."

An odd glimmer crosses her eyes.

"What?" I say roughly.

"Nothing. That's just what my therapist used to advise. Baby steps."

She goes quiet for a long moment, and then the most brilliant smile fills her face and lights up the room. It's the first time Hannah has smiled at me like that, a smile that truly reaches her eyes, and it makes my heart clench in the strangest way.

"You're a pretty good guy, Garrett. You know that?"

A good guy? I wish. Fuck, if she could read my mind and see all the dirty images flashing inside it, if she knew all the wicked things I want to do to her, she'd probably recant that statement.

"I have my moments," I answer with a shrug.

Her smile widens, and my chest cracks wide open.

I know in that moment that I'm in trouble.

I agreed to help her not just because I'm her friend, but because I'm a *man*. And when a woman asks you to have sex with her and give her an orgasm, you don't think about it. You say *hell yes*.

Well, she got the orgasm. She did. And I know I'm going to get the sex. I will.

But right now, all I want is for this girl to smile at me again.

26

Hannah

Stop right there!" a sharp voice booms as I hurry toward my bedroom. "Where do you think you're going, young lady?"

I spin around, startled to find Allie lying on the couch in our common area, balancing one of her icky juice cups on her knee. In my haste, I hadn't even noticed her.

"What are you doing home?" I ask in surprise. "I thought you have econ on Wednesdays."

"It got cancelled because the prof has Ebola."

I gasp. "Holy shit! Are you serious?"

She snickers. "Well, no. I mean, maybe. He sent out an email saying he's come down with an *illness*—" she uses air quotes "—but he didn't say what the illness was. I like to imagine it's something bad, though. Because then he won't be able to teach for the rest of the term and we'll all get automatic A's."

"You are an evil person," I inform her. "And one day that voodoo black magic of yours is going to come back to haunt you. Seriously, don't come crawling to me when you get Ebola. Anyway, I have to go. I just popped in to drop off my stuff before I head to rehearsal."

"No way, Han-Han. You're going to sit your pretty butt down on this couch, because we need to have a little chat."

"I really can't be late for rehearsal."

"How many times has *Cass* been late for rehearsal?" she challenges.

Good point.

With a sigh, I walk over to the couch and flop down. "Okay.

What's up? And make it snappy."

"Fine, you want snappy? How's this—what on God's green planet is going on with you and Garrett?"

My mouth snaps closed. Crap. Busted. I mean, I *had* texted her last night saying "*over at Garrett's—be home late*" but Allie lives in her own Sean-centered bubble for so much of the time that I'd been hoping she wouldn't bring up the subject.

"Nothing's going on," I answer.

Ha, if by "nothing" I mean "I went over to his house and we both got naked and masturbated in front of each other and then I had an orgasm and *he* had an orgasm and it was the best feeling *ever.*"

Allie sees right through my feeble attempt at lying. "I'm going to ask you this one time, and one time only—Hannah Julie Wells, are you dating Garrett Graham?"

"No."

She narrows her eyes. "Fine. I'm going to ask you twice. Are you dating—"

"I'm not dating him." I sigh. "But we are fooling around."

Her jaw falls open. A second ticks by, then another, and then her blue eyes light up in victory. "*Ha*! I *knew* you were into him! Oh my God! Hold my juice—I think I need to break out in a happy dance! Do you know how to do the running man? If so, can you teach me *right now*?"

I laugh. "Oh God, please don't do a happy dance. And it's not a big deal, okay? It'll probably fizzle out soon."

Yeah, when I go out with Justin.

And double crap—this is the first time since Dean's birthday that Justin has even crossed my mind. I've been entirely focused on Garrett, on the way he turns me on, the things I want to do with him. But now that I'm reminded of my impending date, I experience a sharp tug of guilt.

Can I really go out with someone else after what Garrett and I did last night?

But... It's not like I'm dating Garrett. He's not my boyfriend, and there's no way he considers me his girlfriend, so...why not?

Still, the urge to cancel on Justin refuses to go away, but I push it aside as Allie continues to gush about the awesomeness of this hookup.

"Did you sleep with him? Oh, please say yes! And please say that it was good! I know you and Devon didn't have Brangelina-level chemistry in the sack, but from what I've heard, Garrett Graham has some serious moves."

Yep. He certainly does.

"I didn't sleep with him."

She looks disappointed. "Why not?"

"Because...I don't know, because it didn't happen. We did other stuff." My face burns hotter. "And that's all I'm saying about the subject, okay?"

"Not okay. BFFs are supposed to tell each other everything. I mean, *you* know everything about my sex life. You know about the time Sean and I tried anal, and you know how big Sean's dick is—"

"Which is above and beyond TMI," I interject. "I love you to death, but I never, ever wanted to know about the butt sex, and I definitely could've lived without you bringing out a ruler and demonstrating the size of your boyfriend's penis!"

Allie pouts. "You're the worst. But don't worry, I'll get all the dirty details eventually. I'm very good at prying out details."

It's true. She is. But she's not getting a single one right now.

Rolling my eyes, I stand up. "All right, are we done here? Because I really need to go."

"Fine, go. And no, we are not done." She grins at me. "We won't be done until you bust out that ruler and put an end to the age old question, *how big is Garrett Graham's—*"

"Goodbye, perv."

The first thing I see when I walk into the choir room fifteen minutes later is a cellist.

Question: How do you know when things have spiraled out of your control?

Answer: When you find a cellist in your rehearsal space and don't even bat an eye.

Ever since MJ endorsed Cass's choir idea, I've given up on arguing with either one of them. At this point, they can do whatever the hell they want—AKA whatever the hell *Cass* wants—because I simply don't have the mental energy to play his game.

"You're late." Cass tsks with disapproval as I unzip my coat.

"I know."

He waits for me to apologize.

I don't apologize.

"Hannah, this is Kim Jae Woo," MJ says with a hesitant smile. "He's going to be accompanying you guys during the second verse."

Uh-huh. Of course he is.

I don't bother asking when this decision was made. I just nod and mutter, "Sounds good."

For the next hour, we concentrate only on the middle section of the song. Normally Cass would be stopping us every two seconds to criticize something I've done, but today the brunt of his criticism lands on poor Kim Jae Woo. The Korean freshman shoots me a panicked look every time Cass bitches at him, but all I can do is offer a shrug and a sympathetic smile.

It's sad. I've lost all enthusiasm for this song. The only thing that brings me comfort now is the knowledge that if we don't win the scholarship thanks to Cass's theatrics, I'll get a second chance in April during the spring showcase.

At two o'clock, Cass calls an end to rehearsal, and I breathe a sigh of relief as I pull on my coat. When I step into the hall, I'm startled to find Garrett standing there. He's wearing his Briar jacket and holding two coffee cups, and he greets me with a crooked smile that makes my pulse race.

"Hey!" I wrinkle my forehead. "What are you doing here?"

"I stopped by your room, but Allie said you were rehearsing, so I figured I'd come by and wait until you were done."

"You were standing out here the whole time?"

"Naah, I grabbed some coffee and wandered around for a bit. Just got back now." He glances past my shoulder into the music room. "Is rehearsal over?"

"Yep." I take the cup he hands me and pop the plastic lid. "We have a cellist now."

Garrett's lips twitch. "Mmm-hmmm. And I bet you're positively *thrilled* about that."

"More like indifferent."

A sharp voice snaps from behind me. "You're blocking the door, Hannah. Some people have somewhere to be."

Rolling my eyes, I move away from the doorway and allow Cass and Mary Jane to exit. Cass doesn't spare so much as a look at me, but when he notices who I'm talking to, his blue eyes fly in my direction.

"Cass, have you met Garrett?" I ask politely.

He warily turns back to the tall, strapping hockey player at my side. "Naah, I haven't. Nice to meet you, man."

"You too, Chazz."

My duet partner stiffens. "It's Cass."

Garrett blinks innocently. "Oh, sorry—wasn't that what I said?"

Cass's nostrils flare.

"So I hear you're singing a duet with my girl," Garrett adds. "I hope you're not giving her any trouble. I'm not sure you know this, but my Han-Han has a bad habit of letting people walk all over her." He arches one dark brow. "But you wouldn't do that, right, Chazz?"

Despite the pang of embarrassment his words evoke in me, I'm also fighting hard not to laugh.

"It's. Cass."

"That's what I said, no?"

There's one long moment of very obvious macho posturing as the two guys stare each other down. As I expect, Cass is first to break the eye contact.

"Whatever," he mutters. "Come on, MJ, we're gonna be late."

As he drags the sweet blond girl away like a piece of luggage, I turn to Garrett with a sigh. "Was that necessary?"

"Fuck yeah it was."

"Okay. Just checking."

Our eyes lock, and a burst of heat goes off inside me. Oh boy. I know exactly what he's thinking right now. Or rather, what he's thinking about *doing.*

Me.

I'm thinking the same damn thing.

I might have told Allie that this thing between us would fizzle out, but at the moment, it's blazing even hotter than it did last night.

"My place?" he murmurs.

Those two words, low and husky, make my thighs clench so

hard I'm surprised I don't pull a muscle.

Rather than answer—my throat has clogged with desire—I take the coffee from his hand and proceed to dump both our cups in the trashcan behind him.

Garrett chuckles. "I'll take that as a yes."

27

Hannah

I have no idea what was said during the car ride to Garrett's townhouse. I'm sure we talked. I'm sure I saw the scenery whizzing past the window. I'm sure I even breathed oxygen in and out of my lungs like a normal person. I just don't remember any of those things.

The second we stumble into his bedroom, I loop my hands around his neck and kiss him. Forget baby steps. I want him too bad to go slow, and my hands fumble for his belt buckle before his tongue even enters my mouth.

His husky laughter tickles my lips, and then strong hands cover mine to stop me from undoing his belt. "As much as I appreciate the enthusiasm, I'm gonna have to slow you down, Wellsy."

"But I don't want to go slow," I protest.

"Tough cookies."

"Tough cookies? What are you, my grandmother?"

"Does she say *tough cookies*?"

"Well, no," I confess. "Nana swears like a sailor, actually. Last Christmas she dropped a *motherfucker* bomb at the dinner table, and my dad nearly choked on his turkey."

Garrett barks out a laugh. "I think I like Nana."

"She's very sweet."

"Uh-huh. Sounds like it." He tilts his head. "Now can we stop talking about your grandmother, Ms. Mood Killer?"

"You killed it first," I point out.

"Naah, I just changed up the pace." His gray eyes go molten

hot. "Now get on the bed so I can make you come."

Oh. My. God.

I scramble onto the mattress so fast it brings another laugh to Garrett's lips, but I don't care how eager I look. The nerves I felt last night aren't wreaking havoc on my stomach today, because my whole body is trembling with need. In the back of my mind, it *does* occur to me that maybe it won't happen again, at least not from Garrett's touch, but oh man, I'm dying to find out.

He settles beside me and thrusts his hand in my hair as he kisses me. I've never been with a guy who's this rough with me. Devon treated me like I might shatter, but Garrett doesn't. I'm not a fragile piece of china to him. I'm just…me. I love how excited he gets, the way he pulls my hair if my head isn't exactly where he wants it to be, or how he bites my lip when I try to tease him by depriving him of my tongue.

I sit up only so he can whip my shirt off, and then he uses one hand to unsnap my bra with the kind of Garrett dexterity I've come to expect. The second he takes off his own shirt, I press my lips to his chest. I didn't get to touch him yesterday, and I'm starving to know what he feels like, what he tastes like. His flesh is warm beneath my lips, and when my tongue darts tentatively over one flat nipple, a husky groan escapes his lips. Before I can blink, I'm on my back and we're kissing again.

Garrett cups my breast, toying with my nipple between his fingers. My eyelids flutter closed and in this moment, I don't care if he's looking at me. I only care about how good he's making me feel.

"Your skin feels like silk," he murmurs.

"Did you steal that line from a Hallmark card?" I crack.

"Nope, just stating a fact." His fingers skim the undersides of my breasts. "You're soft and smooth and perfect." He lifts his head to give me a wry look. "My calluses are probably scratching the shit out of you, huh?"

They are, but it's the kind of erotic scraping that makes my heart pound. "If you stop touching me, I'll punch you."

"Naah, you'll just break your hand if you do that. And I happen to like your hands." With a wicked smile, he takes my right hand and places it directly over his crotch.

The hard bulge beneath my palm is so tempting I can't help but stroke it. Garrett's features stretch tight. A second later, he quickly removes my hand. "Oh hell. Bad idea. I'm not ready for this to end yet."

I snort. "Aw, is someone quick on the trigger?"

"Shut it, woman. I can go all night long."

"Uh-huh. Sure you can—"

He cuts me off with a blistering hot kiss that ends with me gasping for air. Then a naughty gleam lights his eyes again, and he bends his head to kiss my nipple.

A shockwave of pleasure blasts from my breast to my core. When Garrett's tongue darts out and swirls around the distended bud, I all but float away. My breasts have always been sensitive, and right now, they're a bundle of tight, crackling nerve endings. When he sucks my nipple deep in his mouth, I see stars. He shifts to my other breast, giving it the same thorough attention, the same lazy kisses and teasing licks.

Then he begins kissing his way south.

Despite the excitement surging through my blood, I experience a wave of anxiety. I can't help but remember all the times Devon did this exact same thing, kissing his way down my body. Or how much time he spent between my legs when intercourse didn't seem to do it for me.

But thinking about my ex right now is *not* what I ought to be doing, so I banish all thoughts of Devon from my mind.

Garrett's breath tickles my belly button as his tongue grazes my belly. I can feel his fingers trembling as he undoes the button of my jeans. I like knowing that he might be nervous, or in the very least, that he's as excited as I am. He always comes off as so cool and self-assured, but right now, right here, he looks like he's struggling to hold on to the last thread of his control.

"Is this okay?" he whispers, sliding my jeans and panties down my hips. Then his breath hitches, and I feel a tad self-conscious as his hungry gaze fixes between my legs.

I inhale slowly and say, "Yes."

The first brush of his tongue against my folds is like an electric current shooting up my spine. I moan so loudly that his head lifts abruptly.

"Tuck's home," he warns, humor dancing in his eyes. "So I suggest we use our indoor voices."

I have to bite my lip to stop from making noise, because what he's doing to me...holy mother of pearl. So. Good. He circles my clit with his tongue, then licks it in soft, slow strokes that drive me absolutely wild with desire.

I suddenly remember how Allie confessed that she had to "train" Sean to do this because he used to go all motorboat on her clit from the word *go*. But Garrett needs no training. He allows my pleasure to build, going slow and making me crazy, making me beg.

"Please," I whimper when the tempo once again becomes excruciatingly leisurely. "More."

He raises his head, and I'm pretty sure I've never glimpsed anything sexier than the sight of his glossy lips and burning gray eyes. "Do you think you can come like this?"

I surprise myself by nodding. I don't think I'm lying, though. I'm wound up so tight I'm like a cartoon bomb about to detonate.

With a low growl of approval, he leans down and wraps his lips around my clit. He sucks hard, simultaneously pushing one finger inside me, and I go off like a rocket launcher.

The orgasm is a thousand times more intense than the orgasms I've given myself, maybe because my body knows I wasn't the one who made it happen. *Garrett* did this. Garrett turned my limbs to jelly and sent this wave of sweet, pulsing satisfaction racing through me.

When the incredible sensations finally abate, they leave behind a warm rush of peace and a strangely bittersweet feeling. What happens next is something I've only seen happen in movies and it embarrasses the crap out of me.

I start to cry.

In a heartbeat, Garrett climbs up my body and searches my face in concern. "What's wrong?" His expression goes stricken. "Oh shit. Did I hurt you?"

I shake my head and blink through the onslaught of tears. "I'm...crying...because..." I breathe deeply. "Because I'm happy."

His features relax, and now he looks like he's trying not to laugh. His jaw twitches as he meets my eyes. "Say it," he orders.

"Say what?" I use the corner of his blanket to wipe the moisture staining my cheeks.

"Say *Garrett Graham, you are a sex god. You have achieved what no other man ever has. You—*"

I punch him in the shoulder. "Oh my God, you're *such* a jerk. I will never, ever say those words."

"Sure you will." He smirks at me. "Once I'm through with you, you'll be shouting those words out from the rooftops."

"You know what I think?"

"Women aren't supposed to think, Wellsy. That's why your brains are smaller. Science proves it."

I slug him again, and a howl of laughter flies out of his mouth. "Jeez. I'm *kidding*. You know I don't actually believe that. I worship at the shrine of womanhood." He dons a solemn face. "Okay, tell me what you think."

"I think it's time I shut you up."

He snickers. "Yeah? How do you plan on—" He hisses when I cup his package and give it a hearty squeeze. "You're evil."

"And you're a cocky jerk, so I guess we both just have to deal."

"Aw, thanks for noticing how cocky I am." He smiles innocently, but there's nothing innocent about the way he thrusts his erection into my hand.

Suddenly I don't feel like teasing him anymore. I just want to see him come apart. I haven't stopped thinking about the way he looked last night when he...

My sex clenches at the memory.

I tackle his belt buckle, and this time, he lets me undo it. In fact, he falls onto his back and lets me do whatever the heck I want.

I undress him as if I'm unwrapping a shiny gift, and once I have him naked, I take a moment to admire my prize. His body is long and sleek, boasting a golden skin tone instead of the pasty white you see on so many of the guys at Briar. I run my fingers over his rock-hard abs, smiling when his muscles quiver beneath my touch. Then I trace the tattoo on his left arm and ask, "Why flames?"

He shrugs. "I like fire. And I think flames look cool."

The response amuses me, but it also impresses me. "Wow. I was expecting to hear about the bullshit meaning behind it. I swear, every time you ask someone about their tattoo, they tell you it means "courage" in Taiwanese or something, when we both know it probably means "potato" or "shoe" or "stupidly intoxicated." *Or* they give you a whole spiel about how they hit rock bottom x many years ago but worked their way through it and this is why they have a phoenix rising from the ashes tattooed on their back."

Garrett laughs before going serious. "I guess this isn't the time to tell you about the tribal tattoo on my shin. It means eternal optimist."

"Oh God. Really?"

"Nope. Totally lying. But it'd serve you right for getting all judgy about people's ink."

"Hey, sometimes it's nice to hear that someone got a tattoo just because they like it. I was complimenting you, dumbass." I lean forward and kiss the flames circling his biceps, which, I have to admit, do look pretty cool.

"Hell yeah, keep complimenting me then," he drawls. "But make sure to use your tongue when you do it."

I roll my eyes, but I don't stop what I'm doing. I drag my tongue over the black flames, then kiss my way to his chest. He tastes like soap and salt and man, and I love it. So much that I can't stop licking every frickin' inch of him.

I know he's enjoying my very thorough exploration as much as I am because his breathing becomes ragged, and I can feel the tension rippling through his muscles. When my mouth concludes its journey by brushing against the tip of his penis, Garrett's entire body goes rigid.

I look up and find glazed gray eyes peering back at me. "You don't have to...do that...if you don't want to," he says gruffly.

"Huh. Then it's a good thing I want to, isn't it?"

"Some girls don't like to."

"Some girls are idiots."

My tongue touches his hard flesh, and his hips snap off the bed. I lick his smooth, engorged head, savoring the taste of him, learning his texture with my tongue. When I draw the tip into my mouth and suck gently, he makes a tortured noise deep in his throat.

"Jesus, Wellsy. That feels..."

"It feels what?" I tease, looking up at him.

"Un-fucking-believable," he croaks. "Don't ever stop. I mean it. I want you to keep blowing me for the rest of your life."

Is his growly request good for my ego?

Naah.

It's *great* for my ego.

Since he's too big to take all the way in my mouth, and I'm

not a deep-throat expert, I wrap my fingers around the base of him, sucking and pumping in unison, my pace alternating between slow and teasing and fast and urgent. Garrett's breathing grows more and more labored, his groans growing more and more desperate.

"Hannah," he chokes out, and I feel his thighs tighten and know he's about to climax.

I've never swallowed before, and I'm not brave enough to try it now, so my hand takes over as I stroke him to release. With a husky grunt, Garrett arches his spine, and wetness spurts onto my fingers and his stomach. His face is mesmerizing and I can't tear my gaze off it. His lips are parted, cheeks taut. His eyes are a hazy swirl of gray, like a thick mass of clouds gathering before an impending storm.

Several seconds later, his body relaxes, practically sinking into the mattress as a sated sigh rumbles from his mouth. I love seeing him like this. Limp and spent and still having trouble breathing.

I grab some tissues from the box on the nightstand and wipe him up, but when I try to get up to throw out the tissues, he yanks me down and kisses me hard. "Jesus...that was incredible."

"Does that mean we get to have sex now?"

"Ha. You wish." He wags a finger at me. "Baby steps, Wellsy. Remember?"

I pout like a six-year-old. "But we *know* I can have an orgasm. You just saw it."

"Actually, I felt it on my tongue."

My heart skips a beat at his crude description. I fall silent for a moment, and then I let out a defeated breath. "Will this change your mind?" I scowl at him, then begin the reluctant recitation. "Garrett Graham, you are a sex god. You have achieved what no other man ever has. You are...insert more glowing reviews here." I lift one eyebrow. "*Now* can we have sex?"

"Absolutely not," he says cheerfully.

Then, to my sheer and total dismay, he hops off the bed and picks up his discarded jeans.

"What are you doing?" I demand.

"Getting dressed. I have practice in thirty minutes."

As if on cue, someone pounds loudly against Garrett's door. "Yo, G, we've gotta take off!" Tucker calls.

I snatch the blanket in a panic, desperate to cover myself up, but Tucker's footsteps are already retreating.

"If you want, you can hang out here until we get back," Garrett offers as he pulls his shirt on. "I'll only be gone a few hours."

I hesitate.

"Come on, stay," he begs. "I'm sure Tucker will be cooking up something good for dinner, so you can stick around and I'll drive you home afterward."

The idea of being alone in his house is...weird. But the idea of eating a home-cooked dinner instead of hitting up the dining hall sounds pretty damn tempting. "Okay," I finally relent. "I guess I can do that. I'll put on a movie or something while you're gone. Or maybe take a nap."

"I will allow either of those options." He glares at me. "But you are not, under any circumstances, allowed to watch *Breaking Bad* without me."

"Fine, I won't."

"Promise..."

I roll my eyes. "I promise."

"G! Move your ass!"

In the blink of an eye, Garrett walks over and plants a quick kiss on my lips. "I've gotta go. See you later."

Then he's gone, and I'm alone in Garrett Graham's bedroom, which is, well, I'll just say it—it's surreal as hell. I never even spoke to the guy before midterms, and now I'm sitting naked on his bed. Figure that one out.

I'm surprised he's not worried about me snooping around and finding his porn stash, but when I stop to think about it, I realize it's not that surprising at all. Garrett is the most honest, straightforward person I've ever met. If he has porn, he probably doesn't bother hiding it. I bet it's all neatly organized in a clearly labeled folder right on his computer desktop.

I hear voices and footsteps downstairs, and then the front door creaks open and slams shut. After a few seconds, I get up and put my clothes back on, because I'm not comfortable walking around naked in a room that's not my own.

I opt against taking a nap, because I feel oddly energized after that orgasm. And *that's* more surreal than everything else, the knowledge that I actually had an orgasm with a guy.

Devon and I tried to make that happen for eight long months.

Garrett did it after two hookup sessions.

Does this mean I'm fixed?

That question is way too philosophical to be pondering in the middle of the afternoon, so I push it aside and go downstairs to get a drink. But once I enter the kitchen, inspiration strikes. Garrett and his teammates are probably going to be exhausted when they get home. Why let Tucker slave over the stove when I'm already in the kitchen with nothing but time on my hands?

A quick exploration of the fridge, pantry and cupboards reveals that Garrett wasn't kidding—cooking *does* happen here, because the kitchen is stocked with ingredients. The only recipe I know off the top of my head is my grandmother's three-cheese lasagna, so I gather up all the necessary items and pile them on the granite counter. I'm about to get cooking when something else occurs to me.

Pursing my lips, I fish my phone out of my back pocket and pull up my mother's number. It's only four o'clock, so I'm hoping she hasn't left for work yet.

Luckily, she picks up on the first ring. "Hey, sweetie! This is a lovely surprise."

"Hey. Got a sec?"

"I've got five whole minutes actually," she replies with a laugh. "Your father's driving me to work tonight, so he has the honor of cleaning all the snow off the car."

"You guys are already getting that much snow?" I say in horror.

"Of course we are. It's gl—"

"I swear to God, Mom, if you say global warming, I'm hanging up," I warn her, because as much as I love my parents, their global warming lectures drive me up the wall. "And why is Dad driving you? What happened to your car?"

"It's in the shop. The brake pads needed to be replaced."

"Oh." I absently open a box of lasagna sheets. "Anyway, I wanted to ask you about Nana's lasagna recipe. It serves eight, right?"

"Ten," she corrects.

Frowning, I think about all the food Garrett shoveled into his pie hole when he came to the diner last week, then multiply that by four hockey players and...

"Crap," I mutter. "I still don't think that's enough. If I wanted to serve twenty, do I just double the ingredients, or is there a different way to calculate it?"

Mom pauses. "Why exactly are you cooking lasagna for twenty people?"

"I'm not. But I am feeding four hockey players who I imagine have the appetites of twenty people."

"I see." There's another pause and I can practically hear her smiling over the line. "Is one of these four hockey players someone...special?"

"You can just ask me if he's my boyfriend, Mom. You don't have to be cheesy about it."

"Fine. Is he your boyfriend?"

"Nope. I mean, we're kinda seeing each other, I guess—" *Kinda? He just made you come!* "—but we're friends more than anything."

Friends who make each other come.

I silence the annoying voice in my voice and swiftly change the subject. "Do you have time to quickly talk me through the recipe?"

"Of course."

Five minutes later, I hang up the phone and start preparing dinner for the guy who made me come today.

28

Garrett

The house smells like an Italian restaurant when I walk through the door. I turn to Logan, who shoots me a WTF look, and I shrug as if to say *fuck if I know*, because I honestly don't know. I bend down to unlace my scuffed black boots, then follow the mouthwatering aroma to the kitchen. When I reach the doorway, I blink like I've just stumbled upon a desert mirage.

Hannah's sexy ass greets my eyes. She's angled over the oven door, wearing Tuck's pink oven mitts as she pulls a steaming pan of lasagna off the middle shelf. At the sound of my footsteps, she glances over her shoulder and smiles. "Oh, hey. Perfect timing."

All I can do is gape at her.

"Garrett? Hello?"

"You made *dinner*?" I sputter.

Her cheerful expression falters slightly. "Yeah. Is that okay?"

I'm too stunned—and genuinely touched—to answer.

Fortunately, Dean appears in the doorway and answers for me. "Baby doll, that smells fantastic."

Tucker trails in after Dean. "I'll set the table," he pipes up.

My three roommates lumber into the kitchen, Tucker and Dean going to help Hannah, while Logan stands beside me, looking amazed.

"She cooks too?" he sighs.

Something about his tone—well, not *something*, since it's the unmistakable note of longing that causes my guard to shoot up ten feet. Fuck. He can't actually be into her, can he? I figured he just wanted to sleep with her, but the way he's looking at her right now…

I don't fucking like it.

"Dude, keep it in your pants," I mutter, which summons a chuckle from Logan, who obviously knows what I was thinking and my opinion about said thoughts.

"Shit, this looks amazing," Tucker says as he stands over the lasagna dish with a knife and serving spatula.

The five of us settle at the table, which Hannah actually took the time to not only clean, but cover with a blue-and-white tablecloth. Aside from my mother, no female has ever cooked dinner for me before. I kinda…like it.

"So are you dressing up tomorrow?" Tucker asks Hannah as he heaps a modest-sized square of lasagna onto her plate.

"For what?"

Tuck grins. "Halloween, dumbass."

Hannah lets out a groan. "Oh crap. That's *tomorrow*? I swear, I have no concept of time."

"My costume suggestion for you?" Dean chimes in. "Sexy nurse. Actually, fuck that, we live in the modern world—sexy *doctor*. Oooh, or sexy navy pilot."

"I'm not dressing up as sexy anything, thank you very much. It's bad enough that I'm stuck passing out drinks at the dorm crawl."

I chuckle. "Shit, you got roped into doing that?" The annual Halloween dorm crawl involves people popping into a dorm, getting free drinks, and then moving on to the next building. I've heard it's actually a lot more fun than it sounds.

She sticks out her chin glumly. "I did it last year too. It sucked. You guys better stop in at Bristol House if you're planning on going."

"I'd love to, gorgeous," Logan says in a flirty tone that makes me stiffen. "Don't expect G here to show up, though."

She looks over at me. "You're not going out on Halloween?"

"Nope," I reply.

"Why not?"

"Because he hates Halloween," Dean informs her. "He's scared of ghosts."

I flip him the bird. But rather than own up to the real

reason I hate October thirty-first with every fiber of my being, I just shrug and say, "It's a pointless holiday with silly traditions."

Logan snickers. "Says the Fun Police."

Tucker finishes serving everyone, then sits down and shoves a fork into his lasagna. "Motherfucker, that's good," he mumbles between mouthfuls.

After that, all conversation ceases to exist, because the guys and I are ravenous after three hours of shooting drills, which means we've turned into cavemen. We waste no time demolishing the lasagna, garlic bread and Caesar salad Hannah made for us. And I mean *demolishing*. There's barely half a serving left in the pan by the time we're through with it.

"I knew I should have tripled the recipe," Hannah says ruefully, staring at the empty dishes in wonder. Then she tries to get up to clear the table, at which point Tucker all but bodychecks her out of the kitchen.

"My mama taught me manners, Wellsy." He gives her a stern look. "Someone cooks for you, you clean. Period." His head swivels to the doorway just as Logan and Dean try to sneak out. "Where're you ladies going? Dishes, assholes. G, you get a free pass since you have to drive our lovely chef home."

In the hall, I plant my hands on Hannah's waist and crook my neck to kiss her. "Why can't you be taller?" I grumble.

"Why can't you be shorter?" she counters.

I brush my lips over hers. "Thanks for cooking dinner. That was really sweet of you."

A blush tints her cheeks. "I figured I owed you...you know..." The pinkish tinge darkens to red. "Because you're a sex god and all."

I chuckle. "Does that mean every time I give you an orgasm you'll cook me a meal?"

"Nope. Tonight was a one-time deal. No more home-cooked meals for you." She stands on her tiptoes and brings her mouth to my ear. "But I still get the orgasms."

Like I could ever, *ever* say no to that.

"Come on, I'll drive you back. You've got an early class tomorrow, right?" I'm surprised to realize that I actually know her schedule.

I'm not sure what's happening between us. I mean, I agreed to help her with her sex problem, but...problem solved, right? She got what she wanted from me, and we didn't even need to have sex to make it happen. So technically, there's no reason for her to sleep with me. Or even keep seeing me, for that matter.

And me…well, I don't want a girlfriend. My attention is and has always been focused solely on hockey, graduating, and the draft I'm planning on entering come graduation. Not to mention impressing the scouts who are already starting to show up at our games. Now that the season is in full swing, this means more practices and games and less time to devote to anything—or anyone—other than hockey.

So why does the thought of not spending any more time with Hannah bring the oddest clench of regret to my gut?

She tries to take a step down the hall, but I tug on her hand and kiss her again, and this time it's not a peck. I kiss her hard, losing myself in her taste and her heat and every damn thing about her. I never expected her. Sometimes people sneak up on you and suddenly you don't know how you ever lived without them. How you went about your day and hung out with your friends and fucked other people without having this one important person in your life.

Hannah breaks the kiss with a soft laugh. "Get a room," she teases.

I decide it might be time to reevaluate my stance on girlfriends.

Hannah

"Bwahahahahaha! Happy Halloweeeeen!"

I turn away from the closet—where I was just in the process of trying to find a Halloween-esque outfit that's not a costume because I fucking hate dressing up—and gawk at the creature gracing my doorway. I can't make heads or tails of what Allie is wearing. All I see is a skintight blue bodysuit, lots of feathers, and…are those cat ears?

I steal Allie's trademark phrase by demanding, "What on

God's green planet are you supposed to be?"

"I'm a cat-bird." Then she gives me a look that says, *uh-doy*.

"A cat bird? What is…okay… *why*?"

"Because I couldn't decide if I wanted to be a cat or a bird, so Sean was like, just be both, and I was like, you know what? Brilliant idea, boyfriend." She grins at me. "I'm pretty sure he was being a smartass, but I decided to treat the suggestion as gospel."

I have to laugh. "He's going to wish he suggested something less ridiculous, like sexy nurse, or sexy witch, or—"

"Sexy ghost, sexy tree, sexy box of Kleenex." Allie sighs. "Gee, let's just throw the word *sexy* in front of any mundane noun and look! A costume! Because here's the thing, if you want to dress like a ho-bag, why not just go as a ho-bag? You know what? I hate Halloween."

I snort. "Then why are you going to the party? You should go hang out with Garrett. He's sulking at home tonight."

"Really?"

"He's anti-Halloween," I explain, but saying it out loud doesn't feel right.

I got the strangest feeling last night that he has a more serious reason for hating Halloween rather than just "it's a pointless holiday." Maybe something terrible happened to him many moons ago on Halloween night, like he got egged by hooligans when he was a kid. Oooh, or maybe he watched *Halloween* and was then plagued with nightmares that lasted for weeks, which is what happened to me when I watched my first and only Michael Myers movie at the age of twelve.

"Anyway, Sean's waiting for me downstairs, so I'm taking off now." Allie pops over and smacks a huge kiss on my cheek. "Have fun handing out drinks with Tracy."

Yeah, right. I'm already regretting agreeing to help Tracy with the dorm crawl. I'm not in the mood to wait around all night for drunken college kids to wander into Bristol House so I can hand them drinks and Jell-O shooters. In fact, the more I think about it, the more I'm tempted to back out, especially when I picture Garrett at home by himself, scowling at his reflection in the mirror or throwing a tennis ball against the wall like they do in prison.

Rather than continue my search for a non-costume costume, I duck out of my dorm and walk across the hall to knock on Tracy's door.

"Coming!" She appears nearly a minute later, running a comb through her curly red hair with one hand and applying white powder to her cheeks with the other.

"Hey," she chirps. "Happy Halloween!"

"Happy Halloween." I pause. "So listen…how badly will you hate me if I bail on the dorm crawl? And then when I add insult to injury and ask to borrow your car?"

Disappointment floods her eyes. "You're not coming? Whhhhhhy?"

Shit, I really hope she doesn't start crying. Tracy is the kind of girl who bawls at the drop of a hat, though in all honesty, I think her tears are of the crocodile variety because they always dry up way too fast.

"A friend of mine is having a bad night," I say awkwardly. "He could use the company."

She gives me a suspicious look. "And does this friend go by the name Garrett Graham?"

I smother a sigh. "Why would you think that?"

"Because Allie said you guys are dating."

Of course she did.

"We're not dating, but yes, he's the friend I'm talking about," I admit.

To my surprise, Tracy breaks out in a huge grin. "Well, why didn't you lead with that, dum-dum? Of course I'm going to let you off the hook if it means you get to go and fuck Garrett Graham! Note to you—I will be living vicariously through you, because Oh. My. God. If that hottie so much as *smiled* at me, my panties would probably melt away."

I don't want to touch even a single part of that response, so I ignore it altogether. "Are you sure you'll be okay?"

"Yeah, I'll be fine." She waves a hand. "My cousin is visiting from Brown, so I'll just recruit her."

"I heard that!" a female voice shouts from inside the room.

"Thanks for being so cool about this," I say gratefully.

"No prob. Hold on a sec." Tracy disappears, then comes back a moment later with her car keys dangling from her index finger. "Hey, so I don't know how you feel about sex tapes, but if you get a chance, record every single thing you do with that boy tonight."

"I most definitely will *not*." I take the keys and grin at her.

"Have fun tonight, babe."

Back in my room, I grab my phone from the living room couch and text Garrett.

Me: *U home?*

Him: *Yup.*

Me: *Bailing on the dorm crawl. Can I come by?*

Him: *Glad u came to your senses, baby. Get your ass over here.*

29

Garrett

When the front door creaks open, I'm more than a little apprehensive, because I half expect Hannah to appear in some ridiculous-ass costume in an attempt to spread the Halloween cheer and lure me to that dorm party.

Fortunately, she looks like regular-old Hannah when she pops her head into the living room. Meaning she looks fucking gorgeous, and my dick immediately salutes her. Her hair is tied in a low ponytail with her bangs swept to one side, and she's wearing a loose red sweater and black yoga pants. Her socks, of course, are neon pink.

"Hey." She flops down beside me on the couch.

"Hey." I sling my arm around her and plant a kiss on her cheek, and it feels like the most natural thing in the world.

I have no idea if I'm the only one feeling this way, but Hannah doesn't pull away, nor does she tease me about how fucking boyfriendly I'm acting. I take that as a promising sign.

"So why'd you flake out on the party?"

"I wasn't in the mood. I kept picturing you crying here alone and pity won out."

"I'm not crying, jackass." I point to the boring-ass milk documentary that's flashing on the TV screen. "I'm learning about pasteurization."

She stares at me. "You guys pay *money* to subscribe to a gazillion channels and *this* is what you choose to watch?"

"Well, I flipped by it and saw a bunch of cow udders, and, well, you know, it turned me on, so—"

"EW!"

I burst out laughing. "Kidding, babe. If you must know, the batteries in the remote died and I was too lazy to get up and change the channel. I was watching this wicked-awesome miniseries about the Civil War before cow udders came on."

"You're really into history, huh?"

"It's interesting."

"Some of it. Other parts, not so much." She rests her head on my shoulder and I absently toy with a strand of hair that's come loose from her ponytail. "My mom bummed me out this morning," she confesses.

"Yeah? Why?"

"She called to tell me that they might not be able to leave Ransom for Christmas, either."

"Ransom?" I say blankly.

"That's where I'm from. Ransom, Indiana." A bitter note creeps into her voice. "Also known as my own personal hellhole."

My mood instantly goes somber. "Because of...?"

"The rape?" She smiles wryly. "You can say the word, you know. It's not contagious."

"I know." I swallow. "I just don't like saying it because it makes it feel...real, I guess. And I can't stomach the thought that it happened to you."

"But it did," she says softly. "You can't pretend otherwise."

A short silence falls between us.

"So why can't your parents come to see you?" I ask.

"Money." She sighs. "Just in case you were cozying up to me because you thought I was some heiress, you should know that I'm at Briar on a full scholarship, and I get financial aid for expenses. My family is broke."

"Get out." I point to the door. "Seriously. Get out."

Hannah sticks out her tongue. "Funny."

"I don't care how much money your family has, Wellsy."

"Says the millionaire."

My chest stiffens. "I'm not a millionaire—my father is. There's a difference."

"I guess." She shrugs. "But yeah, my parents are buried under mountains of debt. It's..." She trails off, and I glimpse a flash of pain in her green eyes.

"It's what?"

"It's my fault," she admits.

"I highly doubt that."

"No, it really is." Now she sounds sad. "They had to take out a second mortgage to pay for my legal fees. The case against Aaron, the guy who—"

"Who better be in jail," I finish, because I honestly can't hear her say the word *rape* again. I just can't. Every time I think about what that bastard did to her, white-hot rage floods my stomach, and my fists tingle with the urge to hit something.

Truth is, I've worked my entire life to keep my temper in check. Anger was the one constant emotion I felt growing up, but luckily, I found a healthy outlet for it—hockey, a sport that allows me to pound on opposing players in a safe, regulated environment.

"He didn't go to jail," Hannah says quietly.

My gaze whips to hers. "Are you fucking kidding me?"

"No." Her eyes take on a faraway light. "When I got home that night...the night it happened...my parents took one look at me and knew something bad had happened. I don't even remember what I said to them. All I remember is that they called the police and took me to the hospital, and I got a rape kit done, got interviewed, interrogated. I was so embarrassed. I didn't want to talk to the cops, but my mom told me I had to be brave and tell them everything, so they could stop him from ever doing that to anyone else."

"Your mom sounds like a very smart woman," I say hoarsely.

"She is." Hannah's voice shakes. "Anyway, Aaron was arrested, and then released on bail, so I had to see that bastard's face in town and at school—"

"They let him go back to school?" I exclaim.

"He was supposed to stay one hundred meters away from me at all times, but yeah, he went back." She offers a grim look. "Did I mention that his mother is the mayor of Ransom?"

Shock spirals through me. "Fuck."

"And his father is the parish leader." She laughs humorlessly. "His family pretty much runs the town, so yeah, I'm surprised the cops even arrested him in the first place. I heard his mother raised hell when they showed up at their house. Sorry, their *mansion*." She pauses. "Long story short, there were a bunch of preliminary hearings and depositions, and I had to sit across from him in court and look at his smug face. After about a month of that bullshit, the judge finally decided there wasn't sufficient evidence to take it to trial, and he dismissed the case."

Horror slams into me harder than any hit Greg Braxton could dish out. "Are you serious?"

"As a heart attack."

"But they had the rape kit, and your testimony..." I sputter.

"All the medical exam showed was that there was blood and tearing—" She blushes "—but I was a virgin, so his lawyer claimed that the act of losing my virginity could've caused it. After that, it was Aaron's word against mine." She laughs again, this time in amazement. "Actually, it was my word against his and three of his friends."

I frown. "Meaning?"

"Meaning his pals lied under oath and told the judge I willingly took drugs that night. Oh, and that I'd been throwing myself at Aaron for months, so *of course* he couldn't resist taking what I was offering. The way they were going on, you'd think I was the biggest druggie whore on the planet. It was humiliating."

I didn't know the meaning of blind rage until this very moment. Because the mere thought of Hannah being forced to suffer through all that makes me want to murder everyone in that small town hellhole of hers.

"It gets worse," she warns when she notices my expression.

I groan. "Oh God. I can't hear any more."

"Oh." She awkwardly averts her eyes. "I'm sorry. Forget it."

I quickly grasp her chin and force her to look at me. "Figure of speech. I need to hear this."

"Okay. Well, after the charges were dropped, the whole town turned against me and my parents. Everyone was saying some pretty awful things about me. I was a slut, I seduced him, I framed him, all that fun stuff. I ended up having to be home-schooled for the rest of the semester. And then Mayor Mom and her pastor husband sued my family."

My jaw hardens. "Fuck no."

"Fuck yeah. They claimed that we caused their son emotional distress, slandered him, a bunch of other bullshit I can't remember. The judge didn't award them everything they wanted, but he decided that my parents had to pay for Aaron's family's legal fees. Which means they had to pay for *two* sets of legal fees."

Hannah visibly swallows. "Do you know how much our lawyer charged for every day he spent in court?"

I'm scared to hear it.

"Two grand." Her lips twist in a bitter smile. "And our lawyer was *cheap*. So imagine how much Mayor Mom's lawyer billed a day. My parents had to get that second mortgage *and* take out a loan to cover the leftover costs."

"Shit." I can literally feel my heart splinter in my chest. "I'm sorry."

"They're stuck in that fucking town because of me," Hannah says flatly. "Dad can't quit his job at the lumberyard because it's steady work and he needs the money. But at least he's working in the next town over. He and my mom can't drive into Ransom without dealing with dirty looks or nasty whispers. They can't sell the house because they'll lose money on it. They can't afford to see me this year. And I'm too much of an asshole to go back and see *them*. But I can't do it, Garrett. I can't ever go back there."

I don't blame her. Hell, I feel the same way about my father's house in Boston.

"Aaron's parents still live there. He still visits them every summer." She looks at me with a helpless expression. "How am I supposed to go back there?"

"Have you been back at all since you left for college?"

She nods. "Once. And halfway through that visit, my dad and I had to go to the hardware store, and we ran into two of the fathers of Aaron's friends, the pieces of shit who lied for him. One of the dads made a rude comment, something like, oh look, the slut and her father shopping for nails, because she sure likes to get nailed. Or something stupid like that. And my dad *snapped*."

I suck in a breath.

"He went after the man who said it, smashed his face in pretty good before the fight was broken up. And of course, a deputy just *happened* to be walking past the store at that moment, and he arrested my dad for assault." Hannah's lips tighten. "The charges were dropped when the hardware store owner came in and said my dad was provoked. I guess there are at least a couple honest people left in Ransom. But yeah, I haven't been back since. I'm scared that if I do, I might bump into Aaron and then... I don't know. *Kill* him for what he's done to my family."

Hannah rests her chin on my shoulder, and I can feel the

waves of sadness radiating off her body.

I have no idea what to say. Everything she described is so brutal, and yet...I understand. I know what it's like to hate someone that much, to run away because you're scared of what you might do if you see that person's face. What you might be capable of.

My voice is raspy as hell as I blurt out, "The first time my father hit me was on Halloween."

Hannah's head snaps up in shock. "What?"

I almost don't keep going, but after the story she just told me, I can't hold back. I need her to know that she's not the only one who's experienced that kind of anger and desperation. "I was twelve when it happened. It was a year after my mom died."

"Oh my gosh. I had no idea." Her eyes go wide, not with pity, but with sympathy. "I got the feeling you don't like your dad—I heard it in the way you talk about him—but I didn't realize it was because..."

"Because he beat the shit out of me?" I fill in, my tone dripping with resentment. "My father isn't the man he pretends to be for the world. Mr. Hockey Star, family man, all that charity work he does. He's perfect on paper, huh? But at home, he was...fuck, he was a monster."

Hannah's fingers are warm as she laces them through mine. I squeeze them, needing a physical distraction from the tight ache in my chest.

"I don't even know what I did to piss him off that night. I came home from trick-or-treating with my friends, and we must have spoken about something, he must have yelled about something, but I don't remember. All I remember is the black eye and the broken nose, and being so stunned that he'd actually laid a hand on me." I laugh callously. "After that, it happened on a regular basis. He never broke any bones, though. Nope, because that would lay me out, and he needed me to be able to play hockey."

"How long did it go on for?" she whispers.

"Until I got big enough to fight back. I'm lucky, I only got wailed on for three, maybe four years? My mother lived through it for fifteen. Well, assuming he started hitting her the day they met. She never told me how long it actually went on for. Honestly, Hannah?" I meet her eyes, ashamed of what I'm about to say.

"When she died of lung cancer..." I'm sick to my stomach now. "I was *relieved*. Because it meant she didn't have to suffer anymore."

"She could have left him."

I shake my head. "He would've killed her before he let that happen. Nobody leaves Phil Graham. Nobody divorces him, because that would leave a black stain on his pristine reputation, and he can't have that." I sigh. "He doesn't drink or have problems with substance abuse, if that's what you're wondering. He's just...sick, I guess. He loses his temper at the drop of a hat, and the only way he knows how to solve problems is with his fists. He's a fucking narcissist, too. I've never known anyone who is so full of himself, so fucking arrogant. My mother and I were just props to him. Trophy wife, trophy son. He doesn't give a shit about anyone but himself."

I have never told anyone about this before. Not Logan or Tuck. Not even Birdie, the master of keeping secrets. Anything related to my father, I keep to myself. Because the sad truth is, too many people out there would be tempted to sell the story to make a few bucks. It's not that I don't trust my friends, I do, but when you've already been disappointed by the one person you're supposed to trust most in your life, you're not exactly keen on giving people any kind of ammunition over you.

But I trust Hannah. I have faith that she won't tell anyone about this, and as my confession hangs in the air, it's like a load has been lifted off my chest.

"So yeah," I say roughly, "the last time I celebrated Hallo-fucking-ween, I got the shit kicked out of me by my own father. Not a happy memory, huh?"

"No, it's not." Her free hand rises to stroke my jaw, which is covered with stubble because I was too lazy to shave today. "But you know what my therapist used to tell me? The best way to forget a bad memory is to replace it with a good one."

"I'm pretty sure that's easier said than done."

"Maybe, but there's no harm in trying, is there?"

My breath lodges in my throat when she climbs into my lap. You'd think it would be impossible for me to get hard when we've just had the most depressing conversation known to man, but my dick thickens the moment her firm ass settles over it. The kiss she gives me is soft and sweet, and I groan in disappointment when her mouth suddenly leaves mine.

I don't stay disappointed for long, though, because the next thing I know, she's kneeling on the floor in front of me and freeing my cock from my sweatpants.

I've gotten a lot of blowjobs. That's not a brag, it's just the truth. But when Hannah's mouth finds me, my balls draw up tight and my cock throbs with excitement, pulsing like it's the first time a girl's tongue has ever touched it.

The tip of my dick damn near blows off when the wet heat of her mouth surrounds me. One small, delicate hand caresses my thigh as she works me over with her mouth. Her other hand is curled tightly around my shaft, her thumb rubbing the sweet spot under the head of my dick, and each long suck pushes me deeper into pure, blissful oblivion.

My hips start to move. I can't stop them. Can't stop myself from driving deeper into her mouth and tangling my fingers in her hair to guide her. She doesn't seem to mind, though. My frantic thrusts bring a moan to her lips, and the sexy sound vibrates through my shaft and zings up my spine.

The hot suction drives me crazy. I can't remember a time when I didn't want this girl. When I wasn't fucking *desperate* for her.

It's only when I open my eyes that I register where we are. My roommates are at a party, but we have an early morning practice and a game tomorrow, which means they won't be out late tonight. Which means they could walk into the living room at any second.

I touch Hannah's cheek to stop her. "Let's go upstairs. I have no idea when the guys are coming home."

She stands up without a word and holds out her hand to me.

I take it, and then I lead her upstairs.

Hannah

Garrett leaves the light off.

He locks the door behind us, and I can see his eyes shining in the darkness. He strips so fast it makes me laugh, and then he's naked in front of me, his muscular body a shadowy blur as he takes a step toward me.

"Why are you still dressed?" he grumbles.

"Because not everybody is as proficient at getting naked as you are."

"It's not that difficult, babe. Here, let me help you."

I shiver when he snakes both hands beneath my shirt and slowly drags it up to my collarbone. He plants a soft kiss between my bra cups before pulling the shirt over my head. Rough fingertips skim my hips and tickle the top of my mound as he drops to his knees, drawing the cotton fabric of my yoga pants down with him.

All I can see is his dark head hovering inches from my thighs, and it's such an erotic sight, so fucking hot, that I can hardly breathe. When his mouth grazes the sensitive nub that is already swelling with desire, a bolt of pleasure nearly knocks me off my feet, and I grip the top of his head to steady myself.

"Okay, nope," I announce. "I'm never gonna be able to stay upright if you're doing that to me."

With a chuckle, Garrett stands up and scoops me into his arms as if I weigh absolutely nothing.

We land on the bed with a thud, laughing as we lie on our sides facing each other. We're both naked and it feels like the most natural thing in the world.

When he speaks, it's so nonsensical I'm genuinely caught off-guard. "I thought your name started with an M."

"You thought my name was *Mannah*?"

Garrett snickers. "No, I thought your name was Mona, or Molly, or Mackenzie. Anything with an M."

I don't know whether to be insulted or amused. "Okay…"

"For almost two months, Hannah. I went two months without knowing your name."

"Well, we didn't know each other."

"You knew *my* name."

I sigh. "Everyone knows your name."

"How did I go so long without noticing you, damn it? Why did it take seeing a stupid A on your midterm to make me notice?"

He sounds so genuinely upset that I scoot closer and kiss

him. "It doesn't matter. You know me now."

"I do," he says fiercely, and then he slides lower and captures one of my nipples in his mouth. "I know that when I do *this...*" he sucks hard, a moan flies out of my mouth, and he releases my nipple with a wet *pop.* "...you moan loud enough to wake the dead. And I know that when I do *this*, your hips are going to start rocking, like they're searching for my cock." He licks my other nipple, flicking his tongue over it, and sure enough, my hips rock involuntarily and my sex clamps around aching emptiness.

Garrett props himself up on one elbow, his biceps flexing against my shoulder. "I also know that I like you," he says gruffly.

A laugh shudders out. "I like you too."

"I'm serious. I really fucking like you."

I'm not sure how to respond, so I simply grab the back of his head and bring him down for a kiss. After that, everything becomes a blur. His hands and lips are everywhere, and a wave of pleasure sweeps me away to a beautiful place where only Garrett and I exist. He leaves me only to reach for the drawer next to his bed, and my pulse races because I know what he's getting, what's about to happen. The tear of plastic breaks the darkness and I glimpse a flash of him rolling on a condom, but rather than get on top of me and take control, he moves onto his back and hands me the reins.

"Ride me." His voice is raspy, trembling with need.

Gulping, I climb onto his lap and grip his penis with one hand. He's long and thick and imposing, but this position allows me to control how much of him to take. My pulse gallops like a racehorse as I sink down on him. I experience the most delicious stretching sensation as I lower myself inch by inch, until he's all the way inside, and suddenly I'm full. So damn full. My inner muscles clutch his erection, ripple around him, and he unleashes a desperate sound that rings through my body.

"Oh fuck." Garrett's fingers dig into my hips before I can move. "Tell me about your grandmother again."

"Now?"

His voice comes out strained. "Yes, now, because I don't know if anyone has ever told you this before, but you are tighter than a—okay, nope, not gonna think about how tight you are. What's Nana's name?"

"Sylvia." I make a valiant effort not to laugh.

His breathing grows audibly labored. "Where does she live?"

"Florida. Retirement home." Beads of sweat break out on my forehead, because Garrett is not the only one close to losing it here. The pressure between my legs is unbearable. My hips want to move. My body craves relief.

Garrett releases a long, ragged breath. "Okay. I'm good." His white teeth gleam in the shadows as he grins up at me. "Permission to proceed."

"Thank. God."

I lift myself up and slam down so hard we both groan.

This kind of blinding need is new to me. I ride him in a fast, furious pace, but it's still not enough. I need more and more and more, and eventually I'm just grinding against him, because I've discovered that when I lean forward and do that, my clit brushes his pubic bone and intensifies the pleasure.

My breasts are crushed against his rock-hard chest. He's so masculine, so fucking addictive. I kiss his neck, and find his skin hot beneath my lips. He's burning up, his heartbeat hammering wildly against my breasts, and when I lift my head slightly and see his face, I'm held captive by his expression, the taut stretch of his features and the intense pleasure glittering in his eyes. I'm so focused on him that when the orgasm hits me, it catches me by total surprise.

"*Ohhh*," I cry out, sagging against him as a rush of sweet bliss races through my body.

Garrett rubs my back as I gasp in pleasure. My sex contracts, milking his hard shaft, and his fingers dig between my shoulder blades as he curses. "Hannah...oh fuck, baby, that's hot."

I'm still catching my breath when he starts thrusting upward, fast and deep, his hips snapping up as he fills me, over and over again until finally he gives one final thrust and groans. His features tighten, dark brows drawn together as if he's in pain, but I know he's not. I kiss his neck again, sucking on his feverish flesh as he trembles beneath me, holding me so tight he traps all the air in my lungs.

After we've both recovered and the condom is disposed of, Garrett crawls beside me and spoons me from behind. The heavy weight of his arm makes me feel safe and warm and treasured. So does the way he flattens his palm on my belly and absently strokes my naked flesh. His lips press into the nape of my neck, and I can honestly say I've never been more content in my life.

"Stay over tonight?" he murmurs.

"Can't," I murmur back. "I have to return Tracy's car."

"Tell her it was stolen," he offers. "I'll vouch for you."

I laugh softly. "No way. She'd kill me."

Garrett rests his cheek on my shoulder, rotating his hips so that his semi-hard cock rubs against my butt. He sighs happily. "You've got the sweetest ass on the planet."

I have no idea how we got to this point. One day I was telling him to get lost, the next, I'm snuggling in bed with him. Life is so frickin' weird sometimes.

"Hey," he says a while later. "You don't work Friday nights, right?"

"No. Why?"

"We're playing Harvard tomorrow." He hesitates. "Maybe you want to come to the game?"

I hesitate too. I feel like I'm getting in over my head. I told him things tonight that I've never told anyone, and I'm pretty sure his confession about his father isn't something too many people know, either. I don't want to ask him what it all means, though. I'm terrified that I'm reading too much into it.

I'm terrified of making it real.

"You can take my Jeep," he adds, his voice gruff. "I'll be riding on the bus with the team, so it'll just be sitting in my driveway anyway."

"Can I bring Allie?"

"Sure." He kisses my shoulder, and a shiver runs through me. "Bring anyone you want. We could use the support, actually. Away games suck because nobody's ever cheering for us."

I swallow the odd little lump in my throat. "Okay. Yeah…I guess I can do that."

We go quiet again, and I suddenly become aware of the hard ridge poking against my butt. His very obvious erection makes me laugh. "Really, dude? Again?"

He chuckles. "What was that you were saying about my stamina the other day? Shame on you. *Dude*."

Still laughing, I roll over and plaster myself to his warm, hard body. "Round two?" I murmur.

His lips find mine. "Fuck yeah."

30

Hannah

"I can't believe this is happening," Dexter announces—for about the millionth time—from the backseat of Garrett's Jeep.

Next to Dex, Stella sighs and voices her agreement—also for the millionth time. "I know, right? We're in Garrett Graham's car. Part of me is tempted to go Carrie Underwood on it and carve my name into his leather seats."

"Don't you dare!" I order from the driver's seat.

"Relax, I won't. But I feel like if I don't leave my mark on this car, nobody will ever believe I was in it."

Hell, *I* can't believe she's in it. I wasn't surprised when Allie jumped on the chance to come to Cambridge with me, since she's still on the quest for details about Garrett, but I was startled when Stella and Dex insisted on coming along.

So far during this car ride, both of them have asked me at least twice if Garrett and I are dating. I've replied with my standard response—*we just hang out sometimes*. But it's getting harder to convince even myself of that.

We blast music for the rest of the drive. Dex and I sing along, and our harmonies are ridiculously awesome—why didn't I ask *him* to duet with me, damn it? Allie and Stella can't stay on key to save their lives, but they join in for the choruses, and we're all in high spirits when I pull into the parking lot of the hockey center.

I've never been to Harvard before, and I wish I had more time to explore the campus, but we're running late as it is, so I usher my friends inside because I don't want us to lose out on finding seats. I'm floored by how big and modern the arena is and how many people are here tonight. Luckily, we find four empty seats near the Briar team's side of the rink. We don't bother hitting up concessions since we ate a shit ton of corn chips in the car.

"Okay, so how does this game work again?" Dexter asks me.

I grin. "Seriously?"

"Yes, seriously. I'm a black kid from Biloxi, Han-Han. What the fuck do I know about hockey?"

"Fair enough."

As Allie and Stella chat about one of their acting classes, I give Dex a quick rundown of what he can expect. And yet when the players hit the ice, I realize my explanation hasn't done it justice. This is the first hockey game I've seen in person, and I don't expect the roar of the crowd, the deafening blare of the PA system, the lightning fast speed of the players.

Garrett's jersey is #44, but I don't need to look at the number to know which black-and-silver-clad player he is. He's the center of the starting line, and the second the ref drops the puck, Garrett wins the opening faceoff and snaps the puck back to Dean, who I thought was a wing but is apparently a defenseman.

I'm too busy watching Garrett to focus on any of the other players. He's...mesmerizing. He's already tall without skates on, so the added height makes him appear massive. And he's so fucking fast I have a tough time keeping my gaze on him. He flies down the ice, chasing the puck that Harvard has stolen from us and checking the opposing player like a pro. Briar takes an early lead, thanks to a goal by a player the announcer refers to as "Jacob Berderon," and it takes me a second to realize he means Birdie, the dark-haired senior I met at Malone's.

The clock on the scoreboard ticks down, but just when I think Briar will shut out Harvard in the first period, one of the opposing forwards gets a fast snapshot past Simms to tie the game.

As the period ends and the players disappear into their respective tunnels, Dex pokes me in the ribs and says, "You know what? This ain't half bad. Maybe I should start playing hockey."

"Can you skate?" I ask him.

"Naah. But it can't be that hard, right?"

I snort. "Stick to music," I advise. "Or if you're really

determined to get into sports, play football. Briar could use you."

From what I've heard, our football team is putting up the worst record the school has seen in years, winning only three of the eight games they've played so far. But Sean said they still have a chance to make it to the post-season if they, and I quote, "get their motherfucking shit together and start winning some motherfucking games." It makes me feel sorry for Beau, who I genuinely enjoyed talking to at the party.

The moment I think about Beau, Justin's face swooshes into my head like a gust of wind.

Shit.

We have a dinner date Sunday night.

How the *hell* did I forget about that?

Because you were too busy having sex with Garrett?

Yep, that's it.

I bite my lip as I debate what to do. I haven't thought about Justin all week, but that doesn't trump the fact that I've been thinking about him all *semester*. Something drew me to him in the first place, and I can't just ignore that. Besides, I don't even know what's happening between me and Garrett. He hasn't brought up the whole boyfriend/girlfriend thing. I don't know if I *want* to be his girlfriend.

I have a type when it comes to guys. Quiet, serious, moody. Creative, if I'm lucky. Plays music is always a plus. Smart. Sarcastic but not in a snide way. Unafraid to show his emotions. Someone who makes me feel…at peace.

Garrett has some of those qualities, but not all of them. And I'm not sure *peaceful* is the accurate word to describe how I feel when I'm with him. When we're arguing or shooting wisecracks back and forth, it's like my whole body is wired with electricity. And when we're naked…it's like an entire Fourth of July fireworks display going off inside me.

I think that might be a good thing?

Fuck, I don't know. My track record with guys isn't exactly a series of successes. What do I know about relationships? And how can I be certain that Justin *isn't* the guy I should be with if I don't go out with him at least once?

"So why do they call it the crease?" Dex asks in fascination after the second period commences. "And why does it sound so dirty?"

On my other side, Allie leans in to grin at Dexter. "Babe, *everything* about hockey sounds dirty. Five-hole? Poke check? Backdoor?" She sighs. "Come home with me one time and listen to my dad yell *Jam it in!* over and over again when he watches hockey, and then you can talk to me about dirty. Not to mention *uncomfortable.*"

Dex and I laugh so hard we almost fall out of our chairs.

Garrett

As the guys and I shuffle out of the guest locker room after the game, we're still riding the high of crushing the home team. Even though it's one of our sophomores who landed that last beauty of a goal that secured our win, I've decided that Hannah is my good luck charm and must now attend all of our games, because the last three times we played Harvard, we got our asses handed to us.

We agreed to meet outside the arena after the game, and sure enough, she's waiting there for me when I walk outside. She's with Allie, along with a dark-haired chick I don't recognize and an enormous black guy who I'm amazed isn't on the football team. Because he should be. Maxwell would come in his pants if he had a monster like that on his O-line.

The moment Hannah spots me, she wanders away from her friends and walks over to me. "Hey." She looks surprisingly shy, and she hesitates, as if she's not sure if she should hug or kiss me.

I solve her dilemma by doing both, and as I brush my lips over hers, I hear a victorious "I knew it!" echo from her friends' direction. The exclamation comes from the girl who isn't Allie.

I pull back to grin at Hannah. "Keeping us a secret from your friends, huh?"

"Us?" She raises her eyebrows. "I didn't realize we were an *us.*"

Now is definitely not the time to discuss the status of our relationship—if it even is one—so I just shrug and say, "How'd you like the game?"

"It was intense." She smirks at me. "I notice you didn't score a goal, though. Slacking much?"

My grin widens. "I sincerely apologize for that, Wellsy. I promise to do better next time."

"You'd better."

"I'll score a hat trick just for you, how about that?"

My teammates shuffle past us and head for the bus waiting twenty feet away, but I'm not ready to leave Hannah yet. "I'm glad you came."

"Me too." She sounds like she really means it.

"Are you busy tomorrow night?" The team has another game tomorrow, but it's an afternooner, and I'm dying to get Hannah alone again so we can...yeah. "I thought we could hang out after I get back from—" I stop talking when a shadow appears in my periphery vision, and my shoulders set in a tight line when I spot my father descending the front steps of the building.

This is the point of the evening I dread. Time for the big nod, followed by the silent walk-away.

As if on cue, I get the nod.

But not the walk-away.

My father startles the shit out of me by saying, "Garrett. A word."

His deep voice sends a chill up my spine. I fucking hate the sound of his voice. I hate the sight of his face.

I hate every goddamn thing about him.

Hannah's expression creases with concern when she sees my face. "Is that...?"

Instead of answering, I take a reluctant step away. "I'll be back in a minute," I mumble.

My father is already halfway down the parking lot. He doesn't even turn around to check if I'm following him. Because he's Phil fucking Graham, and he can't imagine someone *not* wanting to be around him.

Somehow my stiff legs carry me in his direction. I notice several of my teammates lingering at the door of the bus, watching us curiously. A few of them are visibly envious. Jesus. If they only knew what they were jealous of.

When I reach him, I don't bother with pleasantries. I just scowl and speak in a terse voice. "What do you want?"

Like me, he gets right to the point. "I expect you to come home for Thanksgiving this year."

My shock manifests itself in the form of a sharp laugh. "No, thanks. I'll pass."

"No, what you will do is come home." A dark look hardens his features. "Or I will drag you home."

I genuinely don't know what's happening right now. Since when does he give a shit whether I come home or not? I haven't been back once since I left for Briar. I'm in Hastings during the school year, and I spend my summers working sixty-hour weeks for a construction company in Boston and saving every last penny, which I then use to pay for rent and groceries because I don't want to take any more of my father's money than I absolutely have to.

"Why the hell do you care what I do for the holidays?" I mutter.

"You're needed at home this year." He's speaking through clenched teeth, as if he's enjoying this even less than I am. "My girlfriend is cooking dinner, and she requested your presence."

His girlfriend? I didn't even realize he had a girlfriend. And how fucking sad is it that I know nothing about my own father's life?

The way he phrased it doesn't escape me, either. *She* requested my presence. Not him.

I meet his eyes, the same shade of gray as my own. "Tell her I'm sick. Or hell, tell her I died."

"Don't test me, boy."

Oh, he's busting out the *boy*, huh? That's what he always called me right before his fists pummeled my gut, or smashed my face, or broke my nose for the hundredth fucking time.

"I'm not coming," I say coldly. "Deal with it."

He moves in closer, his eyes gleaming beneath the low brim of his Bruins cap as his voice lowers to a hiss. "Listen up, you ungrateful little shit. I don't ask much of you. In fact, I don't ask *anything* of you. I let you do whatever the fuck you want, I pay for your tuition, your books, your equipment."

The reminder makes my stomach seethe with anger. I keep a spreadsheet on my computer that documents everything he's ever paid for so that when I gain access to my trust, I'll know the precise amount to write on the check I plan on handing him before I tell him *good riddance*.

But tuition for next term needs to be paid in December, the month before my trust comes in. And I don't have enough in my savings account to cover the full amount.

Which means I'm stuck being indebted to him for a little while longer.

"All I expect in return," he finishes, "is that you play like the champion you are. The champion I *made* you." An ugly sneer twists his mouth. "Well, it's time to pay up, son. You *will* come home for Thanksgiving. Understood?"

Our eyes lock.

I could kill this man. If I knew I could get away with it? I would actually kill him.

"Understood?" he repeats.

I give a curt nod, and then I stalk away without looking back.

Hannah waits for me near the bus, worry clouding her green eyes. "Is everything okay?" she asks quietly.

I draw in a ragged breath. "Yeah. It's fine."

"Are you sure?"

"It's fine, babe. I promise."

"Graham, get your ass on the bus!" Coach shouts from behind me. "You're holding everyone up."

Somehow I manage to force a smile. "I've gotta go. Maybe we can hang out tomorrow after my game?"

"Call me when you're done. I'll see where I'm at."

"Sounds good." I drop a kiss on her cheek, then head for the bus, where Coach is impatiently tapping his foot.

He watches Hannah as she makes her way back to her friends, then shoots me a wry smile. "She's cute. Girlfriend?"

"No idea," I confess.

"Yeah, that's how it usually is with women. They hold all the cards and we're just clueless." Coach slaps me on the arm. "Come on, kid. Time to hustle."

I take my usual seat next to Logan near the front of the bus, and he gives me a funny look as I unzip my jacket and lean my head back.

"What?" I mumble.

"Nothing," he says lightly.

I've known the guy long enough to figure out that a "nothing" from Logan means something entirely different, but he pops in his iPod earbuds and proceeds to ignore me for most of the ride. It isn't until we're ten minutes from Briar that he abruptly yanks out his earphones and turns to look at me.

"Fuck it," he announces. "I'm just gonna come out and say it."

Wariness circles my insides like a turkey vulture. I sincerely hope he's not about to confess that he has a thing for Hannah, because shit will get awkward real fast if he does. I glance around, but most of my teammates are either sleeping or listening to music. The seniors in the back are laughing at something Birdie has just said. Nobody is paying any attention to us.

I lower my voice. "What's up?"

He lets out a weary breath. "I debated saying anything at all, but fuck, G, I don't like seeing anyone get played for a fool, especially my best friend. I figured I should wait until after the game, though." He shrugs. "I didn't want you to be distracted on the ice."

"What the hell are you talking about, man?"

"Dean and I ended up at Maxwell's house last night for his Halloween thing," Logan confesses. "Kohl was there, and..."

I narrow my eyes. "And what?"

Logan looks so uncomfortable that my guard soars another twenty feet. He's never one to beat around the bush, which means shit must be serious.

"He said he's going out with Wellsy this weekend."

My heart stops. "Bullshit."

"That's what I thought, but..." Another shrug. "He insisted it was true. I figured I should tell you about it, you know, just in case he's not talking out of his ass."

I swallow, my mind running a million miles a second. *Bullshit* continues to be my thought of choice, but a part of me isn't so sure. The whole reason Hannah is even in my life is because of fucking Kohl. Because she was interested in *Kohl*.

But that was *before*. Before she and I kissed—

She still went to the party to see him after the kiss.

Right. I gulp again. Well, it was after the kiss but before everything else. The sex. The secrets we shared with each other. All the *cuddling*.

Told you cuddling was a mistake, dude.

My inner cynic wreaks havoc on my brain, bringing a rush of weariness to my chest. No, Kohl had to have been bullshitting. There's no way Hannah would agree to go out on a date with him without telling me.

Right?

"Anyway, just thought you should know," Logan says.

It's damn difficult to speak past my tight-as-fuck throat, but I manage one mumble of a word. "Thanks."

31

Hannah

Garrett texts me just as I'm getting ready for bed. Allie and I literally walked through the door five minutes ago, and I'm surprised to hear from him again tonight. I figured he'd crash the moment he got home from the game.

Him: *Need to talk to u.*

Me: *Now?*

Him: *Yes.*

O-kay. It might be a text message, but it's hard not to extrapolate his tone. And his tone is most definitely pissed off.

Me: *Um, sure. Call me?*

Him: *Actually, I'm at your door.*

My head snaps toward my open doorway, half expecting to find him there. Then I feel silly because I realize he means the door to our dorm and not my bedroom. Still, this *must* be serious, because Garrett doesn't usually show up unannounced.

Queasiness eddies in my stomach as I walk past the common area to answer the door. Sure enough, Garrett is standing behind it. Still wearing his hockey jacket and sweatpants, as if he rushed right over instead of going home to change first.

"Hi," I greet him, gesturing for him to come inside. "What's going on?"

He gazes past me at the empty living room. "Where's Allie?"

"She went to bed."

"Can we talk in your room?"

The queasiness gets worse. I can't decipher his expression at all. His eyes are shuttered, and his tone is completely devoid of emotion. Does this have something to do with his father? I couldn't hear their conversation earlier, but their body language had conveyed some serious aggression. I wonder if maybe they—

"Are you going out with Justin this weekend?"

Garrett voices the demand the moment I close my bedroom door, and I realize in dismay that this has *nothing* to do with his dad.

And everything to do with me.

Surprise and insta-guilt war inside me as I meet his eyes. "Who told you that?"

"Logan. But he heard it from Kohl."

"Oh."

Garrett doesn't move. He doesn't unzip his jacket. He doesn't even blink. He just keeps his gaze locked on mine. "Is it true?"

I gulp. "Yes and no."

For the first time since he got here, his expression flashes with emotion—annoyance. "What the hell does that mean?"

"It means he asked me out, but I haven't decided if I'm going or not."

"Did you say you would?" There's a grim edge to his tone.

"Well, yes, but—"

Garrett's eyes blaze. "You actually said yes? When did he ask you?"

"Last week," I admit. "The day after Beau's party."

His face relaxes. Just slightly. "So it was before Dean's thing? Before you and I…?"

I nod.

"Okay." He takes a breath. "Okay. Not as bad as I thought." But then his features turn to stone again and his nostrils flare. "Wait—what do you mean, you haven't decided if you're going?"

I give a helpless shrug.

"You're not fucking going, Hannah!"

His sharp voice makes me wince. "Says who? *You*? Because last I checked, you and I aren't dating. We're just fooling around."

"Is that what you really—" He stops, his mouth twisting in a scowl. "You know what? I guess you're right. I guess we're just fooling around."

I can barely keep up with the jumbled thoughts racing through my brain. "You said you don't do girlfriends," I say weakly.

"I said I don't have time for a girlfriend," he shoots back. "But guess what—priorities change."

I falter. "So you're saying you want me to be your girlfriend?"

"Yeah, maybe that's what I'm saying."

My teeth sink into my lower lip. "Why?"

"Why what?"

"Why would you want that?" I bite my lip harder. "You're all one-track about hockey, remember? And besides, we argue too much."

"We don't argue. We bicker."

"It's the same thing."

He rolls his eyes. "No, it's not. Bickering is fun and good-natured. Arguing is—"

"Oh my God, we're arguing about the way we argue!" I interrupt, unable to stop from laughing.

Garrett's shoulders relax at the sound of my laughter. He takes a step toward me, searching my face. "I know you're into me, Wellsy. And I'm definitely into you. Would it really be so bad if we made this thing official?"

I gulp again. I hate being put on the spot, and I'm too confused to make sense of anything right now. Acting on impulse isn't something I do often. I never make decisions without giving them careful thought, and although other girls might break out in cartwheels at the thought of making things "official" with Garrett Graham, I'm more pragmatic than that. I didn't expect to like this guy. Or to have sex with him. Or to be in the position where he might be my boyfriend.

"I don't know," I finally say. "I mean, I didn't really think about you and me in terms of dating. I just wanted to..." My cheeks grow warm "...explore the attraction and see if...you know. But I didn't think any farther ahead than that." My confusion triples, turning my mind to mush. "I have no idea what this even is, or where it could go, or..."

As I trail off, I notice Garrett's expression, and the hurt in his eyes cuts into me like a knife.

"You don't know what this is or where it could go? Jesus, Hannah. If you..." He lets out a shaky breath, his broad shoulders sagging. "If you honestly don't know, then we're wasting our time. Because I know *exactly* what it is. I—" He halts so abruptly it gives me whiplash.

"You what?" I whisper.

"I—" He stops again. His gray eyes darken. "You know what? Forget it. I guess you're right. This was all about exploring the attraction." He sounds increasingly bitter. "I'm just your sex therapist, right? Actually, no, I'm your fucking fluffer."

"Fluffer?" I say blankly.

"Like in porn," he mutters. "They bring in the fluffer to suck off the dudes between takes so they stay hard." Anger colors his tone. "That was my job, right? To get you nice and hot for Kohl? To get you ready to bone him?"

Indignation prickles my skin. "One, that's disgusting. And two, that's not fair and you know it."

"I don't know a damn thing, apparently."

"He asked me out before I slept with you! And I probably wasn't even going to go!"

Garrett barks out a harsh laugh. "You *probably* weren't going to? Yeah. Thanks for that." He takes a step to the door. "You know what? Just go on the damn date. You got what you wanted from me. I guess *Justin* can take it from here."

"Garrett—"

But he's already gone. Not just gone, but making his exit known as he slams my door, thuds through the suite, and slams that door too.

I stare at the empty space he was taking up a second ago.

I know exactly what it is.

Garrett's hoarse words echo in my head, and a vise of emotion constricts my heart, because I'm pretty sure I know exactly what it is too.

And I'm scared that because of my split-second moment of indecision, I just threw it all away.

32

Garrett

The temperature seems to have dropped twenty degrees from when I walked into Bristol House to when I stormed out of it. A frigid gust of wind blasts me in the face and chills the tips of my ears as I trudge toward the parking lot.

See? *This* is why I avoid the whole girlfriend drama. I should be over the fucking moon tonight because the team crushed Harvard. Instead, I'm pissed off and frustrated and more upset than I expected to be. Hannah's right—we were just fooling around. Same way I was fooling around with Kendall, or the chick before her, or the chick before that. I didn't even bat an eye when I ended it with any of them, so why the hell am I so bummed right now?

Thank fuck I got out of there, though. I had been seconds away from making a complete fool of myself. Saying things I shouldn't be saying, maybe even *begging*. Jesus. If that's not a sign of some serious pussy-whipping right there then I don't know what is.

I'm halfway to my Jeep when I hear Hannah call out my name.

My chest clenches. I turn around and see her racing down the path from Bristol to the lot. She's still in her PJ's—plaid pants and a black T-shirt with yellow music notes decaled on the front.

I'm tempted to keep walking, but the sight of her bare arms and cold-flushed cheeks pisses me off even more than our fight had. "Jesus Christ, Hannah," I mutter when she reaches me. "You're gonna catch a cold."

"That's a myth," she shoots back. "Cold weather doesn't cause colds."

But she's visibly shivering, and when she wraps her arms around herself and starts rubbing her bare skin to keep warm, I rumble in annoyance and hurriedly unzip my jacket.

Gritting my teeth, I drape the coat over her shoulders. "Here."

"Thanks." She looks as annoyed as I feel. "What the hell is wrong with you, Garrett? You can't just storm off in the middle of a serious discussion!"

"There was nothing left to discuss."

"Bullshit." She angrily shakes her head. "You didn't even let me talk!"

"Yes, I did," I answer flatly. "And trust me, you said plenty."

"I can barely remember *what* I said. You know why? Because you totally caught me off-guard and didn't even give me a second to *think* about it."

"What's there to think about? You're either into me, or you're not."

Hannah makes a frustrated noise. "You're not being fair again. Just because *you* suddenly decide you're ready for a relationship and that we should be together doesn't mean that I'm going to squeal like a sorority girl and say, *wheee, yay!* You clearly had time to think about it, and absorb it, but you didn't give me any time at all. You just barged in and made accusations and ran out."

I experience a pang of guilt. She has a point. I *did* come over tonight fully knowing what I wanted from her.

"I'm sorry I didn't tell you about the Justin date," she says quietly. "But I'm not going to apologize for needing more than five frickin' seconds to think about the possibility of you and me being a couple."

My breath comes out in a white puff that quickly gets carried away by the wind. "I'm sorry I ran off," I concede. "But I'm not sorry that I want to be with you."

Those beautiful green eyes probe my face. "Do you still want that?"

I nod. Then I gulp. "Do you?"

"Depends." She slants her head. "Will we be exclusive?"

"Fuck yeah," I say without hesitation. The thought of her

seeing anyone else is like a machete to the gut.

"Are you okay with taking it slow?" She shifts awkwardly. "Because with the showcase coming up, and the holidays, and exams, and your game schedule...we'll both start to get busy and I can't promise to see you every second of the day."

"We see each other when we see each other," I say simply.

I'm surprised by how calm I sound, how composed I'm staying when there's a herd of excited butterflies thumping in my stomach and shouting *hells yeah* at top-volume. Jeez. I'm about to complicate my life by inviting a girlfriend into it, yet somehow I'm one hundred percent cool with that.

"Then okay." Hannah smiles at me. "Let's make it official."

A dark cloud obscures some of my happiness. "What about Justin?"

"What about him?"

"You told him you'd go out with him," I say through clenched teeth.

"Actually, I canceled the date before I came out here."

The dumb butterflies inside me take flight again. "You did?"

She nods.

"So you're not all hot for him anymore?"

Humor dances in her eyes. "I'm hot for *you*, Garrett. Only you."

Just like that, my anxiety dissolves into a burst of pure joy that brings a grin to my lips. "Damn right you are."

Rolling her eyes, she moves in and rubs her cold cheek against my chin. "Now can we please go inside? I'm freezing my butt off and I need my fluffer to warm me up."

I narrow my eyes. "Excuse me?"

She blinks innocently. "Oh, I'm sorry. Did I say fluffer?" Her smile lights up her whole face. "I meant *boyfriend*."

Sweetest words I've ever heard in my life.

33

Hannah

Life is good.

Life is wonderfully, amazingly, *scarily* good.

These past two weeks of dating Garrett have been a blur of laughter and cuddling and hot sex, intermingled with real life events like classes and studying, rehearsals and hockey games. Garrett and I forged a connection that caught me by surprise, but even though Allie continues to tease me about my sudden about-face when it comes to the guy, I don't regret my decision to date him and see where things go. So far, it's been working out great.

But see, here's the thing about life. When it's *this* good?

Something inevitably goes bad.

"I know this is an inconvenience," says Fiona, my performing arts advisor. "But I'm afraid there's nothing I can do except advise you to speak directly to Mary Jane and—"

"No way," I cut in, my stiff fingers curling around the arms of my chair. I stare at the pretty blond woman across the desk, and wonder how she can possibly describe this atom bomb of a disaster as an *inconvenience.*

And she wants me to talk to Mary Jane?

Fuck. That.

Because why the *fuck* would I talk to the stupid, brainwashed bitch who just ruined any chance I had of winning a scholarship?

I'm still reeling from what Fiona told me. Mary Jane and Cass *dumped* me. They actually got permission to kick me out of the duet so that Cass can sing it as a solo.

What the *hell*.

Yet in the back of my mind, I'm not even surprised. Garrett had warned me something like this could happen. I had worried about it myself. But never in a million years had I expected Cass to do this *four weeks* before the showcase.

Or that my advisor would be *totally fucking cool with it*.

I grit my teeth. "I'm not talking to Mary Jane. It's obvious she's made up her mind about this."

Or rather, that *Cass* had made it up for her, when he'd cajoled her into speaking to our respective advisors and blubbering about how her composition is suffering in its duet form and that she's pulling it out of the showcase if it's not a solo. Of course, Cass had quickly pointed out that it would be egregious to waste a perfectly good song, and he'd *graciously* offered to let me sing it. At which point, Mary Jane insisted that it should be sung by a male voice.

Fuck you very much, MJ.

"So what am I supposed to do now?" I ask in a tight voice. "I don't have time to learn a new song and work with a new songwriter."

"No, you don't," Fiona agrees.

Normally I appreciate her no-nonsense approach, but today it makes me want to slug her.

"Which is why, given the circumstances, Cass's advisor and I agreed to bend the rules for you. You won't be teaming up with a composition major. We've agreed—and the faculty head signed off on it—that you can sing one of your own compositions. I know you have a lot of original songs in your repertoire, Hannah. And in fact, I think this is a great opportunity for you to showcase not just your voice, but your songwriting abilities." She pauses. "However, you'll only be eligible to win the performance scholarship, since composition isn't your major."

My mind continues to spin like a carousel. Yes, there are a few originals I can sing, but none of them are even close to being performance-ready.

"Why isn't Cass being penalized for this?" I demand.

"Look, I can't say I approve of what Cass and Mary Jane have done, but unfortunately, this is one of the drawbacks of duet work." Fiona sighs. "Every year there's at least one duet partnership that breaks down right before the showcase. Do you remember Joanna Maxwell? She graduated last year?"

Beau's sister.

I nod.

"Well, her duet partner bailed *three days* before the senior showcase," Fiona confides.

I blink in surprise. "Really?"

"Oh, yeah. Let's just say it was pure chaos around here for those three days."

My spirits lift, just a bit, when I remember that not only did Joanna win the scholarship, she also caught the eye of an agent who later got her that audition in New York.

"You don't need Cassidy Donovan, Hannah." Fiona's voice is firm, ringing with reassurance. "You thrive as a solo performer. *That's* your strength." She gives me a pointed look. "As I recall, that's exactly what I advised at the beginning of the term."

Guilt warms my cheeks. Yep. I can't deny it. She *had* told me her concerns about the project from the start, but I had allowed Cass to convince me that we would be a powerhouse together.

"You'll have whatever you need to prepare," she adds. "We'll rearrange the schedule so you'll have access to rehearsal space whenever you need it, and if you require accompaniment, any number of orchestra students can help you out. Is there anything else you think you might need?" A tiny smile tugs on her lips. "Trust me, Cass's advisor isn't happy about this either, so if there's something you want, tell me now and I can probably make it happen for you."

I'm about to shake my head, but then something occurs to me. "Actually, there is something I want. I want Jae. I mean, Kim Jae Woo."

Fiona furrows her brow. "Who?"

"The cellist." I stick out my chin in fortitude. "I want the cellist."

Garrett

"I *cannot* believe he did that!" Allie sounds livid from her side of the booth, her blue eyes blazing as she looks up at Hannah.

My girlfriend wears that I'm-trying-really-hard-not-to-show-how-furious-I-am-right-now expression, but I can sense the volatile emotions radiating from her body. She smooths out the bottom of her apron. "Really? Because I can totally believe it," Hannah answers. "I bet this was his plan all along. Drive me crazy for two months and then screw me over right before the show."

"Fuckin' Cass," Hannah's friend Dexter mutters from his seat next to Allie. "Someone needs to give that boy a good ass-kicking." Dex glances at Logan and me. "Can't one of you hockey players do it? Rough him up a bit?"

"Gladly," Logan says cheerfully. "What's his address?"

I jab my friend in the side. "We're not beating anybody up, jackass. Not unless you want to face Coach's wrath—and a suspension." I turn to Hannah with a rueful look. "Don't worry, I'm beating him up in my head, baby. That counts, right?"

She laughs. "Sure. I'll allow it." She tucks her order pad in her apron pocket. "I'll be right back."

As Hannah heads for the counter, I admire her ass for so long it gets me three loud snickers from my companions. And don't get me started on how weird it is to be sharing a booth with my best friend and *Hannah's* best friends.

I was certain that Hannah's artsy friends would be all condescending and frigid around me—especially after she told me what they think about Briar's jock crowd—but I think my natural charm has won them over. Allie and Dex already treat me like we've been buds for years. Stella, who discovered her passion for hockey during the Harvard game, now texts me every other day to ask hockey questions. And while that dude Jeremy is still a bit snarky whenever I see him, his girlfriend Megan is pretty cool, so I'm willing to give him a few more chances to not be a dick.

"She's pissed," Logan remarks as he watches Hannah chatting with the cook behind the pick-up counter.

"She should be," replies Dex. "Seriously, what kind of selfish douchetard dumps his duet partner right before a show?"

Logan snickers. "Douchetard? I'm totally stealing that phrase."

"She'll be fine," Allie says confidently. "Hannah's originals are awesome. She doesn't need Cass."

"No one needs Cass," Dex agrees. "He's like the human being equivalent of syphilis."

As everyone laughs, I tune them out and focus my attention on Hannah. I can't help but remember the first time I came to Della's, with the sole purpose of persuading Hannah to tutor me. It was only a little more than a month ago, yet I feel like I've known her forever.

I don't know what I was thinking taking that whole anti-girlfriend position. Because having a girlfriend? Fucking rocks. Seriously. I get to have sex whenever I want without having to work for it. I have someone to vent to after a shitty day or a devastating loss on the ice. I can make the worst jokes on the planet and chances are Hannah will laugh at them.

Oh, and I love being with her, plain and simple.

Hannah returns to our booth carrying our drink orders. Or rather, Allie and Dex's drink orders. Logan and I asked for sodas, but what we get is water.

"Where's my Dr. Pepper, Wellsy?" Logan whines.

She levels him with a stern look. "Do you know how much sugar is in a soft drink?"

"A perfectly acceptable amount and therefore I should drink it?" supplies Logan.

"Wrong. The answer is *too damn much*. You're playing Michigan in an hour—you can't get all hopped up on sugar before a game. You'll get a five-minute energy boost and then crash halfway through the first period."

Logan sighs. "G, why is your girl our nutritionist now?"

I pick up my water glass and take a sip of defeat. "Do *you* want to argue with her?"

Logan looks at Hannah, whose expression clearly conveys: *you'll get a soda over my dead body*. Then he looks back at me. "No," he says glumly.

34

Hannah

My phone meows just after midnight, but I'm not asleep. In fact, I'm not even in my PJ's yet. The second I came home after work, I grabbed my guitar and got right back to work again. Now that Cass has thrown a selfish, vindictive wrench into my life, things like "sleep" and "relaxing" and "not panicking" don't exist anymore. For the next month, I'm pretty much going to be a walking basket case, unless I magically find a way to juggle school, work, Garrett, and singing without having a nervous breakdown.

I put down the acoustic and check the screen. It's Garrett.

Him: *Can't sleep. You up?*

Me: *Is this a booty call?*

Him: *No. Do u want it to be?*

Me: *No. I'm rehearsing. Totally stressed.*

Him: *All the more reason for this to be a booty call.*

Me: *Keep it in your pants, dude. Why can't u sleep?*

Him: *Whole body hurts.*

Sympathy flutters through my belly. Garrett had called earlier to say they'd lost the game, and apparently he'd taken some brutal hits tonight. Last time we talked, he was still icing his entire torso.

I'm too lazy to type, so I dial his number and he answers on the first ring.

His husky voice slides into my ear. "Hey."

"Hey." I lean back against my pillow. "I'm sorry I can't come over and kiss all your boo-boos, but I'm working on the song."

"It's okay. There's only one boo-boo I want you to kiss, and you sound too distracted for that." He pauses. "I'm talking about my dick, by the way."

I choke down a laugh. "Yep. I got that. No need to clarify."

"Did you decide which song you're going to sing?"

"I think so. It's the one I sang to you last month when we were studying. Do you remember it?"

"Yeah. It was sad."

"Sad is good. Packs more of an emotional punch." I hesitate. "I forgot to ask you earlier—was your dad at the game?"

A pause. "He never misses one."

"Did he bring up Thanksgiving again?"

"No, thank fuck. He doesn't even look at me when we lose, so I wasn't expecting him to be chatty." Garrett's voice is thick with bitterness, and then I hear him clear his throat. "Put me on speakerphone. I want to hear you sing."

My heart squeezes with emotion, but I try to hide the response by donning a casual tone. "You want me to sing you a lullaby? Aren't you precious."

He chuckles. "My chest feels likes it got hit by a truck. I need a distraction."

"Fine." I hit the speaker button and reach for my guitar. "Feel free to hang up if you get bored."

"Baby, I could watch *you* watching paint dry, and I still wouldn't be bored."

Garrett Graham, my own personal sweet-talker.

I settle the acoustic on my lap and sing the song from the top. My door is closed, and although the walls in the dorm are paper-thin, I'm not worried about waking Allie. The first thing I did after Fiona told me about the duet was give Allie a pair of ear plugs and warn her that I'm going to be singing late into the night until the showcase.

Weirdly enough, I'm not angry anymore. I'm *relieved.* Cass

had turned our duet into the kind of flashy, jazz-hands performance that I despise, so as infuriating as it is to get dumped, I've decided I'm better off not having to sing with him.

I run through the song three times, until my voice goes hoarse and I finally have to stop to chug the bottle of water on my nightstand.

"Still here, you know."

Garrett's voice startles me. Then I laugh, because I honestly forgot he was on the line. "I couldn't put you to sleep, huh? I don't know if I should be flattered or insulted."

"Flattered. Your voice gives me chills. Makes it impossible to fall asleep."

I smile, even though he can't see me. "I need to figure out what to do about that last chorus. End high or low on the last note? Oooh, and maybe I should switch up the middle section too. You know what? I have an idea. I'm hanging up now so I can figure it out, and you need to go to sleep. Night, dude."

"Wellsy, wait," he says before I can hang up.

I take the phone off speaker and bring it to my ear. "What's up?"

I'm greeted by the longest pause ever.

"Garrett? You there?"

"Uh, yeah. Sorry. Still here." A heavy breath reverberates through the line. "Will you come home with me for Thanksgiving?"

I freeze. "Are you serious?"

Another pause, even longer than the first. I almost expect him to rescind the invitation. And I don't think I'd be upset if he did. Knowing what I do about Garrett's father, I'm not sure if I can sit across a dinner table from that man without reaching over to strangle him.

What kind of man hits his own son? His *twelve-year-old* son.

"I can't go back there alone, Hannah. Will you come?"

His voice cracks on those last words, and so does my heart. I let out a shaky breath and say, "Of course I will."

35

Hannah

Garrett's father's house is not the mansion I expected it to be, but a brownstone in Beacon Hill, which I suppose is Boston's equivalent of mansion living. The area is gorgeous, though. I've been to Boston several times, but never to this ritzy part of it, and I can't help but admire the beautiful nineteenth-century row houses, brick sidewalks and quaint gas lamps lining the narrow streets.

Garrett barely said a word during the two-hour drive into the city. Tension has been rolling off his suit-clad body in steady, palpable waves, which has only succeeded in making me even more nervous. And yes, I said *suit-clad*, because he's wearing black trousers, a crisp white dress shirt, and a black jacket and tie. The expensive material fits his muscular body like a dream, and even the perma-scowl on his face doesn't take away from his sheer hotness.

Apparently his father demanded he wear a suit. And when Phil Graham found out his son was bringing a date, he requested that I also dress formally, hence my fancy blue dress, which I wore to last year's spring showcase. The silky material falls to my knees, and I paired it with four-inch silver heels that made Garrett grin when he showed up at my door, as he informed me that he might now actually be able to kiss me standing up without getting a crick in his neck.

We're greeted at the front doors not by Garrett's dad, but by a pretty blonde in a red cocktail gown that flutters around her ankles. She's also wearing a lacy black overlay with full sleeves, which I find odd because it's like a million degrees inside the house. Seriously, it's *hot* in here, and I waste no time shrugging out of my pea coat in the elegant parlor.

"Garrett," the woman says warmly. "It's wonderful to finally meet you."

She appears to be in her mid-thirties, but it's hard to judge because she's got what I like to call "old eyes." Those deep, wise eyes that reveal a person has lived through several lifetimes already. I'm not sure why I get that sense. Nothing about her elegant outfit or perfect smile hints that she's seen hard times, but the trauma survivor in me immediately feels an odd kinship with her.

Garrett answers in a brusque, but polite voice. "It's nice to meet you too…?"

He lets that hang, and her pale blue eyes flicker with unhappiness, as if she's realized that Garrett's father hadn't told his son the name of the woman he was dating.

Her smile falters for a beat before steadying. "Cindy," she fills in. "And you must be Garrett's girlfriend."

"Hannah," I supply, leaning in to shake her hand.

"It's a pleasure to meet you. Your father is in the sitting room," she tells Garrett. "He's very excited to see you."

Neither Cindy nor I miss the sardonic snort that sounds from Garrett's direction. I squeeze his hand in a silent warning to be nice, all the while wondering what she means by "sitting room." I always assumed that sitting rooms were where rich people gathered around to drink their sherry or brandy before sauntering into their thirty-seat dining rooms.

But the interior of the brownstone is a lot larger than it looks from the outside. We walk past two rooms—a living room, and yet another living room—before we reach the sitting room. Which looks like…another living room. I think about my parents' cozy split level in Ransom and how that measly three-bedroom house has nearly bankrupted them, and it brings a rush of sorrow. It doesn't seem fair that a man like Phil Graham should have all these rooms and the money to furnish them, while good people like my parents are working so hard to keep their roof over their heads.

When we walk in, Garrett's dad is in a brown wing-backed chair, balancing a tumbler of amber liquid on his knee. Like Garrett, he's wearing a suit, and the resemblance between them is jarring. They have the same gray eyes, the same strong jaw and chiseled face, but Phil's features seem sharper, and he has wrinkles around his mouth, as if he scowled one too many times and his muscles froze in that position.

"Phil, this is Hannah," Cindy says cheerily as she settles on the plush loveseat next to Phil's chair.

"It's nice to meet you, Mr. Graham," I say politely.

He nods at me.

That's it. A *nod.*

I have no idea what to say after that, and my palm goes clammy in Garrett's hand.

"Have a seat, you two." Cindy gestures to the leather sofa near the electric fireplace.

I sit.

Garrett remains standing. He doesn't say a word to his father. Or to Cindy. Or to me.

Oh fuck. If he's planning on keeping up this silent routine all night, then we're in for one long and awkward Thanksgiving.

Absolute silence stretches between the four of us.

I rub my damp hands on my knees and try to smile, but I feel like it might actually be a grimace. "So…no football?" I say lightly, glancing at the flat screen mounted on the wall. "I thought that was a Thanksgiving tradition." God knows it's all my family does when we go to Aunt Nicole's for the holiday. My uncle Mark is a rabid football fan, and even though the rest of us prefer hockey, we still have a good time watching the all-day game fest on TV.

Garrett, however, refused to show up any earlier than he had to, so the afternoon games have already been won and lost. I'm pretty sure the Dallas game is just starting, though.

Cindy is quick to shake her head. "Phil doesn't like football."

"Oh," I say.

Cue: more silence.

"So, Hannah, what are you majoring in?"

"Music. Vocal performance, to be exact."

"Oh," she says.

Silence.

Garrett rests his shoulder against the tall oak bookcase near the door. I sneak a peek in his direction and notice that his expression is completely vacant. I sneak a peek in Phil's direction and notice that his expression is the same.

Oh God. I don't think I'll be able to survive this night.

"Something smells wonderful—" I start.

"I should go check on the turkey—" Cindy starts.

We both laugh awkwardly.

"Let me help you with that." I practically dive to my feet, which is a big oh-no-no when you're wearing four-inch heels. I sway for one heart-stopping moment, terrified I'm going to topple over, but then my equilibrium steadies and I'm able to take a step without falling.

Yep, I'm a terrible girlfriend. Uncomfortable situations make me nervous and itchy, and as much as I want to stick by Garrett's side and help him through this hell of a night, I can't stomach the thought of being trapped in a room with two males whose animosity is tainting all the oxygen in the room.

Shooting Garrett an apologetic look, I trail after Cindy, who leads me into a large, modern kitchen with stainless steel appliances and black marble counters. The delicious aromas are stronger here, and there are enough tin-foil-covered dishes on the counter to feed an entire third-world country.

"Did you cook all this?" I exclaim.

She turns with a shy smile. "I did. I love to cook, but Phil rarely gives me the chance to do it. He prefers to dine out."

Cindy slips on a pair of plush mitts before opening the oven door. "So how long have you and Garrett been seeing each other?" she asks conversationally, setting the enormous turkey pan on the stovetop.

"About a month." I watch as she lifts the aluminum foil off the massive bird. "What about you and Mr. Graham?"

"A little over a year now." Her back is turned to me, so I can't see her expression, but something about her tone raises my guard. "We met at a charity event I was organizing."

"Oh. Are you an event planner?"

She sticks a thermometer into the breast area of the turkey, then the legs, and her shoulders visibly relax. "It's ready," she murmurs. "And to answer your question, I *was* an event planner, but I sold my company a few months ago. Phil said he misses me too much when I'm at work."

Um. What?

I can't imagine ever giving up my job because the man in

my life *misses me too much when I'm at work*. To me, that's a red flag if I ever saw one.

"Oh. That's...nice." I gesture to the counter. "Do you want me to help you heat everything up? Or are we not eating right away?"

"Phil expects to eat the moment the turkey is ready." She laughs, but it sounds forced. "When he sets a schedule, he expects everyone to follow it." Cindy points to the large bowl by the microwave. "You can start by heating up the potatoes. I still need to make the gravy." She holds up a gravy mix packet. "Usually I make it from scratch using the turkey juices, but we're strapped for time, so this will have to do."

She turns off the oven and places the turkey on the counter before turning her attention to the gravy. The wall over the stove is covered with hooks of pots and pans, and as she reaches up to grab one, her lacy sleeves ride up, and either I'm imagining it, or there's bluish-black bruising on the undersides of both her wrists.

As if someone grabbed her. Hard.

Her arms come down and the sleeves cover her forearms, and I decide that the black lace was playing tricks on my eyes.

"Do you live here with Mr. Graham or do you have your own place?" I ask as I wait for the mashed potatoes to finish nuking.

"I moved in with Phil about two weeks after we met," she admits.

I *have* to be imagining things, because there's no way that chord in her voice is bitterness, right?

"Oh. That's kind of impulsive. You guys hardly even knew each other, huh?"

"No. We didn't."

Okay, I'm not imagining it.

That's *absolutely* bitterness.

Cindy glances over her shoulder, an unmistakable flicker of sorrow in her eyes. "I'm not sure anyone ever told you this, but spontaneity has the tendency to backfire on you."

I have no clue how to respond.

So I say, "Oh."

I get the feeling I'm going to be saying that word a lot tonight.

36

Garrett

He hits her.

The son of a bitch hits her.

It only takes thirty minutes in Cindy's company for me to reach that conclusion. To pick up on the signs. I see it in the way she flinches whenever he touches her. Just slightly, and probably unnoticeable to anyone else, but it's the same way my mother would respond each time he came near her. It was almost like she was anticipating the next strike of his fist, or his palm, or his fucking foot.

But that's not the only warning sign Cindy is broadcasting. The long-sleeved lacy thing over her red dress is a dead giveaway—I've fucked enough sorority girls to know that you don't match white heels with a black jacket. And then there's the spark of fear that flicks through her eyes whenever my father so much as twitches in his chair. The sad droop of her shoulders when he tells her that the gravy is too watery. The slew of compliments she gives him because she's obviously trying to keep him happy. No, to keep him *calm*.

We're halfway through dinner, my tie is choking the life out of me, and I'm not certain I can control my rage anymore. I don't think I can make it to dessert without attacking the old man and demanding to know how he can possibly do this to another woman.

Cindy and Hannah are chatting about something. I have no clue what it is. My fingers grip my fork so tight I'm surprised it doesn't snap in half.

He tried to talk to me about hockey earlier when Hannah

and Cindy were in the kitchen. I tried talking back. I'm sure I even managed to form proper sentences, with subjects and predicates and all that shit. But from the second Hannah and I walked into this godforsaken house, my mind has been somewhere else. Every room holds a memory that brings bile to my throat.

The kitchen is where he broke my nose for the first time.

Upstairs is where I got the brunt of it, usually in my bedroom, where I don't dare venture tonight because I'm scared the walls might close in on me.

The living room is where he slammed me against the wall after my eighth-grade league didn't make it to the playoffs. I noticed he hung a painting over the hole in the drywall, though.

"So yeah," Hannah is saying. "Now I'm singing a solo, which is what I should've done in the first place."

Cindy makes a sympathetic noise with her tongue. "This boy sounds like a selfish ass."

"Cynthia," my father says sharply. "Language."

There it is again—that flinch. The weak "I'm sorry" should come next, but to my surprise, she doesn't apologize.

"You don't agree, Phil? Imagine you were still playing for the Rangers and your goalie left you in the lurch right before the first game in the Stanley Cup series."

My father's jaw stiffens. "The two situations aren't comparable."

She quickly backpedals. "No, I guess they're not."

I shovel a forkful of mashed potatoes and stuffing into my mouth.

My father's cool gaze travels to Hannah. "How long have you been seeing my son?"

From the corner of my eye, I see her shift in discomfort. "A month."

He nods, almost like he's pleased to hear it. When he speaks again, I realize precisely what he's pleased about. "It's not serious, then."

Hannah frowns.

I do, too, because I know what he's thinking. No, what he's *hoping*. That this thing with Hannah is just a fling. That it'll fizzle out sooner rather than later and then I can go back to focusing exclusively on hockey.

But he's wrong. Hell, I was wrong, too. I thought having a

girlfriend would distract me from my goals and split my focus, but it hasn't. I love being with Hannah, but I haven't lost sight of hockey, either. I'm still bringing it in practice, still smoking my opponents on the ice. This last month has shown me that I can have Hannah *and* hockey in my life, and give both of them the attention they deserve.

"Did Garrett tell you he's planning on entering the draft after graduation?" my father asks.

Hannah nods in response.

"Once he gets drafted his schedule will become even more hectic. I imagine yours will, too." My father purses his lips. "Where do you see yourself after graduation? Broadway? Recording an album?"

"I haven't decided yet," she replies, reaching for her water glass.

I notice that her plate is empty. She's finished all her food, but hasn't asked for seconds. Neither have I, though I can't deny that Cindy's cooking is fucking fantastic. I haven't eaten a turkey that juicy in years.

"Well, the music industry is a tough one to break into. Requires a lot of hard work and perseverance." My father pauses. "And an incredible amount of focus."

"I'm well aware of that." Hannah's lips form a tight line, as if she has a million more things to say but is forcing herself not to.

"Professional sports is the same way," my dad says pointedly. "Requires that same level of focus. Distractions can be costly." His head tips toward me. "Isn't that right, son?"

I reach for Hannah's hand and cover her knuckles with my palm. "Some distractions are worth it."

His nostrils flare.

"Looks like everyone has finished eating," Cindy blurts out. "How about some dessert?"

My stomach churns at the thought of spending even another second in this house. "Actually, Hannah and I have to go," I say roughly. "The weather forecast called for snow tonight so we want to head back before the roads get bad."

Cindy's head swivels to the floor-to-ceiling window on the other side of the dining room. Beyond the glass, there isn't a speck of white in the air or on the ground.

But God bless her, she doesn't comment on the snow-free

state of the street. If anything, she looks almost relieved that this uncomfortable evening is about to come to an end.

"I'll clear the table," Hannah offers.

Cindy nods. "Thanks, Hannah. I appreciate it."

"Garrett." My father scrapes his chair back. "A word."

Then he walks out.

Fuck him and his fucking *words*. The bastard didn't even thank his girlfriend for the lovely meal she prepared. I'm so goddamn sick of this man, but I swallow my anger and follow him out of the dining room.

"What do you want?" I demand once we enter his study. "And don't bother ordering me to stay for dessert. I came home for Thanksgiving, we ate some turkey, and now I'm leaving."

"I don't give a shit about dessert. We need to talk about that girl."

"That girl?" I laugh harshly. "You mean Hannah? Because she's not just some girl. She's my *girlfriend*."

"She's a liability," he snaps.

I roll my eyes. "How do you figure?"

"You lost two of your last three games!" he roars.

"And that's her fault?"

"Damn right it is! She's making you lose sight of the game."

"I'm not the only player on the team," I say flatly. "And I'm not the only one who made mistakes during those games."

"You took a costly penalty in the last one," he spits out.

"Yeah, I did. Big fucking deal. We're still number one in our conference. Still number two overall."

"Number two?" He's shouting now, his hands forming tight fists as he takes a step toward me. "And you're happy with being number *two*? I raised you to be number *one*, you little shit!"

Once upon a time, those blazing eyes and red cheeks would have made me flinch, too. But not anymore. Once I turned sixteen and gained two inches and forty pounds on my father, I realized I no longer had to be afraid of him.

I'll never forget the look in his eyes the first time I fought back. His fist had been coming toward my face, and in a moment of clarity, I realized I could *block* it. I didn't have to stand there and take the abuse anymore. I could dish it right back at him.

And I did. I still remember the satisfying crunch of my knuckles when they connected with his jaw. Even as he'd growled in fury, there'd been genuine shock—and *fear*—in his eyes as he'd stumbled backward from the force of the impact.

That was the last time he ever raised a hand to me.

"What are you going to do?" I taunt, nodding at his fists. "Hit me? What, you're tired of taking it out on that nice woman out there?"

His entire body goes stiffer than granite.

"You think I don't know you're using her as your punching bag?" I hiss out.

"Watch your fucking mouth, boy."

The fury in my gut boils over. "Fuck you," I hurl out. My breathing goes shallow as I stare into his enraged eyes. "How could you lay a hand on her? How could you lay a hand on *anyone*? What the *fuck* is the *matter* with you?"

He stalks toward me, stopping when we're a mere foot apart. For a second I think he might actually strike me. I almost *want* him to. That way I can strike back. I can smash my fists into his pathetic face and show him what it's like to get beat on by someone who's supposed to love you.

But my feet stay rooted in place, my hands pressed tightly against my sides. Because no matter how badly I want to do it, I will never lower myself to his level. I will never lose control of my temper and be like *him*.

"You need help," I choke out. "Seriously, old man. You need some fucking help, and I really hope you get it before you hurt that woman any more than you already have."

I stagger out of his study. My legs wobble so hard it's a miracle they manage to carry me all the way to the kitchen, where I find Hannah rinsing plates at the sink. Cindy is loading the dishwasher. Both women glance over at my entrance, and both their faces go pale.

"Cindy." I clear my throat, but the massive lump remains. "I'm sorry to steal Hannah away, but we have to go now."

After a long beat, the blonde's head jerks in a quick nod. "That's fine. I can do the rest."

Hannah shuts off the faucet and approaches me slowly. "Are you okay?"

I shake my head. "Can you go wait in the car? I need to talk to Cindy for a moment."

Rather than leave the kitchen, Hannah walks back to

Cindy, hesitates, then gives the woman a warm hug. "Thank you so much for dinner. Happy Thanksgiving."

"Happy Thanksgiving," Cindy murmurs with a strained smile.

I reach into the inner pocket of my jacket and extract my keys. "Here. Get it started for us," I tell Hannah.

She exits the room without another word.

Taking a breath, I cross the tiled floor and stand directly in front of Cindy. To my horror, she reacts with that tiny, fearful flinch I've been witnessing all night. As if this is a *like father, like son* situation. As if I'm going to…

"I'm not going to hurt you." My voice cracks like a fucking egg. I feel sick that I even have to assure her of that.

Panic floods her eyes. "What? Oh, honey, no. I didn't think…"

"Yes, you did," I say quietly. "It's okay. I'm not taking it personally. I know what it's like to…" I swallow. "Look, I don't have a lot of time here, because I need to get the hell out of this house before I do something I might regret, but I just need you to know something."

She uneasily lets go of the dishwasher door. "What is it?"

"I…" Another deep gulp and then I get right to the point, because really, neither one of us wants to be having this conversation. "He did it to me and my mom, too, okay? He abused us, physically and verbally, for years."

Her lips part, but she doesn't say a word.

My heart squeezes as I force myself to keep going. "He's not a good man. He's dangerous, and violent, and…sick. He's sick. You don't have to tell me what he's doing to you. Or hell, maybe I'm wrong and he's not doing anything—but I think he is, because I see it in the way you act around him. I acted that way too. Every move I made, every word I said…everything I did was rooted in fear, because I was desperate for him not to beat the shit out of me again."

Her stricken look is all the confirmation I need.

"Anyway." I inhale deeply. "I'm not going to drag you out of here over my shoulder, or call the cops and tell them there's domestic abuse going on in this house. It's not my place, and I won't interfere. But I need you to know a couple things. One—it's not your fault. Don't you ever blame yourself, because it's all on him. You did nothing to invite his criticism and his verbal attacks, and you didn't fail to meet his expectations because his expectations are fucking *impossible* to meet." My chest seizes so hard my ribs ache. "And two, if you ever need anything, anything at all, I want you to call me, okay? If you need to talk, or if you want to leave him and need someone to help you pack or move or whatever, call me. Or if he...does something and you need help, for fuck's sake, call me. Can you promise to do that?"

Cindy looks stunned. Completely and utterly stunned. Her blue eyes are glassy, and she starts blinking fast, as if she's trying to ward off tears.

The kitchen becomes as silent as a funeral home. She just stares at me, blinking wildly, the fingers of one hand toying with her sleeve.

After what feels like an eternity, she gives a shaky nod and whispers, "Thank you."

Heat blasts from the air vents when I slide into the driver's seat. Hannah has started the engine and she's already buckled up, as if she's as desperate to get away from here as I am.

I put the car in drive and speed away from the curb, needing to put distance between me and that brownstone. If I'm lucky enough to play for Boston one day, I plan on living as far away from Beacon Hill as possible.

"So...that was kind of brutal," Hannah remarks.

I can't stop the laugh that shudders out. "Kind of?"

She sighs. "I was trying to be diplomatic."

"Don't bother. That was a nightmare from start to finish." My fingers curl around the steering wheel so tightly my knuckles turn white. "He hits her."

There's a beat of silence, but when Hannah answers, it's with regret and not surprise. "I thought that might be the case. Her sleeves rode up in the kitchen and I thought I saw some bruises on her wrists."

The revelation sends a fresh bolt of anger whipping through me. Damn it. A part of me was still hoping I might be wrong about Cindy.

Silence settles between us as I head for the highway ramp. My hand rests on the gearshift, and Hannah covers it with hers.

She strokes my knuckles, her gentle touch easing some of the pressure in my chest.

"She was scared of me," I mumble.

This time, Hannah *does* sound surprised. "What are you talking about?"

"When I was alone in the kitchen with Cindy, I took a step closer and she flinched. She *flinched*, like she was scared I might hurt her." My throat clogs up. "I mean, I get it. My mom was jumpy, too. So was I. But…fuck. I can't believe she thought I was capable of hurting her."

Sadness softens Hannah's voice. "It's probably not just you. If he's abusing her, then she's probably scared of *anyone* who comes near her. I was the same way for a while after the rape. Jumpy, nervous, suspicious of everyone. It was a long time before I was finally able to relax around strangers, and even now, there's still things I won't do. Like drink in public. Well, unless you're there to play bodyguard."

I know that last line is an attempt to make me smile, but it doesn't. I'm still preoccupied by Cindy's reaction.

In fact, I don't feel like talking anymore. I just…can't. Fortunately, Hannah doesn't push me. I love that about her, how she never tries to fill silences with forced conversation.

She asks if I'm okay with music, and when I nod, she plugs in her iPod and loads up a playlist that *does* make me smile. It's the classic rock set I emailed her when we first met, though I notice she doesn't start it from the first song. Because the first song happens to be my mother's favorite, and I'm pretty sure that if I hear it right now, I'll burst into tears.

Which just goes to show that Hannah Wells is…amazing. She's so fucking attuned to me, my moods, my pain. I've never been with anyone who can read me so well.

An hour goes by. I know it's an hour because that's how long the playlist lasts, and when it ends, Hannah puts on a different mix, which makes me smile too because it consists of a whole lot of Rat Pack, Motown and Bruno Mars.

I'm calm now. Well, calm*er*. Every time I feel like I'm relaxing, I remember Cindy's fear-ridden eyes and the pressure squeezes my chest again. As uncertainties eddy in my gut, I force myself not to dwell on the one question that keeps pricking at my brain, but as I speed off the exit ramp and drive toward the two-lane road that will take us to Hastings, the question pops up again and this time I can't bat it away.

"What if I'm capable of it?"

Hannah turns down the volume. "What?"

"What if I'm capable of hurting someone?" I ask hoarsely. "What if I'm just like him?"

She answers with absolute conviction. "You're not."

Misery crawls up my spine. "I have his temper, I *know* I do. I wanted to strangle him tonight." I press my lips together. "It took all my willpower not to throw him into a wall and beat him to death. But it wasn't fucking worth it. *He's* not worth it."

She reaches for my hand and laces her fingers through mine. "And that's why you're not like him. You *have* that willpower, and that means you don't have his temper. Because he can't control his. He lets the anger fuel him, drive him to hurt the people around him, people who are weaker than him." Her grip on my hand tightens. "What would you do if I pissed you off right now?"

I blink. "What do you mean?"

"Let's pretend we're not in the car right now. We're in my room, or your house, and I...I don't know, tell you that I slept with someone else. No, I tell you that I've been sleeping with the entire hockey team since the second we met."

The thought makes my insides clench.

"What would you do?" she prompts.

I turn to her with a frown. "I'd end it and walk out the door."

"That's it? You wouldn't be tempted to hit me?"

I recoil in horror. "Of course not. Jesus."

"Exactly." Her palm moves gently over my cold knuckles. "Because you're not like him. No matter how angry someone made you, you wouldn't hit them."

"That's not true. I've gotten into a brawl or two on the ice," I admit. "And one time I punched a guy at Malone's, but that's 'cause he said some nasty shit about Logan's mom and I couldn't *not* throw down for my friend."

She sighs. "I'm not saying you're incapable of violence. Everyone is capable of it. I'm saying you wouldn't hurt someone you love. At least not intentionally."

I pray to God she's right. But when you inherited your DNA

from a man who *does* hurt the people he loves, who the hell knows.

My hands start to shake, and I know Hannah feels it because she squeezes my right hand to steady it. "Pull over," she says.

I frown again. We're driving down a dark stretch of road, and even though there are no other cars in sight, I don't like the idea of stopping in the middle of nowhere. "Why?"

"Because I want to kiss you, and I can't do that when your eyes are on the road."

An unwitting smile springs to my lips. Nobody has ever asked me to pull over before so they can kiss me, and although I'm exhausted and pissed off and sad and who knows what else, the thought of kissing Hannah right now sounds like pure fucking heaven.

Without another word, I pull off onto the shoulder, move the gearshift to park, and flick the emergency blinkers.

She slides closer and grasps my chin. Delicate fingertips stroke my stubble, and then she leans in and kisses me. Just the fleeting touch of her lips, before she pulls back and whispers, "You're not like him. You will never be like him." Her lips tickle my nose before kissing the tip of it. "You're a good person." She plants a tiny kiss on my cheek. "You're honest and kind and compassionate." She lightly bites my bottom lip. "I mean, don't get me wrong, you're a total dick sometimes, but it's a tolerable kind of dickishness."

I can't stop a grin.

"You're not like him," she repeats, firmer this time. "The only thing you two have in common is that you're both gifted hockey players. That's it. You are *not* like him."

Jesus, I needed to hear that. Her words penetrate that terrified place in my heart, and as the pressure in my chest dissipates, I cup the back of her head and kiss her hard. My tongue slides into her mouth and I groan happily, because she tastes like cranberries and smells like cherries and I fucking love it. I want to kiss her all night, for the rest of my fucking life, but I haven't forgotten where we are at the moment.

I reluctantly break the kiss—just as her hand sneaks toward my crotch.

"What are you doing?" I croak, then groan again when she rubs my aching cock over my trousers.

"What does it feel like?"

I grab her hand to still its movements. "I don't know if you're aware of this, but we're sitting in the car on the side of the road."

"No, really? I thought we were on an airplane on our way to Palm Springs."

I choke out a laugh, but it turns into a wheeze when the temptress beside me strokes me again. She squeezes the head of my cock, and my balls tighten, little zings of heat racing through me. Oh hell. This is *so* not the time, but I have to know if she's as turned on as I am, and I can't stop my hand from drifting to her knee. I caress the baby-soft skin of her thigh before slipping my hand under her dress.

I cup her over her panties and moan when I feel the damp material against my palm. She's wet. Really wet.

Somehow I manage to yank my hand away. "We can't do this."

"Why not?" An impish twinkle dances in her eyes, which doesn't surprise me, because I'm quickly discovering that Hannah is adventurous as hell once she lets down her guard and trusts someone.

And it still floors me that it's *me* she trusts.

"Anyone can drive by." I pause meaningfully. "Including a police patrol."

"Then we better be fast."

Before I can blink, she unzips my pants and slides her hand inside my boxers. My eyes promptly roll to the top of my head.

"Get in the backseat," I burst out.

Her eyes widen, then fill with delight. "Really?"

"Hell, if we're going to do this, we might as well do it right," I answer with a sigh. "Go big or go home, remember?"

It makes me laugh how quickly she dives into the backseat. Chuckling, I pop the glove box and grab the strip of condoms stashed there, then join her in the back.

When she sees what I'm holding, her jaw drops. "Are those condoms? Okay, I think I might be mad about this, except I probably shouldn't be because it's very helpful right now. But...*seriously*? You keep condoms in your *car*?"

I shrug. "Of course. What if I'm driving along one day and come across Kate Upton stranded on the side of the road?"

Hannah snorts. "I see. Is that your type then? Busty blondes with curves to spare?"

I cover her body with mine and prop my elbows on either side of her. "Naah, I prefer busty brunettes." I bury my face in her neck and nuzzle her skin. "One in particular. Who, by the way, also has curves to spare." My hands slide down to her waist. "And tiny hips." I glide my palms underneath her and squeeze her round bottom. "And a grabbable ass." I move one hand between her legs. "And the tightest pussy on the planet."

She shivers. "You have the dirtiest mouth."

"Yeah, but you still love me."

Her breath hitches. "Yeah. I do." Her green eyes shine up at me. "I love you."

My heart damn near explodes as those three sweet words hang between us. Other girls have said that to me before, but this time it's different. Because it's Hannah saying it, and she's not just any girl. And because I know that when she says she loves me, she actually means me—Garrett—and not Briar's hockey star, or Mr. Popularity, or Phil Graham's son. She loves *me*.

It's difficult to speak past the enormous lump in my throat. "I love you, too." It's the first time I've told a woman I love her, and it feels so damn right.

Hannah smiles. Then she pulls my head down and kisses me, and suddenly we're not talking anymore. I push her dress up and yank my trousers down. I don't even take off her panties, I just shove the crotch aside, roll on a condom with one hand, and guide my cock to her opening.

She moans the instant I enter her. And I wasn't kidding about how tight she is. Her pussy clutches me like a vise and I see stars, so close to losing it I have to will the climax away.

I've fucked girls in my car before.

I've never made love to one.

"You're so beautiful," I mumble, unable to take my eyes off her.

I start to move, dying to go slow and make it last, but I'm painfully aware of our surroundings. A Good Samaritan—or worse, a cop—might spot the Jeep and think we need roadside assistance, and if they decide to approach us, they'll get an eyeful of my bare ass, see my hips pumping and Hannah's arms clutching my back.

Besides, in this position, it's hard to maneuver. All I can

manage is fast, shallow strokes, but Hannah doesn't seem to mind. She makes the sexiest noises as I move inside her, breathy sighs and shaky whimpers, and when I hit this one certain spot inside her, she moans so loudly I have to clench my ass cheeks to stop from coming. I can feel the orgasm hurtling toward me, but I want her to come, too. I want to hear her cry out and milk me dry as her pussy spasms around me.

I reach between us and press my thumb on her clit, rubbing it gently. "Give it to me, baby," I rasp in her ear. "Come for me. Let me feel you coming around my cock."

Her eyes squeeze shut, hips rising to meet my hurried thrusts, and then she cries out in pleasure, and I come so hard my vision wavers and my mind fragments into a million pieces.

When the mind-shattering pleasure finally abates, I register what song is playing in the car.

My eyes fly open. "Did you re-download One Direction?"

Her mouth twitches. "No..."

"Uh-huh. So why is "Story of my Life" playing?" I demand.

She pauses, then lets out a big sigh. "Because I like One Direction. There. I said it."

"You're lucky I love you," I warn her. "Because I wouldn't stand for it otherwise."

Hannah grins. "You're lucky *I* love *you.* Because you're a total asshole and there aren't a lot of girls who'd put up with it."

She's probably right about the asshole thing.

She's definitely right about the lucky part.

37

Hannah

"I don't like this," I declare. "I mean it, babe, my legs are starting to hurt. I told you, I'm not flexible."

Garrett's laughter vibrates through my body. My *naked* body, I should add, because we're in the middle of having sex. Which I just confessed to not liking.

Maybe I *am* a mood killer.

But you know what, I don't care. I'm still vetoing this position. Garrett kneels in front of me, and my ankles are up on his shoulders. And maybe if he wasn't a big strapping hockey player, my legs wouldn't feel like they're resting on top of the frickin' Empire State building and be cramping the living hell out of me.

Still laughing, Garrett leans forward and my muscles breathe a sigh of relief as I slide my legs down and hook them around his ass. Immediately, the angle changes, and a moan slips out of my mouth.

"Better?" he says huskily.

"Oh my God. Yes. Do that again."

"I have no idea what I did."

"You twisted your hips, like...*ooohhh*...yeah, like that."

Every time he fills me, my core clamps around his erection. Every time he retreats, I feel empty, achy, desperate. I'm addicted to this guy. To his kisses and his taste, to the feel of his short hair beneath my fingers, and the smooth sinew of his back when I dig my nails into it.

His hips flex and his breathing quickens, and he thrusts

harder, deeper, turning my vision into a white haze. Then he reaches to the place where we're joined and rubs my clit, and off we go. He comes first, but keeps pumping inside me even as he trembles in release. His climax sets me off and I tremble even harder, biting my lip to stop from crying out so I don't alert his roommates to the delicious sensations coursing through my body right now.

Afterward, he rolls on his back and I lie on top of him, scaling his body like a monkey as I plant little kisses on his face and neck.

"Why do you always have so much more energy after sex?" he grumbles.

"Don't know. Don't care." I smack kisses all over him, until he's laughing in delight. I know he likes the attention, and it's a good thing he does because I can't stop giving it to him. For some reason, I turn into an affection monster when I'm around him.

Life is good again. A week has passed since Thanksgiving, and Garrett and I are still going strong. We've been busy, though. All our final papers are due soon, including the one for Tolbert's class, which I've been helping Garrett with. His practice schedule is just as jam-packed as ever, and so is mine as I prepare for the showcase. But hey, at least I'm finally excited about it again.

Jae and I came up with an arrangement that I love, and I'm confident I'm going to put on a hell of a performance. But I still haven't forgiven Cass and Mary Jane for what they did. MJ has texted several times asking if we can meet up and talk, but I've been ignoring her, and since Fiona got me my own rehearsal space in one of the senior choir rooms, I haven't run into MJ or Cass since they dumped me.

And the icing on the I-love-my-fucking-life cake? My dad called last week with some good news—my parents are meeting me at Aunt Nicole's for Christmas. I've already booked my ticket, and I can't wait to see them, but I'm disappointed that Garrett can't come with me. I invited him, but the dates didn't work out because the team's got a game scheduled the day after I leave, and another one two days before I get back. So Garrett will be spending the holidays with Logan, who is apparently from a town twenty minutes from Hastings.

Loud pounding on Garrett's door jolts me out of my happy thoughts. The door is locked so I'm not worried about anyone barging in, but I still reach for the blanket out of habit.

"Sorry to interrupt, boys and girls," Logan calls out, "but it's time to put your p's and v's away. Gotta go, G."

I shoot Garrett a blank look. "P's and v's?" Half the time I can barely make sense of Logan's made-up acronyms and abbreviations.

Garrett grins at me. "Oh come on, really? Even *I* got one. It's grade school shit."

I think it over, then blush. "How exactly does one put away their vagina?"

He snickers. "Ask Logan. Actually, please don't." He slides out of bed and wanders around searching for his clothes. "Are you coming to the game after rehearsal?"

"Yeah, but I don't think I'll make it before the second period. Argh. By the time I get to the arena, it'll probably be standing room only."

"I'll get someone to save a seat for you."

"Thanks."

I pop into the bathroom, freshen up, and come out to find Garrett on the edge of the bed, leaning over to put on a pair of socks. My heart skips a beat at the sight of him. Messy hair, biceps flexing, red splotches on his neck from where I nibbled on it. He's frickin' gorgeous.

Five minutes later, we leave his house and go our separate ways. I have Tracy's car, so I drive back to campus for rehearsal. Now that Cass is out of the picture, I can finally enjoy singing again.

And I do. My own personal cellist and I hammer out the ending of the song, and a couple hours later, I'm driving toward Briar's hockey center. I texted Allie to see if she wanted to come to the game with me, but she's busy with Sean, and my other friends are buried under mountains of schoolwork, which makes me grateful that I got a head start on mine. Most of my courses are performance or music theory, so I've really only had to focus on the British Lit and Ethics papers, both of which are almost done.

I get to the arena later than I hoped. The third period has just started, and I'm dismayed to see 1-1 flashing on the scoreboard, because Briar is playing a Division II team from Buffalo tonight. Garrett had been confident the game wouldn't be at all competitive, but apparently he was wrong.

There's an empty seat waiting for me behind the home team's bench courtesy of a senior named Natalie. Garrett has mentioned her before, but I haven't met her until now. Apparently she's been dating Birdie since freshman year, which is impressive. A lot of college relationships don't seem to last that long.

Natalie is funny and sweet, and we have a good time watching the game together. When Dean takes a particularly hard hit that sends him sprawling across the ice, we both gasp in alarm.

"Oh my God," Natalie bursts out. "Is he okay?"

Fortunately, Dean is fine. He shakes it off and jumps up, skating toward the Briar box for a line change. The moment Garrett hits the ice, my pulse speeds up. He's a force to be reckoned with. Fast footwork, skilled stickhandling, hard hitter. His first pass connects with Birdie's stick and they fly across the blue line into the zone. Birdie dumps the puck and Garrett chases it. So does the other team's center, and elbows are thrown behind the crease as the Buffalo forward tries to gain the upper hand.

Garrett comes out victorious and zips around the net, snapping off a quick shot. The goalie stops it easily, but the rebound bounces directly in Birdie's path. He slaps the puck right back at the goaltender, whose glove whips up a second too late.

Natalie leaps to her feet and cheers herself hoarse as Birdie's goal lights the scoreboard. We hug excitedly, then hold our breaths as the last three minutes of play tick by. The other team scrambles to gain possession of the puck, but Briar's sophomore center wins the next faceoff and we dominate the rest of the game, which ends with a final score of 2-1.

Natalie and I walk toward the aisle, jostled in all directions as we're shuffled down the stairs like cattle.

"I'm so glad you're with Garrett," she gushes.

The comment makes me smile, because she's only known me for twenty minutes. "Me too," I answer.

"Seriously. He's such a great guy, but he's so fricking intense when it comes to hockey. He hardly drinks, doesn't gets serious with anyone. It's not healthy to be *that* focused on something, you know?"

We leave the rink but don't head to the arena exit. Instead, we make our way through the crowd toward the hallway that leads to the locker rooms so we can wait for our guys. Garrett Graham is *my guy.* It's a surreal thought, but I like it.

"That's why I think you're good for him," she says. "He looks so happy and relaxed every time I see him."

My spine stiffens when I spot a familiar face in the crowd.

Garrett's father.

He's twenty feet away from us, headed in the same direction as we are. His baseball cap rests low on his forehead, but that doesn't stop him from getting noticed, because a group of guys in Briar jerseys quickly approach him for an autograph. He signs their jerseys, then a photo that one of them hands him. I can't see the picture, but I imagine it's an action shot of him from his glory days, just like the ones I saw framed in his house. Phil Graham, hockey legend.

Now living vicariously through his son.

I'm so focused on my hatred for Garrett's father that I don't pay attention to where I'm walking, and a startled laugh leaves my mouth when I bump into someone. Hard.

"I'm sorry. I wasn't watching where—" The apology dies on my lips when I notice who I bumped into.

Rob Delaney looks as stunned as I feel.

In the split second that our eyes lock, I turn into an ice statue. Shivers wrack every inch of my body. My feet are frozen in place. Wave after wave of horror slams into me.

I haven't seen Rob since the day he testified in court—*on my rapist's behalf.*

I don't know what to say. Or do. Or think.

Someone shouts, "Wellsy!"

I turn my head.

When I turn it back, Rob is hurrying away like he's trying to outrun a bullet.

I can't breathe.

Garrett comes up beside me. I know it's him because I recognize the gentle sweep of his hand on my cheek, but my gaze stays glued to Rob's retreating back. He's wearing a Buffalo State jacket. Does he go there? I never bothered finding out what happened to Aaron's friends. Where they went to college, what they're doing now. The last time I had any contact with Rob Delaney, it was indirectly. It was when my dad attacked Rob's father in the hardware store in Ransom.

"Hannah. Look at me."

I can't tear my eyes off Rob, who hasn't made it out the door yet. The group of friends he's with stop to talk to a few people, and he tosses a panicky glance over his shoulder, paling when he realizes I'm still staring at him.

"Hannah. Jesus. You're white as a sheet. What's wrong?"

I guess I'm pale, too. I guess I look like Rob. I guess we've both just seen a ghost.

The next thing I know, my head is wrenched to the side as Garrett's hands clutch my chin to force eye contact.

"What's going on? Who is that guy?" He's followed my gaze, and now he's watching Rob with visible mistrust.

"Nobody," I say weakly.

"Hannah."

"It's nobody, Garrett. Please." I turn my back to the door, effectively eliminating any temptation to look Rob's way.

Garrett pauses. Searches my face. Then he sucks in a breath. "Oh fuck. Is it...?" His horrified question hangs between us.

"No," I say quickly. "It's not. I promise." My lungs burn from lack of oxygen, so I force myself to take a deep breath. "He's just a guy."

"What guy? What's his name?"

"Rob." Nausea circles my belly like a school of sharks. "Rob Delaney."

Garrett's gaze moves past my shoulder, which tells me that Rob is still here. Damn it, why can't he just leave already?

"Who is he, Hannah?"

Hard as I try, I can no longer pretend that my whole world hasn't been knocked off kilter.

My face collapses and I whisper, "It's Aaron's best friend. He's one of the guys who testified against me after the—"

Garrett is already stalking away.

38

Garrett

My blood roars between my ears. I hear Hannah calling after me but I can't stop moving. It's like I'm watching the world through a red mist. I've gone on autopilot, turning into an asshole-seeking missile that travels in a straight path toward Rob Delaney.

The bastard who helped Hannah's rapist get off without so much as a slap on the wrist.

"Delaney," I call out.

His shoulders tense. Several people glance our way, but there's only one person I'm interested in at the moment. He turns around, dark eyes momentarily flickering with panic when he notices me. He saw me talking to Hannah. Probably figured out what she told me.

He says something to his friends and takes a hasty step away from the group, and my jaw turns to stone as he warily approaches me.

"Who the hell are you?" he mutters.

"Hannah's boyfriend."

His expression conveys unmistakable fear, but he still tries to play it off cool. "Yeah? Well, what do you want?"

I draw a calming breath. It doesn't calm me down. At all. "I just wanted to meet the asshole who aided and abetted a rapist."

There's a long moment of silence. Then he scowls at me. "Fuck off. You don't know shit about me, man."

"I know everything about you," I correct, my whole body trembling with barely-restrained fury. "I know you let your friend drug my girl. I know you stood by while he took her upstairs and hurt her. I know you committed perjury afterward to back him up. I know you're a piece of shit without a conscience."

"Fuck off," he says again, but his bravado wavers. He looks stricken now.

"Really? *Fuck off*? That's all you have to say? I guess that makes sense." I swallow the acid coating my throat. "You're a fucking coward who couldn't defend an innocent girl. So why would you have the balls to defend yourself?"

The bitter accusations trigger his anger. "Get out of my face, man. I didn't come here tonight to get railed on by some dumb jock. Go back to your slut girlfriend and—"

Oh *hell* no.

My fist snaps out.

After that, everything is a blur.

People are shouting. Someone grabs the back of my jacket, trying to yank me off Delaney. My hand throbs. I taste blood in my mouth. It's like an out-of-body experience that I can't even describe because I'm not there. I'm lost in a haze of unchecked anger.

"Garrett."

Someone slams me into a wall, and I instinctively release a right hook. I glimpse a flash of red, hear my name again, a sharp, emphatic "*Garrett*"—and my vision clears in time to see the blood spurting from the corner of Logan's mouth.

Oh shit.

"G." His voice is low and ominous, but there's no mistaking the worry swimming in his eyes. "G, you've gotta stop."

All the oxygen in my lungs shudders out in a rush. I glance around and find a sea of faces staring at me, hear hushed voices and confused whispers.

And then Coach appears, and I'm suddenly hit with the gravity of what I've just done.

Two hours later, I stand in front of Hannah's door, and I barely have enough strength left to knock.

I can't remember the last time I reached this level of intense exhaustion. Instead of a post-game celebration with my team tonight, I sat in Coach's office for more than an hour and listened to him shout at me for starting a fight on school property.

Which, by the way, earned me a one-game suspension. To be honest, I'm surprised the punishment wasn't stiffer, but after Coach and a few other Briar officials got the whole story out of me, they decided to go easy on me. Hannah had given me permission to tell them about her history with Delaney, insisting that she didn't want them to think I was some psycho who went around attacking random hockey fans for no good reason, but I still feel like a shit for sharing her trauma with my coach.

One-game suspension. Jesus. I deserve a helluva lot worse.

I wonder if my dad has heard about the suspension yet, but I know he must have. I bet he has someone at Briar on his payroll to feed him information about me. Luckily, he wasn't around when I left the arena, so I was spared from dealing with his wrath tonight.

Logan was there, though, waiting for me outside, and I've never been more ashamed in my life as I apologized to my best friend for hitting him. But Hannah had also given me the okay to share the truth with Logan, and after I told him who Rob was and why I went after him, Logan was ready to go after Rob himself, and then he apologized to *me* for pulling me off the bastard. That's when I realized how much I fucking love the guy. He might be crushing on my girlfriend, but he's still the best friend I've ever had. And hell, I can't even fault him for the girlfriend-crushing part because why *wouldn't* he want to be with someone as incredible as Hannah?

I'm nervous as hell when she opens the door to let me in, but she surprises me by immediately throwing her arms around me. "Are you okay?" she says urgently.

"I'm fine." It sounds like I'm speaking through a mouthful of gravel, so I clear my throat before continuing. "I'm sorry. I'm so fucking sorry, baby."

She tilts her head to look up at me, regret etched into her face. "You shouldn't have gone after him."

"I know." My throat closes up. "I couldn't stop myself. I kept picturing that bastard sitting on the witness stand, calling you a whore and saying you took drugs and seduced his friend. It made me sick." I weakly shake my head. "No, it made me *crazy*."

She takes my hand and leads me to her room, closing the door behind her before joining me on the edge of the bed. She reaches for my hand again, and gasps when she sees the state of my knuckles. They're cracked and caked with blood, and even though I washed my hands thoroughly before coming here, the little cuts have opened up and are now dribbling with blood.

"How much trouble are you in?" she asks.

"Not as much as I deserve. One-game suspension, which shouldn't hurt the team too bad. Our record is solid enough that we can afford a loss if it comes down to that. And the cops weren't called because Delaney refused to press charges. The Buffalo coach tried to get him to change his mind, but he told everyone that he provoked me."

Her eyebrows shoot up. "He did?"

"Yeah." I let out a breath. "Too much of a hassle dealing with the police, I guess. He probably just wanted to go back to whatever hole he crawled out of and pretend it never happened. Just like how he pretended that his best friend didn't hurt you." Bile bubbles in my throat. "How the fuck is that fair, Hannah? Why aren't you angrier? Why aren't you *furious* that your rapist is walking around free? And his slimy friends are the ones who *helped* him get off."

She sighs. "It's *not* fair. And I *am* angry. But...well, *life* isn't always fair, babe. I mean, look at your father—he's every much a criminal as Aaron is, and he's not in jail either. If anything, he's still revered by every hockey fan in this country."

"Yeah, because nobody knows what he did to me and my mom."

"And you think if they knew, they'd stop idolizing him? Some of them might, but I guarantee you that a lot of them won't care, because he's a star athlete and he won lots of games, so that makes him a hero." She shakes her head sadly. "Do you realize how many abusers are walking around unpunished? How many rape charges are dropped because of 'insufficient' evidence, or how many date rapists get away with what they've done because the victim is too scared to tell anyone? So yeah, it's not fair, but it's also not worth agonizing over."

Sorrow clogs my throat. "You're a better person than I am, then."

"That's not true," she chides. "Remember what you told me on Thanksgiving? How your father isn't worth your anger and revenge? Well, that's the best revenge right there, Garrett. Living well and being happy is how we get over the shit in our past. I was raped, and it was awful, but I'm not going to waste my time or energy either, not on some pathetic, screwed-up guy who couldn't take no for an answer, or his pathetic friends who thought he deserved to be rewarded for his actions." She sighs again. "I put it all behind me. You really didn't have to confront Rob on my behalf."

"I know." Tears sting my eyes. Shit. The last time I cried was at my mom's funeral, when I was twelve years old. I'm embarrassed that Hannah is witnessing it, but at the same time, I want her to understand why I did it, even if it means falling apart in front of her. "Don't you get it? The thought of anyone hurting you rips me apart." I blink rapidly, fighting the tears. "I didn't realize it until tonight, but...I think I was broken, too."

Hannah looks startled. "What do you mean?"

"I was broken before I met you," I mumble. "My entire life revolved around hockey, and being the best, and proving to my father that I didn't need him. I didn't let myself get close to girls because I didn't want to be distracted from my goals. And I knew that if I did get close to someone, I'd leave them in heartbeat once I got drafted. I didn't let a single person in, not even my closest friends, and then you came along and I realized just how fucking lonely I've been."

I drop my head on her shoulder, so tired of...of everything.

After a beat, she pulls my head into her lap and strokes my hair. I curl into her, my voice muffled against her thigh. "I hate that you saw me lose it tonight." A rush of self-loathing sears my flesh. "You told me I wasn't capable of hurting you, but you *saw* what I did tonight. I didn't go over there planning on hitting him, but he was so fucking smug, and then he called you a...he said something nasty, and I snapped."

"You lost your temper," she agrees. "But that doesn't change the way I feel about you, or what I think about you. I said you'd never hurt me, and I still believe that." Her voice shakes. "God, Garrett, if you knew how badly I wanted to rip his eyes out tonight..."

"But you didn't."

"Because I was in shock. I didn't expect to see him there." Her fingers slide over my scalp in a soft caress. "I don't want you to hate yourself for this."

"I don't want you to hate me for it."

She bends down and brushes her lips over the top of my head. “I could never hate you.”

We stay this way for a while, with her fingers in my hair and my head in her lap. Eventually she coaxes me into bed and I slide between the sheets fully clothed. We’re spooning now, except she’s the one holding *me* and I’m too fucking tired and ashamed to move.

I fall asleep with her hand stroking my chest.

39

Hannah

The next morning, I leave Garrett asleep in my bed and get ready for work. Although I'm still shaken up over what happened last night, I meant every word I said to him. I *don't* blame him for losing his temper. In fact, some spiteful part of me is glad that Rob took a fist to the face. He deserves it after what he did to me. Lying under oath, providing testimony that allowed the case against Aaron to be dismissed...what kind of person does something so cruel and vindictive?

But I know Garrett is upset about what he did, and I know I'm going to have to work hard to make him see that he's not the monster he thinks he is.

But I also can't bail on work, so Operation Reassurance will have to wait.

Once I'm dressed and ready to go, I sit on the edge of the bed and touch Garrett's cheek. "I have to go to work," I whisper.

"Mmmddrv...yuou...?"

I deduce that he's offering to drive me, and a smile tugs on the corner of my mouth. "I've got Tracy's car today. Go back to sleep if you want. I'll be back around five."

"'Kay." His eyelids flutter and a second later he's asleep again.

I make myself a cup of instant coffee in the kitchen and chug it to jumpstart my barely functioning brain. My gaze shifts to Allie's bedroom door, which is wide open. The glimpse of her perfectly made bed worries me only for a second, because when I check my phone, I find a text from last night that tells me Allie spent the night at Sean's frat house.

My shift at the diner is chaotic from moment one. The breakfast crowd arrives in droves and it's a good two hours before the rush finally dissipates. I don't even have time to take a breath once it clears out, because Della asks me to reorganize the supplies under the counter before the lunch rush hits. I spend the next hour on my knees, moving stacks of napkins and packets of sugar from one shelf to another, and switching the coffee mug shelf with the drinking glass shelf.

When I hop to my feet, I'm startled to find a man sitting on the stool directly in front of me.

It's Garrett's father.

"Mr. Graham," I squeak in surprise. "Hi."

"Hello, Hannah." His voice is as chilly as the December air outside the diner. "We need to talk."

We do?

Shit. Why do I have a feeling I know *exactly* what he wants to talk about?

"I'm working," I answer in an awkward tone.

"I can wait."

Double shit. It's only ten o'clock and I'm not off until five. Is he actually going to sit around and wait for *seven* hours? Because there's no way I'll be able to get through my shift if he's in the diner, staring at me the whole time.

"Let me see if I can take a break," I say hastily.

He nods. "It won't take long. I assure you, I only need a few minutes of your time."

I don't know if that's a promise, or a threat.

Gulping, I pop into the back office to talk to Della, who signs off on a five-minute break after I tell her that my boyfriend's father has something urgent to discuss with me.

The moment Mr. Graham and I step outside, I get the answer to that age-old promise vs. threat question—because his body language emits some serious menace.

"I bet you're quite pleased with yourself."

I frown. "What are you talking about?"

He shoves both hands in the pockets of his long black coat, and he looks so much like Garrett it's actually kind of upsetting. But he doesn't sound like Garrett, because Garrett's voice isn't this harsh, and Garrett's eyes definitely don't carry this much animosity.

"I've been with a lot of women, Hannah." Mr. Graham laughs, but without an ounce of humor or a shred of warmth. "You think I don't know what an ego boost it is for a woman when she has two men fighting over her?"

Is *that* what he thinks last night was about? That Garrett and Rob were fighting a duel for my love? Jesus.

"That's not why they were fighting," I say weakly.

His lips curl in a sneer. "Oh really? So the fight had *nothing* to do with you?" When I don't answer, he laughs again. "That's what I thought."

I don't like the way he's looking at me with such blatant hostility. And I wish I hadn't forgotten my gloves inside, because my hands feel like two blocks of ice.

I shove them in my pockets and meet his eyes. "What do you want?"

"I want you to stop distracting my son," he says briskly. "Do you realize he's facing a one-game suspension for that stunt? Because of *you,* Hannah. Because instead of concentrating on winning games, he's panting over you like a puppy dog and fighting battles on your behalf."

My throat tightens. "That's not true."

He takes a step closer and I'm genuinely frightened for a moment. I chastise myself for it, though, because come on, he's not going to hurt me when we're out in public. When the diner window is right behind me and anyone can see us.

"I see the way he looks at you, and I don't like it. And I certainly don't like that you've divided his attention. Which is why I've decided you're no longer going to be seeing my son."

I can't stop a laugh of disbelief. "With all due respect, sir, but that's not your decision to make."

"You're right. It's going to be *your* decision."

My stomach lurches. "What does that mean?"

"It means you're going to break up with my son."

I gape at him. "Um...no. I'm sorry, but no."

"I thought you'd say that. It's all right. I'm confident I can change your mind." Those cold, gray eyes bore into my face. "Do you care about Garrett?"

"Of course I do." My voice cracks. "I love him."

The confession brings a flash of annoyance to his eyes. He

studies my face, then makes a derisive sound. "I believe you mean that." He shrugs dismissively. "But that just means you want him to be happy, don't you, Hannah? You want him to succeed."

I have no idea where he's going with this, but I know that I hate him for it.

"Do you want to know why he's succeeding right now? What enables him to do that?" Mr. Graham smirks. "It's because of me. Because *my* signature is on the tuition checks I send to Briar. He goes to school because of me. He buys his textbooks and pays for his booze because of me. His car? Insurance? Who do you think makes the payments for that? And his gear? The boy doesn't even have a job—how do you think he's able to live? Because of *me*."

I feel sick. Because now I *do* know where he's going.

"I generously allow him these luxuries because I know his goals align with mine. I know what he wants to achieve, and I know he's capable of achieving it." His jaw hardens. "But we've hit a little speed bump, haven't we?"

He gives me a pointed stare, and yep, *I'm* the speed bump.

"So this is what's going to happen." His tone is deceptively pleasant. Garrett is right. This man *is* a monster. "You're going to break up with my son. You won't see him anymore, you won't remain friends with him. This will be a clean break with absolutely no further contact. Do you understand?"

"Or what?" I whisper, because I need to hear him say it.

"Or I cut the boy off." He shrugs. "Bye-bye tuition and books and cars and food. Is that what you want, Hannah?"

My brain snaps into overtime, rapidly running over my options. I'm not about to let some asshole blackmail me into ending things with Garrett, not when there are clearly other solutions available to us.

But I haven't given Phil Graham enough credit, because apparently he's not just a jerk, but a mind reader.

"You're considering what will happen if you say no?" he guesses. "Trying to think of a way you can still be with Garrett without him losing everything he's worked so hard for?" He chuckles. "Well, let's see, shall we? He can always apply for financial aid."

I silently curse him for raising the idea that had just entered my mind.

"But wait, he didn't qualify for financial aid." Graham looks like he might actually be enjoying himself. "When your family's income is as substantial as ours, schools don't give you money, Hannah. Believe me, Garrett applied. Briar turned him down on the spot."

Shit.

"A bank loan?" Garrett's father suggests. "Well, that's hard to get approved for when you have no credit or assets."

My brain scrambles to keep up. Garrett *must* have credit, though. Some kind of income. He told me he works during the summer.

But Mr. Graham is like a sniper, shooting down every thought that enters my head.

"He gets paid in cash for his construction work. What a pity, huh? No record of income, no credit, not needy enough to warrant help from Briar." He *tsks* with his tongue and I almost smack him in the face. "So where does that leave us? Oh, right, the other option you're considering. My son will find a job and pay for his own education and expenses."

Yep, that idea has also occurred to me.

"Do you know how much an Ivy League education costs? Do you think he can pay that kind of tuition working part-time?" Garrett's father shakes his head. "No, he'll have to work full-time in order to do that. He might be able to keep attending school, but he'll have to drop hockey, won't he? And how happy will he be then?" His smile chills me to the bone. "Or let's assume he can juggle it all—full-time job, school, and hockey…there won't be much time left for you, will there, Hannah?"

Which is exactly what he wants.

I feel like I might throw up. I know he's not fucking around. He *will* cut Garrett off if I don't do what he says.

I also know that if Garrett found out about his father's threat, he'd tell him to fuck right off. He'd pick me over the money, but that only makes me sicker, because Mr. Graham is right. Garrett would have to drop out or work his ass off, which either means no hockey altogether, or no time to focus on hockey. And I *want* him to focus on it, damn it. It's his *dream*.

My mind continues to spin.

If I break up with Garrett, Mr. Graham wins.

If I don't break up with Garrett, Mr. Graham still wins.

Tears well up in my eyes. "He's your *son*…" I choke on the

words. "How can you be so cruel?"

He looks bored. "I'm not cruel. I'm just practical. And unlike some people, I have my priorities in order. I've invested a lot of time and money in that boy, and I refuse to see all that hard work go to waste over a piece of coed pussy."

I flinch in repulsion.

"Get it done, Hannah," he says harshly. "I mean it, don't fucking test me, and don't think I'm bluffing." His icy stare pierces my face. "Do I look like a man who bluffs?"

Acid burns my throat as I slowly shake my head. "No. You don't."

40

Garrett

Hannah has been avoiding me for days. She's playing it off like she's busy, and yeah, she has work and rehearsal, but she's been working and rehearsing since the moment we started dating and it sure as hell hasn't stopped her from coming by for a quick dinner, or chatting on the phone with me before bed.

Ergo—she's fucking avoiding me.

I don't need to be a Mensa member to know that it's because of the way I went after Delaney. That's the only reason I can think of for why she might be upset with me, and I'm not sure I blame her. I shouldn't have hit the guy. Especially not in the arena in front of hundreds of witnesses.

But the thought that she might be...I don't know...*scared* of me now...

It kills me.

I show up at her dorm unannounced because I know that if I text her beforehand, she'll give me some excuse about how busy she is. I know she's home because I pulled the most pathetic move on the planet by texting Allie to find out, followed by the dick move of begging her not to tell Hannah I'm coming over because I have a surprise for her.

I'm not sure Allie bought it. I mean, girls talk, so it stands to reason that Hannah told her best friend about whatever's bugging her.

As I expect, Hannah doesn't look happy to see me at her door. She doesn't look pissed off, either, which makes me uneasy, especially when I notice the glimmer of regret in her eyes.

Shit.

"Hi," I say gruffly.

"Hi." Her throat bobs as she swallows. "What are you doing here?"

I suppose I can pretend that everything is all right, that I just stopped by to see my favorite girl, but that's not who Hannah and I are. We've never tiptoed around the truth before, and I'm not about to start now.

"I wanted to find out why my girlfriend is avoiding me."

She sighs.

That's it. A *sigh*. Four days of zero physical contact and minimal text messages and all I get from her is a sigh.

"What the hell is going on?" I demand in frustration.

She hesitates, her gaze darting toward Allie's closed door. "Can we talk in my room?"

"Sure, as long as we actually fucking *talk*," I mutter.

We go to her bedroom and she shuts the door. When she turns to face me, I know exactly what she's going to say.

"I'm sorry I've been acting so weird. I've just been doing some thinking…"

Holy shit. She's breaking up with me. Because *nobody* starts a sentence with "*I've just been doing some thinking…*" without ending that sentence with, "*and I don't think we should see each other anymore.*"

Hannah lets out a breath. "And I don't think we should see each other anymore."

Even though I'm expecting it, the quiet words stab me in the heart and send a tornado of pain spiraling through me.

She hurries on when she notices my expression. "It's just…things are moving too fast, Garrett. It's barely been two months and we're already at the I-love-you stage, and it's so super serious all of a sudden, and…" She looks frazzled and sounds upset.

I, on the other hand, am neither frazzled nor upset.

I'm devastated.

I choke back the bitterness lining my throat. "Why don't you say what you really mean?"

She frowns. "What?"

"You said you didn't hate me for losing my temper with Delaney, but that's what all this is about, right? It scared you. It made you see me as some reckless caveman who can't control his violent urges, right?"

Shock fills her eyes. "*No.* Of course not."

The conviction in her voice makes me falter. It's so easy for me to read this girl, and as I search her eyes, I can't find even a hint that she might be lying to me. But…fuck. If she's not pissed about Delaney, then why the *hell* is she doing this?

"We're moving too fast," she insists. "That's what this is about."

"Fine," I say tersely. "Then let's slow it down. What is it you want? You want us to see each other only once a week? Stop crashing at each other's places? What do you want?"

I thought my heart couldn't throb any worse than this, but then she stabs another sword of agony into it.

"I want us to see other people."

All I can do is stare at her. I'm afraid of what might come out of my mouth if I try to talk.

"I mean, I've only had one serious relationship before you, Garrett. How do I know what love is? What if there's something more out there…someone else…something…*better*, I guess."

Sweet Jesus. She just keeps twisting the knife deeper and deeper.

"College is all about exploring your options, right?" She's talking so fast now that it's difficult to keep up. "I'm supposed to be meeting people and going on dates and finding out who I am and all that stuff, or at least that's what I was hoping to do this year. I didn't expect you and I to get together, and I really didn't expect it to get so serious, so fast." She shrugs helplessly. "I'm confused, okay? And I think what I need right now is some time to…you know…to think," she finishes feebly.

I bite the inside of my cheek until I taste blood in my mouth. Then I draw a long, unstable breath and cross my arms. "All right, so let me get this straight—and feel free to correct me if I'm wrong. You fell in love with me and didn't expect it, so now you want to date other people and fuck other guys—sorry, you want to *explore*, just on the off chance that you meet someone who is *better* than me."

She averts her gaze.

"Is that what you're saying?" My voice is cold enough to freeze everything south of the Equator.

After an eternity of silence, she looks up.

Then she nods.

I'm pretty sure she hears the massive *crack* in my chest as my heart splits open like a watermelon. God knows she's the one responsible for it.

In the back of my mind, a little voice whispers, *This is wrong.*

No fucking kidding, asshole. There's nothing *right* about this.

"I'm going to leave now." I'm amazed that my paralyzed vocal cords allow me to speak. I'm not amazed by the naked anger in my tone. "Because I honestly can't look at you right now."

A tiny breath puffs out of her mouth. She doesn't say a word.

I stagger to the door, my brain and heart and motor functions eerily close to shutting down on me, but I manage one hoarse parting line as I reach the threshold. "You know what, Wellsy?" Our gazes lock and her lips tremble as if she's trying not to cry. "For someone who's so damn strong, you really are a fucking coward."

Alcohol. I need some fucking alcohol.

There's no alcohol in the fridge.

I barrel up the stairs two at a time and burst into Logan's bedroom without knocking. Fortunately, he's not in the middle of boning some nameless puck bunny. I wouldn't have cared if he was. I'm a man on a mission, and Logan's closet is the mission.

"What the hell are you doing?" he demands as I throw open the closet door and reach for the top shelf.

"Taking your whiskey."

"Why?"

Why? *Why?*

Maybe because my chest feels like someone scraped it with a dull razorblade for the past ten years? And then they took that razorblade and shoved it down my throat so it would tear up my windpipe and shred my insides. And then to add insult to injury, they ripped my heart out and threw it on the ice so an entire hockey team could slash it up with their skates.

Yup. So that's where *I'm* at right now.

"Jesus Christ, G, what's going on?"

I find Logan's Jack Daniels bottle underneath an old hockey helmet and curl my fingers around it. "Hannah dumped me," I mumble.

I hear Logan's shocked breath. A bitter, spiteful part of me wonders if he's happy by the news. If he thinks this might be his golden opportunity to move in on my girlfriend.

Sorry. My *ex*-girlfriend.

But when I turn around, I find nothing but sympathy flashing in his eyes. "Shit, man. I'm sorry."

"Yeah," I mutter. "Me too."

"What happened?"

I twist off the bottle cap. "Ask me again when I'm shit-faced. Maybe I'll be drunk enough to tell you."

I swallow a deep swig of whiskey. Normally the alcohol would burn its way down to my gut. Tonight I'm too numb to feel it.

Logan stops asking me questions. He wanders over and snatches the whiskey from my hand. "Well." He sighs before raising the bottle to his lips and tipping his head back. "Then I guess we're getting shit-faced."

41

Hannah

I knew I would be a basket case for the rest of the semester, but I didn't expect it to be because of the hollow cavern in my chest that used to hold my heart.

I haven't seen or spoken to Garrett in a week. A week is not a long time. I've noticed that as I get older, time seems to fly by in hyper-speed. You blink, and a week has passed. Blink again, and a year has gone by.

But ever since I broke up with Garrett, time has reverted back to the way it was when I was little. When a school year felt like forever, and a summer never seemed to end. Time has slowed down, and it's excruciating. These past seven days may as well be seven years. Seven *decades.*

I miss my boyfriend.

And I hate my boyfriend's father for putting me in this impossible situation. I hate him for making me break Garrett's heart.

You want to explore, just on the off chance that you meet someone who is better than me.

Garrett's bleak recap of my lying-through-my-teeth breakup speech continues to buzz in my brain like a swarm of locusts.

Someone better than him?

God, it *killed* me to say that. To hurt him like that. The bitter taste of those words still burns my tongue, because damn it, *someone better than him*?

There's *no one* better than him. Garrett is the best man I've ever known. And not just because he's smart and sexy and funny and so much sweeter than I ever gave him credit for. He makes me feel *alive*. Yeah, we bicker, and sure, his cockiness drives me crazy sometimes, but when I'm with him, I feel whole. I feel like I can drop my guard completely and not have to worry about getting hurt or taken advantage of or being afraid, because Garrett Graham will always be there to love and protect me.

The only silver lining to this awful mess is that the team is winning again. They lost the game that Garrett missed thanks to his suspension, but they've played two more since then, including one against Eastwood, their conference rival, and they won both. If they keep going the way they're going, Garrett will get what he wants—he'll lead Briar to the championships in his first year as captain.

"Oh God. Please don't tell me that's what you're wearing tonight." Allie marches into my bedroom and frowns at my outfit. "No. I forbid it."

I glance down at my ratty plaid pants and sweatshirt with the collar cut off. "What? No." I point to the garment bag dangling from the hook behind my door. "I'm wearing that."

"Ooooh. Let me see."

Allie unzips the bag and proceeds to oooh and aaah over the strapless silver dress inside it. Her animated reaction is a testament to how out of it I've been this week. I was pretty much in a trance when I drove to Hastings to buy this dress for the showcase, and although it's been hanging on my door for *four* days, I never bothered showing it off to Allie.

I don't *want* to show it off. Hell, I don't even want to wear it. The winter showcase starts in two hours and I could not care less. The entire semester has been building up to this one stupid performance.

And I could not. Care. Less.

When Allie notices my disinterested face, her expression softens. "Aw, Han-Han, why don't you just call him?"

"Because we broke up," I mumble.

She nods slowly. "And why is that again?"

I'm too depressed to give her the same bullshit excuse I dished out a week ago. I haven't confessed to Allie or my friends the real reason I ended things with Garrett. I don't want them knowing about his asshole father. I don't want to *think* about his asshole father.

So I told them, and I quote, "it didn't work out." Four measly words, and they haven't managed to pry a single detail out of me since.

My stony silence drags on long enough for Allie to shift in discomfort. Then she sighs and says, "Do you still want me to do your hair?"

"Sure. If you want." There is zero enthusiasm in my voice.

We spend the next thirty minutes getting ready, though I don't know why Allie bothers dressing up. *She's* not the one who has to get up on stage and sing in front of hundreds of strangers.

Though, out of curiosity, how exactly does one sing a heartfelt ballad when their heart has been crushed to dust?

I guess I'm about to find out.

The backstage area of the main auditorium is chaotic when I wander in. Students rush past me, some carrying instruments, all dressed to impress. Panicky voices and brisk orders echo all around me, but I barely register them.

The first face I see belongs to Cass. Our gazes hold for a beat and then he walks over, looking like a million bucks in a black suit jacket and a salmon-colored dress shirt with the collar propped up. His dark hair is styled to perfection. His blue eyes offer no trace of remorse or apology.

"Great dress," he remarks.

I shrug. "Thanks."

"Nervous?"

Another shrug. "Nope."

I'm not nervous because *I don't care*. I never thought I was one of those wimpy girls who walks around like a zombie after a breakup and bursts into tears at even the smallest reminder of her true love, but depressingly enough, I totally am.

"Well, break a leg," Cass says once he figures out I'm not interested in making conversation.

"You too." I pause and, not under my breath, mutter, "Literally."

His head sharply turns toward me. "Sorry, I didn't hear that last part."

I raise my voice. "I said, *literally*."

Those blue eyes darken. "You're a real bitch, you know

that?"

A laugh flies out. "Uh-huh. *I'm* the bitch."

Cass scowls at me. "What, you want me to apologize for talking to my advisor? Because I'm not going to. We both know the duet wasn't working out. I just had the balls to do something about it."

"You're right," I agree. "I should be thanking you. You actually did me a huge favor." And no, I'm not being sarcastic. I mean every word.

His self-righteous expression wavers. "I did?" Then he clears his throat. "Yes, I *did*. I did both of us a favor. I'm glad you're able to recognize that." His trademark smirk resettles on his lips. "Anyway, I need to find MJ before the performance."

He saunters off, and I head in the opposite direction in search of Jae. All the sound checks were done this morning, so everything's pretty much good to go. Since I'm the last junior to perform, I get to wait around with my thumb up my ass until they call my name. Cass, of course, is opening the junior showcase. He must've sucked someone's dick to get that slot, because it's the best one in the line-up. That's when the judges are still bushy-eyed and excited, eager to start *judging* after sitting through the sophomore and freshman performances, which don't qualify for scholarships. By the time the last junior hits the stage—go me!—everyone is tired, anxious to stretch their legs or grab a smoke before the senior performances begin.

I pop my head into a few dressing rooms looking for Jae, but he's nowhere to be found. I hope my cellist hasn't deserted me, but if he did…well…I don't care.

I miss Garrett. I can't go five seconds without thinking about him, and the reminder that he's not in the audience tonight is like a karate chop to the neck. My windpipe closes up, making it impossible to breathe.

"Hannah," a meek voice calls out.

I stifle a sigh. Shit. I'm *so* not in the mood to talk to Mary Jane right now.

But the little blonde dashes over to me before I can make my escape, trapping me in the doorway of the dressing room I was about to enter. "Can we talk?" she blurts out.

The sigh escapes. "I don't have time for that right now. I'm looking for Jae."

"Oh, he's in the green room on the east stage. I just saw him."

"Thanks." I start to walk off, but she blocks my path. "Hannah, please. I really need to talk to you."

Annoyance clamps around my throat. "Look, if you're trying to apologize, don't bother. Apology not accepted."

Hurt flashes in her eyes. "Please don't say that. Because I really am sorry. I'm so, so sorry for what I did. I shouldn't have let Cass talk me into it."

"No kidding."

"I…I just couldn't say no to him." A helpless chord wobbles her voice. "I liked him so much, and he was so attentive and encouraging, and he insisted that the song was meant for one performer and that *he* was the only one who could do it justice." Mary Jane's entire face collapses. "I shouldn't have gone behind your back. I shouldn't have done that to you. I'm…so sorry."

It doesn't escape me that she's using the past tense in regards to Cass. And although I'm a jerk for doing it, I can't help but laugh. "He dumped you, didn't he?"

She avoids my eyes, her teeth sinking into her lower lip. "Right after he got the solo."

I don't pity a lot of people. I mean, sympathy? I hand that out freely. Pity is reserved for someone I truly feel sorry for.

I pity Mary Jane.

"Should I bother saying *I told you so*?" I ask.

She shakes her head. "No. I know you were right. And I know I was stupid. I wanted to believe that someone like him was actually interested in someone like me. I wanted it to be true so badly that I screwed up my friendship with you."

"We're not friends, MJ." I know I'm being harsh, but I guess my tact filter broke at the same time my heart did because I don't bother softening my tone or censoring my words. "I would never screw over a friend like that. Especially over a *guy*."

"Please…" She gulps. "Can't we just start over? I'm so sorry."

"I know you are." I offer a sad smile. "Look, I'm sure eventually I'll be able to talk to you without thinking about all this shit, maybe even trust you again, but I'm not there yet."

"I get it," she says weakly.

"I really need to find Jae." I force another smile. "I'm sure

Cass will do a great job with your song, MJ. He might be an asshole, but he's a damn good vocalist."

I dart off before she can respond.

I track down Jae and we hang out backstage until the show starts. After weeks of non-stop rehearsing, we've become friends, though Jae is still as shy as ever and afraid of his own shadow. But he's only a freshman, so I'm hoping he comes out of his shell once he adapts to college life.

The freshman and sophomores are up first. Jae and I stand in the wings, stage left, watching as performer after performer takes the stage, but I have trouble concentrating on what I'm hearing and seeing.

I'm not in the mood to sing tonight. All I can think about is Garrett, and the agony in his eyes when I broke up with him, the slump of his shoulders when he left my dorm.

I have to remind myself that I did it for *him*, so that he can stay at Briar and play the game he loves without having to worry about money. If I had told him about his father's threats, Garrett would have chosen our relationship over his future, but I don't want him to work full-time, damn it. I don't want him to drop out, or quit hockey, or stress about making rent or car payments. I want him to go to the pros and show everyone how talented he is. Prove to the world that he's on the ice because he *belongs* there, and not because his father got him there.

I want him to be happy.

Even if that means I have to be miserable.

There's a short intermission after the last sophomore performs, and backstage is hit with pandemonium again. Jae and I are nearly knocked off our feet as a never-ending stream of robe-clad students pour onto the stage. I realize they're the members of Cass's choir.

"That could've been us." I grin at Jae as we watch the choir get in position on the dark stage. "Cass's army of minions."

His lips twitch. "I think we dodged a bullet."

"Me too."

When the show starts up again, this time I'm giving it my full attention, because the prodigy that is Cassidy Donovan has graced the stage. As the pianist plays the opening chords of MJ's song, I experience a twinge of jealousy. Damn, it's such a great song. I bite my lip, worried that my simple little ballad falls short compared to Mary Jane's beautiful composition.

I can't lie. Cass sings the hell out of the song. Every note, every run, every frickin' *pause*, is absolute perfection. He looks great out there, sounds even better, and when the choir joins in and goes all *Sister-Act* on the place, the performance kicks into a whole new gear.

There's only one thing missing—*emotion*. When MJ first played the song for me, I *felt* it. I felt her connection to the lyrics and the pain behind them. Tonight, I feel nothing, though I'm not sure if that's because of a failure on Cass's part, or if letting Garrett go robbed me of the ability to feel emotions.

But I sure as hell am feeling *something* when I settle behind the piano thirty minutes later. As the haunting strains of Jae's cello fill the stage, it's like a dam breaks inside me. Garrett is the first person I sang this song to, back when it was rough and choppy and nowhere close to polished. And Garrett is the one who listened to me rehearse it and hone it and perfect it.

When I open my mouth and start to sing, I'm singing it for Garrett. I'm transported to that peaceful place, my happy little bubble where nothing bad ever happens. Where girls don't get raped and sex isn't hard and people don't break up because abusive assholes force them to. My fingers tremble on the ivory keys and my heart squeezes with every breath I take, every word I sing.

When I'm done, silence crashes over the auditorium.

And then I get a standing ovation.

I rise to my feet, and only because Jae walks over and forces me to so we can take a bow. The spotlight blinds me and the cheers deafen me. I know Allie and Stella and Meg are out there somewhere, on their feet and screaming their lungs out, but I can't see their faces. Contrary to what movies and television shows lead you to believe, it's impossible to make eye contact with a face in the crowd when a blast of light is hitting you in the eyes.

Jae and I leave the stage and head for the wings, and someone instantly swallows me in a bear hug. It's Dexter, and his smile takes up his entire face as he congratulates me.

"Those better be happy tears!" he says.

I touch my cheek, surprised to feel moisture there. I hadn't even realized I was crying.

"That was spectacular," a voice bursts out, and I turn to see

Fiona marching toward me. She sweeps me into her arms and hugs me. "You were breathtaking, Hannah. Best performance of the night."

Her words don't ease the tight ache in my chest. I manage a nod and mumble, "I need to use the ladies' room. Excuse me."

I leave Dex, Fiona and Jae staring after me in confusion, but I don't care, and I don't slow down. Fuck the ladies' room. And fuck the rest of this showcase. I don't want to stand around and watch the senior performances. I don't want to wait for the scholarship ceremony. I just want to get the hell out of here and find a private place to cry.

I sprint toward the exit, my silver ballet flats slapping the hardwood floor in my desperate need to flee.

I'm five feet from the door when I smack into a hard male chest.

My gaze flies up and lands on a pair of gray eyes, and it takes a second to realize I'm looking at Garrett.

Neither one of us speaks. He's wearing black trousers and a blue button-down that stretches across his broad shoulders. His expression is a mixture of shining wonder and endless sorrow.

"Hi," he says gruffly.

My heart does a happy somersault, and I have to remind myself that this isn't a happy occasion, that we're still broken up. "Hi."

"You were…brilliant." Those beautiful eyes go a bit glassy. "Absolutely beautiful."

"You were in the audience?" I whisper.

"Where the fuck else would I be?" But he doesn't sound angry, just sad. Then his voice thickens and he murmurs, "How many?"

Confusion slides through me. "How many what?"

"How many guys have you dated this week?"

I jerk in surprise. "None," I blurt out before I can stop myself.

And I regret it instantly, because a knowing glimmer fills his eyes. "Yeah, I didn't think so."

"Garrett—"

"Here's the thing, Wellsy," he interrupts. "I've had seven whole days to think about this breakup. The first night? I got wasted. Seriously fucking trashed."

A jolt of panic hits me, because it suddenly occurs to me that he might have hooked up with someone else when he was drunk, and the thought of Garrett with another girl *kills* me.

But then he keeps talking and my anxiety eases. "After that, I sobered up and wised up and decided to make better use of my time. So...I've had seven whole days to analyze and reanalyze what happened between us, to dissect what went wrong, to reexamine every word you said that night..." He slants his head. "Do you want to know the conclusion I reached?"

God, I'm terrified to hear it.

When I don't answer, he smiles. "My conclusion is that you lied to me. I don't know why you did it, but trust me, I intend to find out."

"I didn't lie," I lie. "We really were moving too fast for me. And I really do want to see other people.

"Uh-huh. Really?"

I put on my most insistent tone. "*Really.*"

Garrett goes quiet for a moment. Then he reaches out and lightly strokes my cheek before pulling back and saying, "I'll believe it when I see it."

42

Hannah

Christmas break doesn't come soon enough. I am literally a mess as I board the plane to Philly—dressed in sweats, sporting bedhead, and covered with stress zits. Since the showcase, I've run into Garrett three times. Once at the Coffee Hut, once in the quad, and once outside the Ethics lecture hall when I came to pick up my graded paper. All three times, he asked me how many guys I've dated since our breakup.

All three times, I panicked, blurted out some excuse about being late, and ran off like a coward.

Here's the thing about breaking up with someone under false pretenses. They don't buy your bullshit unless you actually turn around and do the thing you said you wanted to do. In my case, I need to be dating a whole bunch of randoms and getting my exploration on, because that's what I told Garrett I wanted, and if I don't put my money where my mouth is, he'll know something's up.

I suppose I could ask someone out. Go on a very public date that Garrett will no doubt hear about and convince the guy I love that I've moved on. But the thought of being with anyone other than Garrett makes me want to throw up.

Fortunately, I don't have to worry about any of that right now. I've gotten a reprieve, because I'll be spending the next three weeks with my family.

I get on the plane, and for the first time since Garrett's father issued his punishing ultimatum, I'm finally able to breathe.

Seeing my parents is just what I needed. Don't get me wrong, I still think about Garrett non-stop, but it's a lot easier to distract myself from the heartache when I'm baking Christmas cookies with my dad or being dragged into the city for a day of shopping with my mom and aunt.

On our second night in Philly, I told my mom about Garrett. Or rather, she wrestled it out of me after she caught me moping in the guest room. She informed me that I looked like a hobo who'd just crawled out from under the boardwalk and proceeded to shove me in the shower and force me to brush my hair. After that, I spilled my guts, which prompted Mom to launch what she's now calling Operation Holiday Cheer. In other words, she's crammed a gazillion holiday activities down my throat, and I love her dearly for it.

I'm not looking forward to going back to Briar in three days, where Garrett is undoubtedly planning his own not-so-covert op—Operation Get Hannah To Admit She Was Lying. I just *know* he's going to try to win me back.

I also know it won't take much effort on his part. All he has to do is look at me with those gorgeous gray eyes, flash that crooked grin of his, and I'll break down in tears, throw my arms around him, and tell him everything.

I miss him.

"Hey, sweetie, are you coming down to watch the ball drop with us?" Mom appears in the doorway and holds up a bowl of popcorn enticingly, and I'm reminded of the first time I spent the night at Garrett's, when we stuffed ourselves full of popcorn and watched hours of television.

"Yeah, I'll be down soon," I answer. "I just want to change into comfy clothes."

Once she walks off, I climb off the bed and dig around in my suitcase for a pair of yoga pants. I wiggle out of my skinny jeans and replace them with the soft cotton pants, then head downstairs to the living room, where my parents, my aunt and uncle, and their friends Bill and Susan are all lounging on the L-shaped couches.

I'm spending New Year's Eve with three middle-aged couples.

Par-ty.

"So, Hannah," Susan pipes up, "your mother was just telling me that you won a prestigious scholarship recently."

I feel myself blushing. "I don't know about prestigious. I mean, they give them out every year for the winter and spring showcases. But yeah, I did win."

Take that, Cass Donovan, my inner smug monster shouts.

I hadn't planned on going back to the auditorium after I ran into Garrett at the showcase, but Fiona ended up catching me just as I was trying to sneak out and dragged me back to the stage. And yep, I can't deny that hearing my name announced at the scholarship ceremony gave me a total victory high. And I'll never forget the outrage on Cass's face when he realized they hadn't called *his* name.

Now I'm five grand richer, and my parents can take a breather because I'll be able to pay my residence and meal expenses on my own for this upcoming semester.

At ten to midnight, Uncle Mark puts an end to our chatter by unmuting the television so we can watch the Times Square celebration. Aunt Nicole hands out cardboard noisemakers with pink streamers on them while my mother passes around handfuls of confetti to everyone. My family is cheesy, but I wouldn't trade them for anything in the world.

My eyes are surprisingly misty as we all count down along with the announcer on the TV. Then again, maybe the tears *aren't* surprising, because when the clock reaches zero and everyone screams "HAPPY NEW YEAR!" I remember that the strike of midnight doesn't just indicate the start of a new year.

January 1st is also Garrett's birthday.

I clamp my lips together to stop the rush of tears, forcing a laugh as my father spins me around in his arms and kisses my cheek. "Happy New Year, princess."

"Happy New Year, Dad."

His green eyes soften when he notices my sad expression. "Aw, kiddo, why don't you pick up the phone and call that poor boy already? It's New Year's Eve."

My jaw drops, and then I swivel my head at my mother. "You told him?"

She at least has the decency to look guilty. "He asked why you were mopey. I couldn't *not* tell him."

My dad chuckles. "Oh, don't blame your mom, Han. I

figured it out all by myself. You've been so miserable I knew it had to be boy trouble. Now go wish him a happy new year. You'll regret it if you don't."

I sigh. But I know he's right.

My pulse speeds up as I hurry upstairs. I fish my cell phone out of my purse, then hesitate, because really, this is *not* a good idea. I broke up with him. I'm supposed to be moving on and seeing other people and blah fucking blah.

But it's his *birthday*.

I exhale a shaky breath and make the call.

Garrett answers on the first ring. I expect to hear noise in the background. Chatter, laughter, drunken yells. But wherever he is, it's as quiet as a church.

His husky voice tickles my ear. "Happy New Year, Hannah."

"Happy birthday, Garrett."

There's a slight pause. "You remembered."

I blink through my tears. "Of course I did."

There are so many other things I want to say to him. *I love you. I miss you. I hate your father.* But I tamp down the urge and say nothing at all.

"How's the dating going?" he asks cheerfully.

My stomach goes rigid. "Uh…it's great."

"Yeah? Doing lots of exploring? Conducting a thorough search for the meaning of love?"

There's a mocking note there, but more than anything, he sounds amused. Smug, even.

"Yep," I say lightly.

"How many guys have you dated?"

"A few."

"Awesome. I hope they're treating you right. You know, opening doors for you, laying their jackets on the ground so you can walk over puddles, that kind of stuff."

God, he's such a jackass. I love him.

"Don't worry, they're all very chivalrous," I assure him. "I'm having a blast."

"Good to hear." He pauses. "I'll see you in a few days. You can tell me all about it."

He hangs up, and I curse under my breath.

Damn it. Why is he pushing this? Why can't he just accept

that it's over between us and focus on his stupid hockey team?

And how the hell am I going to convince him I don't want to be with him when I can't even convince myself?

43

Hannah

My second day back on campus, I embark on my own mission: Operation Believe It When You See It. Because clearly the only way I can convince Garrett to back off is to prove to him that I'm in the process of moving on, which means I need to find a guy to go out on a date with. Stat.

The first opportunity arises when I pop into the Coffee Hut to grab a hot chocolate. It's snowing like a bitch outside, and I stomp the snow off my boots on the mat by the door before heading for the back of the line. That's when I notice that the guy in front of me looks familiar. When he places his order and moves to the pick-up counter, I get a flash of his profile and realize it's Jimmy. Jimmy...what's his last name again? Pauley? No, Paulson. Jimmy Paulson from British Lit and the Sigma party. Perfect. We've got history. We're practically in a relationship.

"Jimmy, hey," I greet him after I order my drink and join him at the counter.

He visibly stiffens at the sound of my voice. "Oh. Hey." His gaze darts around the coffee shop, as if he doesn't want anyone to see us talking.

"So, listen," I start, "I was just thinking, we haven't really talked since that party back in October..."

The barista plops a foam cup in front of Jimmy, who snatches it up so fast I don't even see his hand move.

I hurry on. "I thought it would be nice to catch up and..."

He's already edging away from me. Jesus, why does he look so terrified? Does he think I'm going to shiv him or something?

"...I was wondering if maybe you want to grab a coffee sometime," I finish.

"Oh." He inches farther away. "Uh. Thanks for the offer, but...uh, yeah, I don't drink coffee."

I stare at the coffee cup in his hand.

He follows my gaze and gulps. "I'm sorry, I have to go. I'm...meeting someone...all the way on the other side of the campus and it's...uh, far, so I'm kind of in a hurry."

Well, at least he's not lying about being in a hurry—because he flies out the door like an Olympic sprinter.

Okay, that was...weird.

Frowning, I get my hot chocolate and go outside, heading in the direction of Bristol House. It's slow going because the snow is falling faster than the campus maintenance crews can shovel it, and my boots sink into two feet of it every time I take a step. But the forced leisurely pace allows me to encounter another element of weirdness. When I was dating Garrett, people said hello and waved to me all the time. Today, everyone I pass seems to be going out of their way to avoid me, particularly the guys.

Is this what disgraced Amish people feel like when they've been shunned? Because everyone is looking right through me, and I don't like it.

I also don't understand it.

As I make my way to the dorms, I decide to give Dexter a call and see if he wants to go out tonight. Maybe to Malone's—no, wait, Garrett might be there. Another bar in town, then. Or the college rec hall. Anywhere I might be able to meet a guy.

I approach Bristol just as opportunity number two exits the building next door. It's Justin, and unlike the rest of the world, he actually lifts his hand in a wave.

I wave back, mostly out of relief that *someone* looks happy to see me.

"Hey, stranger," he calls, making his way over to me.

He's sporting that rumpled, rolled-out-of-bed hair, and yet I don't find it so adorable anymore. It just makes him look like a slob. Or maybe a phony, because I'm pretty sure I can see gel in his hair, which means he must've taken the time to create the I-don't-care style. Which makes him a fucking liar.

I meet him halfway. "Hey. How was your break?"

"Good. Not much rain in Seattle this time of year, so I had

to settle for a shit ton of snow instead. Went snowboarding, skiing, hot-tubbing. Fun times." Justin's dimples pop out, and they do nothing for me.

But...hell, he's the only guy who's so much as looked my way today. Beggars can't be choosers, right?

"Sounds fun. Um, so—"

Nope.

Nope, nope, nope. Just...nope.

I can't go there. Not with *this* guy. Garrett helped me make Justin jealous back in October. I *canceled* a date with him when I realized I wanted to be with Garrett. And I know how much Garrett dislikes Justin.

There's no way I can open this Justin door, not just because my feelings for him are non-existent, but because it would be like sticking a knife in Garrett's chest.

"So hi," I finish. "Yeah...I just came over to say hi." I hold up my hot chocolate cup as if it's somehow a part of this conversation. "I'm going inside to drink this. Good to see you."

His annoyed voice chills my back. "What the fuck just happened?" he asks.

The guilt pricking at my stomach spurs me to turn around. "I'm sorry," I say with a sigh. "I'm such an asshole."

A wry smile plays on his lips. "Well, I didn't want to say it, but..."

I walk back to him, my gloved hands still wrapped around my cup. "I never meant to lead you on," I admit. "When I said I'd go out with you, I really wanted to at the time. I mean it." Pain lodges in my throat. "I didn't expect to fall for him, Justin."

Now he just looks resigned. "Do people ever *expect* to fall for someone? I think it just kinda happens."

"Yeah, I guess so. He...snuck up on me." I meet his eyes, hoping he can see the genuine regret I'm feeling. "But I *was* interested in you. I never lied about that."

"*Was*, huh?" He sounds sad.

"I'm sorry," I say again. "I'm...damn it, I'm a mess, and I'm still in love with Garrett, but if you ever want to start over, as friends, I'm one hundred percent on board. We can talk Hemingway sometimes."

Justin's lips twitch. "How do you know I like Hemingway?"

I give him a faint smile. "Um. Well, I may have done some

recon back when I had a crush on you. See? I wasn't lying about that."

Rather than make a cross with his hands and shout *Stalker!*, he chuckles softly. "Huh. I guess not. That's good to know, at least."

After an awkward silence, Justin shoves his hands in his jacket pockets. "All right. I'm up for giving this friend thing a shot. Text me if you ever want to grab coffee sometime."

He wanders off, and a weight lifts off my chest.

Upstairs in my dorm, I congratulate myself on a potential disaster averted and return to mulling over my mission. Allie doesn't get back from New York until tomorrow. Stella is out of town, too. When I text Dex, he vetoes a hangout session because he's cramming for his last exam. When I message Meg, she says she has plans with Jeremy.

Sighing, I scroll through my phone contacts until a name sparks my interest. Actually, the more I think about it, the more I like the idea of making this call.

Allie's boyfriend picks up after several rings. "Hey, what's up?"

"Hey. It's Hannah."

"No kidding," Sean cracks. "Your number is in my phone."

"Oh, right." I hesitate. "So listen, I know Allie isn't back from her dad's yet, but I was wondering if..." I trail off, then blurt out, "What are you doing tonight? Do you want to hang out?"

My best friend's boyfriend falls silent. I don't blame him. I've never called him to hang out without Allie before. For that matter, I've never *called* him, period.

"You realize this is weird, right?" Sean says frankly.

I sigh. "Yes."

"What's going on? Are you just bored or something? Or is this a fucked up hit-on-your-friend's-boyfriend kinda thing? Wait—is Allie listening in?" Sean raises his voice. "Allie, if you're there, I love you. I would never, ever cheat on you with your best friend."

I snort into the phone. "She's not on the line, dumbass, but that's good to know. And trust me, I'm not hitting on you. I...well...I was hoping we could hang out with some of your frat brothers tonight. Maybe you could, you know, set me up with one of them."

"Are you serious?" he exclaims. "No fucking way. You're too

good for any of those idiots, and I'm pretty sure Allie would kill me if I hooked you up with one of them. Besides..." He clams up abruptly.

"Besides what?" I demand.

He doesn't answer.

"Finish that sentence, Sean."

"I'd rather not."

"I'd rather you did." My suspicion snaps into overdrive. "Oh my God." I gasp. "Do you know why every guy on campus is suddenly treating me like I have an STD?"

"Maybe?" he says.

"Maybe?" When he doesn't answer, I groan in frustration. "I swear to God, if you don't tell me what you know, I'll—"

"Okay, okay," he interrupts. "I'll tell you."

And then he does.

And my response is a loud shriek of outrage.

"He did *what*?"

Twenty minutes later, I burst through the doors of Briar's hockey arena. Cold air immediately slaps my cheeks, but it doesn't succeed in cooling the fire burning inside me. It's five-thirty, which means Garrett and the team have just finished practice, so I bypass the rink doors and march right to the locker rooms in the back of the building. I'm so pissed off that my whole body is trembling from the force of my anger.

Garrett has officially stepped over the line. No, he's so far past the line that I can't even *see* the stupid line. And there's no way I'm letting him get away with this ludicrous, juvenile bullshit.

I reach the locker room door as one of the players walks out of it.

"Is Garrett in there?" I bark.

He looks startled to see me. "Yeah, but—"

I bulldoze past him and grab the door handle.

The guy protests from behind. "I don't think you should go in th—"

I burst into the locker room and—

Penises!

Sweet Jesus.

Penises *everywhere*.

Horror slams into me as I register what I'm seeing. Oh God. I've stumbled onto a penis convention. Big penises and small penises and fat penises and penis-shaped penises. It doesn't matter which direction I move my head because everywhere I look *I see penises.*

My mortified gasp draws the attention of every penis—er, guy, in the room. In a heartbeat, towels snap up and hands cover junk and bodies shuffle around, while I stand in the front of the room blushing like a tomato.

"Wellsy?" A bare-chested Logan grins at me, one shoulder propped up against his locker. It looks like he's trying very hard not to laugh.

"Penis—*Logan*," I blurt out. "Hi." I do my best to avoid making visual contact with the half naked males milling in the room, all of whom are either grinning in amusement or blanching in alarm. "I'm looking for Garrett."

With a barely restrained smirk, Logan hooks his thumb at a doorway in the back, which I assume leads to the showers because steam is rolling out of it.

"Thanks." I shoot him a grateful look and head in that direction, just as someone emerges from the steamy space.

Dean appears and I see his penis.

"Hey, Wellsy," he drawls. Completely unfazed by my presence, he strolls naked toward his locker as if finding me in here is a daily occurrence for him.

I charge forward, debating whether I should close my eyes, but luckily all the showers have saloon-type doors and are divided by partitions. As I march down the tiled floor, heads swivel my way. One of the heads belongs to Birdie, whose eyes widen when I walk past him.

"Hannah?" he squeaks.

I ignore him and keep walking until I spot a familiar back. My gaze conducts a quick double-check, and yep, golden skin, tattoo, dark hair. It's Garrett, all right.

At the sound of my footsteps, he twists around and gapes at the sight of me. "Wellsy?"

I stalk up to the half-door, level him with my meanest scowl, and shout, "What is the *matter* with you?"

44

Garrett

I'm grinning like the town idiot. And now is *not* the time to be grinning like the town idiot, not when I'm buck naked in a room full of showering dudes and my girlfriend is glaring daggers at me. But I'm so happy to see her that I can't control my facial muscles.

My eyes eat up the sight of her. Her gorgeous face. Dark hair pulled back in a ponytail with a pink hair thingie. Infuriated green eyes.

She's so damn hot when she's mad at me.

"It's nice to see you too, baby," I answer cheerfully. "How was your break?"

"Don't you *baby* me. And don't ask about my break because you don't *deserve* to know about it!" Hannah glowers at me, then shifts her attention to the three hockey players in the neighboring stalls. "For the love of Pete, would you guys just rinse off and skedaddle already? I'm trying to yell at your captain."

I choke back a laugh, which ends up spilling out when my teammates snap to attention like they've been issued a command by a drill sergeant. Showers turn off and towels come out, and a moment later, Hannah and I are alone.

I shut off the faucet and turn around. The shower door does a good job of hiding my downstairs area, but all Hannah has to do is peek over and she'll get an eyeful of my quickly hardening dick, who is unbelievably happy to see her.

But she doesn't sneak a peek. She simply keeps glaring at me. "You invoked a campus-wide hands-off law? Are you *kidding* me?"

I'm not at all remorseful as I meet her eyes. "Of course I did."

"Oh my God. You are unbelievable." She shakes her head in disbelief. "Who *does* that, Garrett? You can't just go around and tell all the guys at this school that they're not allowed to touch me or you'll kick their asses!"

"I didn't tell *all* the guys. Do I look like I have that kind of time?" I flash a grin. "I told a few key people and made sure they spread the word."

"What, if you can't have me no one else can?" she says darkly.

I snicker. "Well, that's just insane. I'm not a psycho, babe. I was doing it for your sake."

Her jaw drops. "How the hell do you figure *that*?"

"Because you're in love with me, and you don't want to date anyone else. But see, I was afraid your stubborn self would try to do it just to back up your cover story, so I had to take some preventative measures." I prop my forearms on the stall door. "I knew if you went out with anyone else you'd end up regretting it, and then you'd feel like an ass when you finally came to your senses, and, well, I wanted to spare you all that pain and suffering. You're welcome."

She looks stunned for a moment.

Then she starts to laugh.

Jesus, I've missed the sound of her laughter. I'm tempted to hop over the little door and kiss the crap out of her, but I don't get the chance.

"What the *hell* is going on in here?"

Hannah jumps in surprise when Coach Jensen appears in the shower area.

"Oh, hey, Coach," I call out. "Not what it looks like."

His dark brows knit in a displeased frown. "It looks like you're taking a shower in front of your girlfriend. In my locker room."

"Okay, then yeah, it's what it looks like. But I promise, it's all very PG. Well, except for the fact that I'm naked. But don't worry, no kinky shit is going to happen." I grin at him. "I'm trying to win her back."

Coach's mouth opens, then closes, then opens again. I can't tell if he's amused or pissed or ready to wash his hands of this whole thing. Finally, he nods and opts for option number three. "Carry on."

Coach shakes his head to himself as he ambles off, and I turn back to Hannah in time to see her trying to sneak away.

"Oh, hell no," I announce. "No way, Wellsy." I snatch my towel and wrap it around my waist as I stumble out of the stall. "You're not running off on me."

"I came here to yell at you," she stammers, her gaze dipping to her feet. "And now I'm done yelling at you, so..."

She yelps when my wet hands cup her cheeks to force her to look at me. "Great, you're done yelling. Now I want you to *talk* to me, and you're not leaving until you do."

"I don't want to talk."

"Tough cookies." I search her agonized expression. "Why did you break up with me?"

"I already told you—"

"I know what you told me. I didn't believe you then and I don't believe you now." I set my jaw. "Why did you break up with me?"

A shaky breath leaves her mouth. "Because we were moving too fast."

"Bullshit. Why did you break up with me?"

"Because I wanted to see other people."

"Try again. Why did you break up with me?"

When she doesn't answer, frustration blasts through me, and I react by crashing my mouth down on hers. I kiss her roughly, desperately, the days and weeks of missing her catching up to me and pouring out in the form of deep, hungry kisses that leave us both breathless. She doesn't pull away. She just kisses me back with the same unchecked passion, her hands clinging to my wet shoulders like she's lost at sea and I'm her life preserver.

That's how I know she still loves me. That's how I know she missed me as much as I missed her. And that's why I wrench my mouth away and whisper, "Why did you break up with me?"

Her anguished gaze locks with mine. Her bottom lip quivers, and as several seconds tick by, I wonder if she's going to answer me. I wonder if—

"Because your father told me to."

The shock almost knocks me off my feet. As my equilibrium turns into a seesaw, I drop my hands to my sides and stare at her, unable to comprehend what I just heard.

I swallow. Then I swallow again. "What?"

"Your father told me to end it," she admits. "He said that if I didn't, he'd—"

I hold up my hand to silence her. I'm too stunned to listen. Too enraged to move. I force myself to breathe. Long, calming breaths that help steady my wonky balance and clear my foggy head. Then I exhale in a slow rush and run a hand through my damp hair.

"Here's what's going to happen," I say quietly. "You're going to wait outside for me while I get dressed, and then you and I are going to—I don't care where we go. Your dorm, my car, *anywhere.* We're going to go somewhere, and you're going to tell me every word that son of a bitch said to you." I take another breath. "You're going to tell me *everything.*"

Hannah

Garrett doesn't say a word as I recount everything that happened between his father and me. We're in my room because the arena is closer to the dorms than it is to Garrett's house, and he was in too much of a hurry to have this conversation. But all he's done so far is loom over me with his arms crossed and his brow furrowed, listening intently as my confession spills out of my mouth like confetti.

I can't stop talking. I recite his dad's threats verbatim. I explain why I went along with them. I beg him to understand that I did it because I love him and want him to be successful.

And through it all, Garrett says nothing. He doesn't even blink.

"Will you please say something?" I mumble when I've finished talking and he still hasn't said a word.

His gray eyes fix on my face. I can't tell if he's angry or annoyed, if he's disappointed or upset. All those emotions would make sense to me.

But the response I get?

Makes no sense at all.

Garrett starts to laugh. Deep, husky rumbles that bring a frown to my lips. His brow relaxes and his arms fall to his sides as he sinks down on the bed beside me, his broad shoulders trembling with mirth.

"You think this is funny?" I demand, genuinely offended. I've been a total misery zombie this past month, and he finds it *amusing*?

"No, I think it's a damn shame," he says between chuckles.

"What's a shame?"

"This." He gestures between us. "You and me. The whole fucking month we missed out on." He lets out a heavy sigh. "Why didn't you just *tell* me?"

My throat closes up. "Because I knew what you would say."

Another chuckle pops out of his mouth. "I highly doubt that, but okay, humor me. What would I have said?"

I don't understand his weird-ass reaction, and it's making me uneasy. "You would have told me that you didn't care if your father cut you off, because you're not going to let him control you, or *us*."

Garrett nods. "Yup, you're on track so far. What else?"

"Then you would have said you care about me more than you care about his stupid money."

"Yup."

"And you would have let him cut you off."

"Right again."

My stomach lurches. "He said you aren't eligible for financial aid, and that you wouldn't be able to get a bank loan."

Garrett nods again. "Both true."

"You would have had to clean out your savings account to pay for next term's tuition, and…and then what? We both know you can't afford rent and expenses and car payments when you're not working, so that means you would need to get a job and—"

"I'm gonna stop you there, baby." The smile he gives me is infinitely tender. "So…let's back up. I let my father cut me off. Ask me what I would've said next."

I bite the inside of my cheek. A little too hard, so I soothe the sting with my tongue. "What?"

Garrett leans closer and sweeps his fingertips over my

cheek. "I would've said, *Don't worry, babe, I'm turning twenty-one in a few weeks, and my grandparents left me a trust fund that I can access on January 2nd.*"

I suck in a shocked breath. "Wait—what?"

He lightly pinches my bottom lip, shaking his head in frustration. "My grandparents left me an inheritance, Hannah. My dad didn't know about it because my mom signed all the papers behind his back. Gran and Gramps hated the old bastard—they really fucking hated him—and they saw how controlling he was when it came to me and hockey. They were afraid he might try to access the trust and do whatever he wanted with the funds, so they made sure I was taken care of. They left me enough money to pay my father back for everything he's ever paid for. Enough to pay for the rest of my education, and all my expenses, and probably enough to sustain me for a few years once I graduate."

My mind reels. I'm having trouble processing the information. "Really?"

"Really," he confirms.

As the significance of what he's just told me sinks in, I experience a flood of pure horror. Sweet baby Jesus. Is he telling me I broke up with him for *no reason*?

Garrett sees my expression and chuckles. "I bet you feel pretty stupid, huh?"

My mouth falls open, but I can't formulate any words. I can't believe... I'm so... God, he's right. I'm so fucking stupid.

"I was trying to do the right thing." I moan miserably. "I know how important hockey is to you. I didn't want you to lose that."

He sighs again. "I know, and trust me, that's the only reason I'm not pissed off at you right now. I mean, I'm annoyed to shit that you didn't just talk to me about it, but I understand why you didn't." His eyes flash. "That asshole had no right to do that. I swear, I'm going to—" He stops and puffs out a breath. "Actually, I'm going to do absolutely nothing. Not worth my time and energy, remember?"

"Does he know about the trust fund now?"

A triumphant gleam enters his eyes. "Oh, he knows. My grandparents' executor couriered him a check yesterday. I estimated what I owed him and threw some extra cash on top of it, and he called last night and yelled at me for about twenty minutes before I hung up on him." Garrett's tone goes serious. "Oh, and there's something else you should know—Cindy dumped his ass."

Shock and relief war inside me. "Really?"

"Yup. Apparently she packed her bags a week after Thanksgiving and never looked back. That was another reason he was so pissed off on the phone. He thinks we said something to make her leave." Garrett's cheeks hollow in anger. "Son of a bitch still can't take responsibility for anything he does. He can't fathom how it might be *his* fault that she left."

My head continues to spin. I'm happy Cindy extricated herself from that abusive relationship, but I'm not happy about the month Garrett and I were apart. I'm not happy that I allowed Phil Graham to scare me into giving up the guy I love.

"I'm sorry," I say softly. "I'm so sorry, Garrett. For everything."

He reaches for my hand. "Yeah, me too."

"Don't you dare apologize. You have nothing to be sorry about. *I'm* the one who tried to be all heroic and broke up with you for your own good." I groan. "God, I can't even be selfless without screwing it up."

He snickers. "It's okay. At least you're hot. And don't get me started on your stripper tits."

I squeak when he suddenly cups my breasts over my sweater and gives them a hearty squeeze.

He makes a contented little noise as he rubs his palms over my quickly hardening nipples. "Oh, I've missed these. You don't know how fucking much."

A laugh flies out. "Seriously? You're going straight to second base when we haven't even officially gotten back together?"

His lips latch onto my neck, and his tongue darts out for a teasing lick. "As far as I'm concerned, we were never broken up." Then he nibbles on my earlobe, eliciting a flurry of shivers. "So the way I see it, we could hug and kiss and cry, which will take about, what, twenty minutes? And then twenty more minutes where I forgive you and you vow your undying love to me. Maybe ten minutes of you giving me head to make up for all the time we've lost—"

I punch him in the arm.

"But what's the point of wasting more time when we can get right to the good part?"

My lips quiver in amusement. “And what exactly is the good part?”

Before I can blink, I’m on my back with the deliciously heavy weight of Garrett’s body on top of me. He flashes his trademark grin, that sexy crooked smile that never fails to make my heart pound, and then his mouth covers mine in a hungry kiss.

“*This—*” He sucks on my lower lip and rotates his hips seductively “—is the good part.”

I wrap my arms around him and hold him tight against me, and it’s so familiar, so wonderfully perfect, that the love in my heart overflows and stings my eyes. “I love you, Garrett,” I choke out.

His husky voice tickles my lips. “I love you, Hannah.”

Then he kisses me, and everything in my world is right again.

45

Hannah

March

"Why is your ex-crush in my living room?" Garrett drops the whispered accusation in my ear as he comes up beside me.

My gaze shifts to Justin, who is on the couch playing a complicated-looking shooting video game with Tucker. Then I turn back to Garrett, who looks more amused than pissed. "Because he's my friend, and I invited him. Deal with it."

"You don't think it's kind of a dick move to invite him? I mean, the football team did shit all this season, and now he has to come celebrate with the hockey crowd for making it to the semi-finals? *And* he has to be around the perfect specimen of manhood who stole you away?" Garrett's gray eyes twinkle. "You're a terrible person."

"Oh, shut it. He's happy that you guys are going to the Frozen Four." I bring my lips close to his ear. "And don't tell *anyone* this or I'll kill you, but he's been hooking up with Stella this past month."

"For real?" Garrett's jaw drops as he glances across the room, where Stella, Dex and Allie are in the middle of an animated conversation with Logan and Simms. It's still kind of bizarre seeing my friends interacting with Garrett's friends, but we've all hung out dozens of times over the past three months, so I'm starting to get used to it.

From his spot next to Dex, Logan senses me watching them and lifts his head, and...well, *that's* something I *haven't* gotten used to. The look he gives me burns with unmistakable longing, and it's not the first time he's looked at me like that. When I brought it up to Garrett—just once, in the most awkward conversation ever—he simply sighed and said, "He'll get over it." No anger on Garrett's part, no resentment, just that one measly sentence, which hasn't done much to soothe my worries.

I don't like the idea that Garrett's best friend might have feelings for me, but Logan hasn't tried to make a move on me, and he sure as hell hasn't talked to me about it, so that's a relief, I guess. But I really do hope he gets over whatever he's feeling, because as much as I like the guy, I'm totally and unequivocally in love with his best friend, and that's never going to change.

This semester has been a busy one for us. I'm yet again rehearsing, this time for the spring showcase, and this time it *is* a duet—with Dexter, and the two of us are having a blast working together. Garrett and the team have been killing it in the post season. The championship is next week, and the venue for it just happens to be the Wells Fargo Center, home of the Philadelphia Flyers, which means that, yep, I'm going to be watching the final game live, and staying at Aunt Nicole's for the three days the team is in Philly.

There's no doubt in my mind that the team will crush it. Garrett and the guys have worked hard this season, and if they don't win this final game, I'll eat my hat. Either that, or give my man lots and lots of consolation sex. *Such* a chore.

"Look what the cat dragged in," Garrett says suddenly, and I turn around to see Birdie and Natalie appear in the doorway where Garrett and I are lurking.

Their faces are flushed and their expressions are secretive, leaving no doubt as to why they're late for the party. I give Nat a hug of greeting, then smile at Birdie, who responds to Garrett's taunt with a defensive look.

"Hey, I already told you I'm against this party. It's bad luck to celebrate before you've even won."

"Naah, we've got this in the bag, man." Garrett grins and leans in to smack a kiss on my cheek. "Besides, I've already won the most important prize of all."

I'm pretty sure my cheeks turn into a pair of tomatoes.

Natalie groans good-naturedly, but Birdie, to my surprise, just nods in approval.

"See," Garrett informs us as he slings an arm around my shoulder, "I'm allowed to say stuff like that to Birdie because I know he won't make fun of me."

"Well, he should," I grumble, "because that line was cheesy as hell."

"Oh, shut it," he mimics. "You like it when I'm romantic."

Yep. I really do.

Birdie and Nat wander off to say hi to everyone, but Garrett and I stay in our little corner. He tugs me toward him and kisses me, and even though I'm anti-PDA, it's impossible to think about social etiquette when Garrett Graham is kissing me.

His lips are warm and firm, his tongue hot and wet as he slides it into my mouth for a fleeting taste. I part my lips eagerly, wanting more, but he chuckles and tweaks a strand of my hair.

"Stop being inappropriate, Hannah. We're in *public*."

"Ha. Like I can't see your boner."

His gaze drops to his crotch, and he sighs when he notices the bulge straining against his jeans. "For fuck's sake, Wellsy, you get me hard without me even noticing." He frowns. "Damn it, now I'm gonna have to leave my own party so we can go upstairs and take care of this. Thanks a lot."

I snort. "Dream on. There's no way I'm doing the walk of shame afterward in front of all our friends."

His face collapses. "You're ashamed of me?"

"Don't give me that little boy trickery." I poke him in the chest. "It doesn't work on me anymore."

"Little boy?" he echoes. A wicked smile curves his mouth as he angles his body so that he's facing away from the room. Then he takes my hand and plants it directly over his hard-on. "Does this feel little or boyish to you?"

Shivers fly up my spine. Oh no. Now *I'm* turned on.

As my heart pounds and my body tingles, I let out an annoyed groan and grab his hand. "Fine. Let's go upstairs."

"Nope. I changed my mind about that. We're going to stay down here and enjoy the party."

I drop his hand like a hot potato and scowl deeply. "You're such a vagina-tease."

Garrett laughs. "Yeah, but you still love me."

Tiny butterflies of happiness take flight in my stomach and dance around my heart. I take his hand again and lace our fingers together. "Yeah," I murmur with a smile. "I still love you."

Epilogue

Garrett

My father waits outside the arena when the team bursts out the back doors. Dean had somehow gotten his hands on an old-school boom box, and he has it propped up on his shoulder as Queen's "We Are the Champions" blasts out of the speakers. There's nobody around to hear the victory song but us, and the family and friends who made it out to Philly to watch us play. Applause breaks out as we stroll up like the champions we are, and several of my bonehead teammates take exaggerated bows before heading over to say hello to the people who came out to see us.

I fucking did it. I mean, it was a team effort—no, a team *domination*, because for the first time in years, the Frozen Four championship game was a shutout. Simms didn't let our opponents score. Not even once. And it seems fitting that the three lamplighters on our side came from me, Tuck, and Birdie, respectively.

I'm proud of my team. I'm proud of *myself* for leading us here. It's the perfect end to the perfect season, and it gets a little more perfect when Hannah rushes over and hurls herself into my arms.

"Oh my God! That was the best game *ever*!" she declares before kissing me so hard my lips feel bruised.

I grin at her enthusiasm. "Did you like the little gun-finger I flashed you after that goal? All for you, baby."

She grins back. "Sorry to burst your bubble, but you were actually pointing at the old guy a few seats over. He totally freaked out and started shouting to everyone that you scored that goal for him, and then I heard him ask his wife if maybe you knew that he was just diagnosed with diabetes, so I didn't have the heart to tell him who the goal was really for."

I break down in laughter. "Why is nothing ever simple with us?"

"Hey," she protests. "We're more interesting this way."

I can't argue with that.

From the corner of my eye, I see my father lurking near the bus, but I don't make eye contact with him. In fact, I notice that *nobody* is looking at him. Not me, not Hannah, not any of my teammates. A few months ago, I told the guys the truth about my dad, because the conversation I had with Hannah about life not being fair and my father still being revered had stuck with me. So after the New Year, when one of our sophomore D-men asked me if I could get him a Phil Graham autograph, I could no longer hold it in. I sat the boys down—even Coach was there—and told them everything.

Needless to say, it was damn uncomfortable and pretty fucking intense, but when all was said and done, my teammates proved to me that I'm not just their captain, but their brother. And now, as we all head for the bus, not a single pair of eyes travels in my superstar father's direction.

"I'll see you back at campus?" I say to Hannah.

She nods. "Yep. Uncle Mark is driving me back now, so I should be there around the same time you guys get in."

"Call me when you're home. Love you, babe."

"Love you, too."

I plant one last kiss on her lips, then climb onto the bus and settle in my usual seat next to Logan. As the door shuts and the driver pulls away, I don't glance out the window to look at the tall, surly man who's still standing in the parking lot.

I don't look back these days.

I only look forward.

Author's Note

I loved every second of writing this book, but just like with every project I undertake, I couldn't have done it without the help of some pretty amazing people:

Jane Litte, for beta reading this secret, just-for-fun project, convincing me to share it with other readers, and then holding my hand during my very first self-publishing endeavor.

Vivian Arend, for stepping out of her comfort zone and reading a New Adult book! And for just being plain awesome.

Kristen Callihan, for her invaluable advice and endless cheerleading for this project.

Gwen Hayes, the sweetest, smartest and funniest editor I've ever worked with.

Sharon Muha, for her eagle eyes (and for not complaining every time I send her a gazillion page manuscript and ask for a proofreading rush job).

Sarah Hansen (Okay Creations) for the beautiful cover!

Nina Bocci, my publicist AKA lifesaver, for loving this book as much as I do and making sure everybody heard about it!

And to everyone who read/loved/reviewed/talked about the book—you guys rock. You rock hard.

About the Author

A USA Today bestselling author, Elle Kennedy grew up in the suburbs of Toronto, Ontario, and holds a BA in English from York University. From an early age, she knew she wanted to be a writer and actively began pursuing that dream when she was a teenager. She loves strong heroines and sexy alpha heroes, and just enough heat and danger to keep things interesting!

Elle loves to hear from her readers. Visit her website www.ellekennedy.com and sign up for her newsletter to receive updates about upcoming books and exclusive excerpts. You can also find her on Facebook (AuthorElleKennedy) or follow her on Twitter (@ElleKennedy).

CPSIA information can be obtained at www.ICGtesting.com
Printed in the USA
LVOW07s1020270915

455905LV00018B/710/P